Bravery Not Included

Bravery Not Included

Rise of the Amazons Book 1

Amberly Smith

Kuznya Freelance
Boise, Idaho

Visit author website at www.amberlysmith.com

ISBN-13: 978-0692535738
ISBN-10: 069253573X

Dedication

To all the amazing women in my life but especially to Judy Burdick. Mom, you were my first Amazon. I love you.

Acknowledgements

I want to thank Janis McCurry for believing in me and supporting my efforts. Thank you, Janis.

Also, James from Humble Nations for the beautiful cover. Val Roberts, Sally Fogel, Kyrsten Bell, Cheryl Maude, and all the other patient readers of the early versions of this book. You all rock.

Chapter 1

Being an Amazon didn't automatically make you a morning person. "Whose idea was it to go so f'ing early?" Liesel Grant turned her head so her little sister wouldn't see her stifle another yawn. She could always attribute the moisture in her eyes to the glare of headlights from other cars. Harriett saw anyway and laughed, the dork.

"It'll give us more time to talk." Harry grinned at her sister, annoyingly chipper and fully awake without the aid of caffeine. "This once-a-week get together has been canceled twice."

Liesel could hear the hurt in her sister's voice. "I really am sorry I canceled last week."

"You'd better be. And you can prove just how sorry by buying breakfast." Harriett kept her eyes on the road.

"Crap, Harry. I'll do better—"

"What? Like it's just you?" Her baby sister flipped her golden hair off her shoulder to look at Liesel. Then Harry looked back at the road and sighed. "How long since you've seen Karma for anything but babysitting? She doesn't return my calls and I've not seen her for over a month."

Liesel didn't want to fight. The sun had to be up before people could fight. It was a rule. And if she tried to defend their older sister Karma, they'd fight. It wasn't that she didn't agree with Harriett. She did. But you stuck up for your sister.

Headlights flashed in their eyes again as they took the sharp corner. A Suburban ignored the twist in the road, popped the curb, hit the canal's guardrail and kept going. The sound of steel folding like aluminum foil, ground down Liesel's spine as the Suburban pushed through the metal barrier. The sound, like a fucking dog whistle, had all her senses on full alert. It switched Liesel to ready mode.

"It's going in." Her sister Harry shifted gears and turned the wheel on the old pickup. The central canal would be high and swift with ice runoff. Harry straightened out and headed for the space of missing rail, her headlights cut across the early morning traffic as other cars stopped along the roadside. Before the truck halted, Liesel had her seatbelt off and door open. Harry was right behind her.

The engine's heavy weight had pulled the vehicle nose-down into the water. The back-end of the suburban formed a new dock which swayed as the rapid current battered at its sides.

"They're not coming out," Liesel whispered to her sister. *Oh, please no*. Was there a mom and her children caught in there, the cabin filling with water and fear? She needed to save them.

Harry touched her arm. "Just because you're more powerful than a locomotive," she kept her voice low and looked directly into Liesel's eyes, "doesn't mean you have to play superman. Let the trained professionals handle this."

The addictive drive to run into danger was part of her inner wiring. Add a loved one into the needs-saving category and need turned into instinct-driven process, right along with breathing air and pumping blood. "Harry, promise you'll stay up here." The only reason she wasn't already in that water was Harry.

Harry crossed her arms and glared. There was no time. Every minute the oxygen the passengers needed to live slipped away. Heat flashed across her chest and roared through her head. She needed to save them. Move, move, move. "Stay. Up. Here."

Liesel jumped in feet first and scissored her legs to keep her head above water. It was cold. Colder than drinking-from-the-hose cold. Liesel's chest ached as she drew in a sharp breath. Glacier runoff kicked summer's ass every time. Her sister yelled directions up on the bank, "Let's get your car turned around there. You too. Turn on your lights so we can see."

The twenty foot wide canal was easily fifteen feet deep. The slanted cement sides had cracked from overgrown vegetation. Liesel swam to the rear of the vehicle and pulled herself up on top of the car. Her wet jeans sucked to her legs like frozen saran wrap.

The back door didn't have a handle, so she punched the rear

window and two thirds of the glass crinkled like a massive spider web. Her second punch was at a corner of the window frame, angled slightly so it would bend, giving her a hand hold. Liesel tossed the glass to the side and the vehicle groaned and swayed with a slow-to-accelerate motion as the pressure leveled out. The vehicle's back-end tilted down into the water and Liesel took a deep breath preparing to go under with it.

Even with the headlights from above, she could see little of the interior; a black on black comparison of images. Flat black. Shiny black. Less black. She moved in the less black area and reached the first rear seat. It was empty. As the car finally settled to the bottom of the canal, she bumped against the ceiling and started moving parallel, feeling disoriented.

There was a car seat, but it was empty. Desperate for air, she pushed back through the vehicle for the surface. She surged out of the water like soda in a shaken bottle.

The group of early commuters had rallied Good-Samaritan-style and waited on the bank with blankets. Two large men lay over the edge on their bellies, arms outstretched, ready. Another breath and she went back to the vehicle.

Was there a child floating loose in the darkness?

Was there only a driver left?

More familiar with the lay of the land, she made better time into the vehicle. Her body had adjusted to the cold. The rest of the forward seat was empty. No one in the passenger side. She unclicked the driver's seatbelt. He was big. Maybe three-fifty. Maybe more. She wouldn't be able to pull him back through the rear of the vehicle. Not enough clearance.

How long had she been down here? The sense of disorientation grew and she panicked. It felt like a tangle of burrs clawed up her throat and her sense of reality blinked off like a television, fuzzy grey at the edges. When she opened her mouth, ready to breathe in, large bubbles rippled out around her and she fought the urge a second longer. Turning to face the large windshield Liesel braced herself against the ceiling and kicked the windshield loose.

She pushed for the top, her lungs opening up so large in her chest she felt her ribs strain to keep them in place. She coughed and sputtered as she reached open air, trying to remove water from her mouth and nose while sucking in oxygen for her empty lungs. The current had carried her and the car farther down the canal and the helpful bystanders were trying to establish climbing ropes closer to the new location.

Harry watched from the bank and, seeing that Liesel's arms were empty, jumped into the water to help. Damn it. No.

Going back was hard. Her body told her there was no way she was going down again and she fought it.

The man had floated to the top of the SUV, a tangled twist of limbs. She grabbed hold of him under his arms and tried to pull him out but part of him caught on part of the car. Harry swam past Liesel's right side, perhaps checking that the driver was the only one. Liesel gave a quick jerk and the man came free. She surfaced a foot from the rescue team.

"Is there any more?" someone asked.

"I don't think so. My sister is down checking." Her stupidly brave and completely non-amazon sister. Liesel grasped the high cement wall with her cold finger tips. She realized the psychedelic blur of colors wasn't a precondition of nearly blacking-out but rather emergency lights from a fire engine. The cavalry had arrived.

She placed her feet in the cracks the old tree roots had battled into the sidewall. With the man over her right shoulder, she lifted them both up, using only her left hand and her feet. She handed him up, like a wet ragdoll, kept her hands in place until she was sure they had him.

Then she turned at the waist, more than half out of the water and looked for Harry. Surely she had come up by now.

Nothing.

The vehicle headlights illuminated the opposite bank. Nothing.

Oh, god no. "Harry!" She pulled air in as she released the side. With a flip in the water, using her legs to push off from the canal wall, she swam back to the vehicle. Not Harry. Please not Harry.

An image of Harry, her long blonde hair floating around her like a halo, her lips and eyes blue, dead, filled Liesel's mind. Her heart constricted; a sharp, bloody, jagged ache in her chest.

The suburban had swept farther down the canal so that she was once again entering in the rear. It had been less than ten minutes since she'd started and perhaps only a couple of minutes since Harry had passed her. Way too long. Way too fucking long. Why hadn't she listened and stayed out of the water like Liesel had told her?

Liesel ignored the less black. She ignored the biting sting of the cold current. She ignored the passing of time.

She found Harry underneath the forward seat, her sister held a small bundle. A child? The water suddenly felt thick and warm around her. As if her sister's soul had left her frozen body, heating the water as it withdrew. She opened her mouth to shout 'no' and again the bubbles. The water resisted Liesel's slightest movement, the current determined to press her permanently into the roof.

Liesel wrapped herself around her sister, making sure Harry's limbs were clear and used the flow of the water to push them out the window. She swam to the top of the vehicle then elbowed and kneed to a standing position, desperate to get Harry's head out of the water. Once on top, she carried Harry with one arm beneath her knees, the other behind her head. The bundle, black yarn, cotton and fluff, but no bones, was still in Harry's arms.

They'd floated down the canal even farther. A bridge where the road crossed the canal created a bottleneck. The sudden push against the new barrier lifted the vehicle up. Liesel draped Harry's motionless body over her shoulder; one hundred-fifty pounds of precious sister and dripping canal water.

Liesel bent at the knees then leapt for the bridge's railing. She grasped the bar with her left then right hand, opened her mouth to call for help. Opened and closed, but said nothing.

Harry didn't move but the bundle tumbled loose. Liesel had forgotten everything but Harry. She couldn't reach out to catch it. She watched it spin back to the water and felt Harry slip backward off her shoulder. She let go with one hand to catch her sister.

Help. Yet, she couldn't form the words. Her remaining hand burned across the thick pad of her bottom knuckles. She clenched tighter and told her arm to flex, to lift her and her sister to safety.

She tried to adjust Harry on her shoulder so she could use both hands but was afraid she'd drop Harry. She dug deep, looking for an iron will to match her Amazon strength?

Her hand burned and the veins on her arm popped to the surface and screamed.

Then she found the resolve, the motivation. This was Harry, the only person in this freak-show of life that got her, made her laugh, put up with her shit. Her baby sister and her best friend.

Her abs flexed to granite, her bicep opened and filled with fire. Her arm formed an angle, growing smaller as she pulled her chin up to the bar. 130 degrees, 90, forty-five. Her t-shirt stuck to her skin and her jeans pulled heavy at her hips. She got her feet wedged on the bridge under the metal rail then draped her sister like a wet towel over the top. Keeping herself between Harry and the water, she pulled herself over the rail.

Finally the words came. "Help. Over here."

Liesel's arms were liquid and it was all she could do to get Harry to the flat surface of the bridge's sidewalk without dropping her head against the cement. She didn't trust herself to do CPR compressions. She wouldn't be able to judge how much pressure to use, might snap Harry's sternum or ribs. Her body shivered at the contrast of wet skin and warm morning air.

Liesel tilted Harry's head back and gave her two quick breaths. Then she slid her hand to Harry's throat to check for a pulse. Her hand slipped along Harry's neck. She pulled back from the fear long enough to see that her hand was covered in blood.

"HELP. ME." This time her words were a gurgling shout.

Two more breaths.

Please.

Harry.

Breathe.

A cough was her only warning before Harry started eliminating the water from her lungs. With it came more blood, bile and hacking. Harry's whole body trembled as she leaned to her side.

Liesel pulled Harry into her arms and held her baby sister, pushed her long blonde hair away from her face, and rocked them at the waist slowly. "Help!"

"The...." Harry coughed some more, "The baby?"

"A doll. A Wonder Woman plushy," Liesel told her.

The blood was from Harry's hand. Two of her fingers were black and mangled. "What happened to your hand?"

"I was pulling the guy's leg loose of the seatbelt—"

"When I jerked him free." Oh shit. Oh shit. Liesel hadn't been careful and Harry had almost died. Would she ever learn? "I'm sorry." Her eyes heated and warm tears streaked down her icy cheeks. Her heart throbbed behind her abused ribs and her body shook from her effort to lift herself and Harry onto the bridge. Her teeth knocked against each other and she tightened her jaw to quiet the intrusion.

"A stupid doll, Harry! God damn it. Why the fuck didn't you listen? Why didn't you stay where it was safe?" Liesel's heart pounded at the side of her neck, keeping her airway tight. Black yarn hair and a gold lasso would haunt her; she could still see it spinning down into the water.

"I wanted to help you," Harry whispered.

"It's not your place. I'm responsible—"

"For who?" Harry tried to yell, then coughed and shivered. "Who, Leis? You can't be everywhere. You can't guard everyone."

"I'm sure as hell going to try."

"I won't let you stand alone," Harry closed her eyes and breathed in and out. "I won't leave you."

A firefighter with a medical kit finally reached their side. He wrapped a thermal tarp around them both and started taking Harry's vitals.

"The driver?" Harry asked him.

"Okay. I think he'll be okay," he said. "Who else was in the car?"

"Wonder Woman," the sisters said. Not a baby, not worth the sacrifice her sister had been willing to make.

Liesel squeezed Harry's uninjured hand.

She had to stop using her strength for more than opening stubborn pickle jars. She'd almost lost Harry. Even when she didn't mean to, she exposed her loved ones to danger. How many more people would she hurt? Every time this need pushed at her to save, to defend, to fight, someone got hurt. At those times she couldn't justify it away with discourses on genetics or biology. At those times it looked much more like an addiction. Getting her fix might feel good, but, just like any drug, it was destroying those she loved.

Lab Rat 2.8-12

The summer after her family moved into their tall San Francisco house, Teona and her father tore out the grass and put in a half basketball court. The hoop and key were regulation; the tall shade tree was a bonus.

Positioning her hands for a hook shot, Teona leaped, shot the imaginary ball, landed on the balls of her feet, squatted, stepped to the right and leaped again. She kept a steady rhythm. Her heart rate increasing. Her body warming. Leap, squat, step. As her thighs caught fire and quivered a plea to stop, she pushed herself further. Just fifteen more. She focused her thoughts on Freddy. She wondered if the money she'd gotten on her sixteenth birthday was enough to buy a bus ticket to go and see him. Normal, teenage thoughts ran alongside a count of each repetition.

With basketball season, intramurals and summer camps, Teona almost always practiced with a team. When she didn't, she kept to a strict personal program. She knew she wouldn't make the WNBA by just playing high school ball. Even college wasn't a guarantee.

She'd been at it for hours, switching between squats, free throws and pushups. The sweat rivulets left salt trails on her brown skin. One of her cornrows was coming loose and she pushed the wisps of hair behind her ear.

Afraid of what she could do if she saw them coming, they attacked from behind.

Thronged, fishhook probes spiked into her back. They rapidly delivered two shock pulses. They'd learned their lesson with the girl in Seattle. Two shocks. One wasn't enough.

She caught herself with the first pulse, tearing her hands and knees on the rough blacktop.

With the second—twisting thump of electricity—she banged her head against the ground and lost consciousness.

Chapter 2

A cheeky computer graphic winked next to the member's name.

CornHusker: I nominate Liesel for Queen of the Amazons

Liesel shook her head and typed her response into the chat window.

Oni: No.

Her desk was covered with files, blank DVDs, a bag of Cheetos and three bottles of water. It wasn't nearly as organized as she'd like but it reflected the messy day she'd had. Three new web clients, her first employee rearranging the office and she was all out of soda. Not only was she stressed but she was going through caffeine withdrawal.

Liesel's arms still ached from the bridge; the feel of metal still chilled her palms. She swallowed and pushed the thought away.

Queen of the Amazons. There were so many things wrong with the idea. Queens were figure heads, powerless to make any difference, and definitely not nominated. Especially not by some disembodied typer in Kansas City whose avatar was a talking ear of corn.

CBGB: I 2nd the nomination.

CornHusker: All those in favor type aye!

"Crap," Liesel said. She typed furiously to explain her reasons to decline and to steer the topic back to the monthly meeting. But before she could hit enter, more text scrolled up on the screen.

Eye

Aye

aye

eye

Eye

aye

"Great. Six in favor," she said to herself, but others were 'voicing' in and she realized that it was more than six, as variances scrolled between the ayes too quickly to catch.

Totally Eye

B:B

;)

*!& Yes

She hit enter, sending what she'd already typed and bringing up a clear line to type in. *Oni: This isn't a governing body.*

Her protest was drowned out, only staying on the screen for a second.

This was supposed to be a regular website meeting for HOAX, Home Of the Amazon eXchange. She had created the website to connect women and men with superhuman strength. It gave her an opportunity to share her research. It allowed them to support the newbies.

Kansas City was keeping track. *CornHusker: 118 Ayes so far*

"Shut up and Listen!" She yelled at the computer then hit the macro that typed the same thing. The Aye's continued, pushing her words off the screen.

CornHusker: Crap, I lost count around 315

She did a 'select all' and removed everyone from the chat group then opened a new channel with an opening statement. Meanwhile her instant messenger was making kissing noises. It made the exaggerated smooching noise when someone sent her a message. Why had she ever thought the annoying sound was cute? Her inbox registered thirty-five new messages.

"This is a web community. As owner of the server, web mistress, and creator, I have plenty of titles. This is a monthly meeting to discuss concerns regarding the site and to give an update on my research projects." Enter. Three lines of text. There was an extended pause as people rejoined the chat room.

CornHusker: I'm CONCERNED about the rights of Amazons and think we need a political presence or at least an advocate.

Ringer: If we established a board of directors.

Doohickey: We are almost two thousand members counted

Ringer: like a union or nonprofit organization

The text was being typed at the same time all over the world. It came in disjointed and out of order. Often, in a mad dash to speak first, people broke their responses in two.

CornHusker: YES PRECISELY

Thomas: What are we going to do? Form our own country? Es estúpido!

CornHusker: sorry caps

IndianPrincess: There is a national group of little people

Aqua: only English in chat please

Some members used programs to translate the English into their native tongue.

IndianPrincess: they meet annually and advocate for workplace access

Thomas: mea culpa, only you do not understand the word estúpido.

CornHusker: little people? Like midgets?

K457: vertically challenged

Aqua: go "$^! yourself Thom

Mom242: Language

BridgeMaker: Language

CBGB: Language

IndianPrincess: There is the Native American Rights Fund NARF

Aqua: I humbly apologize Liesel

IndianPrincess: and the ACLU and PFLAG

Thomas: twenty lashes with the soggy noodle

K457: wet

Mom242: wet noodle

CBGB: Indi how do you know about Parents for GLBT?

Liesel called for attention. *Oni: ENOUGH All Right! Stop or I'll restrict everyone's access to read text only.*

The word 'ENOUGH' stayed on the screen for a while then she continued her post. Later she'd pull the profile she had private investigator Jim Griffon do on CornHusker. Maybe his report would shed some light on why the guy was suddenly so hell bent on getting her elected for a nonexistent position.

She flexed her fingers and shrugged her sore shoulders. Harry was fine, and she'd keep telling herself that until the fear went away. Even now she could feel the water swaying below her feet, as if she was still on the submerged SUV and trying to reach the bridge. She swallowed to moisten her dry mouth.

Oni: I will research our options regarding nonprofit/special interest groups and post our choices in two weeks. Then we can discuss it at next month's meeting.

CornHusker: No! Not a month.

A simple right click of the mouse over Corn's name and he could no longer add to the chat.

Global: Form a committee, delegate

Her IM kissed the air.

Row-Ki: I volunteer to research our Global Options

She thought that Row-Ki was the Japanese businessman in Italy. Or was he in England this week? Liesel's stomach hurt and her eyes ached. They had sprung this on her now, without warning and she'd placate them so she could finish the meeting and get back to her paying job. Next month this would blow over.

OFN: and look at receiving minority recognition

What? Shit. That was exactly what she didn't want. The American people would never allow special treatment for people—as they would see it—that already had the advantage. It would be easier to ask for tax cuts, but only for billionaires.

But Amazons didn't have an advantage. Or rather their strength didn't outweigh the disadvantages. Faced with mistrust and unable to understand why they were different, many Amazons struggled to find a place in life where they could be themselves. Where their strength wasn't taken advantage of and exploited.

Oni: I have someone else in mind to handle the global front. Thank you though Row-Ki.

Liesel checked to see if SRS, Sarah Rustle Shift, a lawyer, was online. At the same time she rifled through the folders in her bottom draw to double check SRS's identity. Musso from New York handled her oversee background checks. He had no sense of humor and didn't report his opinions like Griffon did. But he also didn't ask questions about why she wanted a file on an international defense lawyer who once worked for the UN.

Yep, she was thinking of the right member. She was able to keep a good portion of her people straight. Two thousand people and counting and she remembered their names and locations and basic stats. It was eerie. CornHusker was sure it was an ability bestowed on her, like her instinctive knowledge of who was and wasn't an Amazon. Amazingly, it didn't require her to have physical contact. She always just knew. CBGB had dubbed her the Santa Claus of super strength.

The members in the chat room were listed alphabetically. SRS was on. Right below Squeeze.

Oni: SRS are you available to do that?

It was quiet, or there was no new text, as SRS worked on translating. *SRS: I would be most honored.*

Oni: Thank you. Now if we could please go over old business.... I hesitate to ask but any other new business?

Her text stayed put but her IM continued to make kissing noises. She clicked on it to make sure and yep, CornHusker wanted his restriction lifted.

Oni: A few announcements. For those of you who haven't yet, please make sure you turn in your questionnaire by the end of the month. Dr. Sky and Dr. Kandi are using them to trace genetic traits in Amazons and match up genealogy.

Oni: Our own Clara Larkin set a new basketball record for the National League. I don't see her mom on but congratulations. I watched via webcam, great game.

Oni: Now the biggie. The McKinnons are sending me the leather book.

The next part she had typed up earlier and cut and pasted it, a paragraph at a time, into the chat windows. Six lines of text at a time. She allowed time between pastings for the translation programs to do their thing.

Oni: As a reminder: The McKinnon family contacted me about an old manuscript that has been in the family for several generations. In the past they have made several attempts to translate the work. No one was successful.

Her headache worsened by the minute. She rubbed at her eyes, waited for the translators and posted the next paragraph.

Oni: One linguist believed the writing was possibly pre Rosetta stone and that the meaning was lost.

As she worked, her mind ran wild with possible implications. Queen. She was a web-designer and worked in her spare time gathering information on Amazons. Though, lately it wasn't just spare time. With several new financial grants for research from anonymous—and wealthy—benefactors, the research paid more than her designs. People, all over the world, wanted to know why they were Amazons. What being an Amazon meant. Meant, as in deep-meaning-of-life, meant.

She wanted to help these people but she wanted to do it through her books and website, not as some glorified political head. Worst she'd get from a book was a paper cut. Dusty tomes like the *Virgin of Guadalupe*, wouldn't put her family in jeopardy.

Oni: The leather pages have been dated and are only fifteen hundred years old. Post Rosetta stone. As the manuscript was passed down, the family was told that it kept the secrets of the Amazons.

Liesel continued her cut-and-paste of paragraphs. *Oni: I'll be receiving them in about a week but from the scans I've already been sent, I've translated the following section.*

Before posting the next and final paragraph her IM started making kissing noises. Liesel right clicked over CornHusker's name and re-established his full rights in the chat room.

Oni: Corn stop IMing me!

CornHusker: It isn't me.

Liesel pasted the last paragraph then opened the instant message window.

HeartsOnFire: Clara Larkin has been kidnapped.

She read the message twice before it sank in and a third time out loud. She'd watched Clara play basketball less than a week ago. Her outside world raced, the ceiling fan, the blinking cursor, all faster than normal. But internally, deep inside her heart and mind? Molasses. Her veins and lungs pumped at a protracted rate.

A perfect example of why she shouldn't be queen. Not only could she not maintain order in a chat meeting, speak as an advocate, or regulate the actions of others, she couldn't protect these people. Let the reign of Queen Liesel commence.

Chapter 3

The house was a remodeled historical home in Boise's North End. Private investigator Jim Griffon didn't know if it was a Victorian or what the hell it was. But it meant, for once, he would charge full price.

The front yard was green and well-tended. Tall lamps with stone bases and old beveled glass stood on either side of the front oak doors. The beautiful Boise foothills were close enough to touch. The early morning sun clutched the peaks about to pull itself over the top. *Yep, full price.*

A tall redhead opened the door before he could knock and the bubble of satisfaction burst in his chest. It was Liesel Grant. She had him on a monthly retainer to do her background checks. He had similar situations set up with property management companies that wanted a little more than a credit check before renting out their houses. But why have him drive across town if all she needed was her curiosity satisfied?

"Mr. Griffon. This way." Not really a greeting, but not as hostile as he sometimes felt around her. She held the door wide for him to step in, closed it and turned on her heels to walk down the tiled hall. She had lovely legs, smooth and shapely.

Griffon spotted the security panel at the front door, a motion device tucked into a ceiling corner, and a couple of security cameras. There were natural wood accents, overstuffed leather furniture and flowers. It smelled like a store, clean, with a hint of potpourri. But none of the scents of home, like spicy food cooking and sweaty socks.

He preferred to meet clients on his own turf. His west Boise office was two blocks from the Boise Police Department's central office and had enough traffic to make him feel like he was back home in California. Unless Liesel had moved in the last couple of weeks, this wasn't her house. Her home had the permanent sent of delicious and a postage stamp of a front yard, not the landscaped acre this house sat on.

"Sara?" Liesel said as she turned into a dining room.

"I don't know what to.... I've never...." The second woman stopped speaking as Griffon stepped into view, her eyes large. She was perfectly done up, manicured and polished. And she had been crying; her bottom lip still quivered.

Griffon hated crying women. Crying made them incoherent and made his gut cramp. "I'm Jim Griffon. You called my office." He stepped toward the lady, extended his hand. "How can I help?"

"Actually, I called," Liesel said. Oh really? His assistant Max had called with the address and since it was on his way back from the surveillance job, he didn't think about the request for a home visit. He'd need to talk to Max about giving him a heads up if he was going to do a little hand holding with an overly cautious control-freak of a client. A background check did not warrant a home visit.

Liesel didn't have the lean, shiny look of the rich as the sitting lady did. She didn't shake Griffon's hand and no one spoke. Griffon pulled out his smartphone and stylus pen from his briefcase's outer pocket. The action seemed to unpause the two women.

"Why don't you have a seat?" Liesel said, all formal.

"I'm Sara Larkin," the older lady said, "Ms. Grant is a family friend."

Just not enough of a friend to use first names or to realize that Griffon and Liesel already knew each other. He pulled a dining room chair out for her. "Ms. Grant." He could do formal too. She hesitated then sat.

Griffon walked to the opposite side and sat down as well. That was better. More like sitting behind his desk.

"So what do you need help with?"

Sara glanced to Liesel who responded, "Clara Larkin, Sara's youngest daughter, is missing."

"Have you notified the police? Filed a missing person report?"

Liesel handed him a stack of papers. A copy of the police report? How'd she manage that? Case files weren't available to the public until a case was closed and finished prosecuting. He set it next to his briefcase on the table. "How young are we talking? When did she runaway?" Griffon asked.

"Clara is seven. She was taken four days ago," Sara said.

His brain clenched in self-defense. An abduction, not a simple missing person. *Shit on a stick.* And though it had been a whole year since his own kidnapping, his nerves were immediately biting at the bit. He shoved, battered and yelled into submission the rush of memories. He had control. He would deal with this. Find a way to work around this case, around these...emotions.

But before he could process, gather his internal resolve, before he completed the thought that started with—how the hell did they get a police report on an open case—a little girl whispered behind him. "The hairy men took her."

The three adults turned to look at her in the doorway.

"Tara, this is Mr. Griffon. He's a private investigator," Liesel said. "Come sit down with us."

Sara, Tara, Clara. Great. The mother fidgeted in her seat shooting glances between her daughter and Griffon. Was she afraid of him? His rather rough features made people cautious around him, which he thought wise, but his gut said there was more going on here. More than the fucked up mess of a kidnapping.

Tara pulled out a chair on Griffon's left, ruining his 'desk.' He tried giving her a warm smile, not wanting her to be frightened. He figured she was about nine; Amy, his incredible niece, was nine. He couldn't think like that right now. He had to brace himself to apologize but decline. No, he would not find the daughter, no one would.

"Did you see them take your sister?"

She nodded.

"Did you tell the police?"

She nodded again.

Griffon picked up the report, scanning quickly. No sketch of an assailant, no warrants issued, but they had talked to the child. "Mrs. Larkin, the police have more resources, including manpower and frankly, they're free. It's only been four days. You should give them time to work." Only four days, yeah like that wasn't a sleepless lifetime.

The two ladies exchanged looks, and Liesel sighed, as if they were holding a conversation he couldn't hear. Not so odd. Women, like police officers, had their own nonverbal language. "Mrs....Sara wants to do everything she can to find her daughter," Liesel said.

And? He wanted to say, who wouldn't. Griffon turned to Tara and tried to not compare her pale hair to the dark waves of Amy's hair. God, he couldn't do it. Couldn't just walk away. If nothing else he'd find answers, new places to look. He'd share the burden of hope and shoulder some of the pain. He sighed. "What happened?"

"We were doing our homework. Clara screamed." Tara's eyes were unfocused, glassy. "He grabbed me. He had an arm around my neck and one across my face. All I saw were his hairy arms. Then Clara stopped screaming." She started crying, eyes puffy and red, and Griffon choked back a growl. Multiple men, home evasion, definitely a ransom situation rather than a sexual predator who would have grabbed her off the street or taken both girls.

"If I had been stronger...they w-would...maybe they would have taken me."

"Tara." Her mother's voice was sharp.

"Tara, we've talked about this. There's nothing wrong with you," Liesel said.

"But if we were the same...." Tara said.

"Then your parents would be worried about both of you. Besides, you don't know that you're different," Liesel said.

"What do you mean diff--?"

"Mr. Griffon," Sara cut him off, "the police are restricted to jurisdictions and rules." She clasped and unclasped her hands, a complicated process because of her long nails. Her eyes focused at a point on Griffon's chin rather than looking him in the eye. "I want someone out there looking for my daughter. Someone who isn't divided between cases."

Did she think she was his only client? He felt like sighing again. "Let's go back a moment. Doing your homework? It's August."

"The girls attend a year-round private school," Sara explained.

He flipped the report back open, scanning for a video mention, giving himself a moment to think. Sometimes while on the police force, he would get a call for one situation when other things were happening, like a domestic abuse call where drug use was apparent. He had to decide which was important; establishing trust in a victim, or eliminating drugs. Neither was a perfect solution.

In this situation, Clara, the missing seven year old, was the important issue.

"Was there anything on the security cameras?" Griffon asked.

"They only cover the artwork in the entrance hall and since we were home the rest of the security system was off," Sara said.

"So you didn't get anything on tape?"

"They came in through the kitchen."

Griffon looked at Mrs. Larkin then at Tara as he considered. Missing children were hard. Lots of dead ends and almost always death at the end. But he'd been missing once and he had nieces, young and vulnerable.

The memories pushed to the front past his barriers.

The sharp glass had cut Griffon's skin like a tomato. His skin depressed until taut, then slit to allow the sharp point. Ashley had pushed the glass in until he howled. She had pushed until she couldn't feel the glass, felt only blood, sinew, or bone. On Sunday, the other one dug out a pair of pliers and removed the beer bottles. Piece by piece. Digging around the crusty scabs to get to his inflamed skin.

Random flashbacks, just another side effect to having your life fucked over by a pair of psychos. He fisted his hand in his lap, keeping his face impassive. He had control. He resisted the telling urge to wipe his brow.

He coughed into his tense fist. Clearing out the memories and refocusing on the present.

Needing another minute to regroup, he opened his briefcase. The inside looked like a Q creation, but 007 would have had a built-in explode-on-command-option or voice activation. Griffon pulled out his netbook, opening the laptop and switching it on in one motion.

"These are my rates." He slid a card across the table, watched her face to judge her reaction. He pulled a contract from his briefcase.

"You will also be charged for any major travel expenses. Is that acceptable?"

"I'll pay you five times that. Plus all expenses," Sara said.

Griffon's eyebrows went up. Holy hell, who was this kid? A Kennedy love child? But he didn't say anything. With that kind of money, there would be a catch.

"But I want you to work with Liesel."

Uhm, hell no. His last partner had been gunned down. Unfortunately, not by him. When Sara didn't explain, he turned to look at Liesel. There had to be more here than some neighborly referral. Maybe Liesel and Sara had worked together or something and Liesel was recommending the only P.I. she knew. He knew who she was. Knew that Liesel, as a web designer, established elaborate security systems for clients and wanted to make sure they weren't doing anything illegal with it. Liesel was just a local computer geek that lived alone. Hell, he knew more about her than she probably realized but he wanted to make a point for Mrs. Larkin. "Are you with the police?"

"No. Griffon—"

"Are you with the FBI?"

"No, but I—"

"CIA, DEA, military?"

"No, but—"

"Then why would I need your help?" His voice was harsh but he couldn't neutralize it.

"My sister is—" Tara said.

"Different," Sara interrupted.

"How so?" he asked Sara.

She didn't answer, just stared at him. Liesel sighed and flexed her hands. The movement caught Griffon's eye and he watched the white to red flash of color along her knuckles.

Feeling that he wasn't going to get any further with Mrs. Larkin, he turned to really study Liesel. She had nice green eyes, smooth skin and her red hair was long and wavy past her shoulders. She was tall, quite possibly six feet, even without her heels. Best of all, she was just soft enough to be curvy. Today she wore a black V-neck stretchy T-shirt, too big to properly show those curves. He liked what he saw. Always had.

She had a bruise along her neck, faded and yellow and almost hidden by her hair. He'd heard about some car accident from guys still in the department. They said no casualties and only the sister had gone to the hospital for stitches.

"I'll appreciate any help Ms. Grant can give me on finding Clara." He tried to leave it at that diplomatic concession. He felt the need to clarify his position. He would not, *would not*, work with this woman. The fee wasn't worth the stress. And back behind the anger he felt insulted that Mrs. Larkin would suggest that he had a price. A kid needed finding and he'd use all his resources, even Liesel to find and bring her home.

"All expenses and twice my fee." Was he seriously negotiating down his price? Yes, it looked like he was. "It's important Mrs. Larkin that you realize—"

She didn't want to hear his cautionary statement. "Five times, expenses and a thousand retainer."

He lengthened his spine and crossed his arms.

"Liesel trusts you but I don't have the time to build that confidence. So, if need be, I will buy that loyalty and discretion. I want her back, Mr. Griffon, and to me, it's just money."

"For the first week five times the fee but subsequent weeks, if, god forbid, it takes that long? Standard flat fee," Liesel said. Great, a needy client that thought he could work miracles.

He took a couple of notes on his smartphone. Clara's full name and Social Security number, what the father did—he worked for a local microchip company—and how to contact Mrs. Larkin directly. He explained the contract, made the adjustments regarding his fees and printed a copy for Sara. He watched as she read through the contract. Her eyes lingered on sections of the page. Her hand shook as she signed. He passed her his business card.

"I'll call in a few hours with my initial report and to schedule a time I can come back and look around your house."

It didn't escape his notice that the police were also surprisingly missing from this little meeting. The Larkins had to have some serious sway to get a copy of the report and clear out the detectives waiting for a ransom demand. Though after four days and no contact, maybe they just assumed it had gone south, the kidnappers freaking out and killing the only real witness. Maybe no cops meant they had given up.

He shut down his laptop and disconnected the portable printer, and stowed everything—including his advance—back into his briefcase. He loved that briefcase.

Liesel stood when he did. "I need to get going as well. If you need anything Sara, anything."

Sara nodded, in survivor mode, functioning as required but not really living. Tara climbed into her mother's lap and hid her face against Sara's neck.

"I'll walk Mr. Griffon out," Liesel said.

Back down the tiled hall and out the front door. Liesel grabbed a small black purse off an entrance table as they passed.

As soon as the door was closed Griffon asked, "They don't think she was abducted by aliens, do they?" He rubbed the back of his neck, inhaling the early dew-damp air. The approaching heat would quickly eliminate all moisture.

"What?" Liesel said. They turned toward each other halfway down the walk in front of the Larkins' home. And then she smiled and his brain got fuzzy as it shut down and another part of his body powered up. "No, not aliens. Clara is an Amazon."

Liesel smelled inviting, warm. If scent could be different temperatures, she was warm. Not cool or cold. And not so hot he'd get burned by placing his lips to her lovely throat. She leaned around him and waved her hand. Griffon glanced over his shoulder to see two old ladies walking their way decked out in track suits.

"This isn't the best place to explain this. Come on over to my office." She glanced at her watch. "I've got some time before my next appointment." He watched her walk to a scooter, secure a helmet to her head, and start the engine while he stood and gapped at her.

Had she said Amazon? How fuzzy was his brain?

Chapter 4

Liesel's secretary Penelope didn't look up from her ledger as Liesel opened the front door. Liesel needed to buy her secretary a desk. The woman was going to get a serious kink in her neck. Liesel would give the task to Penelope, but the older lady would come back with a cherry wood antique and a very large bill.

Penelope raised a finger to indicate that she had heard Liesel come in but was finishing the entry. The secretary thing was still new, but it made things run smoother.

She wanted to find Clara. She wanted to take a week off and go to McCall with her sister Harry. Even better, she wanted to take Clara and Tara to McCall with Harry. Two sets of sisters reconnecting. All perfectly safe under her watchful eye. Please, let Clara be okay.

Liesel walked around Penelope and into the kitchen, pushing the hair off her neck. "Hot today." The air conditioner kept the three bedroom house tolerable, but it was turning out to be another scorcher.

Her home had been her place of business ever since she started Daemon Designs Web Development. The master bedroom and bath at the left side of the house were separated from the rest of the rooms by a long hallway. Perfect for keeping business in the office area.

"Yes, quite hot." Penelope laid her pencil down and turned to Liesel. "We are going to need to put these on the computer. It would be much faster." She fanned through the previous months' pages. "Once we enter all these back pages."

Liesel took the egg carton out of the fridge and took out a pan. "That's one of the reasons I've hired Anna."

"Hired, fhp," Penelope said. Penelope Glass hadn't reserved judgment with regards to yesterday's new addition. She had a whole month more seniority and had lived a very straight and narrow life. She didn't know what to do with the seventeen-year-old.

"Well, I will be paying her. The judge approved the half minimum wage for her hours of community service." Though the judge might be under the impression that working for Liesel was really working her mom's nonprofit breast cancer group. Liesel got out a bag of pre-cleaned green peppers. "You want some breakfast?"

"It's almost ten. Haven't you eaten?"

Liesel managed to stifle her sigh. "Sure. I ate a piece of toast and drank orange juice before I went running this morning. Then I had another piece of toast, some bacon and an apple after my shower. Now I'm going to have scrambled eggs. Want some?" She refused to hide her appetite from this woman. If the office was in a building and not her home, she might have considered it.

"It might be easier for you to lose weight if you cut back on your intake." Penelope was not quite fifty, never married, no kids, yet had perfected that cautiously sensitive tone mothers used to make suggestions. "With all that food it must be hard for you to run."

Liesel cracked a few eggs in a bowl and pulled out a fork from the drawer to scramble them. "Speaking of Anna." Which of course they hadn't been, but it was as good a way to change the subject as any. "She here yet?"

"She's in filing invoices, which should have taken ten minutes at the most." Obviously she'd been at it a bit longer.

"Hey, Anna. I'm making eggs. Want some?" Liesel yelled. Penelope shook her head, probably lamenting her current work situation. From a plush office downtown, she now worked at a private home where the boss yelled down the hall to get your attention, instead of calling your extension.

Anna Fort-Porter walked down the hall, hands deep in her front pockets, making the loose jeans sag even lower. She had a bellybutton ring, a bar bell through her bottom right lip and one through her left eyebrow. She'd dyed her hair purple-black at one point, but it had grown out. Her dark blond roots were down to her ears, then purple black to her shoulders. "You think I'll be all 'I could eat' insolent pride shit. But I'm not like that." She glared at Penelope. "I'd love some eggs. Thank you for offering."

Liesel turned back to the stove to hide her smile and added some non-stick spray to the heated pan. "How do you want them?"

"What?"

Liesel looked back at Anna. She was staring at Liesel, eyes wide, mouth open.

"Over easy? Scrambled? Sunny?"

"Scrambled is fine."

Penelope was back to her ledgers, ignoring them. Liesel had bluntly shared information about her work and left Anna and Penelope to interpret however they felt comfortable. Anna seemed to view Liesel as an overzealous comic book fan that also did web design. She wasn't sure how Penelope saw her.

Anna was an Amazon and that was a can of hissing snakes Liesel didn't want to open too soon. Finding out the truth while Liesel was answering Griffon's questions, probably wasn't the best time. The judge had contacted Liesel about Anna; had her come to Anna's hearing. No real surprise that Judge Corti would see the similarities between the two women. They might look different and Liesel hadn't had to serve time, but they were both Amazons, they'd both been charged with assault.

"Would you mind getting some plates down?" Liesel nodded to the proper cupboard then poured the eggs, scraping them with a spatula. She probably only had a few more minutes before Griffon showed up then she had a presentation for a client that afternoon. The annual Boise Susan G. Komen Race for the Cure was next weekend, a huge event for her mom's group. And, on top of that, was the delivery of the McKinnon's book. Better not freak about last minute things just yet.

"How did it go this morning?" Anna asked. "With the private dick."

"Not good but not bad." Liesel was quiet a moment, working on the eggs, thinking about the gorgeous Mr. Griffon. Though they'd only worked together on a paper level over the last year she knew he would be able to handle this case. It had taken three days to convince Sara Larkin to work with him. Even after showing the woman the news articles about his miraculous rescue and the at-cost work he did for the women's shelter finding dead beat dads for child support, she still refused. Finally it had come down to Liesel threatening to tell all to the police if Sara didn't seek help. She didn't fully understand the woman's fear. "He's coming over to ask me a few questions."

"Are you a suspect?" Penelope asked.

"If I was, I'm sure the police would have been here to question me by now." Liesel slid half the eggs onto a plate and handed them to Anna.

"Yeah, they'd be all over this place. But no one would think that of you. It would be like suspecting the pope of doing something illegal. Of course, all those catholic priests...."

Liesel lost her appetite. Was Clara being fed? She stared at her plate, pushed her food around.

"I think I'll send you guys on a shopping trip," Liesel said. "A desk for the living room and a few things." Liesel wrote down the list on a post-it. "Think cheap. Anna, I expect you to help Penelope stay in budget."

"Which is?"

"Look at it this way. Spend too much and it comes out of your pay."

The teenager shoveled food as she walked to the sink. She deposited her plate then followed Penelope to the door. Anna whispered a thank you to Liesel as she passed. They slid out as Griffon was walking up the driveway, so they left the door open, nodding a greeting in passing. Liesel leaned against the counter trying to eat her eggs and munching on green peppers. She could see Griffon out the big front window.

He rapped on the door jamb, probably unable to see her at first, because of the glaring sun behind him.

"Come in."

He paused just inside the door to let his eyes adjust to the light change. Liesel crossed to the door to put her shoes on, not wanting to be even slightly at a disadvantage.

"Okay, I'm here. Show me." Prove it, he meant. He looked mean or maybe just mad. His black hair, though short, was curly. He had intense eyes. He looked like a dark Athena warrior, rich olive skin, thick archy eyebrows, strong eyes and plenty of definition beneath his collared shirt. And did she mention his eyes with their dark, inky lashes. Worth a repeat. Top to bottom, WOW. Though, now that she thought about it, she hadn't seen his backside today. He was partially Hispanic, or so Musso's background check had said.

Liesel greeted him without too much of a stumble or pause. The stammering-ogle fest happened earlier. She had watched him walk up to the Larkin's house, her heart fluttering and her body humming its approval. If asked she'd admit to requesting reports in person so she could go to his office and just look at him. But she wasn't volunteering the information.

"Thanks for coming. I know the whole home visit thing.... Thanks. It'll be easier to talk without the Park Avenue set peering out their windows at us."

She led the way into her office and gestured toward a chair. She was proud of this room. The house was a typical ranch style on the Boise Bench, decent lawn with full sprinklers—she would never remember to water otherwise—and plenty of rooms.

However, the office was the best room. Three walls had floor-to-ceiling bookshelves. Four computer towers, a jukebox, two filing cabinets, a tasteful and cheap desk and two overstuffed armchairs. Cramped. Cozy. The chairs didn't match anything else in the room, not even each other. Liesel felt the chairs made the room welcoming, by offsetting the rest of the metal decor. The jukebox, similar to its musical cousin, held hundreds of computer discs. Each disc contained research books and website files.

Griffon ignored the chairs and walked toward the jukebox in the corner. "I heard one of these babies can hold five times the average PC."

"A lot more, actually," she said. He had the same gleam in his eyes that she got when she talked tech. His presence had her nerves jangling.

He checked out her equipment and she checked out his rear. Very nice. She could imagine running her hand over the curve of his ass. Using the new grip to pull him tighter against her heated body. Kissing a trail up the back of each knee.

"You running an internet server?"

Who knew that techno talk could make her even more turned on?

"Among other things." Liesel sat in one of the chairs and watched Griffon prowl the room. She repeated a little mantra in her head to calm herself, feeling flushed. Keep it professional, be confident, no more ogling his ass.

When he didn't say anything else, she added, "I have a computer science degree from Boise State and my design business is growing nicely, as you probably know. I have a very good client base."

He walked around her desk and bent for a closer look at the jukebox. Still, he didn't comment. His Dockers pulled tight across his ass. Oh, my.

"I promise to show you the rest of my toys later, but for now we should get a few explanations out of the way."

He whipped his head around and stared at her, eyes narrowed. He stood and leaned a hip on her desk, crossed his arms. Maybe P.I.s felt suspicious of everyone they worked with. He had to either think she was overly paranoid or that there was more going on than web designing. He'd be even more suspicious if she had only used him for background checks instead of spreading the jobs to Musso as well.

She'd practiced this, said it to others, but it was always awkward at first like a second language she didn't use enough. It sounded stilted, broken, until she got going.

"Everyone has physical things they are born with that makes them different from others. Eye color, ability to roll your tongue, larger lung capacities. Some are born Amazons." She didn't pause to gauge his reaction. "They are not bitten or cursed. It is not something they choose. They are just born different."

Amazons often greeted the knowledge with a sense of relief. But she had seen a wide spectrum of responses, even hostility. And it was even harder to gauge the reaction of a regular human, though nothing was all that average about Griffon.

"So it's a genetic mutation."

She cocked her head and gave a half shrug. "No, no mutants. There have always been Amazons, just like there have always been good-looking men with curly hair." Did she say that? Flirting wasn't professional. *Shit.* She shifted in her seat, keeping her eyes stern, hoping he wouldn't react. "They exist in history, believed to be legend or myth." She gestured at some of her books. "But they are very real."

"So what are we talking about? Superhuman strength?" He left the desk and walked toward the bookshelf closest to him, scanning the spines.

"Superhuman strength, longevity, high metabolism. At least for most." She hesitated to give him the whole story, worried that she would overload him.

"Hatred of men?" he sneered.

Liesel caught her breath, unnerved by the anger from him and her sudden fear. She trusted Griffon, hell she even liked him as a person. She didn't need to be afraid. But boy, he could turn the power of that gaze on a person and have them babbling in their corn flakes for the rest of their lives. "People are not born with hatred. It is taught. So, if a woman hates men, Amazon or not, it is something she has learned." Where was her sharp, watch-it-buddy voice when she needed it?

"So, the Larkins are warrior women?"

"No. One is not born a warrior."

"Ah, it's taught." His voice was rife with derision.

"Just because a boy is tall, doesn't mean he would make a good basketball player. There has to be a desire, a natural grace. Though maybe basketball isn't the right example since Clara does play...." Liesel swallowed back the pain just saying the girl's name created. "She has the build of a ballerina, but has no desire to dance."

"And her mom? She didn't look all that powerful?"

"Mrs. Larkin...Sara...isn't an Amazon. I believe it was passed through the father. You see, there are dominant and recessive genes—"

"I have a minor in biology and have spent more time in CS— crime scene labs—than I ever wanted to. You don't have to talk down to me."

Liesel stared at his hard face, kept eye contact, didn't back down.

"Good. That will make this part easier." She stood and walked toward him. The room was small enough that she had to brush by him to get to her desk. Instead of waiting for him to stand aside, she kept going, her thigh gliding up the length of his, her arm bumping his shoulder. It felt so nice. Now, if only he would stay put so she could do that again.

Liesel pulled out a pen and notepad from her desk and walked back around him. This time he moved out of her way. She sat down on the middle of the desk, doing a little shimmy. She realized that her skirt was hiking up, pulled her thighs together and tried to look prim. Men wore oxford jackets and slacks to look professional. Maybe she should consider it.

She started drawing on the paper and Griffon perched next to her and leaned in. She drew a capital 'A' and a little 'a.'

"The Amazon gene is dominant, while non-Amazon or little 'a' is recessive. Any girl born with 'A' from the father or mother will be an Amazon. However, a son is born with a 'y' chromosome that is dominant to the 'x.' The 'y' makes them male." She drew a series of 'a' and 'x' combinations. "Mrs. Larkin, and we can only assume her parents as well, is 'ax, ax'— receiving a recessive gene and 'x' chromosome from each parent. Mr. Larkin's mother was an Amazon, probably an 'Ax,ax', though we're not sure. She passed that to her son making him an 'ay,Ax', non-Amazon. But all of his daughters will be 'ax,Ax', Amazons."

Of course, that didn't explain the rather complicated double-Amazons, 'Ax, Ax' or 'Ax,Ay.' Or why there was a line of male Amazons. But since she was still working that out herself, it was probably wise to leave that until necessary.

"All of his daughters? What about Tara?"

The man was smart enough to realize the discrepancy and nice enough to remember Tara's name. Major points in Liesel's book. "Tara is an Amazon. The strength doesn't manifest at the same age for everyone."

"During heightened emotional states?" Sarcastic.

Liesel knew he was referring to Dr. Jean Grey's speech from the X-Men movie. She glared at him.

They sat in silence for a while. Griffon sighed. "I'm not saying I believe you—or hell, even understand—but if Amazons are just strong humans, why bring in a P.I. to find a missing one? Don't you have an Amazon task force? A secret connection to the FBI? The First Lady in your pocket?"

Liesel couldn't read his face, but the dark emotions that she saw there made her glad she didn't explain that she too was an Amazon. "There aren't many Amazons left and they are scattered. And the number who actually know they are Amazons is even less."

"Not know? How could you not know?"

"How much do you bench press?"

"What?"

"You know, you lie on your back and...." She demonstrated lifting a bar.

"I know what bench pressing is. I'm trying to understand how that—" He pulled the last few words through his gritted teeth.

"People don't know they are strong, or how strong they are, unless they are tested. Women, raised in a male dominant society, are taught to not display strength. They clean and sew and sit quietly. They do not run or play sports. Or rather they didn't. It has only been in the last hundred years that women have realized that they may be more than just...women. But still there was the stigma of being different, the worry of overshadowing the men they love."

"Overshadowing? How strong are we talking?"

"Stronger than Buffy but not as strong as Superman." Liesel gave a little chuckle but Griffon only frowned. "As in Buffy the Vam—"

"I'm familiar with the show."

"Personally, I'm a Spike fan. Angel is a melodramatic prick."

Griffon gave her another little frown then asked, "So why a P.I.?" His tone was the same as he probably used on incoherent, overwrought victims, as if directing her back to the point of the story.

"Mrs. Larkin has only known Clara was an Amazon for about six months. It's a bit of a shock to watch your daughter lift couches out of the way to find a pair of shoes. And I don't mean lifting one end." Liesel started swinging her legs, tapping them lightly against the desk. "Mrs. Larkin is still struggling with the knowledge. She hired you, I think, because she doesn't want to expose her daughter to the public. If she was kidnapped for....ransom, say and we get her back but meanwhile we've told the government that she is supper strong. I mean, what's to prevent them from taking advantage of that?"

She rubbed the bridge of her nose, then placed her hand on the desk, raised her shoulders in a shrug. She looked at her knees as she thought about the day Clara was taken. "I do know one thing though. It would've taken more than one man to get her out of that house. Especially as quietly as they did."

They were close enough for her to look into his eyes, but he wasn't looking at her. She could feel his thigh next to her hand on the desk. Inches away. He smelled of coffee and the rich erotic smell of his aftershave. He had such long lashes, they curled like his hair. She wondered if all his hair was curly. The heat from his skin felt amazing in the chilly room. The phone rang and Liesel leaned into Griffon's body to reach for the phone.

She'd given him the stock photo view of the situation. He could believe or not.

Chapter 5

Lab Rat 1.8-11

When she woke, Clara Larkin knew she had been asleep a long time. Probably days. The eye crusties stuck like glue to her lashes. Her whole body felt heavy and her mouth tasted like the lint underneath her bed. She knew she wasn't in her pink bedroom and she knew, almost immediately, that she was in danger. The lights above her blazed. Once on a dare, she had looked into the light bulb of the overhead projector Sister Courtney used for spelling tests. Both now and then she saw black smudges across her eyes.

She blinked and tried to look around. She was in a plastic Tupperware square bowl. At least that's what it looked like. Her mom used them to freeze lasagna. "Mommy?"

There were other people, just out of sight.

She yelled this time, "Mommy!"

None of the others turned at the noise.

Griffon sat quietly next to Liesel on the desk as she answered the phone. He didn't consider this as a possible joke. No one he knew would set up such an elaborate scheme just to trick him or get even. All of his enemies, and thankfully there weren't many, leaned toward the shoot-them-in-the-head type revenge. Except for his ex-partner, she hadn't believed in revenge. Ashley had believed in massive retaliation. So Liesel's story of super-humans just didn't fit anywhere.

"Yes, I have time next week...." Liesel spoke into the phone.

Okay, God did some really weird things. People were born with birth defects like extra fingers or brittle bones. But those were all bad things. Griffon had worked with a psychic while on the police force, and since scientists said people only use a percentage of their brain, psychic abilities made sense to him. But a group of women that were extra strong? He was going to hold onto his skepticism awhile longer.

"I'm just not available tomorrow, sir. I am more than willing to...Well, thank you. Yes, please call to schedule that. Goodbye." She shook her head and pushed the end button on the phone, setting it next to her instead of hanging it back on the base.

The computer on the large desk behind them beeped. "Oh, man, it's late," Liesel said.

Griffon looked out the single window. The sun hadn't even reached its peak. "You got some place you have to be?"

"No, it's just that I didn't plan for any of this. Okay, that sounds stupid. You don't plan for kidnapping. What I mean is that I have this whole schedule thing, and I'm really behind today. I have a web presentation this afternoon."

She pushed with her arms and hopped off the desk. Her skirt clung high to her thighs for a moment then settled back to her knees. But not before Griffon saw the top of a lacy stocking. Wasn't that a glorious sight? And his body was thinking, for once, the same thing his brain was. He growled low in his chest, and she jerked and turned at the noise.

"What's the matter?"

He stood too and realized that he was shorter than her, at least with her heels on. "How tall are you?"

"You're growling at me because I'm tall?"

"No, I'm growling at you because you're wearing a sexy pair of stockings. How tall?"

"Six feet. But just barely."

He raised his eyebrows.

"When a girl wishes she was shorter, that 'just barely' is important."

He stepped forward, bringing them closer. "If you want to be shorter, then why do you wear heels?" Griffon made sure his voice was slow and smooth. Sexy. He'd never had problems getting women to his bed. He had learned at an early age what women liked. And he knew that Liesel appreciated what she saw when she looked at him.

"I've got big feet."

Griffon laughed. Talking to Liesel often turned out to be a very rough translation from female to male. A totally arousing, thrilling translation. "And big feet mean?"

"It's harder to find shoes when you've got big feet, less selection." Liesel stepped out of one of her shoes bringing her to eye level and a couple of critical inches closer. "Man, you've got scary eyes."

"Thanks," Griffon said.

"Well, I'm sure you like them. Gives you that intimidating edge. Don't mess around with Jim."

"Sometimes it's nice to be messed with. Then I can mess back." Griffon placed his hand at her waist and ran it over her hip and down her thigh. He watched her eyes dilate and smirked. But the action drew her attention to exactly how close they were standing. She stepped back.

"Mr. Griffon, we're going to be working together—"

"No, we're not."

"But—"

"I don't see any way you can help me." Okay, except for this ache in my groin. And it had been long enough since he'd ached, that it had a bitter sweet quality.

"Well, once you've had a chance to go over the police report and talk to the Larkin family again...."

"I read most of it on my way here. The police are doing their job well, and I'm not going to waste my time or the Larkins' money, no matter how much they have, by doing the work twice. I'll find something, an angle or suspect, which the police aren't working and head in that direction."

"This could be that direction," Liesel said.

"Six months since she realized she was an Amazon and a mother who is secretive? How many people really know?" Besides the lady standing in front of him. Now he just needed his dick to realize she was a suspect and he might be able to keep his head clear enough to do his job.

"Besides me? I don't know. Clara could have told any one of her friends."

"The police have questioned her entire class. Gone door to door in the neighborhood. Nothing. Besides, who would believe her?"

"Anyone who asked for a demonstration." She sounded exasperated. "This isn't a disease or a royal blood line. Strength is a very physical thing."

Didn't he know it. "Maybe she did show someone, but who? I think this was someone looking for a ransom, but the job got botched, so they cut their losses and took off."

Liesel gasped, her hands covering her mouth. Then her eyes turned hard. "You think she's dead." Her eyes glistened and Griffon swore to himself that if she started to cry he could leave, no guilt.

"That is what happens in most of these cases. If there was any hope for her, she would have been found within the first two days." A little shiver went through Liesel's body and Griffon rolled his eyes. "I didn't realize you were so close. You keep referring to her mother as Mrs. Larkin."

"Sara's a silly, closed minded...dope." It was obvious that she had restrained herself from using a harsher word. "But Clara is one of my girls. I feel responsible for her."

Liesel gave a little sniff but no tears leaked out of her eyes. *Thank you, God.* Griffon patted her. Awkward pats, the opposite of seduction. Way to go Griffon.

"I'm going to head to my office, run her stuff through the computer and contact a few people with the police department. I'll call you before I go back over to the Larkin's, let you know if I find anything helpful." It irked to offer that much but better to reassure her than have her sobbing on his shoulder.

She nodded. "Okay." Then she pulled a card from a little brass holder on her desk. "I have a new cell phone number." The business card read Liesel Grant, than had a bunch of weird symbols under her name.

"What are these?" He pointed to the odd symbols.

"It's Greek. It says Amazons."

"So that's what you do, besides the web thing?" Or maybe rather than the web thing. How many background checks had he done for this chick and did all those people think they were Superheroes? "Do you run an Amazon help group or something?"

"More on the 'or something' side. I'm considered the Historian. I'm researching and developing a database on all things Amazon. From Greek mythology to present day genetic research. There is evidence in almost every culture of superhuman warriors that—"

He could tell she was warming to her subject but he couldn't handle any more unbelievable information right now. And it was getting increasingly more difficult to think with his brain. She was passionate about her work. It made her glow and was sexy as hell.

"We'll have to talk more on that someday. Fascinating."

"You're right." She smiled, distracted by her own thoughts.

A beautiful way for a woman to look. Distracted.

Chapter 6

Sara, Clara, Tara, even the maternal grandmother was named Mara. *Shit*. Griffon needed to call his mom and thank her for naming his brother Frank. The Larkins paid their bills on time, except in January after holiday spending. They had lived in Boise for more than ten years. Their trash day was Tuesday and Mr. Larkin collected Pez dispensers. Griffon could find any desired information on the adult Larkins. But, other than their grades at a local private school and birth announcements, there wasn't much on the two girls.

Griffon's office was on Franklin near the police station. A hair shop called 'Bush Whacker' was on his left and a take-and-bake pizza joint was on his right. The office was in a good location and had three exit's including the front door. Plus, the previous leasers, an accounting firm, had a storage cage installed with high-grade chain-link fencing and numeric keypad entry. Griffon kept his arsenal in there.

He typed in the first web address from Liesel's business card. Daemon Designs was a simple three page site describing her services, how to contact her and hyperlinks to sites she had designed or currently maintained. She had a few new links up, all high end elaborate projects. Chick knew her shit. The second web address h.o.a.x.com brought up a blank page asking for a password. Now that was interesting. Griffon stared at the blinking cursor for a moment then typed 'Amazons' and pressed enter. A message came back.

"Nice try. You may try again tomorrow." Griffon read out loud. "What the?" He clicked on the reload button.

The page was no longer blank but had a little cartoon character wagging a single finger back and forth in a 'shame, shame' sort of way. The message below the cartoon read 'Your computer has already tried today and you have now reset your twenty-four-hour time limit.' The website must read and store the IP, internet protocol, address of each computer that tried to access the website. Very smart. But it was fairly easy to change one's address. However, you would only have one more try before you had to reset it again.

Griffon switched programs and ran Liesel's name through the police database as he pulled his hard copy file on her and added it to his growing pile. No arrests. One speeding ticket two years ago. Original license issued at age fifteen, which meant she had lived here at least since then. He flipped through the file and the few pictures she had, reviewing the details, seeing if anything popped out at him. The file also stated she was twenty-eight. She looked younger.

The Larkins' Amazon grandmother was dead, so Amazons could die, but Liesel had said something about longevity. What the hell did that mean? Now that the initial disbelief was wearing off, he had questions; lots of them.

If Liesel had presented the idea of Amazons as some God-blessed, mythical beings, he wouldn't have bought it for a moment. But a genetic difference seemed reasonable. Surely exaggerated but reasonable.

Griffon placed a call to Lieutenant Bit. Lt. Bit was in charge of the Larkin investigation. They exchanged small talk about Bit's kids and Griffon's job. It had been long enough, finally, that the awkward feeling between them was gone. Lt. Bit had rescued him when Griffon's psycho ex-partner had kidnapped him a year ago. A week later she'd gotten her fondest wish, suicide by SWAT.

"You hired that retired Max Wallace, I heard," Lt. Bit said.

Max had retired from the L.A. Sheriff's department. He then did twenty years as an Ada County Sheriff, in Idaho. Now, in his sixties and enjoying money from two retirement funds, Max couldn't stand being at home with nothing to do. He came in each morning, answered Griffon's phone, drank Griffon's coffee and helped on the occasional stake-out. Griffon kept him because he was a wealth of experience and contacts.

"Good guy, Max," Lt. Bit said.

"Yeah," Griffon said. "I've been hired by the Larkins to look for their daughter."

"Good to know they have faith in us."

"It's not like that. Just doing all they can to find her."

"Perhaps. I'm surprised though. Mr. Larkin has been helpful getting the investigation going." Bit's voice was muffled, probably taking a sip of his coffee.

"I don't think he knows his wife hired me."

"Wouldn't it be nice if we could stay out of sticky stuff like that?"

That would be a no-shitter. "So, what you guys got on Clara? Any leads?"

"No. The sister can't give us any details but a white, hairy man. The doors had been left unlocked. It's a nice neighborhood and it was the middle of the afternoon. No one locks doors in the middle of the day around here. Heck, plenty still don't lock them at night. Neighbors saw a 'dirty van' parked out front. Whether it was white or tan is still being debated. I don't even have a partial on the plate just that it was out of state."

"Which state?"

"The neighbor didn't know. Just thought it didn't look like an Idaho plate."

Griffon leaned back in his chair. The screen of his phone was blank, cursor blinking. "That's got to be frustrating."

"Everyone loves this kid. All the neighbors, teachers. Even the checkout clerk at the local grocery store. I've started carrying extra handkerchiefs with me." Griffon knew that Bit was perplexed by the case, not annoyed with the show of emotion. Griffon had never figured out what to do with crying victims but Bit had that knack. Might come with him being married.

"I see the FBI is involved."

"If it had been a grab off the street, they wouldn't touch it. But with them entering the home and taking her specifically.... Guess they're curious and they're using the possible cross state plates as jurisdiction."

"So nothing?" Griffon doodled a little on one corner with the stylus pen as they talked.

"Well, we've got the local channels airing the story a couple of times a day, missing posters. The standard. You know. It brings in a lot of calls, each of which have to be followed up, but nothing promising. We would start a search through the foothills with the dogs, but we don't even have a place to start, so that's kind of pointless."

There were plenty of natural hazards surrounding Boise, the mountains on one side, a desert on the other. Many manhunts required trekking through both extremes for days.

"What about the Larkins themselves?"

"Mr. Larkin is the Police Commissioner's godson or something. We did a cursory search on them but that's all. We'll leave it up to the FBI if they want to pursue that angle. What about you? What do you think of the Larkins?"

"Typical family of four." Griffon figured that was a safe middle of the road answer. He realized he'd written Clara's name over and over. He cleared the screen.

"Well, keep me informed if you find something and let us know if we can help."

"Thanks. I will. See you?" Griffon said.

"Yeah."

They hung up and Griffon tapped his pen against the screen on his lap. Why hadn't the national channels picked up the story? Sure, Boise was small compared to L.A. and New York, but that was why a crime like this seemed so huge. Was someone keeping things quiet or were the Networks not getting the sob story they wanted? With more than a hundred thousand kids missing each year, perhaps this was just one more to add to the list.

Time to call the Larkins. Griffon picked up Liesel's card, tapping its edge on his desk. He did say he'd call her first. He grabbed the phone and dialed her number.

She'd sat so prim next to him on that desk, sending out her warm scent. As he listened to her answering machine he could almost smell her; felt his body flush with desire.

"I'm not available at the moment. Please leave your name and number and I'll return your call. *Contácteme en tres. Yo sólo hablo inglés.*" Was that Spanish? "*Je ne parle pas francais. S'il vous plaît me contacter oni@daemondesigns.com.*" After that Griffon lost track of any kind of pattern. Griffon was sure the last little bit was in Japanese. Each language beside English was slightly computerized rather than Liesel's voice. The machine beeped and he sat silently trying to remember why he'd called.

"Shit, Liesel, who do you have calling you? This is Jim Griffon. You have my number. Nothing new on Clara. I'm going over to the Larkins.'" Griffon didn't know what else to say, so hung up. What would she do if someone left a message in Japanese, which she obviously didn't speak? Heck of a website company that needed Japanese as a language option. Which got him thinking, he'd never processed a background check for anyone other than in the United States. She was way too thorough and cautious to just not do them. Who else did she use? What other secrets was she hiding?

He picked up her folder and headed to the front office. "Hey Max! I need you to do some digging for me."

At seven that night, he sat crossed legged in the middle of little Clara's very pink room.

The china dolls and tea set must have been Sara's doing. Because all the personal things, the ones that had been touched, worn, used, were not girlie at all. Clara had three signed basketballs in her closet, a pile of sport jerseys in her pajama drawer and a very tattered pair of sneakers. The sneakers sat next to a hardly worn pair of Mary Janes. He read a few letters and a postcard Clara had sent home from a sports camp earlier that summer. She sounded like a typical seven-year-old. Her penmanship was better than his.

Tara came to the door and looked at Griffon. "Is your room this pink?" Griffon asked.

"No. Mine's purple." She had a hint of disdain in her voice.

"Do you have any ideas who took her?"

Tara shook her head.

"Was anyone ever mean to her?"

Again the head shake.

"Not even at school? Like a bully?" Griffon lifted a pile of school papers from her miniature desk, rifling through them. He was surprised by Clara's photograph. When he'd looked at the one in the police file, he had expected a bulky, muscular girl with boyish hair. Instead, she was slender, with a pert round face and long dark blonde hair. This photo, of her basketball team, showed how tall she was.

"Well, once a boy tried to kiss her."

"What happened?" Griffon lifted his head.

"The boys chase the girls and try to kiss them during recess. The little kids. I'm too big for that kind of stuff."

Griffon had kissed his first girl that way. It made him smile to remember that kiss. Tara didn't say anything and Griffon realized she was waiting for his response. "Of course."

"Well, Tommy tried to kiss her again and she said she wasn't going to let him. When he caught her, she pushed him really hard. Broke his neck bone."

Griffon gasped at her words. "His what?" Tara pointed to her collar bone. "That's the collar bone."

"Yeah, that one. He couldn't run after the girls for a whole month."

It was a long shot but it was all he had, "Do you remember Tommy's last name?"

Chapter 7

"It wasn't just one collar bone. It was both of them. Clean in two." Max had tracked Tommy Mitchum's dad down to an office off Park Center Blvd., Boise's second downtown. Mr. Mitchum worked the night shift, cleaning. Good thing that private schools had scholarships. As Mr. Mitchum talked, he wound a cord back onto a vacuum cleaner. "Me and his mother worried that it was some sign of disease. You hear about fragile bones, because of leukemia, doing that to kids. But doctor says he's fine."

Mitchum shook his head and continued, "Tommy's been real upset since Clara's been gone."

Park Center pond, surrounded by thousands of Boise's famous evergreen trees, laid three floors below and six feet out the all-glass wall of the office building. Griffon's office was fifteen minutes down the Connector from Park Center. Of course, pretty much everything was fifteen minutes away from everything else in Boise.

"Bit young for love sickness," Griffon said.

"Thought the same. I thought even maybe he had seen something. Heard something and didn't know how to tell anyone. But he says his heart aches when he doesn't see her." Mitchum chuckled. "My son the Casanova. His teenage years are going to be fun."

Griffon decided to pass Tommy Mitchum off to Lt. Bit. There wasn't anything there anyway and if the little boy broke down in front of Griffon, he would have to spend the rest of the day in his favorite electronic store on a spending spree to bolster his spirits again.

Liesel was out running. So what if it was in the general direction of Griffon's office. She wasn't going to go that far. Her goal was six miles. The pedometer on her hip said she was almost to the turnaround point.

She breathed in and out, her rhythm steady like her heartbeat and the pounding of her feet. Even her arms had their own dance steps and moved accordingly. She no longer needed to think about it. Running. She listened instead to the noises around her, what she called 'Early Morning Boise', track three, also known as 'Paperboys and Bakery Trucks.'

The neighborhood had sidewalks—most did—and several yards were being watered by automatic sprinklers, also known as track four.

There were green trees and lawns but there was also a desert surrounding this oasis-like valley. The humidity was nonexistent. The mornings were cool. It would be over a hundred by noon.

Five days. Five days since Clara had been taken. Five days since the online group had voted her in as queen. Life wasn't looking so great. She had this constant feeling of not knowing which direction to go in. She wasn't standing still. Yet she couldn't tell, for the life of her, which direction she was going in.

Cars were parked along the road giving her a natural shield against traffic, though there wasn't much this early. Soon people would be off to work and the cars would be parked someplace else. She turned a corner. The sidewalk was old and a row of hedges and trees hid the house on her left.

Thump, thump. Her rhythm altered because of a tight dipping driveway. The trees, cottonwood, pine, spruce—she didn't know the difference—were determined to reclaim the land. The tree roots had raised the sidewalk. She watched her feet so she wouldn't stumble over the cracks.

"This is not where you usually run."

She didn't hear the words, only reacted to the figure stepping through a hedge at her left, and dropped back from the sidewalk. She reached in her pocket for her mace, which she had forgotten at home. Damn it all to hell and back twice. Her heart, no longer steady, jerked about in her chest like a cell phone set on vibrate.

"Hey!"

A hand reached for her and she panicked. Please, don't let me hurt anyone. She jerked her arm out of his grasp and ran.

Immediately, something sharp and solid hit her mid-shin and she staggered, almost doing a face plant on the cement. Hands grabbed her around the waist and twisted them both to the side. She landed on him, thumping hard against his legs. Using the momentum, she twisted into the hedge on her knees. Leaves and branches smacked her face. She jerked her torso back, trying to regain her feet, but her leg wouldn't support her.

"Liesel."

Her assailant pushed her again and her butt hit the sidewalk. He smacked her hand away from her leg; she hadn't even realized she was reaching for it. He smacked it like the piano teacher had the one and only time she went for lessons. All in the wrist.

She finally looked and saw more than the sweatshirt, broad shoulders and baseball cap.

It was Griffon. Her heart, still on vibrate, began playing 'Mission Impossible', triple time.

"Shit. Oh, Griffon, did I hurt you?" Her hands reached for him. "Please say you're okay."

He jerked back from her hands. They had blood on them, her hands. But it was her blood. No biggie. She wasn't fussed about it.

Breathe and look with the eyes, Liesel told herself. Breathe and make your throat work. Talk without gasping. She realized he may not understand her. "I'm...okay." Breathe and talk. You do it all the time.

"I'm okay." She said again and looked at him, pleading with her eyes. His initial reaction was pulled back behind his mean eyes and stony face. "Are...you okay?"

"Why the hell didn't you yell?"

She pressed her hand to her chest, pressed her heart back in place. He looked haggard and she doubted that he'd slept at all last night.

"If you thought I was an attacker why didn't you yell?" Griffon said.

"I didn't...yell." Not such a long pause that time. She wiped the sweat from her face and felt the heat from her skin.

"Stop that." He snatched her hand away and used his own hand to wipe her forehead. "Let's take a look at that leg." His hand shook.

"Crap. How'd that happen?" The adrenaline, having served its purpose, left and she could feel her leg. It hurt like hell.

"Though why people say that, when no one can really know what hell feels like," she mumbled to herself.

"Are you delirious?" he said.

"It's that or crying." She lifted her head and smiled at him, pleased to see him smile back. Her ponytail was loose and a long tendril fell into her eyes. She left it. Maybe he would reach up and sweep it behind her ear. A girl could hope.

She straightened her leg from its bent position, felt the skin pull around the long gash, but it wasn't bleeding. Not excessively. Her hands grasped either side of her leg, lending support, and she hissed air through her teeth.

"It's turning colors and looks swollen."

"How'd...?" She glanced over her shoulder back at the sidewalk.

Griffon raised up to a crouch.

There was a metal pole sticking up from the sidewalk. Probably the remains of a damaged or removed street sign. "Or damaged and then removed." She turned to look at him, and realized she'd spoken out loud again. "Just trying to help the delusional-non-crying state." She laughed. "Nice of them to tie that decorative orange flag on the hazard."

"I tried to stop you from hitting it."

"Well, that explains the attempt to grab me. But not why you're here. Why did you jump out of the hedge at me?" She added plenty of pissed-off to her voice. She took a deep breath and focused again on her heart rate. It was still racing right along but not because she'd been running.

He pulled his sweatshirt off then his T-shirt. Hello, pretty abs. They rippled and flexed. He had scars—jagged, raised, pink ridges—but before she could do more than register them, he'd pulled the sweatshirt back on.

"Hey."

He misunderstood her outrage. "It's clean. Just put it on this morning." It was brown, the T-shirt. Not black or white. And may have said something, she didn't know. He used the T-shirt to wipe at her leg. Sweet and Romantic? Wrong. Ouch and fudge and gosh darn and air sucked between her teeth.

"I want to make sure you don't have any debris."

"Admit it. You get off making me hurt," she joked.

His hand stilled—the color in his face gone—than continued. "You'll want to get a tetanus shot."

"Had one. Karma's mutt bit me."

"Where?"

"At her house. Being protective."

Griffon snorted, his version of a chuckle. It was remarkably endearing. "No. Where did it bite you? On your body."

"My hand."

She noticed he hadn't needed clarification on who Karma, her older sister, was. Meant he'd gotten around to checking her out. She leaned back, placing her weight on her palms, and let him look at her leg. But he wasn't looking at her leg.

She looked where he did. There were no scars on her hands. She blushed and kept her eyes down. Think of something to say! Probably knew that she hadn't needed stitches. Her mind scampered about. Did he think she was lying? Then she remembered he hadn't answered her. "You haven't told me why—"

"I passed you in my car. I found some rather interesting things in your juvenile record." He flipped the T-shirt over her shoulder and stood. Smooth. Agile. She felt weird staring at him as she leaned back on her hands. She looked at her leg again. It looked better now that he had cleaned away the blood.

"Aren't you going to ask what?"

"Okay, I'll play. Whatever did you find in my past?" She added plenty of Scarlet to her voice, even lifting her head to bat her eyelashes. She was bound to be a suspect. And to bring her even higher on his list of people to investigate, the Police didn't know about her. She wasn't surprised that he'd went searching, just that he'd found something so quickly.

His lips tightened. "Roger Davies. Matthew Caldicott."

"He preferred Matt."

"Were you having words over his name, when you broke his nose and arm?" Exactly how a detective would ask. Had asked.

"Actually, Matt's arm was a sprain. Roger had the broken arm."

"And the broken jaw and the —"

"Look. That was over ten years ago. Point?"

Fuming, Griffon thrust his hands in his pockets. She could see his shoulder muscles jump through the sweatshirt.

"You didn't ask me how I found out," Griffon said.

"I didn't yell. I didn't ask what. I didn't ask how." Her voice rose as she got to her feet. She kept her hands down and low until she was sure of her balance. "I didn't thank you for your help. And I didn't swoon when you took off your shirt. If we stand here long enough, I'm sure you can tell me a few things else I should have done." She was loud. Not yelling. Just loud.

"I—"

"But one thing I want you to know. Right. Now." She poked a finger at his chest. "I contacted you because I knew you were good. You checked on me? I've done my homework too." She turned and started walking back the way she came. At first, the leg was stiff but she was able to walk without a limp by the time she got to the corner. Hurt? Yes it did. But no limp. "I know you were in the military as an MP while getting your associates degree via correspondence and on-base classes. Then you finished your Bachelor degree at San Francisco State University. You received several accommodations and were on the dean's list."

"I want you to tell me what happened to those two guys." He followed but stayed behind her.

"Then you came to Boise and went through the police academy here. Served in a patrol car for-"

"Liesel."

She sighed. "They got married. To each other. Then to really spread the love around, they adopted three kids. The five of them grow sod out in Caldwell. Their latest email was full of happy news." Okay, so the sarcasm and loud voice weren't helping. "How the hell should I know?" Which was her point. What was his? Get to it.

Griffon grabbed her arm then steadied her. "You," he shouted. Then made an effort to control his anger, "know what I mean."

He was angry, so obviously frustrated by her attitude, and he looked exhausted. Yet, he was holding her arm with a gentle hand. He'd prevented her from falling, again. It made her mind race and her heart pound. He stood so close. His mouth was strained from trying to keep his temper. It looked so inviting and the heat pouring off both of them, their hearts still beating hard from their scuffle, it was intoxicating.

So she kissed him. He would push her back in a moment, once he realized what she was doing. Or worse, he'd wait until she stopped and give her that condescending smile, the mouth's equivalent to being patted on the head.

When he didn't pull away, Liesel decided since it would be the last kiss—you can't kiss someone who has patted you on the head— that it had better be worth it. She placed her free hand on his jaw to bring him even closer and opened her mouth to suck on his bottom lip. His mouth opened and she darted her tongue in, just a little. Just so she'd know what it was like to French kiss him. She didn't know why she was kissing him. Because she wanted to, perhaps. The desire was strong and fierce.

He placed his hands on her hips and she pulled her tongue back to her own mouth, waiting for the gentle push he'd give to break the kiss.

Griffon moved his hands around her hips then slid them up her back pulling her into his body and up. He took advantage of her gasp to slip his tongue into her mouth, just a dip, just a tease, like she had. Then deeper, circling. A little shiver went up her spine then echoed in his body. He tasted so good. Hot, spicy, wet. He moved one of his hands into her hair so he could press her closer, coaxing her tongue to follow his back into his mouth.

He pulled back and his eyes looked deep into hers, searching for something. Neither spoke. She was too foggy headed to register what he could be looking for. She stepped away from him, started walking again. She'd kissed him on impulse and wanted to gush with enthusiasm like a teenager over how good it felt. And if they had been on a date maybe she would have. But instead he was here giving her the third degree about her past—like his had been so rosy—because he thought she was involved with the kidnapping. He would think she'd kissed him to distract him, and hell, maybe she had. Liesel, can you screw this up even more?

Resigned to tell him as much as she could remember, she said, "I dated Matt Caldicott my sophomore year of high school. He was a junior and gorgeous and almost popular."

"Matt?" He asked. His voice was metallic and hollow.

She sighed and shook her head. "Roger Davies kept picking fights with him." She could feel the tears and shame, even all these years later. "Called him pansy, faggot. Roger said even *I* could kick Matt's ass." She rounded the corner and pointed across the street at his car. "That you?"

"Yeah."

She headed across, looking as she went for cars. "You'll be giving me a ride, won't you?" She smiled, not expecting an answer.

He clicked his car open and she climbed in, giving her butt a couple of swipes to make sure she wasn't bringing dirt with her into the black mustang.

He didn't start the car. "And?"

"I'm walking to school one morning and...." She fiddled with her seat belt. "I don't even...one minute, normal...then suddenly I was jumped from behind. Three guys on my back. All at the same time." She breathed and looked out unseeingly at the street. "Scared me so bad." The closest she'd ever been to absolutely terrified.

She tugged on her ponytail, finally pulling it out then turned to him. "They formed a circle around me. Made sure I didn't leave. Roger wanted to fight me. Here he is. Huge guy, fists up, and laughing. He says I'm not really a girl. That I can't be because Matt likes boys and if we are sleeping together then...but way more with the colorful slang."

She was quiet for a while. "It's okay to hit me. Women's lib." She had avoided his first couple of hits. "So, we fought, and I thought the other two would join in once he was down. But they just grabbed him and...." carried him to the school nurse, where an ambulance was called. "Made sure he got medical help." She gave a little hand wave to indicate she couldn't find the word.

Griffon was quiet for a long time just staring at her. She refused to look at him.

"And Matt?"

I tried to be careful? She laughed. At herself. "I was angry. I should have waited until I'd cooled off." She shrug. She would have left it at telling-the-bastard-off, but he'd slapped her. She told him to knock it off and when he swung again she made him stop. "Can't go back."

"You got to give me more than that Liesel. Like why."

"I don't know why. Maybe Roger got off beating people up and thought I'd be an easy mark. Maybe he and Matt had fought in the past and he liked to rub Matt's nose in it. When I went to tell Matt, warn him that the other two might come after him?" She laughed. "I was such an idiot. He'd known before it happened and I called him a jerk. He slapped me and I told him he didn't get to touch me, not ever again. He swung at me again and I made him stop."

"You could have walked away. The best fights are the ones you don't have."

"I know that now. But then...I was such a child."

Well now that he knew and so obviously disapproved she could shelf that kiss and her desire. Gee, it was fun while it lasted but they'd both be better off. She was his client and they needed to stay focused on finding Clara.

Chapter 8

The last thing I said to you, remember what it was? Fuck you. You thought it was just me telling you off. You didn't realize it was a promise. Ashley's voice was always clear in Griffon's dreams. But if she had really said that before hitting him over the head, he didn't know. There was a lot that he didn't remember. But it didn't stop his dreams being full of horrid details. She had cracked his skull, but thankfully it had swelled. A good sign for head injuries.

He'd turned Ashley in for taking bribes. Testified in court against her. She was a dirty cop and a power hungry lunatic.

"When did you come to? In the warehouse or the van?"

The van. His hands had been shackled behind him and his ankles were chained to his wrists so he couldn't straighten his legs. But he didn't tell Dr. Brown any of this.

Shrinks should be required to have those long, sloped, backless couches they show on TV. They're not for comfort. The love seat Griffon was sitting on was plenty comfortable. Squishy, deep-sigh, comfort. But sitting on it made you face Dr. Brown. Lots of direct and deep eye contact. Which wasn't happening.

There was no way he could say what happened out loud, let alone while looking at someone.

Instead, he spent most of his sessions talking to the large window over Dr. Brown's shoulder. The view was of downtown Boise. Traffic and trees. No one saw in. He'd checked. And he couldn't see himself reflected back.

"Did you talk to them?" Dr. Brown said.

They had me for four days. Yeah, I had lots to say. To beg. "When I first came to, I tried to talk to them. All calm cop. 'Think about what you're doing.' They said they'd thought long and hard about it."

"How did that—"

Griffon glared. They'd already discussed Griffon's opinion of the popular question 'How did that make you feel?'

Dr. Brown was patient. "How did the Grey Ghost exercise go?"

The week before he did a little contract work for the city of Boise, playing the bad guy during training scenarios. "Good. My body held up. Had the Boise SWAT team dancing through an old manufacturing warehouse."

"With this new case, you'll be working with a woman?"

"Yeah," Griffon said then amended, "Probably."

"How do you feel about that?" He'd asked the question but this time Griffon let him. He was the expert after all.

Hopeful. Scared. Angry. Griffon just shrugged. He remembered his reaction when Liesel's body slid the length of his thigh. It made his balls tighten just thinking about it. And wasn't that the miracle of the week. Followed by that kiss. The kiss had been heaven. Confusing, because what the hell did it mean, but heaven. When they'd meet several months ago, he'd been so focused on just getting the job finished. Building his client list, paying the mortgage, in his own survival mode. He'd noticed Liesel, sure, but he hadn't really *noticed* her.

There was a long silence; the doctor happy to let Griffon just process.

"How is the medication working for you?" Dr. Brown asked.

"I think I'm getting used to it. I don't shake. Still feel anxious."

"Daily?"

"No."

"That's good."

Griffon started imagining the sound of crickets in the silence. His right hand dug at the cuticle of his left thumb. "And with this antidepressant—"

"Effexor."

"There aren't the sexual side effects?" That had been very painful to get out.

"Depression effects all aspects of our life—" Dr. Brown said.

"This is supposed to—"

"It helps. It isn't an instant fix. There is no such thing." Dr. Brown was in his fifties, had lots of experience and he wore Dockers and button down shirts. Griffon picked Brown for two reasons. He was a guy and he was gay. Shit, no. It didn't make sense. But it had. To him. At the time. He liked the guy just fine.

"The doctors, the other ones...." He started digging at a different fingernail, "they said it isn't...that there isn't anything physically wrong." He paused, but he couldn't bear to hear what Dr. Brown would say, so he continued just as the Doc was about to talk.

"I'm healing fine. No damage." You're paying how much an hour? To just stammer around the issue? That should be way helpful. Spit it out. "Nothing is causing my inability to get aroused." All out. Fine. Next. "I worried because I don't even wake up with morning wood. And I miss that, you know. It's not like I jerked off every morning." He made direct eye contact to make sure the doctor believed him. "I didn't. But it's normal. To wake up that way."

"It's reassuring."

"Yeah."

"Did the doctor's suggest trying postage—"

"Stamps? Yeah." Griffon snorted. "Yep. Sure did." But the idea of putting stamps on his dick, to see if they were torn in the morning, was embarrassing as hell. He'd done enough embarrassing things. Thank you god, you absentee father.

"The stamps would indicate that you got erect at night while dreaming. A very normal and healthy process." Nothing embarrassed this guy. It was his total comfort with saying words like 'erect' that made it easier for Griffon.

"All I dream about are those bitches beating the shit out of me with those...." He breathed a few times to calm down. "I don't want to know that shit is getting me hard." He was back to staring out the window. They had wiped his blood on themselves, like war paint. It had been freaky to see Liesel do the same thing. The blood from her leg, smeared on her forehead.

"In times of trauma, especially physical, the body has many ways of coping."

Griffon jerked to his feet—inert to angry-pacing-man in seconds—and Doc didn't shift in his seat. He didn't so much as flinch. Impressive.

"I know all that crap. I worked a few sexual victim cases. You work a little of everything in a small city like Boise. You're required to read all the books on...sexual assault. But knowing it, is different from feeling it." He stood by the window, glad Doc didn't ask him to sit back down.

"Was torturing you all they did? I've wondered if my presumed knowledge of sodomy wasn't—"

"SHUT UP!" He turned and blanched. "Shit, Doc, I'm sorry." That hadn't happened to him, the medical exam said so. But it happened in his nightmares.

"Come sit down."

Squishy, deep sigh, comfort. "You didn't flinch when I stood up. What tips you off? Saw my thigh muscles flex? You knew I was going to stand up."

"It's the eyes. I've had a lot of experience reading people."

"As a therapist." Griffon nodded in understanding.

The doctor corrected him. "Nope. As a gay man. Who is going to be bothered by it? Who thinks they know? Plus, I'm a people watcher." He smiled. "You avoid subjects that make you uncomfortable, by pointing out odd things like thigh muscles."

Officially, no comment.

Lab Rat 5.8-15

Jordan Mathews felt like a kid stuck in the backseat of a station wagon, on the curviest ride of his life, about to hurl. His current physical state had more to do with drinking his losses than being on any trip. As a sophomore at the University of Montana, the only place he was headed was across the university's golf course for another 4.2 miles.

Normally running was routine. His body fit enough and his experience long enough, that he actually enjoyed the build of adrenaline, the sweat running down his body. His mind focused on laps, speed, heart rate, other runners and daydreams. But with his hangover the run battered him. The inside of his mouth salivated; he took short, harsh breaths to keep the food he'd eaten from spraying the grass.

Practice had broken up and he was alone on the field. The sun set early on this side of campus. Tall campus buildings and mountains shadowed the field. He'd been late, and now he had to finish his distance alone.

He groaned as his stomach pitched upward, tightened his lips and puffed air out his nose. No more drinking for him. He'd thought a high metabolism would make a drinking game easy. Wrong. But the new freshman on their cross country team, Jordan's new roommate, had dared him.

Simoné Kennedy, his fiancé, would have loved to see him walking back to campus the night before—a hangover in full effect though he'd barely stopped drinking. A high metabolism had brought the consequences rushing toward him, instead of having the decency to wait for morning.

She attended the University of Michigan Ann Arbor, a Junior majoring in women's studies. He missed having her close but it was important that she got this chance. Montana didn't offer women studies as a major. Michigan was a bit too close to home for him. Plus, once they were married their responsibilities to his family would take so much of their focus. She deserved some freedom.

Two miles left. He stopped just long enough to empty his stomach into the tall weed-like grasses at the base of Mont Sentinel.

Simoné would laugh to see him now. He swirled water from his camel pack and then spit it into the grass as well. People walked the campus paths, or sat outside enjoying the warm weather. Though it was only in the mid-eighties, it was the warmest weather the campus would have until late spring. He drank more water, swallowed and began running again. He couldn't just stop. No one would know he hadn't finished. No one but himself.

To help the last miles go faster, he broke from the track and headed for the forest covered, groomed paths through the campus hills. He conjured his favorite day dream. Simoné wrapped around him, their bodies sweaty from sex.

"Sim, are you going to marry me one day?"

"I don't like that one. The last proposal was better. 'Hey babe! Let's make this legal.'" She laughed. Sweet, he missed her laugh.

"You propose every time we sleep together. And every time I say yes."

"I've asked when we weren't in bed," Jordan said.

"Yeah, the first time. When you really meant it."

"I always mean it. I love you. And one day I'm going to marry you. And not because my family wants us to or because your family wants us to but because-"

She would stop him. She always stopped him when he went off like that. Sometimes she got pretty creative on how, exactly, she made him stop.

He let the day dream dwell for a moment.

Then she would say, "Because I love you." Like there had been no pause.

She was not tall, almost a foot shorter than him. Nor broad, nor loud. Yet she inundated from flesh-tip to bone marrow the very fiber of his body. Overwhelmed, engulfed, and saturated him. And Jordan could only float along with her guiding the way. And that was just her laugh. He loved to make her laugh.

In two weeks they'd have a weekend together. Time to start working on his next proposal.

The trail was hilly and cool and swarming with mosquitoes. A nasty ping to his shin had him cussing and turning back. He'd run all the way to the dorm and it would be just over the required miles. He bent to quickly swipe at the mosquito; the bugger was sucking for all it was worth. And seemed to be...shaped like a dart?

Griffon had the sports camp—which Clara had attended in June—fax him their employment records and spent the night doing background checks on everyone on the list. Max stayed to help. "This is better than a stake out. We can get up and move around and leave to go to the bathroom. Speaking of which," Max headed for the back of the office.

The majority of the list was high school or college kids that volunteered as camp counselors. Some of them hadn't even been there at the beginning of the summer when Clara had. The more permanent staff, a whole list of five people, came out clean. No major criminal records, no large cash inflow or out flow, no subscriptions to porno magazines.

"I'm getting myself a soda, want one?" Max was back and leaning into the mini fridge.

"Toss me a bottle of water." He snagged the bottle out of the air.

"That's where we should look next," Max said as he sat down at his desk and picked up his share of the print outs to read.

"What?" Griffon said.

"Water."

"Max," Griffon warned.

Max liked to torment. "Suppliers to the camp. Who brought in water? Who cleaned the pool? Who delivered food?" Max looked like Sean Connery. Laugh lines, thick white hair combed back from a strong hairline. Easy going attitude. He once said that the looks helped with the women and the go-lucky attitude helped with the men.

"No pool. They're right on the lake at Coeur d'Alene."

"Still, you can see what I mean. We're looking at the first layer with this list." He lifted the pages in his hands. "But the next layer would be supplies."

Griffon stared at the photo on his computer screen of the camp. "What layer is the owners?"

"The next layer."

"Awfully scenic up there," Griffon said.

"I don't like the sticks, too much dirt. Give me a grimy L.A. street any day," Max said.

"Might have to go look myself. Get a feel for it."

"Hell, you'll need to go, whether the weather is nice or not."

"I'm glad you agree. You're in charge until I get back," Griffon said.

"Already packed?"

"Yep, I take the puddle jumper that leaves in four hours."

"Puddle jumpers. I'd rather do a stakeout."

The Coeur d'Alene airport catered to the private flyer and the filthy rich. He was neither and had to fly into Spokane, Washington and rent a car to drive the two hours to the camp. Luckily the rental place had a pickup truck. He couldn't imagine driving into the camp in a car, let alone riding on a school bus. 'Bus Driver', he added to his smartphone and turned through the gate. It was the last week of camp for the summer and the area was swarming with teens heading to breakfast. The camp had six full-length, black top, basketball courts. They were spread out below him as he dipped into camp and pointed the car toward the lake.

Clara wasn't here. A girl of seven would stick out like an underage gambler at the Vegas slot machines. This camp group was one of the oldest sessions they offered. There was no age difference between counselors and campers. The sexual escapades of a co-ed camp caused tears, drama, and headaches. All things on his list of never-evers.

Two of the courts had games going on and from his car it was like watching the Utah Jazz play at the top of the Energy Solutions stadium. They were good.

He parked the truck and grabbed his briefcase. The office was his first stop. The manager was a former NBA player, injured badly his first year. Not on the court but in a car accident, alcohol had been involved, enough alcohol to fill a basketball stadium.

Tall, thin, and solid, the athlete had stayed in shape. He was on the phone as Griffon entered. He'd thought they wouldn't have a landline, looked like he was wrong. He wrote, 'get phone number' on his smartphone and started browsing the walls. There were hundreds of pictures of former campers turned big shots. It looked like they'd had kids from across the country. A bit unexpected for a camp in Idaho. He'd thought the university camps put on by Notre Dame or North Carolina, number 23's alma mater, would have more of a draw. Maybe they were price restricted. He added price comparison to his list.

The same man appeared in many of the photos. Was he a coach? The white, geek look of many coaches like Pete Newell was normal and odd at the same time. But this guy looked like he could play, though a bit short.

"Sorry about that. I'm the camp manager can I help you with

something?" Finally off the phone, the manager turned to greet Griffon.

Griffon kept his back to the man, partly to keep him off balance and partly to keep his best weapon in reserve. "Jim Griffon. Sent you an email."

"Right. Clara, uhm Larkin, you said."

"Who's this guy?" He placed his thumb flat on one of the photos; not giving a fig who the person was. It wasn't like he was pictured with Clara. But Griffon asked so he could judge the Manager's normal, at ease, voice. And also, since he was pictured so many times, Griffon felt a manly, I-should-know-this-famous-sports-figure curiosity.

"Sam Murket, he's a sports agent. Was, really. Getting too old for it I hear."

"He doesn't look all that old, in spite of the white hair," Griffon said.

"I don't know him personally. Those photos were sent by some of my former campers," the manager said. "When you make something of your life, you want to share it with the people who helped you get there."

"And how many have you helped make it?" Griffon stepped to another photo.

"Two WMBA first picks went to camp here. And three of the last ten Wade Trophy recipients." Griffon knew that the Wade Trophy was the basketball equivalent to the Heisman.

"That's impressive. Who's this guy?"

"Michael Jordan?" disbelief.

"No, next to him. His coach. Can never remember his name."

"Oh, uhm, Phil Jackson."

"Yeah, that's right. And how much do you guys charge for the camps?" Griffon said. The man scrambled about his desk to find a price guide and held it out for Griffon. Griffon turned and took the paper, keeping his eyes down to scan the paper.

"And how do you attend AA meetings during the summer?" He looked the man in the eye and dared him to flinch; knowing his steely look intimidated most people. 'Scary eye's' Liesel called them.

The manager's Adams apple bobbed. "I go here in Coeur d'Alene, twice a week. I'm sorry Clara is missing."

"She hasn't been misplaced. She was taken." It was easy to intimidate people. Put them on edge.

"But I had nothing to do with it. Honestly, if I knew something that could help you—" the man said.

"You can help. What's your telephone number?"

The man was shaking by the time Griffon left the office and headed for the physical trainer's cabin, a big red cross painted on its roof. He would recommend that the medic give the poor guy some pain reliever before he left later. Griffon was going to need something himself. His gut said there was nothing here. Just spinning his wheels. Lots of time to waste and plenty of reasons to put off finding Clara. Who was probably dead. Fuck. Sometimes, his job sucked.

Liesel had another phone message from Griffon that morning. "Nothing new on Clara. I'll let you know if I need help." Griffon's way of saying 'Stop calling and nagging me with questions and offers to help.' As the days passed, it was hard not to get discouraged. It was even harder, though, to watch Tara shrink into herself, self-imposed guilt and worry eating her away.

Liesel had plenty of her own guilt. Guilt for lusting after Griffon, even guilt over working on other things instead of just working to find Clara.

Liesel had been so caught up with Clara's disappearance that she had forgotten about the McKinnon book. But her excitement peaked as she and Anna stood next to the kitchen table where the shipping package was ready to be opened.

Anna was ready with a box knife, one she'd pulled from her jean pocket. "So, what's the big deal with this book?" Anna asked.

"I've been hired to translate this...." Liesel couldn't talk for a moment as she opened the box.

It smelled like leather. When the box was closed, no smell. Box opened, and immediately she knew it contained leather. Each 'page' was over a square foot in size. The only thing making them a book was the threaded string laces at the left hand side. Cracked, dry and in some places faded, it was still in remarkably good shape. Along the edge was a continuing scroll-like border of Celtic knots. "I've been hired to translate this for a Scottish family." She didn't realize she'd repeated herself.

She floated a thumb along the edge of the top page. She would wait to touch the pages until she had her gloves on, she didn't want the oil from her skin staining the manuscript. The Celtic knot border hadn't shown in any of the scans Mr. O'Grady had sent. Intrigued, she was unaware of Penelope and Anna working around her.

Liesel remembered when Seamus O'Grady, a McKinnon by marriage, emailed her about the leather book. The e-mail asked if she spoke the Amazon language. Use to weird and often rude reactions to her HOAX website, she'd replied, "I write and read Latin, speak some Greek and I'm learning French."

"I'm looking for someone to translate," Mr. O'Grady's email said. It did include 'Dear Ms. Grant' and a 'sincerely, Seamus O'Grady.' But that was the gist.

"I can recommend a couple of linguists. Which language is it?"

The next email contained a scan of the leather pages. It was written in Gaelic. She'd written the words and a rough translation out in her reply email by referring to an online 'Gaelic to English' dictionary.

Three days of nothing. Then Mr. O'Grady sent a short email requesting to speak with her on the phone.

"Do you want me to help you carry that back to your office?" Anna asked at her elbow.

"What?" She gave her head a shake and smiled at Anna. How long had she been lost in thought?

"Want me to carry that for you? It looks heavy."

Liesel laughed. Then she realized that Anna might take her laughter the wrong way. Before she could explain, Penelope called out from the living room. "You have an IM from...C. B. G. B. You asked me to tell you if he came on." The Instant Message program and concept was new to Penelope, but she was being a good sport about learning it. "Why would someone choose CBGB as a nickname?" Penelope asked.

"I believe it was because Sex Pistols was taken." Liesel was quick to explain when she saw Penelope's startled expression through the kitchen door. "The Pistols were a punk rock band. CBGB was a punk club in New York."

"Oh."

"Anna, if you could put the box in my office? Thanks. I've been waiting to talk to him for days," Liesel said. Anna just nodded.

CBGB's real name was Sergei Sky. Doctor Sergei Sky. He was an ER resident and had the chaotic schedule to go with it.

She didn't know a lot about him, other than that. He was working, when he could, with Dr. Sima Kandi, a geneticist and genealogist. Dr. Kandi was tracking the genetic history of the Amazons. She was the sole reason Liesel knew about the dominant Amazon gene.

In a hurry to talk to Sergei and get back to the leather pages, Liesel sat at the front desk instead of going into her office and clicked on CBGB's IM message.

CBGB: A little bird said you need me. Be still my exhausted heart.

Oni: I'm here. Thanks for contacting me. I know you have almost no time off.

*CBGB: *shrug**

Oni: I've contacted you about this leather book. It indicates that a substance, when used during carrying—I'm assuming pregnancy—prevents the harsher mutations of double-Amazons.

CBGB: We prefer Blue Hairs.

Sergei was a double-Amazon. If two Amazons had children, some of them—having a dominant Amazon gene from each parent—were born with birth defects. It seemed to be random. Known cases included psychic abilities, abnormal eye color, and superhuman senses—hearing, eyesight. Sergei had blue hair. Everywhere.

Oni: It is still up for a vote

As the double-Amazon chat moderator, he had suggested the name Blue Hairs as being cooler than Double Amazons and it had caught on.

CBGB: 58% for, 34% against and the rest undecided. But only doubles should be voting and it isn't something I can tell from a distance. Oh and congratulations on the landslide win, you're Highness.

Oni: It wasn't a win because I wasn't running against anyone. I wasn't running at all.

CBGB: Well, you were caught. I think it's a good idea.

Liesel had turned the task of researching their options over to LegalEagle. He was a corporate lawyer out of Dallas, Texas and the moderator of the over-forty forum. He and SRS would handle the details.

Oni: Back on subject

Liesel yelled for Anna. Penelope, hovering around the desk jumped. "Anna, could you get me the yellow legal pad on my desk?" Liesel smiled at Penelope to let her know she was sorry she'd yelled in her ear.

CBGB: Sorry your highness. So?

Oni: You've been working with Dr. Kandi, with the genetic coding and the genealogy of members.

Anna handed her the notepad and since she was the closest to the phone when it rang, answered it. "Daemon Designs, this is Anna."

CBGB: Got a long way to go with the second but the former continues to hold up against all tests.

Oni: This is a passage from a scan the McKinnons sent

Liesel hit enter to send the text, then flipped through her notes to the proper section. She typed, keeping an eye on Anna and Penelope as they moved about the office. Anna took a message and Penelope was opening the pile of mail.

Oni: "Thus began the war of conquests against the surrounding lands. It would last for many decades. For with each push against our sisters they" what they did, I'm not sure. I only got the top of that page in the scan and it seems to be written in columns, like a newspaper. The next column starts with this "and thus the Mightys were created. Men, children of Zeus, children of Apollo. Among them Hercules and Azure, called so for his skin. We lived for a time, separate. Mightys and Amazons. Men and Women."

CBGB: Azure as in blue? Is it saying that male Amazons are actually a different race? That would explain a lot. Do you think I could look that book over?

Oni: What? You going to come all the way here? You've got the end of your residency.

CBGB: Shhhh, don't say that word, jinx me

Oni: LOL ???sorry?

CBGB: Forgiven. No. I was thinking at the National Conference

Oni: National? It's getting way out of hand as it is. It was supposed to be just me and the website officers

Liesel suffered another moment of panic. Surely, not that many people would come to Las Vegas. Clara was still missing. The Race for the Cure was in two days and she was over a week behind on designs. Dealing with the whole Queen thing could wait.

CBGB: Yeah, but they let slip when and now people are coming.

Oni: I think that the three of us—me, you and Dr. Kandi, can get together. I'll have Penelope schedule it and contact you. Maybe you can figure out what this vague reference to pregnancy means and are there really Mightys or is that just the Male form of the word Amazon.

Her own words blinked on the screen. As she waited for Sergei's reply she looked up. Penelope was watching her. She rubbed her leg self-consciously. Penelope hadn't been in the office when Liesel came back from running the morning she fell, but she still got the feeling that the older lady could see through her pant leg. It was healed, of course. But thinking of her leg made her think of kissing Griffon. Which cued a blush and hot thoughts of his abs plus, as a bonus, awkward tension in the office.

She wasn't sleeping much. When she did she had nightmares of bench pressing in front of congress. She would have preferred hot steamy dreams about Griffon. Or dreams about saving Clara.

Anna placed a message at her elbow. "Your sister, Karma, says to call your sister Harry." Having an odd assortment of siblings herself, Anna didn't think the message needed clarifying.

CBGB: I'm not working with Dr. Kandi anymore. I'll continue sending her my half of the genealogy.

She was startled to see the screen had changed.

Oni: Why not?

After another long pause.

CBGB: I'm just not. Plus, I've been given a grant to study the effects of Parkinson and Seizure medication on previously classified schizophrenics.

Oni: Wow.

Whoa. Blue Hairs—now he had her doing it—who were born with psychic abilities, were often thought to have mental illnesses. Especially when their powers didn't develop until puberty.

CBGB: Yeah. It's the whole reason I became a doctor.

Oni: Keep me posted?

CBGB: Do the same? Send me translations as you go along

Oni: Yeah.

CBGB: Next week, same bat channel.

Sergei logged off. Off to sleep or back to work, his life consisted of little else.

All this new knowledge about the origin of their strengths, an origin that felt dark and twisted, a story about lies and wars and death, would give her people a better understanding of themselves. As she worked the first section, which advocated for secrecy, she wrote each sentence out in Gaelic and double checked her work by posting it on the website and having Google translate it. The author urged the reader to be careful, that exposure made them all vulnerable.

Chapter 9

Lab Rat ?

It was a get-in-and-get-out job. If Freddy Rayne's boss used those words anywhere in his directions, Freddy knew it was a swipe. The legit jobs, complete with paperwork and keys to doors—well, as legit as it came from a man who paid his workers under the table—did not start with 'get into this sealed-tight place' and did not end with a vague and plumb unhelpful, 'then get outta there.'

The office had just installed a new server. Stealing the server rack would pay for a month's rent, Abigail's next set of college books and a week's worth of food. Though if the job went clean, he promised himself he'd get one day—three meals, a full pyramid—of food. Not just what they could afford, but a day of being cracking stuffed.

Freddy crouched down to tie his Nikes and check out the entry points. He'd walked by twice already. The single night employee left for his lunch-hour every day at ten then was gone for over a half hour. It wasn't Freddy's business what they did in such an office. He was to get the server rack and get out. As he finished his third pass of the building he noted the cars in the parking lot. The night jockey's car had car seats in the back, a pile of My Little Ponies and fast food garbage. The strip of office buildings also housed a medical supply company and a personal fitness trainer. Neither business was open past five. A delivery van, parked in the second row, was the 'company car' for the medical supply company. Across the street more strip offices were available for lease.

It would be an easy job. At least for someone strong enough to lift the eight hundred pounds of metal racks and wiring and load it into a high bed truck. Freddy just happened to be one of those people. Beth would drive the truck. He didn't like the idea of bringing one of his two half-sisters along but the half hour timeframe and his lack of a driver's license made her a reliable and necessary choice. He was the youngest but as the only man and as the strongest, he worked hard to keep his sisters safe and as far within the law as he often strayed from it.

The August sun wasn't planning to set anytime soon. And the evening heat was content to lie like a forgotten soggy towel on the bathroom floor over Tampa Bay.

Since there were no houses on the street, not many cars passed. The tightly-sealed would unseal nicely with his crowbar—currently hooked to his belt and hidden down his pant leg.

There went the employee. Freddy signaled Beth and she flipped her visor down, the light flicking back from the vanity mirror.

He walked straight to the rear door. A strut or a jerky jog was the way newbies moved, and declared to the whole vicinity that you were ganking the place.

The crow bar separated the door from its port with a scratchy sclink. And he was in. He heard the truck pull behind him. Beth was supposed to give him ten minutes before pulling around. Skirt, love her, must be in a fluff.

Wearing gloves, he unplugged the power cord and yanked free the lines maintaining the network. The dopes had been suckered into buying Tech U Shit quality equipment. But him knowing better didn't affect his payout, so he'd be keeping the info to himself.

As he pushed behind the server rack, leaving ravine gouges in the linoleum, a hand grasped his forearm.

His tightened muscles, flexed even further. The blood in his veins grabbed the T1 line straight to his gut.

Three men stood between him and the rear door. One of the men held Freddy's crowbar, which he'd left propped against the door jamb.

Not a clean job. Shit. No day of food for him.

"I m-must be in the wrong p-place." The job wasn't worth getting put in J. V. He'd mark it as a wipe and cut his losses. But then it registered that these thugs weren't dressed in casual business clothes like the employee had been or like detectives would. They weren't surprised he was there and they sure as hell weren't trying to stop him.

Ever the talker, Freddy said, "Boss s-sent you?" The stutter made him sound scared but hopefully that would be a good thing. The sound he'd thought was Beth must have been the white medical delivery van. He should have double checked to make sure it was empty.

"We're your escort."

Yeah, because I'm black, young and alone, I'll be turning this into your trusting hands. Fuck a Duck, no. He wasn't stupid.

If the three were related—inbreeding looked possible—their last name had to be Dumbasrocks. The one with the crowbar had a silver GV2 watch around his wrist. The other two had prison tats snaking up their arms—distinguishable by their lack of color and crude design. But enough sizing them up, it wasn't like he'd be picking them out of a line-up. Pawning their asses all over this floor, maybe.

They rushed him. There was no cracking way he would let any of them sight Beth. She'd be safe, always. He would kill to keep her that way. His half hour was almost up; time to execute the 'get outta there' portion of the job.

"And the mighty shall fall and the Amazons shall inherit the earth." Not exactly a direct scriptural quote. Liesel rechecked her translation and adjusted a few words. "The Mighty, once defeated, the Amazons may have the land." That didn't feel correct either.

The Mightys. She tapped her pen against the page, staring at the word. Mighty in Greek was μπορεί and in French Le Puissant. German was Das Mächtige and in Latin....

She turned her eyes to the book case. Where was her Latin dictionary?

She swiveled in her chair, giving a little push with her hands on her desk. She unfolded her legs and was surprised at how stiff they were. The muscles just above her butt cinched and gripped as she stood. She rubbed at the ache, arching her back to stretch and looked at the bottom right of her computer screen to check the time. Crap. She'd been translating for four hours. She'd barely done a column.

The words came easily, as if she had been reading and writing ancient Gaelic her whole life. But it wasn't Gaelic or Greek or Latin. Or so all the experts said. And it wasn't easy. It was gruelingly slow but it held her interest and made life speed by.

She rubbed at her head, wishing it would hurt. The pain would narrow her focus and shut out the rest. But it didn't. She was drained. But no headache. She massaged her leg, thinking about Griffon. He left her messages, sometimes with questions about Clara or Amazons, but mostly 'Nothing yet. I'll keep you posted.' He was slowly documenting Clara's every action over the last year. Including any macaroni crafts made at school and her trips to the dentist.

The worry still gnawed at her but only in the background, she had no other place for it. She still had to build her sites, work the research, wish and hope and wait.

Liesel put down her pen and checked her hair to make sure there wasn't another pen up there.

She walked down the hall to the kitchen. Anna Marie was at the new desk, reading off the computer screen. She looked up as Liesel approached.

"Where's Penelope?" Liesel asked.

It was even hotter today and Anna had forgone the baggy jeans for a short pleated skirt. It was black, but her shirt was a dark olive green. Liesel, in full historian mode, wore loose jean cut-offs and Griffon's brown t-shirt, the one he'd used to wipe her injured knee. The blood had come out but not his scent. The earthy smell was neither overtly masculine nor flowery. It said power. And it felt like a naughty secret to wear it.

"Left. Right at five."

"Hmm." Had Penelope come in to say goodbye? "And you stuck around...?" She pitched her voice up so Anna would know it was a question.

"Do you mind?" Anna pulled her hands from the keyboard.

"Not at all. Want to stay and eat dinner?"

"You know, you don't have to feed me." Defensive, Anna crossed her arms and stared at the front door.

"I'm going to eat and it's nice having company." Liesel shrugged. "But you will be helping cook, so...double bonus for me." She walked through the living room/front office to the kitchen, talking over her shoulder.

They worked in tandem getting stuff out of cupboards and cooking meat. Liesel held a one-sided conversation in hopes of putting Anna at ease. She talked about Harry Potter—who didn't love J.K. Rowling—and high school angst.

"Can I ask you some questions?" Anna asked.

"Of course." No hesitation. It was way too important to get this just right. After knowing Anna for weeks, the young girl was going to finally ask about being an Amazon.

"Why can you read that...book? When no one else has?"

Or maybe not.

"Oh. Was actually wondering that myself." The last sentence came out before she could stop it. She gave a little laugh in hopes to dispel her own tension. She yanked the hair tie out of her hair and threaded her fingers through it. With jerking motions, she re-hooked the ponytail. She'd left her other scrunchie in Griffon's car. Okay, no more thinking about mister sexy and scary.

"Want to do an experiment with me?" Liesel asked.

Shrug. "Whatever." But Liesel could tell that she was intrigued.

The stay-busy plan worked. Help one Amazon since she couldn't yet help another.

Senator Mathews' office was in an average government building. There was the smell of old money, newspaper ink and sweat. "You're from Luke's line?" The Senator asked the young man standing in front of his desk. Washington D.C. had a high population of senators but he had always seen himself as above the numbers. He was The Senator for a reason.

"His grandson, by his fourth wife." The man was the perfect Mighty specimen. Well over six feet tall, athletic with crisp black hair. Dignified. Powerful. He'd make a good addition to the Harvest Team.

"How is my little brother?"

"I don't interact with Luke."

"Of course not." The question had been a test. Luke had gone against the Mighty ways and had been expelled from the family circle.

The Senator needed to verify the man's origin and prove he was capable of the job The Senator was hiring him for. "My son Marcus was the one to recommend you." Marcus was next in line after the Senator to be the Patriarch of the Mightys of North America. As head of a private family, he had the responsibility to maintain that privacy.

"I knew who I was at an early age. I've looked for my true family my whole life." He chose his words carefully and The Senator approved.

"Family. Yes, we are that." He tapped his pencil. "I need you to protect this family. Protect us from exposure."

"Whatever it takes." The man's voice neither altered in pitch nor cadence.

"We want a document recovered and all who've seen it destroyed."

"Which document?"

No hesitancy about killing. Good. "*A History of the Amazons.*"

Chapter 10

It had been four months since Anna Marie Raven Kompfee Fort-Porter had quit smoking, but her hands still shook with need. Her hands and clothes had stopped smelling like Camel Lights. Not because they were what she preferred, the Camels, but because they were easy to swipe from her mom and later from Douglas, one of her step-dads. Slim cigars or pipes with an Italian blend, that's what she got when she had a choice. Especially, if that Italian was mixing in a little Mary Jane. She put her elbows on the table as she ate. It was rude and her six-months-of-the-year-with-mom side rebelled at the very thought, but it hid the shaking hands. So, elbows on the table.

She ran her left hand into her hair, just above her ear, pulled her hand down through the strands, flipping the purple ends out. She watched Liesel for a while, to see if she would take seconds on the spaghetti. For once there was plenty, but it might be for leftovers. She'd always thought leftovers should get his own damn food.

Liesel handed her the bread basket then scooped more noodles onto her plate, passing the noodles as well.

Anna had dyed her hair just before she hit bottom. Her final, fine-you-think-I'm-a-punk, watch-this. Then she'd been arrested for assault. It didn't matter the guy wasn't taking no for an answer; that he'd had his hands all over her. All over. He had no priors and she had broken his jaw, three ribs and his knee cap.

She kept it now, the hair, for two reasons. She put every penny she could away for school. She couldn't afford a haircut. And two, it reminded her, when she looked in the mirror, just how stupid she'd been. She had believed that people saw what they wanted to see. Nope. People saw what you showed them. That's why she only showed Liesel the angst-riddled teenager.

The leather manuscript, diary—whatever they were calling it—intrigued Anna. She had a bag her mother had traveled with. It probably had a style name, but if so, Anna didn't know what it was.

It was big enough to hold comic books, with plenty of room leftover for a camera, art tools, and an umbrella. Her mother always carried an umbrella. Marie Kompfee, her mom, had been a travel writer and an avid X-Men fan. Not that she ever took Anna with her, not even when she died of cancer.

"My mom used to...." write. She couldn't say it. It felt somehow too personal, "—own a leather bag. It was old and worn. Reminds me of that," she nodded her head in the direction of the office. "How old is it?" She stretched her hand toward her glass of milk and watched it shake, hoping Liesel wouldn't notice.

Liesel looked in the direction Anna indicated, as if she might actually see through the walls, her thoughts obviously elsewhere. She shrugged. "Not sure. The family that hired me had it tested. Which I don't totally understand."

Mental moan. Anna couldn't stop the answer forming in her mind. Carbon dating measured the decay of C-14, radioactive carbon, found in all plants and animals. Sometimes she couldn't get her mind to be quiet. The method was developed by Professor Willard Libby, a team member on the nuclear bomb during World War II. After the war and the two nukes to Japan, he tried to figure out how long the damage he'd caused would last. Can't measure that.

That's more than enough, she told herself.

In the 70's, Accelerator Mass Spectrometry was developed to date very small samples of carbon. Grain of rice small. OSL, she couldn't remember what it stood for, was used on things older than 60,000 years.

She bit her tongue, felt the pressure of her teeth throb deep into her mouth. The Dead Sea Scrolls were carbon dated to the first century BC. *Give it a rest, will you.* How did one pronounce spectrometry anyway?

"They were told it is about 500 A. D. But they believe it may have been a copy of a much older document that was deteriorating. Which it is." They looked at each other and Liesel continued, reading the question in Anne's eyes. "It says so. The first page says they found the record. That's what she calls it. The record. And, in an attempt to keep the information safe, she wrote it on leather. But Brigid doesn't say how old it is. The original. Or, for that matter, how she got it. At least not yet."

"How come you think it was a girl? Realistically, only men, and clergy at that, could read and write in the...." She caught herself and closed her mouth. She'd sounded much too smart.

Liesel just gave her a knowing smirk. "She says her name is Brigid and that she is the oldest daughter to a Lord, though I'm not sure of that word. Brigid is a very Celtic name. It is also the name of an Irish fertility and war goddess."

"Cool."

"Yeah. She says that she hopes to finish transcribing it before she is married. I'm hoping the McKinnon family has a record of her. It would be neat."

"But it's not her record?"

"No, it's...well, come on." Anna followed Liesel into the office. Liesel flipped on an extra light. Though the summer sun wouldn't set until almost ten o'clock, the shadows had lengthened.

"Can you read this?" She showed Anna the notebook she'd been using.

Embarrassed, Anna shook her head. "I only read English. I can cuss in Spanish. You pick that up in jay-ve pretty quick."

"But it matches this?" she smoothed a hand over the first leather page.

"Sure. What's it say?" She felt the need to use poor grammar to cover her earlier slip.

"It's in Gaelic. It says, 'Greetings, sister of my heart, sister of my blood. I pray that you are a sister, for these enchantments I put on this text should prevent all others from knowing my words. I am Sheena, the last of my Amazon clan, and had only my mother to guide me in our ways. I have married a good man and carry his child inside me, who I think belongs in the world of mortal men and not in the dwellings of our ancestors.

"This is a long and sad tale but such tales often are when the gods decide to interfere with the lives of men.'

"It's rough. The punctuation...doesn't really translate, so some is a bit adlib on my part." Liesel shrugged and continued. Her voice was lyrical and she read quickly.

""I am not here to tell you that the gods are real. As you read this, you know they are real. Like every generation who hears this story before you, we know the words are true. They are part of our heritage, an ancestral memory. We have no proof, other than this memory, that we cannot access until we hear the tale, for as with all other accounts of gods, all the evidence was lost countless years ago.'"

Liesel stopped reading and said, "That's a huge leap on my part—"

"Just read it." Anna said.

"'No Amazon is sure why the story starts but we know where the story begins. Thousands of years before my birth, there was a kingdom whose success was legendary in its day. A city of learning and magic, of compassion and strength."

"'Zeus, son of Saturn, king of kings, the ruler of the gods of Olympus, saw the city in all its splendor. He came down to the city disguised as a mortal and found the city to be...'"

"Don't stop. It's just gettin' good."

Liesel smiled. "Rogue. It's in Gaelic."

So much for Liesel not calling her Rogue, after the comic book hero. It was why her mom had called her Anna Marie, after the X-Men comic character's alter ego. Anna's half-brother, the one that shared the same mom, was named Logan. Though now, fans knew that Wolverine's name was really James.

Shut up. Stop. Refocus. Liesel was waiting for her to respond.

But Anna just shrugged. "Can't be. The McKinnon Clan would be able to read it. Or, you know, someone they knew."

"But they can't." Liesel smoothed her hands over the leather and it shifted in the light. "To them, it looks like hieroglyphs and it keeps changing."

Anna leaned toward the old leather, smelling cardboard and ink and Liesel's hand soap. Then she saw them. Symbols skittering across the leather but only at the corner of her eyes. The center stayed clear, focused. She turned and the symbols moved to the edge of her vision, finally disappearing off the page. "Wicked. How come...Oh." Her legs folded up under her and her hands shook even harder as she placed them against the ground. There was an enchantment and Anna, a 'sister of my blood,' could read the pages. She was an Amazon. One more label to live up to. One more thing her mother had never told her. One more chance to fail.

She seriously needed a cigarette.

Chapter 11

Griffon figured finding Liesel in the breathing mass of female bodies would be...well, back when he believed that certain things were impossible he would have said his finding her bore a close relationship to impossible. But now his world was turned up on its back and he was flaying like a turtle to right himself.

She'd left bread crumbs, purple ones. Women in purple t-shirts with Boise Amazons in gold lettering. They stood out against the old ladies in pink and the white t-shirts. Perhaps because he was looking for them—and for their source—there seemed to be more of them than any other group. If he'd been here as part of the festivities, or if his trip into the thousands of cars funneling into the parking lots, or if it wasn't so fucking hot, perhaps he'd appreciate the wonder of ten thousand women joining forces to eliminate breast cancer. But he hadn't expected the sheer number or that he'd have to park a mile away. Worse than a pro stadium crowd where at least there were parking garages.

He'd have to recommend the event to some of his military contacts as a great opportunity to practice finding and following someone in a crowd. When everyone was dressed the same. He'd done a similar exercise at the Gay Pride event in San Francisco, him playing mouse for a FBI field team. It took them two hours to find him in the crowd and then once he was spotted he led them on a merry chase. Course that was before Ashley and now crowds had his spine itching and looking for a wall to place his back against. Excess moisture built in his mouth and flushed the palms of his hands. He swallowed and breathed evenly.

Max had called him that morning, laughing his fuzzy ass off. Yesterday Griffon had tried to explain to the hardened and experienced man—who had seen it all—that he was starting to believe in these Amazons. Then this morning's paper includes the headline *Boise Amazons Win Fundraising Competition*.

He swam up stream of the purple shirts and there she was. Her thick red hair was braided, her face bare of cosmetics, glowing. Her own purple t-shirt had faded with wash and ware and she'd removed the regular sleeves, showcasing her toned arms. The look suited her and any doubt he had about her intentions and involvement in Clara's disappearance did not hinder his new ragging libido. Like a kid jumping up and down in excitement and barely contained anticipation, his lust flipped to maximum just looking at her. Good lord.

Race for the Cure was Boise's largest fund-raiser for the research and treatment of breast cancer. Over ten thousand people—mostly women but also children and men—ran or walked for their loved ones. Max had told him all of this over the phone as he continued to rib Griffon for his gullible nature. Gullible, a word not used in relation to Griffon. *Ever*. And yet she'd convinced him, almost.

He weaved his way to the front of her table where she laid out more shirts from a box and greeted participants. A few people in front took one look at him, lowered their heads and hastily retreated. Even though his pissed off vibe was strong their duck-and-cover reaction wasn't a new one. He cleared his throat to get her attention.

"The registration table is around the front of the building." Liesel said, slightly turned to wave and smile at people who called to her across the parking lot. The lot was full of sponsor booths instead of cars. Albertsons's corporate office and the large Park Center Boulevard was the Komen Race starting point. A few days earlier he'd been on the other side of the pond talking to Mr. Mitchum.

Griffon fingered the purple t-shirts on her table. But he didn't feel them, the anger-layer was just below his skin, like the hot white coals of a fire, and muted his sense of touch. "Boise Amazons?" Half distracted, Liesel handed him a brochure.

"Boise Amazons was created by me and my mom, a two time breast cancer survivor. The site is a wealth of information and a great place to go for support during treatment." She handed a t-shirt to a lady as the new person signed her name to a check list. "Members get a t-shirt with yearly membership dues." The new lady had very short hair, a bow kept it from being a high-and-tight military cut. Perhaps a recent chemotherapy patient. Liesel signaled to her mom, Eliza Grant. Griffon recognized her from his search on Liesel, which hadn't uncovered anything about Boise Amazons and breast cancer. Liesel's mom took the new lady and hugged her, whispered words of welcome and congratulations.

Liesel smiled at the pair then turned her attention back to him. He groaned. That sexy smile diffused his anger down to just mad. "Griffon," she gasped, her chest shuddered up. Nice. "Sorry I didn't realize it was you. Is everything okay? Did you find something?" As she asked she came around the table to put a hand on his arm, searching his face with hope and excitement in her eyes.

She looked tired, purple smudges around her overly bright eyes. Was she dehydrated? Stressed? She cared, about Clara, about the thousands of women around him. She'd worked this event for several years and the group placed Eliza, her mom, front and center and didn't so much as mention Liesel. Even the news article lauded the Grant family's effort without mentioning Liesel in anyway. He didn't get her but it was obvious that she cared and valued her privacy. He could relate to that. But he wasn't ready to just jump back on the path of trust.

Before he could demand answers she was mobbed by children. Her body swayed as two bodies plowed into her full force. One a red head the other a pale brunette a bit like his niece Riley, but with long hair and a few inches taller. Though in the few months since he'd seen Riley she'd probably grown and in more than just length.

"I win." The two shouted in unison. The younger, still using Liesel's leg as a pole to swing off of, smiled at Liesel. "Who won Leis?"

"Well clearly it was me who won." Harriett, Liesel's sister, said who had followed her nieces. Harriett pulled on the little girls' arms to disentangle them. Harriett was a tall, gorgeous blonde. There were plenty of photos of her on the internet. Mostly past lovers moaning their loss via social media. Griffon wondered if she knew about the pictures. Griffon waited for his body to stir and though he appreciated what she was equipped with, he only felt curiosity.

Liesel tried to turn back to Griffon.

More people, who must have also been family, gathered around her. Her mom, two sisters and six nieces and nephews were in various stages of donning their purple t-shirts.

Shit, he didn't want to see this side of her. She untangled a sleeve to help the redheaded girl dress while absently taking a guard position with the other adults, kids in the center. Did they even realize the protective body language the four naturally shifted into? Like watching the secret service fan out to optimize the ability to play bullet sponge around the president. He knew firsthand how families reacted to abductions; the need to shelter. But this seemed more ingrained.

He reached for Liesel's arm to regain her attention and the others responded, shifting their own positions and stance. On guard. It rang plenty of memory bells with his own military training.

"They're about to start," Harriett said. She took the hands of her younger nieces and led the way to the starting line, a huge arch of pink balloons.

"Boise Amazons? Had a nice laugh at how easy it was to convince me?" Griffon said quietly.

"What?" Liesel finally registered that Griffon was pissed. He saw the change in the stretch across her shoulder muscles, the sharp focus of her eyes.

"You said—".

Her older sister spoke over him, "Leis." Karma grabbed her arm and steered her toward the start.

The Grant family stood between a group of ladies, their black t-shirts asking you to 'Save Our Tatas', and a father and son walking for a loved one, her picture, bald head covered with a scarf, on both of their backs, 1979-2011. Christ.

At the blast of an air horn, the mass of bodies began moving forward. Like air plane passengers, all standing at once and then realizing there was only one exit, they did a stuttering shuffle of hurry and wait.

Plenty of time to answer Griffon's questions. "Explain."

"It should only take me an hour. You could wait—" Liesel said.

"No. I could not." He took her arm and tried to steer her out of the mass of moving, gabbing ladies.

Her sisters, tempers flaring, started toward Griffon but Liesel quickly waved them off. Oh yeah, these people might look like civvies, but their actions suggested an awareness of his physical threat. Paranoid or very protective. Or both.

"I'm finishing this walk." She pried his fingers loose then stumbled. He caught her elbow to steady her and sighed.

"Fine. You can explain while we walk." He still held her elbow and stroked his thumb across her skin before he let go. He couldn't resist the temptation and saw, though briefly, the awareness and desire flared in Liesel's eyes as well.

Liesel scooped up a little girl, smiled at the child's mother and tied the girl's shoes before placing her back down. He doubted they even knew each other—no purple shirt at least—yet the mom thanked Liesel and continued forward.

"Boise Amazons, right." She took a deep breath. "Amazon is a Greek word meaning 'without breast.' Legends say Amazons would remove the right breast of female children at birth, so it wouldn't interfere with their archery. Which is total bumpkiss. Modern archers don't have any problems with boobs getting in the way." Liesel's cheeks flushed as Griffon looked down at her chest. She had a very nice pair.

The mass of bodies picked up their pace then came to a halt as traffic ahead of them stopped as well. There was sweeping waves of noise as a helicopter flew overhead from a local TV station. A cheerleading squad from a local high school was cheering along the side lines, encouraging the walkers, giving high fives to the ladies in pink.

"I was in college when my mom was diagnosed the second time. All these women she met during treatment really leaned on each other." Liesel wiped sweat off the back of her neck, more from the heat then from exertion. The crowd had picked up speed and they moved around the slower walkers as Liesel spoke. "My college classes were on web design. So, I created this web group called Boise Amazons. For breast cancer fighters. Everyone has a rank." She pointed to a lady they were about to pass. "Private, for first timers. Captain, for those in chemo. And Veteran, like my mom, when they are deemed cancer free. Even civilian, for family members that need a place to talk. We choose Amazon because not all of the ladies survived whole."

His anger or response to this—*her story*—Well, he was willing to wait and see what she would say. Mostly he observed. If you watched you learned. "Anyway. It was just a message board at first and a group that met each year at, well, here, at the race. Then we sold t-shirts to members and that paid for the site. We just kept getting bigger. We started selling shirts and stuff to people all over the United States, donating profits to research." She pulled her own shirt down so he could see it. 'Boise Amazons' in big gold letters and smaller, in black, 'Breast Warriors.'

Why? Why abuse himself with this heat and this woman? He could be beating his head against the wall that was this case instead of walking in this heat surrounded by women. His claustrophobia was showing. He was jostled from the sides and he clenched his fists breathing through his nose. A self-inflicted test, that's what this was. Could he be surrounded, pressed in by women and not freak out? He was doing just fine. Sure he was. He swallowed.

They had reached the water station, the half-way point, and he realized they'd left her family behind. Alone in anonymity. He should kiss her again. See if his previous reaction was just a fluke. Griffon had remained silent, his breathing hardly altered by her rapid walking. He passed her a cup of water as they walked past the water station, then took one for himself.

"Thanks."

"The Larkins?" He did another impatient nod and Liesel laughed. She liked him. He knew interested woman when he say one. He'd figured that out early in life.

His adrenaline was pumping. The cool breeze blowing across the Park Center pond and the Boise River, made the hot August day almost bearable. And Boise's huge trees provided intermittent shade.

"I'm getting there. I monitored all the message boards and chat groups. And even from the beginning, I would get some weird emails. 'Are you a real Amazon?' or 'I thought this would be for strong people.'" She didn't return a greeting from a fellow participant that called out, focused on internal thoughts.

"That last one always made me angry. It takes a lot to decide to fight cancer. But then I started getting ones addressed to me and...."

She was quite for a long time.

"Anyway, emails." She brushed loose hair behind her ear. "I realized there were people, men and women, all over the world, that were super strong. That couldn't eat enough to stay full. That lived until they were a hundred and fifty. Then I was approached to do some research, given grants to find evidence that they existed in history."

He did his best just to keep up, focused on her words and tried to not trample the people around him as he followed her.

"After a year I quit my day job designing websites for a local company, turned the Boise Amazons over to my mom. I started Demon Designs and started my research. I have a few translators working for me. Translating old papers from Japan and Central America."

"That explains your answering machine." His tone was neutral, not giving anything away.

"Yes. It gives my email address and explains I only speak English."

"That's admirable. This," he gestured to the people around them, "is great." He said it grudgingly, sarcastic. She had been a college student with aspirations of nerddom—he didn't think that with derision, being a techno geek himself—and stumbled upon an ancient race of superheroes and she didn't exploit them. Or did she? Her story explained why an ink fingered computer geek would be researching Amazons and hosting a website for fanatics. Yet, it felt like there was more to it.

"Is there any leads with Clara?" Liesel said.

Griffon sighed. The FBI were analyzing carpet fibers, though that only came in handy when you had a suspect's carpet to compare it to. Griffon and Max were tracing back the maid service that cleaned the Larkin's house and he called Clara's sister Tara 'just to shoot the breeze' every day. "No, no leads."

"What about the sport's camp?"

"The local blue are investigating her teachers and family. The camp wasn't being checked so I looked it over." He rubbed at his forehead then shook his head. "If there's something there I haven't found it." Normally he wouldn't have admitted that he was struggling with a case. Normally he didn't get aroused by a client. Normal didn't seem to apply.

"When are you done here?"

They'd looped back around and were almost to the finish line, another arch of pink balloons. "We usually finish around 2:30," Liesel said.

"I have questions; things I need for Clara." He looked around him, getting the skin crawly panic as his mind took in exactly how many people engulfed him. He was done. Time to go. He would crow to Doctor Brown about his little triumph, walking with his back to all these strangers. But first he needed to leave her with something of his worries. Paint a more realistic expectation so there would be less shattered hope to heal when they solved this case.

"Seven hundred thousand kids go missing each year. Only 100 are kidnapped like Clara was. A fifth, 20,000 a year, are found. Found dead." He looked at her, searching her eyes. Looking for guilt or fear. "The rest aren't found."

"I know Clara's still alive."

It never rained in August. Okay, Liesel thought, it must rain somewhere in August but not in Boise. But it was still August and it was pouring rain. Huge drapes of rain being dragged across the night sky, so thick that you saw it coming, before it pounded the pavement and muffled all other noise. Liesel stood on Griffon's uncovered porch, the rain thundering down her back and head and knocked for the second time. She stood to one side under his porchlight but it offered no cover only light. His black mustang was under the covered carport to the side of the brick house, so he must be home. She'd gone to his office first then tried calling. Again. But his number was busy and had been for half an hour.

He hadn't called that afternoon. Not that she'd worried. But now she needed him.

Rivulets of water streaked down her face, she blinked to keep it out of her eyes. The back end of the drape of rain passed over the house, and the dark, cloudy sky above her was empty. Though wet, she wasn't cold, it was definitely hot enough to be August. She knocked a third time, then ran her hands through her hair and gave her head a shake, sending water in every direction just as Griffon opened the door.

"Is it raining? In August?" He was wearing pajama bottoms, thin flannel ones, and another brown t-shirt. His hair was spiky from his pillow and his cheek was shadowed with whiskers. Her stomach muscles clutched and her cheeks flushed with heat. She resisted the urge to fan herself.

"Exactly my point. I don't know who's responsible but I plan on filing a complaint." Liesel stared at his chest and watched in amazement as his small nipples tightened through his t-shirt. Maybe it was cold, at least out of Griffon's bed.

"Do you know what time it is?"

"I'm not sure. However, I see another sheet of rain heading this way." Liesel bounced on the balls of her feet waiting for him to invite her in.

"How did you find my home address?" The rain swept up his yard toward her.

"In the phone book." She said it in a rush, hoping he would then let her in, but too late, the rain pelted her. "Mr. Griffon!"

Seeing him at the Breast Cancer event, a public place, surrounded by thousands, felt different, distant. It had been hard sharing so much with him and not telling him she was an Amazon. Especially since she had no distinct reason not to tell him. Just fear. Fear of rejection. Now, within seconds, the private situation—just the two of them—and the sexual pulse came thundering back.

He smirked at her. "If you're going to bang on my door at eleven o'clock at night, you shouldn't call me mister." She considered pushing past him to get out of the harsh rain but he must have read her mind because he leaned both forearms on the door jam, literally filling the door way, looking sexy and playful.

"Griffon, please." Liesel pushed her wet hair out of her face. "There's been another kidnapping."

Chapter 12

Dr. Savon had always seen architecture as one of the many artistic forms. The government paper-pusher who had designed this building with its high-tech labs had absolutely no artistic talent. The doctor stood next to Sam Murket in front of a panel of security monitors.

"A bit old for the project." Dr. Savon said as they watched the new lab rat get tossed into the cell. Tall with muscles was just the type of body he preferred. Shave them down for science, another form of art, and open them up to see what was inside. Truly fascinating. This particular peach reminded him of a high school bully he'd known. Of course most of his patients did. He smiled. "We don't even have a blood sample like the other ones."

"This one's the same," Murket said.

"I believe that is what you said about number six."

"No, that is what the blood sample showed. He probably was on something he didn't want showing up. So, he had one of *them* do the blood test for him."

"Maybe the coroner will figure out what he was on, when they find the xylazine and detomidine," Dr. Savon said.

"Is that going to be a problem for us?" Sam asked.

"Shouldn't. Equine sedatives are fairly easy to obtain. If you know what you are doing. They are common enough not to be traced back to any particular region." Dr. Savon would find a way to get that coroner's report. He would add it to his personal files.

Savon continued. "But you're sure about this one?" The new rat would get a number, naturally, but for now it was just a chance to rile Murket.

"I know a natural athlete when I see one."

"Because they are so different from you?"

Murket jerked Savon up by his lab coat. His toes barely touched the ground. He did his best to look frightened, sorry for what he'd said. He couldn't press his body against his attacker or Murket would know how aroused Savon was. There would be time to remember the fear later.

"I brought you in on this project Doctor. I'll be expecting results. Positive results. The buyers are getting antsy." Murket let go of his lab coat.

Dr. Savon did his best to sound disdainful and pompous. But he couldn't quiet hide his excitement. "What they can do...it's amazing. Their bodies' high metabolism may require us to up the calorie intake of their feedings."

"We don't want them too strong," Murket said.

"They are well contained." Oh, but wouldn't it be exciting if they got loose. Very scary. He shivered and Murket let him go. "As you know, this building was used by the government to—"

"Their metabolism?"

"Right. They process all chemicals very quickly and efficiently. That's why we've used the equine sedatives. Nothing else kept them under long enough." Savon kept his vernacular in line with his audience's ability to comprehend. "Six, he had an allergic reaction and the epinephrine was delivered too late." Ah, the poor thing. But the other athletes Murket and his henchmen had gathered were perfect subjects for Savon.

"And when we're done with them?" Murket said.

Realistically they could maintain their lab rats for several years. "Well, we do have a cancelation plan. What do you athletic types call it? Sudden death overtime. I see it as more as a plan b." He showed Murket the switch on the security panel. The big red one. "Shut the vault and walk away."

Fort Knox style steel doors with NASA seals would block off all exits. The henchmen would have to build their own escape tunnel, like scurrying rats, past the red switch and to safety.

"Nothing will get out and by the time they manage to get in...." Oh, the image. Savon's heart heated and thumped blood throughout his body, rushing endorphins and adrenaline to all the best places. Emaciated carcasses decaying in chunks. His engorged penis ached spectacularly. The smell Savon could only imagine.

He gasped and panted and came in his pants. He hunched his shoulders and hacked, digging for an inhaler. He didn't have asthma but the inhaler was a great cover, so was his lab coat. All jocks thought that all nerds had asthma. And acting was another art form.

"Shit. Come in." Griffon stepped out of the way, his playful mood gone. "What's happened?"

"Another girl. This time in San Francisco." Liesel stared down at her feet and the puddle she was creating on his wood floor.

"Any witnesses? Did they take her the same way as Clara?"

"Well, not really." Liesel hedged. She kept her eyes on her feet hoping to avoid the accusatory glare she was sure Griffon was wearing.

His voice was no longer concerned but cranky. "Instead of us playing twenty questions, how about you just tell me what happened."

"Mr. and Mrs. Johnson called me. Their daughter Teona is missing. They thought she had run off with a boyfriend she had met online, but then they got my memo and started asking neighbors." She spoke her thoughts out loud, all in a rush. "There was a white van and some guys hanging around the day she left. I checked online and Freddy hasn't heard from her." She realized she was doing a bad job of it and finally looked up at Griffon's face.

He had his arms crossed over his chest, face tight, nostrils flaring. His eyes were dilated. He was angry at her unhelpful chatter. Liesel shivered.

"Sorry." He said, "Let me get you a towel." She waited until he had turned his back to head down the hallway, and started shucking her clothes. Sandals, t-shirt and shorts. She looked about for a place to wring them out, then figured she'd already created a puddle, and it wouldn't hurt to add to it. She had finished with the clothes, hanging them on hooks on the back of the door, and was just wringing out her hair when Griffon came back down the hall. He was looking at the towels in his hands. "I figured you might need a couple...." His eyes took her in all at once and he spun on his heel.

"Sorry. If you had wanted...You could have...What are you doing?"

"What's the problem? I'm wearing black panties and a black bra. Practical bra and panties. My bikini shows more." She shook her head at his back. "I just didn't think it would bother you, I'm sorry if I offended you." Okay, he thought she was seducing him, and if it worked, then of course that had been her intention all along. But really, she just hadn't thought about it. Her mind too full of Clara, Teona and Anna.

"If you go to a pool you expect half naked women, you don't plan on them popping into your living room in the middle of the night. Unless you're dreaming." She could see his shoulders lifting in heavy breaths. "I can't even remember why you're here." Griffon turned around. Did she see desire in his eyes? Men didn't look at her, let alone like that. She was too tall. Too...curvy.

"You okay?"

He groaned. "Yeah."

"Can I have one of those towels now?"

"They're all too small."

"I beg your pardon!"

"You'll need something that covers you from chin to toes to do me any good."

Liesel smiled. "Give me the towel Griffon. "

He handed her a towel and kept eye contact, let the heat and appreciation show from his hooded eyes. Liesel toweled off and ducked her head as heat rushed to her cheeks, her heart beat an echo through her body.

"Explain about Tina."

"Teona." Liesel wrapped a towel around her torso then flipped her head forward to dry her damp hair. She dropped the towel on the floor and used her bare foot to move it around and sop up the water. "Okay, Teona is one of my girls. A year ago, well a couple actually, I started an online group for teenagers. A place where they could ask questions and talk to each other with privacy. It's a sub group of HOAX." Griffon nodded.

"Teona is a member. When I heard about Clara, I sent an email and snail mail letter to all...well, to everyone I had listed. Members directly, parents and guardians for anyone under age. Including Teona's parents." Liesel bent at the knee and picked up the towel, then passed it to Griffon.

"Keep going." He bunched the towel in his hands and headed to what she supposed was the kitchen.

Liesel took a moment to look around her. She stood in a large rectangular room Griffon had sectioned in half to serve as both a living room and dining room. To her far left was a wood fireplace, and to her right an archway. She heard him dump the wet towels in a sink. The only other door was to the hallway across from her.

The decor was in transition. He still had remnants of dorm furniture, like the bookshelves made of unfinished plywood. But he also had a new love seat.

"The memo explained what happened and asked for any information." She raised her voice to make sure he heard her, lowering it as he came back into the room. "The Johnsons got it yesterday and started asking questions. They found out that there was in fact a white van, so they called me. I advised them to inform the police. Meanwhile, I checked with Freddy, Teona's friend online, who hasn't heard from her. Then I called the Larkins. They said I just missed you. I checked your office then came here."

"And I appreciate the visit but why couldn't we have had this conversation over the phone?"

Like all those messages she'd left? The day she'd been out running and they'd kissed, that happened nearly seven days ago. Add this morning at the walk-a-thon, it equaled three times that she had seen Griffon face to face. Clara had been gone almost two weeks and Liesel had been unable to react to her instinctive urge to do something. Save her. Help. She was losing sleep and felt all kinds of guilt that when she'd hear about Teona she felt relief. Another clue, a chance to act, to actually do *something* instead of wait.

"I tried that and your voice mail on your cell phone is full."

"Oh, yeah." He hooked his thumbs in the waistband of his pajama pants and yawned into his shoulder, blinked a couple of times. "Do you want to sit?" He tilted his head to indicate the kitchen table.

"Thanks." Liesel sat, trying to stay covered as much as possible.

"Do you want coffee?"

"Do you have milk?"

He nodded.

"I'd love a glass of milk."

He headed for the kitchen again, flipping lights as he went. "So what do the Larkins think? You guys already called the police of course."

"Well, actually...."

He stopped halfway into the kitchen and turned back to look at her. "What do you mean?"

"Do I still get that glass of milk after I tell you?"

"That bad? I better get the glass of milk first."

She waited until he came back to the table, a glass of milk in each hand. Liesel's stomach growled in approval, but it always growled, so she ignored it and took a couple of swallows of milk. "The Larkins don't want us to call the police."

"You mean Sara doesn't want."

"No, actually she told her husband. Finally." She shook her head. "Mr. Larkin cried. I think he feels it's his fault that she was taken, being the one who has the Amazon gene."

Griffon shook his head and muttered something that sounded like 'Amazon genes.'

"They both think it is a hate crime and feel that exposure from the media would endanger their daughter."

Griffon nodded. "The police and media are not the same things."

"I agree. I'm going to let you handle passing on the new information to the right people. You're bound to know better than me who's trustworthy." She emptied her glass of milk and eyed Griffon's still full glass. Then took a mental inventory of her kitchen. Guess it was drive through for her. "But that brings me back to why I'm here and didn't just keep trying your phone. The Larkins want us to go to San Francisco and talk to the Johnsons."

"No."

"But wouldn't that be the next logical step to this investigation? As a P.I. don't you ever track people down in other states?"

"Yeah. I'll be going to San Francisco. I'll be continuing this investigation. I'll be talking to the Johnsons. You'll be staying here." His face was hard and his cold.

Liesel, she chided herself, don't be such a ninny. When intimidated, brazen your way through it. "I'm going." She said. "I'll allow you to come with me."

Griffon jerked his head back at her arrogance. "Give me one good reason to take you."

"I'll give you three." She started spinning her empty glass on the table. Little circles and whirling noise. "First, you won't get your bonus and high fee from the Larkins if you don't. They want to give you another thousand for going to San Francisco with me. Second," The glass spun, three complete rotations. "I'm your 'in.' Being an Amazon is still fairly new to these people and they're cautious around strangers who would exploit their daughter." The glass slowed and teetered back and forth. "Third, Freddy was pretty mad to hear about Teona. You may need my protection."

Startled, he laughed out loud then switched glasses with her. Unabashed, she drained his as well and smiled at him. "I wish your laughter meant you were taking it well."

"Leis, you're going to protect me? That's kind of sweet."

Liesel sighed, frustrated by his attitude and worried what his reaction would be to her story. Guess it was time she found out. "He's going to be trouble. His history is a bit more than colorful. Don't get me wrong, he's a good kid, but when you grow up in tough places—"

He interrupted her. "He who?"

"Freddy."

"Freddy's a guy?"

"Yeah." She drew the word out slow. Duh implied.

"A regular guy? I thought you were talking about Amazons. Now I'm insulted." He crossed his arms and leaned back in his chair.

"He is an Amazon."

"Since when have there been male Amazons?" His tone was fierce. It was odd how his voice swung back and forth so readily between tones. But the emotion you heard, unlike most people, didn't really tell you how he felt. Liesel saw it more like a tool, a way for Griffon to get what he wanted.

"Well, my studies show that there may have always been male--"

"Amazons are women."

"In Greek Mythology, yes. In comic books. But we aren't dealing in myth." Liesel sighed and splayed her hands into her hair, tugging, felt the damp strands twist and knot around her fingers. Sometimes there was just so much information she didn't know how much and what to tell. Plus, with the McKinnon leather, she didn't know if they were really Amazons or these Mightys it talked about. "Amazon men can only be born from other Amazon males."

"My head is conjuring all kinds of weird possibilities with that one. You better clarify."

"In order to be an Amazon and a guy, the Amazon gene must be attached to the y chromosome, because, as I've stated, the y chromosome is dominant to the x. So, a male Amazon," Liesel drew 'Ay, x' into the perspiration of her glass, angling it so he could see. "passes the 'Ay' to all his sons, making them male Amazons. Whereas 'Ax' males are carriers of the Amazon gene and not Amazons themselves. They pass the Amazon gene to their daughters."

"Right. Of course." He stood and grabbed both glasses and walked back to the kitchen. "How strong we talking about?"

"Depends on the person." Liesel followed him to the kitchen, and leaned a hip on the door jamb as he rinsed the glasses and set them in the dishwasher. "Humans have a base strength level. With training, exercise, they can be stronger than average." He turned and leaned back against the counter, crossing his arms. "An Amazon's base level is just higher."

"You're worried that some guy's going to kick my ass, because his girlfriend is missing." Yep, she'd insulted him.

"Freddy is just fifteen, and though fairly level headed, I don't want him to get involved and hurt. Tempers and male egos do that sometimes. Get in the way, that is." She said it to point out his rising agitation, to dare him to prove her wrong. She tugged at the towel, whishing it had pockets so she could put her hands someplace and settled on twisting her fingers together behind her back. He stared at her with his head titled to the side, puzzling, deciding on something. He'd pulled his bottom lip into his mouth on one corner. Sexy.

She knew exactly how his mouth would taste. Heat spread across her palms as she thought of sliding them into his shirt, chasing the heat from his bed. She'd kiss him until his lips were soft and his eyes were liquid. She stepped toward him and he looked at her, really looked for a moment. His eyelids slid down and he smiled, perhaps remembering or fantasizing too.

She couldn't decide why she was hesitating. He was sending signals—probably, she wasn't the best signal reader—and they could be kissing right now. But they hadn't talked about what happened. Their kiss, her fights in high school. What if he thought she was violent?

"We need to pack."

Which meant he was letting her come. "Yeah."

She dropped the towel at his feet and he spread his hands over her ass, pulled her closer. "Almost dry."

She slid her arms up to his shoulders. "Can I kiss you?" He had his hands on her ass and yet she was asking? Ugh.

His smile turned smug and he pulled her against him; this slow press and shift to line up all the right parts, teasingly slow. But when he kissed her, this intense, devouring kiss, fast and aggressive, she gasped her surprise and felt desire jerk at her core. His erection pressed against her thigh. She thrust against him and laughed when he groaned. He slid one hand into her hair so he could tilt her head and kiss along her jaw and up to her ear. His other hand slid down into her panties at the back, cupping her bare ass and pulling her more firmly against him. Want, wet and heavy, filled her body.

She felt her eyes roll back and could only hold on. She didn't have any condoms on her. Would he settle for a hand job if he didn't have any somewhere? Was she really doing this? Finally going after this man she'd thought was hot for months?

"Why you?" He'd gone still but she didn't notice for a few seconds, her fingers threaded through his thick dark hair. She kissed his cheek bone, jaw, chin, mimicking his moves. But when he pulled his hand up, out of her panties, she realized he'd gone all quiet.

"This Johnson family won't know me." Shrug of the shoulders. "Do you think any of my clients do before a job? They hire me based on a recommendation from a previous client or because of a phone conversation with me."

Liesel took a half step back and opened her mouth, but nothing came out. She was still all tingly from their kiss. He raised his hands in a gesture to stop though all she'd done was blink stupidly at him. "I know you're coming, I'll deal. Might even enjoy the fringe benefits. But why you? Why do the Johnsons trust you? It can't be that they got your name off of some website their daughter visits."

Fringe benefits? That sounded promising. *Stop grinning like an idiot.* He was tight with suspicion and she couldn't mess this up. Lot more at stake here than getting her itch scratched from the outside.

Liesel sighed and lowered her arms to her side. "Have you ever been in the foothills?"

He groaned. "Oh, Leis just...." She liked that he called her that. Leis, like they were friends.

"Look, I'm going to tell you. I happen to tell stories. It's my way. So follow along, okay?"

His nod was stiff.

"It's not like you're doing anything else." It was cold without him pressed against her.

He quirked an eyebrow at her, playful. "Yes, I've done search missions in the foothills."

"When I was twelve and Karma was twenty-two, we went up to Idaho City with her two oldest kids. We went to the hot springs to swim and the A-frame for milkshakes." The pool and drive thru diner had been two big attractions, but were now closed.

"Then we thought we'd go for a drive, turned off some dirt road between Robbie and Thorn Creeks." At his nod she knew he knew the area.

She picked the towel up off the floor and added it to the pile in the sink. "We stopped to look around, get the kids out and let them play. Karma and I climbed out and she opened the back door to get the oldest, Jessa out and I tried to get Karese out but my side was locked. Then the car started to roll." They had laughed first and Karma had hurried to get back in the car, sliding a bit on all the pine needles, but the driver's door was locked. It was the scariest thing in the world to watch her sister panic. Karma never. Ever. Freaked. Karma was confident, steadfast.

"It started rolling down the side of the mountain. My sister got in front of the car and pushed it back up the hill. It was only a few feet but she didn't just stop it until we could get Karese out. She pushed it back up the incline."

Griffon's face was a tight unreadable mask, guarded. Liesel continued. "We're not talking a little Geo-metro, this was a big black tank. Though color doesn't really matter...." A bit off topic; she really was tired. "We both chalked it up to adrenaline. You can do amazing things when it means saving lives. But I knew it was more than that. She wasn't sore or hurt or even winded."

Liesel couldn't hold his gaze a moment longer. "I started reading about famous women in history. I guess I was looking for something." She shrugged. "Joan of Arc, Molly Brown. But none of them were strong, just brave. Then I came across Greek Amazons. Silly, conflicting tales of warrior women." Liesel bit her tongue and felt the last of the heat from their kiss flit away as his eyes hardened even further.

"The Johnsons?" He did that impatient nod thing, which made her smile. Griffon growled. She had heard him growl at the Larkins and knew exactly how he had felt then, wanting to growl in frustration herself. But this time it was almost a purr and it made the little hairs on the back of her neck stand up.

She gently popped him in the arm. "I'm trying." She shook her head at him. "I realized, when I was in high school, that I was strong. Really strong. Maybe I was like my sister and we just had this natural strength. But I couldn't 'not' lift things. I mean, almost nothing was too heavy. Well, obvious things like cars and busses and stuff, but regular things like...." Griffon straightened to attention, ram rod straight, no longer leaning back against the counter. His eyes grew darker and narrowed. A little shiver went through Liesel's body. I think I might actually be afraid of him, she thought. And if so, why the hell do I want to jump his bones?

Hadn't he known, when he'd read about the fights? About the damage that Matt and Roger had taken? Didn't he guess when she explained about the Boise Amazons? Of course, she'd purposely postponed spelling it out for him. And now she'd have to deal with the consequences.

"So, you're an Amazon." Yeah. Right. He didn't believe her.

"Yeah."

"You have this high metabolism. That's why you're always eating."

"If I was less active, I wouldn't need to eat so much but I run six miles almost every day and I want to keep my curves."

He shook his head with his eyes closed, as if he was trying to dislodge water from his ears. His face was very readable now. He was angry and it made Liesel's heart wrench.

"Thanks for taking the time to tell me now." Sarcastic. Griffon tightened his muscles, arms, chest, stomach, thighs then slowly relaxed each. It was beautiful to watch him flexing his body. "I want full access to the website and all your research. Tonight."

"As soon as I get home."

"I'll be leaving on the first flight in the morning. Don't be late and don't over pack." His voice was all hard unwelcoming edges. His eyes lowered to her chest and she realized her nipples were still hard and straining against her bra. He stayed with his back to the counter, eyes focused on her.

"There's a flight direct to San Francisco at 9:30. I can come by and pick you up at eight?"

"That'll work." He stayed behind her as they left the kitchen. She felt the heat from his eyes prickle up her back as she turned away.

"Now that you're dry, I'll get some sweats or something for you to wear."

"I'm pretty sure I have a longer in-seam then you, but shorts or whatever." She shrugged and Griffon headed back down the hall. Liesel was relieved about the clothes, there was no way she could go to McDonald's in her underwear.

He came back with a beat up pair of jeans and a white, fruit of the loom type t-shirt. Please let them fit, Liesel quietly pleaded, she couldn't bear the embarrassment. She slipped into his pants, her bare skin going from slight tingle to raging vibration as the denim covered each inch. They fit snug and low on her hips and came just to her ankle. The shirt showed her black bra but she decided she didn't care.

"Thanks for the clothes. See you in a few hours." She slipped into her sandals and gathered her wet clothes, letting herself out of the house.

Chapter 13

"My bio says I'm a construction worker's son. Like I raised myself above some lowly beginning by going to college on a track scholarship. The truth of it though is that my father is an engineer and co-owns a construction company." Jordan Mathews sat with his whole left side pressed against the clear wall. Though clear, it was as solid as steel. A little girl sat on the other side. Her left cheek pressed against the glass a few inches away from his.

She had finally stopped crying.

He kept talking. "My grandfather and all my uncles are ranchers. Spiked Circle. Biggest cattle ranch in the mid-west. They have a small dairy operation, too." She kept eye contact and he wondered if she even spoke English.

The people on either side of their two boxes were in the lab. The men had come in, tranquilized them, and dragged them out over an hour ago. They dragged them by their ankles, not caring if their heads bumped along behind them. If this was some government facility they would be dressed in scrubs and carry them out on a stretcher. This was good news and bad news. If this wasn't the government, then someone would be looking for them. The government was good at covering things up. But since the bad guys weren't worried about head injuries, they weren't planning on keeping them either. Most ominous was their lack of secrecy. The minions of the evil idiot addressed each other by name and Jordan had seen each of their faces.

"How many?" Her voice was soft but free of tear jags. "How many uncles?"

"Three regular, two great." Jordan said. English. Thank goodness.

"You have two Amazon uncles?" Her eyes got so big, the light of his box reflected in her pupils. They were a washed out gray and her dirty blonde hair hung tangled and limp past her shoulders. From the look of her, they hadn't let her shower since she'd been brought here.

"What?" Jordan smiled. "No. My father had three brothers, and my grandfather had two brothers." He paused searching her eyes again. "I think they are all...Amazons."

How did this girl know about Amazons? Something he had only known for a couple of months. Was that why they were here, because they were Amazons? But he was a Mighty. Hell, he was The Mighty.

"Do you have brothers?"

"No." Jordan said, half distracted.

"I have a big sister. Tara's almost ten." Her eyes started watering again. "I wish she was here."

"Did they take her too?"

"I don't think so. I don't know." They kept close to the wall. Even just a foot away from the glass and they wouldn't be able to hear each other.

When Jordan had come to a few hours ago he'd raged at the walls, using all of his strength to pound and charge the walls. Bruised and hungry, he was still enclosed in a very thick Plexiglas box. The floor was cold linoleum which he'd torn and pulled up in the corn to reveal cement below. The door was almost seamless to the wall and retracted up through the ceiling. The only way out was to the lab.

Jordan had hazy memories of being strapped to a table, though he hadn't struggled, surrounded by beeping medical equipment. He'd thought he had fallen running and was in the hospital. No big deal. Just the standard oohs and awes when he healed quickly and back to the track within the week. He'd been aware but unable to react. They'd probably given him the date rape drug.

He didn't want to think about the things they might have done. Just took blood and monitored his heart. At least that's what he kept telling himself. But his balls ached like when Cynthia Rowgalski had kneed him in the crotch for making eyes at another girl. And his dick itched. He didn't want to think about his dick.

"Have you talked with anyone else?" Jordan asked.

She shook her head. "I didn't know we could. I tried to with the girl in that one." She pointed to the cube on her other side. Cube sounded better than cell or cage to Jordan. "But we couldn't hear each other."

Jordan hadn't been able to hear the girl crying at first. He saw her cringe against the walls, her shoulders jerking, as the men took the other girl. He sat next to her on his side trying to comfort and was surprised to hear her.

"What's your name?" He asked her now.

"Clara Larkin." Her eyes gleamed with tears for a moment but she kept them from falling.

"I'm Jordan Mathews." He whispered, feeling odd to reveal that. To say it out loud. These people didn't know him by that name.

"Hi." She smiled for the first time and Jordan felt a welling of...He didn't know what to call it. He only knew he would do anything to protect her.

"Is there more of us?" The room was only lit within their cubes.

"I've seen them take a few from down there." She pointed behind Jordan. Her last couple of words were harder to hear, as she pulled away from the wall. The men had come and left from Clara's side of the large area.

They were both silent.

She spoke but the words didn't break the silence. "What? I can't hear you."

"I need to go potty." She blushed and pointed to the plastic paint bucket in her cube. Jordan had one two. He found it odd to be in such elaborate cages and not have toilets.

"How about we go at the same time. We can turn our backs so the other doesn't see. Then in ten minutes we come back here, okay?" She nodded and they broke apart.

Jordan stood above his bucket and tried to think of going on the ranch. You got off your horse and you peed in the fields, only the cows could see you. But here it felt like a hundred eyes were watching and his equipment wasn't working. Finally he started going and the pain rocked him forward with a jerk, just barely keeping the urine stream in the bucket. He threw his head back and yelled. What the hell had they done to him?

He gave himself a little shake to make sure he was dry, and pulled back up his jogging uniform. He hoped he didn't have to go again for a week. He put his bucket over by the door, then went to sit back by the wall, keeping his eyes lowered to give Clara privacy.

"Jordan?" He looked up at Clara. Her cheeks were still pink.

"Uh huh?"

"I'm done."

"Good." Jordan racked his brain for something else to talk about. Anything to distract both of them. "Do they feed us?"

She shrugged. "They gave us oatmeal this morning. The big hairy one had a big tray of bowls and they opened the doors one at a time. Then they brought you in." Who knows how long he was in the cube before he woke up.

Then he thought of something, "How many bowls on the tray?"

"Seven. I counted them. I can do math, even algebra." Clara said. "That's how old I am. Seven."

That would mean seven cubes past his, Jordan thought, and at least one on the other side of Clara. That meant at least ten people in Plexiglas cubes. Why?

"How long have you been here?" he asked.

"I don't know. They only bring food in the morning and I've eaten eleven bowls." Eleven days. Eleven days for a little girl to not know where she was or why she was here. Eleven days not to talk to anyone else. No wonder she had cried.

"I'm here now. I'm going to look out for you." He hated his need to say it. He couldn't stop them from taking her to the lab, he couldn't stop the others. He was trapped and so was she. But he had to say it.

The three highest ranked Mathews sat at the kitchen table—Patriarch Senator Jacob Mathews and his brother's. The last time all three had been in a room together—and it wasn't Thanksgiving—was when they'd lost two Mightys in the 9/11 attack of the World Trade

Towers.

Sitting on the other side of the table, was Christopher Mathews and his older cousins, the twins, Julius and Marcus. Marcus would be the next Patriarch.

But there was even more men, more Mightys. The old marred oak table looked like it had become the Supreme Court justice bench. And Mrs. Idun Mathews, Jordan's mother, was on trial. Her husband, Jordan's Father, Gus and Jordan's only cousin Julius Michael—Mikey—sat in one of the deep leather sofas. All but Mikey, were well over six feet tall, with broad shoulders and blonde, sun kissed hair.

"You were the one that insisted he go away to college." The accusing tone was from Senator Mathews, as Patriarch of the Mightys all deferred to his command.

"He wanted to go. I supported his decision." Idun, unlike the many Mrs. Mathews before her, had not been preapproved for the role. Even after twenty-two years, they didn't approve of her. She'd passed more than her eye color to her only child. Her son. The next King of the Mightys.

"He should have gone to Georgetown," Marcus Mathews said. He'd been waiting for the Senator to die and had, by all indications, a long wait to be the Patriarch.

They'd had this 'discussion' before. The volume was the only thing that varied.

"Where you could keep an eye on him?" Idun said. He was such a great kid. Couldn't they see how dedicated he was to all of them? He loved this family but felt a deep responsibility to learn as much as he could.

"Where he would have been safe," Julius corrected. Julius never spoke before Marcus had a chance to say something. It was the only way Idun could tell the twins apart.

"We don't know that he isn't safe. Did you call the Kennedys?" Jordan's 'Mrs. Mathews' had been picked, groomed, and approved. Idun prayed every day in gratitude that the two young adults actually liked each other.

"What do you think I am? Of course we had somebody check the

Kennedy's," Senator Mathews said. He meant, 'sent a thug to pound on the door and search the place.' He had flown in from D.C. immediately upon receiving word that Jordan was gone. Hate this family as much as she did, for once she was grateful for their over protective natures. They wouldn't rest until Jordan was found.

The Senator continued, "We could've had him married and presiding over business by now, if you hadn't interfered."

"He. Is. Nine. Teen. Years. Old." In the Mathews family—in all Mighty ruling families—the future Patriarch was the oldest male of each generation. Jordan's father, Gus had been the youngest son of a second son. Yet, of all his cousins, his son had been born first and was destined to take over the family. If she had known before she got pregnant, she would have waited. She would have realized that Marcus's wife, Tanya, was secretly waiting. But she hadn't known and Gus, gentle and tender, had cowed to his family and not told her. "When he is ready to lead this family, when he is ready to marry, he will."

"This isn't helping." Gus stood from their couch and reached out to clasp Idun's hand. "We need to send out the guards. We have a network of contacts. Let's for once, put it to use." He stroked Idun's hand, knowing in his quiet way, what she needed. His support.

"I'll take you to the airport," Karma told Liesel. It wasn't like she was offering, it was a command.

"No, we'll be fine. I'll just get a taxi," Liesel said. She sat with her sisters in her bedroom. Or rather they sat and she walked from closet to suitcase and packed. It was just after one in the morning, not an unusual time for the sisters to be together.

"Yeah, I'm sure one of the twenty we have here in the Treasure Valley will be available," Harriett said. She liked to make snide comments about how small Boise was but had never wanted to live anywhere else. A little television on a plant stand was set to an all-sport news channel and Harriett looked up once in a while to get the scores.

The sports announcer droned in the background. "The University of Montana's track star has refused to test a third time and has filed a case against the—"

"Turn that stuff off." Karma said, reaching for the remote. "I don't know why you watch that stuff." It had long been an issue between them. Karma thought only guys (i.e. idiots) watched sports. Harriett liked them because it gave her something to talk to her coworkers about or so she said. Liesel figured she watched for the same reason Liesel did. The tight assed athletes and the excitement of victory, in that order.

Liesel folded her tan skirt in the suitcase then checked it off on the clipboard.

"Oh, Liesel, you've got a packing list." Karma groaned and grabbed the clipboard from Liesel. "Look Harry, it's titled business packing list. It even has the file name where it's stored on her computer." Karma tilted it so Harry could see it, then shook her head and glared at the clipboard.

Liesel ignored her sister. She pulled a black linen bag out of the adjourning bathroom, careful to cover it's detailed content label, and placed it in the suitcase under the tan skirt. She grabbed a handful of fries and peered over Karma's shoulder to see what was next.

"I told you she was cracking up. You need to come over more and not to just dump the kids on Saturdays. I think she misses you. I do." Harriett took the clipboard and smiled at the list. It didn't just say, two pair of pants, it said black slacks with boot leg cut and tan full length skirt with modest slit. Liesel didn't own that many clothes. She only had the two pair of black slacks and the tan skirt was her only tan skirt.

Yes, it was over kill but she couldn't seem to help it.

"I like watching Karma's kids. Especially when Jessa comes. She's so helpful with the rest and Johnny C. has done wonders with my yard." Karma had six kids, two girls, two boys then two more girls. They were spread out, the oldest seventeen and the youngest five. They varied greatly in appearance due to the fact that there were four fathers to account for them. Karma wasn't currently married. "Did mom come over to watch them?" Even though Jessa was seventeen, Karma was still determined to have her kids watched twenty-four seven.

"Yeah. She says to take an umbrella." Karma stretched and yawned on the bed.

"You're in trouble Leis, you don't have umbrella on the list. Better update the file and reprint it." Harriett handed the clipboard back to Liesel, her eyes twinkling. Karma was Liesel's senor by ten years and Harriett was just two years the baby of the family. Yet, Liesel had more in common with Karma. For one, they got quiet and surly when they got tired. Harriett acted silly and laughed at the simplest things. Liesel had always felt that being the same made it harder for her and Karma to get along.

"Ha. Ha." Liesel made a few more checks to the list and wrote umbrella at the bottom.

"Oh, stop. Will you." Karma nudged Liesel with her toes. "What's gotten into you?"

"Nothing," Liesel said defensively. "I'm just trying to get a better handle on my life."

"There was nothing wrong with your life, Liesel." Harriett chuckled and rubbed her eyes. "Maybe a little dull but at least you're content." Liesel gave Harriett a whack with the clipboard.

"Where're you working in the morning?" Liesel asked Harry.

"They keep sticking me on road improvement jobs. Utter bump kiss. I don't mind the heat so much, but I wish I could do a building. They got a contract for one on Broadway and Front. I want that one bad."

"It'll come." That was Karma's way of reassuring her sister, but she didn't put much sincerity to the words. The nonphysical, ladylike, feminist couldn't understand why Harry would work in a sweaty, dangerous, mind numbing career.

Karma switched her attention back to Liesel. Harry blew out a short breath from her nose and looked down at the floor. Karma said, "Leis, you don't have to take the job. No one's going to fault you, if you say no."

Queen, interesting job title. "Yeah." In went her last blouse and the umbrella. Check. Check. "Well, I'm still thinking about it. Right now I need to help the Larkins and the Johnsons find their daughters. Then we'll see."

"Kids disappear every day. I see it all the time at work." Karma was a social worker and volunteered at the women's shelter whenever she could. "Maybe it's just coincidence that they are both Amazons."

Harriett had been fiddling with the straps on Liesel's bag but stilled at Karma's words. Liesel flipped the suitcase closed and zipped it. "Maybe. But keep an extra eye on your kids while I'm gone."

No one said anything. Liesel put the suitcase and carry-on by her bedroom door.

"So, tell us about this P.I.? Is he cute?" Harriett pumped her eyebrows up and down.

"Yeah." Liesel's cheeks were hot. Again. God that kiss. And his hands. She needed to keep it together or her sisters would want details and she'd never get them to go home.

"Yeah, kind of cute or yeah, oh baby!?" Harry said.

"Closer to the 'oh, baby' side." Now she was definitely blushing.

"Where does his brain reside? In his crotch or in his head?" Karma said.

Yeah, like she had room to talk with her taste in men. "Well maybe it visits his crotch but it seems to stay above his shoulders. He was a really good cop and he came highly recommended from one of the girls off the site. I've actually worked with him for a while." Liesel sat between her sisters on the bed. She tried to decide how to wrap things up. She wanted to do some translating before she left in the morning. The tricky part was getting them to leave, without them knowing she planned to stay up all night. She ate the rest of her fries and eyed the apple pie she had bought too.

"Sounds good to me. You'll save the girls, fall deeply in love and have plump little cherubs running around here in no time," Harriett said.

"I am definitely not ready to marry. Especially if I accept—" Liesel said.

Harry interrupted, her outrage feigned. "Marriage? You aren't even dating. It could take you years to find the right one and know if you're ready. How will you ever know the quality of the finished product, if you don't have test runs? What am I saying? You have to get a product to test it." Harriett got a wicked glint to her eye then laughed at her own words.

Liesel looked at her little, sleep drunk sister. "I think you need some sleep or your crew is going to be hounding you tomorrow about giggling like a girl."

"You're right, I need to go. But think about what I said. This 'good' guy might be good for you." Harriett stood and headed for the front of the house. "Come on Karma! I'm tired." Karma would make sure Harriett got home, still protective of her littlest sister even though she was fully grown.

"I'm going to take you to the airport." Karma reminded her, well aware that Liesel had yet to agree. Karma put her fists on her hips. Liesel and Harriett called it her mommy-pose, but she only used it to boss her sisters.

"Fine. I told Griffon I'd pick him up by eight."

"Harry means well Leis but watch this guy. Okay? They rarely are any good at all."

Chapter 14

Griffon rolled out of bed at seven-thirty. He flipped the blankets that he'd pushed to the bottom of the bed up to the top and headed for the bathroom. Being tangled in bedding didn't induce the nightmares—they came regardless—but it sure as hell didn't help. He shoved clothes into his old army issued duffel bag, which he kept half packed for traveling, and called his assistant. He told Max about Teona and had him make hotel reservations. Griffon was just getting out of the shower and pulling on pants, when Liesel banged on his door. He grabbed a t-shirt, opened the door and told her he'd just be a moment. He left the door open and pulled the shirt on as he headed back to put on his Nikes and grab his bags. His second bag was the biggest and held all of his gadgets.

A part of him, the 'on purpose part', registered her reaction to his scars. She looked with interest but didn't ask him to explain.

He hadn't thought Liesel was an Amazon. She didn't look like Xena or Wonder Woman. She'd gotten hurt. Even when he found a copy of her JV record, he thought there must have been an explanation. Perhaps the injuries had been exaggerated, or she'd used a bat or something in the fight. She was a book worm, a geek, from the ink on her fingers, to the sloppy and relaxed way she dressed. She was clumsy. But he realized now, that he hadn't wanted her to be an Amazon. So, he'd ignored the signs. Dr. Brown was going to love this.

He was strongly attracted to Liesel but a women who was physically stronger than him? No way in hell was he going down that road again. A flash, a brief glimpse of his nightmares flared to the front of his thoughts.

The bile stuck in his throat. He was desperate to keep all the fluids he could. He had lost enough through the blood and the DAMN FUCKING TEARS *he couldn't stop. Day three and there wasn't anything left in his stomach. Urine dried to his legs, his lips cracked. Dry heaves would take more energy than he had to give.* He didn't remember his first week in the hospital. His body shut down and focused on healing.

He stepped into the bathroom and took a moment just to breath. He didn't dream at all last night. He didn't know if he was relieved or disappointed that he hadn't had a wet dream after that fucking hot kiss. Why her? Did he hate himself that much?

He got his mental shit together and stepped out into the living room. "Ready."

"Great. My sister insisted on taking us to the airport."

He didn't mean to place a label so quickly, but if he could spot a cop a mile off, social workers weren't any harder.

"Griffon. Karma." She didn't add labels or explanations and grabbed his gadget bag to load up into the back.

He kept his eyes on Karma. "Morning."

"Mr. Griffon." She gave a little nod.

The three of them piled into the car with the ladies up front. They started talking about the great success this year's Komen Race for the Cure had been.

He thought about the coffee shops past airport security, craving caffeine. In a break of conversation, he cleared his throat. "I appreciate you taking us to the airport."

"No problem."

"So, you work for the State?" Just to prove to himself that he was right.

"Social Services."

"Of course."

Karma looked in the rearview mirror at him in the backseat. Her expression clearly said 'what's that supposed to mean?'

He and his brother Frank had been pretty good at keeping the SS out of their lives. Though, maybe if Social Services had been around when the neighborhood housewives came calling, he'd have a different outlook on the SS. Karma looked over at Liesel to share her thoughts but then rolled her eyes. Griffon could see Liesel marking items off a list on a small notepad. She should really switch to digital.

-#-

Griffon inhaled the salty air; San Francisco's airport was built right on the water. It felt good to be home. Griffon had grown up in a shitty inner city neighborhood. A neighborhood where the housewives had defined desperate. They had been more than willing to teach a young boy a few tricks.

The city did hold a few positive memories like his college years, his stint in the military.

They rented a car, a black nondescript, but the biggest sedan that the rental car company offered. Griffon watched as Liesel stretched her legs out in the passenger seat, obviously liking the fact that she had plenty of room for her 36 inseam. Griffon knew her length because he had a 34 in seam and the jeans were just a tad short. They'd looked amazing on her. She should wear jeans all the time. In fact, that was all she should wear. A pair of his jeans. Nothing else.

His foot pressed the gas and he jerked the wheel to change lanes. Liesel looked his way but didn't say anything. He was all for women's right to vote and hold a job, they made great nurses and accountants and stuff. But they didn't belong in positions of power. Here she was, just sitting next to him, even being mad at her, his body still responded. He had seen a potential for a fun relationship, a steady girl he could...well, have fun with. But she had power, and experience had taught him that women couldn't handle power. Oh, yes, the lesson of experience was harsh. He didn't want to be controlled.

Yet, he kept think about all those purple t-shirts. The way she was with Tara. Then the thoughts twisted back on themselves. He hated this.

He flipped the turn signal as he cornered the block, feeling the tightness on the wheels.

"You look like you know your way around."

"I grew up in San Francisco."

"I'd ask you what part, that does seem like the next step, but I wouldn't know what it meant." She read signs as they sailed through traffic.

"A bad part." Griffon supplied anyway.

She made no comment for a while then asked, "Are we almost there?" a note of panic in her voice.

That surprised him. Where was her confidence? She always handled things in a very straightforward, confident way. "Couple of blocks." He stopped for a light. Unlike the Larkins it looked like the Johnsons lived in a lower working class neighborhood. Lawns were cut but yellow. Various cars parked in driveways and on the street rather than behind garage doors.

"Can we stop at a service station or something? I want to freshen up." Was she worried about impressing these people; people that lived in this neighborhood? He took a moment to survey her clothes. They were nothing fancy, a skirt and blouse.

"Why? You look fine and if you need to pee I'm sure the Johnsons have a bathroom."

She gave him a glare. The light changed. "Just pull over a minute."

"No." Okay, he reasoned with himself, he was still angry. But he was driving and this was his investigation. A second later, he wished he'd pulled over, it would have been safer.

She flipped off her shoes, pulled out her purse and pulled down the visor. Then she ran her hands through her hair, fluffing it, and ran a tube of lip stick over her mouth. Griffon reminded himself to watch the road and missed the car in front of him by jerking to a quick stop. Unfazed, she continued grooming. She flipped the visor closed and shimmed her skirt up her thighs, revealing another pair of skin tone stockings with lacy tops. Starting at the toes she straightened and pulled the stockings up, working over her knee to her thigh and repeating the process with the other. "I'm going to have to buy another pair, these are losing their elasticity."

They looked great to Griffon.

She flipped her skirt back over her knees and smoothed her blouse into her waistband. "Ready."

A driver behind them leaned on his horn and shouted something out his window. Griffon put his foot back on the gas and started watching for house numbers.

Chapter 15

The Johnsons' house looked like it had been built before the earthquake and fire of 1906. Not that it was dirty, it was rather quite nice, even had a small patch of green grass out front but it looked broken and about to topple. It survived the natural disaster but Griffon wasn't sure it was still alive.

He made note of a few elements, like placement of windows, proximity of neighbors, height of wood fence, cement steps that lead to the front door. Liesel rang the doorbell, gave her hair a flip and squared her shoulders.

A lady in her late thirties dressed like a school teacher answered the door—denim overall dress with apples and a country blouse. It must be in the standardized dress code for all grade school teachers. And, Griffon noted, she was black. Her skin, eyes and hair were a dark brown. "Ms. Grant. Please come in." She hollered over her shoulder as she opened the door wide for them. "Herschel, she's here."

What? Not 'they're here?' Griffon thought, a little petulantly, even to his own inner ear.

Mrs. Johnson's husband came into the small entryway. He looked haggard, his eyes heavily lined with fatigue and weeping. He shook Liesel's hand, his eyes watering, he blinked to clear them. "We're glad you came. I'm Herschel Johnson and this is my wife Betty."

"It's nice to meet you. I wish it was for different reasons."

They nodded.

"This is Jim Griffon, he's a private investigator that is working on this case with me."

"Oh dear, Ms. Grant, you didn't hire him on our account did you?" Betty still had a bit of southern to her voice.

"I wish I had such resources, this would be the best opportunity to use them. The Larkins have hired him."

They shook Griffon's hand, Herschel's palm rough with calluses, and thanked him for coming.

"Can we maybe sit?" Liesel was using her business tone, or so Griffon had dubbed it. She'd used it in her office when she spoke about genetics and later at his home. She pulled it out over the phone when she wanted another background check.

"There is a tangle that needs fixing." Betty glanced quickly to her husband then back at Liesel. "Freddy's here," she whispered. "But he wouldn't say why. Just 'I'm Freddy.' That's it."

"You let him in of course?" Liesel asked.

"Almost didn't actually," Herschel said. He didn't expound on his statement.

"How long has he been here?" Liesel said.

"Ten, fifteen minutes. " Herschel rubbed the back of his neck and looked toward the back of the house.

"Let's all go into the kitchen," Betty said and Liesel placed a reassuring hand on her shoulder and followed her into the back of the house.

Sitting at the table was a tall boy, his knees barely fitting under the table. He was black, but compared to the Johnsons, he looked pale, several shades lighter. He wore a white t-shirt and low slung jeans, but not so low that his boxers showed above the waistband. The tennis shoes were Nike's and on his skinny wrist was a silver, expensive looking watch.

The boy looked undernourished, hollow checks and shoulder blades visible beneath the t-shirt. Liesel had said he was growing up in a tough place. Griffon bet anything, it was a place where meals didn't come all that regular. With his high metabolism, he looked scrawny instead of thin. Griffon would suspect heroin—he had that look—if it wasn't for the eyes. His eyes were smart, watchful. The eyes gleamed as they looked at Liesel, but the rest of the face stayed stiff. Then he took in Griffon, and Griffon knew he was weary and guarded. Smart kid.

"Freddy? I'm Liesel Grant. I'm glad you made it safely."

Freddy didn't shrug or nod or say anything at all. Liesel pulled out a chair next to him and sat. She placed a hand on his forearm that rested on the table. They exchanged a look and Liesel sat up prim in her seat. Her voice was still all business but now had more Vice Principal and less Den Mother.

"Freddy this is Mr. and Mrs. Johnson, Teona's parents. Mrs. Johnson is a school teacher for special needs children and Mr. Johnson works construction. Mostly steel work, I hear." She waited a moment, perhaps to see if he would speak. "They love Teona," she whispered, "I do too." Again the wait. Freddy looked over her shoulder at the Johnsons then at Griffon. Freddy narrowed his eyes and looked as mean as possible.

His mouth worked for a moment. "I w-wanna h-help."

"Good," Liesel said and turned toward Betty, nodding approval at the lady. Griffon turned to look as well and was relieved to see Herschel's bewilderment mirrored his own. Wasn't enough that women had a sixth sense, why did they have to be strong as well? He ground his teeth and growled. It wasn't all that loud but Freddy heard it and straightened in his seat. His best 'I'm not afraid of you' face he could manage. Liesel touched his arm and his eyes swung back to hers.

"Do you have a place to stay?"

Freddy was about to speak when Betty chimed in. "Why, he's staying here. Isn't he Herschel?"

"We'd be glad for the company." A wise man always follows his wife's lead, when it comes to that sixth sense.

Liesel looked at Freddy and waited.

"Th—thanks."

And then the light went on in Griffon's head, it wasn't nerves that made his voice hesitate. Freddy had a stutter. An Amazon that stuttered.

Betty had everyone sit down in the small tight kitchen as she hustled about making sandwiches and getting drinks, chattering the whole time about having lunch together. Griffon pulled his smartphone and stylus pen out and spoke for the first time. "Thank you Betty, it's very nice of you. I'll just ask a few questions, okay?"

"You a cop?" Not a syllable out of place, but it was rushed, as if Freddy was afraid to linger too long.

"Was," Griffon said.

"Oh, I'm sorry." Liesel flushed. "Freddy this is Mr. Jim Griffon. He's a private investigator."

"He one of us?" Freddy asked. Again, no stutter. It must depend on how comfortable he felt.

"A human being? Yes. At least I haven't detected any gills or suction cups." She smiled at Griffon. "However, just to make sure everything is clear. Mr. Griffon is not an Amazon but does understand that both Clara and Teona are. Though we don't know if that is a coincidence yet or not."

"You can call me Griffon." He addressed his words to Freddy.

Freddy nodded.

Griffon wrote down who the detective assigned to Teona's case was, had both Johnsons run through the day Teona had left and their reactions and what they had done since. "You were okay with her leaving to see Freddy?"

Freddy's hands were on the table. One hand ran over the knuckles of the other, back and forth, in a slow rhythm. Not switching hands, in a circle, but a rocking. Back and forth.

"She'd talked about it for months and we said she could go. We just wanted to clear it with Freddy's parents." Betty had placed enough sandwiches on the table to feed them all twice, or so Griffon figured. When Freddy picked up his third, she got up and started making peanut butter and jelly, having run out of lunch meat, like it was totally natural to feed a bottomless pit. She also opened a bag of chips. "We didn't realize until later that Freddy lived on his own."

"The night before we argued about it." Herschel was still working on his first sandwich, but he ate it with an air of distraction; knowing he needed to eat but not tasting it. Liesel stopped after her second one but took a hand full of the chips.

"Some of her clothes were gone and so was her wallet, we figured she'd left. Hoped she'd call in a couple of days when she wasn't mad any longer about us not letting her go; let us know she was okay," Herschel said.

"Does she have a cell phone?"

"No, and just the family computer."

Griffon turned to Freddy next. "Anyone else that she would have gone to see?"

Freddy shook his head.

"Was there someone who disliked her? Maybe talked smack about her when she wasn't logged on?"

Freddy broke a chip in half and dropped both pieces onto his now empty plate, his jaw working. "I d-did some ch-checking." He waited, looking at Griffon from beneath his eyebrows because his head was still lowered. Griffon out waited him. "Nobody th-that looked...." he took a deep breath and got out very clear, "suspicious." Freddy shrugged. "She was all excited about s-some basketball g-game. Kept telling me she c-couldn't come see me yet. Had to wait for the okay. Doin' chick stuff to get ready for s-school." He shrugged then raised his head. "I don't know what you lookin' fo' but if ya tell us," he glanced at the Johnsons. "'bout Clara, we'll see a sim-, a sim—" he gave up on the word, "something in common."

Definitely a smart boy. Fifteen and living on his own? How? Not that Griffon couldn't think of a few ways. There were all kinds of ways to earn money on the streets. He wondered which ones Freddy was doing.

"Good idea. Clara is seven, blond, blue eyed, tall for her age. Has an older sister, and gets good grades. But other than statistics like that, I don't know much about Clara. Liesel do you?"

"She's only been registered for about six months." Everyone but Griffon nodded and he figured it must have to do with her website. "She was young to chat online but her mom got on once a week and read and responded to the message boards. Both Clara and Teona are paternal partial Amazons."

She looked at Griffon. "That means their fathers were recessive carriers and that neither of their mothers seem to be Amazons." She took a swallow of her milk, and had a contemplative expression. "I don't think they ever met. Different ethnicities, different religions." She shrugged and said quietly. "I don't know."

"Mrs. Johnson, how long have you known your daughter was," he couldn't bring himself to say special, that sounded like she was disabled and Amazon was just wrong too, "different?"

"Not until she was twelve. She wanted to play optimist football. If you can imagine such a thing. You know, pre-teen football. We worried she'd get hurt but she was real good. She could out throw all the other boys and even the coach. Which he didn't like. So instead we got her to play basketball."

"There was other little things," Herschel added.

"Like?" Griffon asked.

"Oh, she could do things the neighborhood kids couldn't. Climb and run and lift. Like when we moved here, she had just turned thirteen. Remember that Betty? She could carry two boxes, when I could only carry one. I've always been proud of that," Herschel said.

"She saved that kid," Freddy said.

Herschel turned and looked at him a moment. "Teona told you about that?"

Betty started to cry silently, big tears rolling down her cheeks. Liesel reached across the table and placed her hand over Betty's, her skin flushed white as she squeezed. Griffon focused on Herschel.

"She was watching a couple of our neighbor's kids. The youngest was climbing on a bookshelf, pulled the whole thing down on his head. Teona caught it, solid oak that thing was, and put it back against the wall." Herschel gave a little laugh. "She then got a stud finder out of my tool box and hammered long nails through the back of that book case and into the wall. Then covered the holes by putting the books back." Herschel beamed and wiped a tear from the corner of his eyes.

Liesel smiled. "Didn't she think the owners would be able to tell?"

"She said there was so much dust on them books that there was no way anyone in that family actually read," Betty said. Her eyes were empty again, and Griffon relaxed the grip on his phone.

"When I came on home that day, I was angry that she would disobey. Would go and see Freddy. But then when we realized; when we started talking to the neighbors...I feel so guilty. She'd been taken...and I'd doubted."

No more tears. His nightmares were filled with them.

He needed out. Now. "Do you mind if I have a look at her room?"

Chapter 16

Griffon followed Herschel's instructions. Jogging up the stairs, in full retreat. Third floor, the whole floor. So, no need to tell which door, there wasn't one.

One wall of Teona's room was plastered with posters of Lisa Leslie, Los Angeles Sparks number 9 and Detroit's number 32, Swin Cash. But it was—almost—artistic, rather than a slap-them-on-the-wall-job. Double bed in the corner, a punching bag in a different corner. The bag was lumpy and smooth in the right places. He gave it a push and watched it spin from the ceiling.

A picture of a cheerleader was crumpled and duct taped to the punching bag. He took the picture down, added it to a pile of papers on her desk.

Both of the missing girls played basketball, both were Amazons, and that was it. Maybe it was a psycho fan out to build the perfect team.

Griffon wrote, 'Which position do they play?' on his phone.

No broken or knocked over furniture. No scuff marks on the wood floor or tares in the blanket on her bed. No signs of a struggle. He placed the cheerleader and the papers from her desk into his briefcase. There were team photos, a scattering of movie tickets, some tampons, and a Nora Roberts romance in the top drawer of her night stand.

He couldn't smell her, in this room. Didn't hear her voice. The room was empty and the promising teen was probably dead.

Could there really be no connection to Liesel? She hadn't left the state of Idaho in the last six months. So she couldn't have taken Teona, but what about on her orders?

When Griffon came back into the kitchen a few moments later, the four of them still sat at the table, quiet. But his presence spurred Liesel into action. "I wrote down the hotel phone number. Plus, Griffon's cell number. If you can think of anything else, please call us." She slid her chair back.

"I'm c-coming, too. I want to help." Freddy stood up, almost knocking his chair down.

Griffon was about to turn him down when Liesel said, "Good."

Uhm, no.

"G-good?" Freddy had expected a protest, too.

"Did you bring any equipment with you?"

"Almost all of it." He indicated three large cardboard boxes stacked in the hall. It seemed to be only consonants that gave him trouble. And it wasn't so much a double sound, when he stuttered, like two g's, but rather a push to get the sound out and that made it sharp and long.

"One day you're going to have to tell me how you got from Tampa Bay to San Francisco, with that much stuff, in one night." Liesel said.

He smiled at her and looked for the first time like he really was only fifteen.

"Anything Griffon or I need computer wise, any searches, etc. we'll be calling you. Meanwhile, if you could monitor the chat groups and message boards? See if anybody has heard from Teona. Or, heaven forbid, if there is anybody else missing."

Freddy was already opening boxes and lifting out computer parts. "C-can I set up in h-here, ma'am?" Freddy asked Betty. She nodded. "Thank you ma'am."

"How much of this stuff is hot?" Liesel whispered to Freddy, but in the small kitchen everyone heard. Griffon looked for a hint of sexual overture in her touch of the young man but saw nothing but a supportive respect.

"I b-bought the monitor." Another boyish grin. Liesel popped him on the arm. Griffon realized it must be an affectionate gesture. She'd done the same to him.

She hugged the parents and Griffon shook their hands. Before they left, Freddy was already running wire to the DSL connection in Teona's room. Griffon didn't want to know what else Freddy did at the Johnsons or if it was legal.

Liesel could have demanded the boy stay out of the way. Instead, she was careful of Freddy's pride without sounding condescending.

Griffon pulled the front door shut. "Tough kid."

"Yeah," Liesel said.

"I thought you grew up in Boise."

Liesel looked at him and waited for him to explain.

"Well, I thought you'd be surprised by that. By kids living on their own," Griffon said.

"I've seen my share of life."

She was quiet until they were both in the car. "Freddy isn't that uncommon. His father beat his mother, the whole time talking about pulling his punch so he wouldn't kill her like the last two. The bastard. He liked that he was stronger than his daughters, who of course aren't Amazons. But then Freddy got older and started protecting his mom. Well, I don't have all the details of course, but Freddy got out." Liesel put her seatbelt on.

"He lives with his two sisters in a one room apartment. They all work full time to pay for rent and for the oldest to go to college. They're taking 'turns' he says. He won't tell me who he works for but I know it's under the table and that they use his strength to their advantage."

"Like to hurt people?"

She shook her head. "No. Like moving stuff. Fridges, pianos. I don't know if it's stuff they're stealing or if it's making deliveries."

"Doesn't eat enough."

"Probably wants it to be fair for his sisters. Equal."

He inserted the key and shifted his body towards her. He looked at her face, really looked. Then asked, "Is that important?"

"Yeah."

Chapter 17

The plan was to check into the hotel then split up. Griffon was going to the police station to talk with Detective Barnaby, the officer in charge of Teona's case. Liesel would go back to the Johnsons neighborhood to re-question the neighbors. She wrote down Griffon's instructions to take the trolley and bus back.

She needed time to process the weird morning. The easy way Freddy submitted to Liesel's tone, the odd reverence from the Johnsons. Griffon had asked why her. She was one of them. They trusted their own but it was beyond that. They saw her as their leader and expected her to lead. She didn't get it.

The hotel gave them adjourning rooms. Each room had two double beds, bathroom, bureau with a TV and a small sitting area with table and chairs. Standard but clean and they had an Ethernet connection so she booted up her laptop and called Harriett while she waited to log in.

"Oh Leis, I'm so glad you called." Harriett sounded frantic.

"Is everyone okay? Mom—" The latest test results. With breast cancer, there was always 'test results' to worry about.

"Yes. Yes." Harry interrupted. "Everyone is fine but your house was broken into."

"I've only been gone a few hours." Liesel sat down heavily on her hotel bed. A strange focused and yet murky feeling filled her. Her hands clutched tightly to the phone, needing the double support to keep it next to her ear.

"I'm working the Clarke project just a few blocks away, so I came over to raid your fridge. I hope that was okay."

"Harry! Yes, that's why you have a key. Keep going, what did they take?" Her mind shuffled through random trivia. She'd locked the back door and the front. It was Sunday, so Penelope wouldn't be in until Monday morning. Her electronics were all insured and backed up off site.

"I brought in your paper and went to lay it on your desk. I noticed the window was broken. The alarm had been deactivated and one of your file cabinets has a broken lock. I don't know what is missing."

"Which cabinet?"

"K thru R."

"There was a leather manuscript in the glass front cabinet. Is it still there?" Please be there.

"That cabinet's empty."

Shit. Shit. She-It.

"Did you call—?"

"Yes, I called the police," she sounded exasperated. "They took some prints and said you would just need to file the report of what's missing when you got back. They asked...."

"Harry? I didn't hear what you said." Liesel's hands shook. She would have to call the McKinnons, or rather Mr. O'Grady. Then contact her insurance company. She had high coverage because of the extensive computer equipment she owned and the rare books, but she doubted 'priceless and irreplaceable' was covered. Mr. O'Grady had paid her a down payment on the translation, which she would return, but she didn't even care. All that information. About herself, about the others. She felt angry and sad and everything in between.

She realized her sister had spoken again. "I'm sorry Harry, I totally missed that. I'm just not taking anything in."

Harry sighed. "What about that girl, Anna? Would she have stolen it?"

"No."

"Well, I guess it makes more sense for her to take the electronics but...."

"No, she wouldn't. She's never lied to me. Besides, she had a key." So did Penelope. She would call Penelope next and ask her to go into the office, see what else was missing. She could even start working on the insurance. The duty of calling Mr. O'Grady was all Liesel's.

Liesel thanked her sister and was about to get off the phone when she remembered. "Harry!"

"What? Shit, don't yell. Scare me to death."

"Are you there? At my house?" Liesel asked.

"No, I'm on my way home—"

"GO BACK! Please, can you go back and check." She couldn't wait for Penelope. "I was working last night. I copied my notes before I filed them. The copies, I think I left them in the copier. In the multi-function-thingy." Her breath came in excited jumps, her grip on the phone tightened even further. Her palms were hot and moisture made them slide along the handle.

"You stayed up after we left? Leis, why aren't you sleeping?"

"Not now Harry."

"Fuck yes, now! Talk to me. I've just flipped a U-turn on Overland. In heavy traffic. Start talking."

It spilled out and she was crying. They'd grown up together, not only as sisters but as surrogate mothers. Their own mom, often too sick to go to Harry's games, too sick to edit Liesel's papers, knew only of her younger daughters' triumphs. When it came to the broken hearts, navigating the bullies at school, failing or falling, they'd had each other. She pressed the phone to her ear and tucked her head into the crook of her arm to hide from the world.

She told Harry everything; the missing kids and kissing Griffon. And in a very quiet voice, she told her best friend that she was afraid. Because they wanted her to be queen. They wanted her to turn the desperate need into meaning, make it acceptable to risk their lives. Give them a banner to fight beneath. Permission to save the day. Thousands of people, at risk, by her command.

They fought then. Old ground covered until thread bare. Whose fault it was that Harry had gotten hurt. "It was an accident, Leis." Her tone had plenty of attitude. Sisters can be such a pain in the ass.

They both sighed. For a while nothing was said. Her head ached like a hangover, dehydrated from crying.

"You were meant to help these kids, Leis."

"I don't believe—"

"In anything. Fine. That's your choice."

"Don't be mad, Harry."

Harry talked over her. "But you should believe in yourself. I do."

"I believe in you, Harry."

"Thanks."

"Harry, I—"

"I'm here." Liesel heard the slam of Harry's truck door. "I boarded up the window. I've got the replacement ordered and I'll install it. I expect dinner and a movie as a thank you. And not that multi-plex, but the local theater with the popcorn included in the price."

Liesel laughed and stood up. Then she sat back down. Please let them be there.

"Legal pad? Six pages on the copy machine?"

"Yes." Liesel said. The blood rushed back into her hands and she almost dropped the phone.

Griffon called Max once he reached his room. "Hey Max, can you call that FBI contact you've got. See who they have on the Larkins' case. Feel him out."

"How's he supposed to feel? Silky?" Max said.

"Make sure he's...open to the unusual."

"How unusual we talking?" Max, Griffon thought, the man of questions.

"I don't know yet," Griffon said. He rubbed the back of his hand across his eyebrows.

"Did I ever tell you about that vampire cult I worked in California?"

"Okay, maybe not that weird." Griffon could hear Max chuckle. "Call my cell when you've got anything."

"Might take some time. My guy just retired."

Griffon disconnected the call. Two nights ago, in the blood drenched world of Griffon's nightmares, Ashley called him Clara. That night Clara had been the one hung from the ceiling by chains. And Griffon, Griffon had stood along the cloudy perimeter of dreamland and watched as Ashley used sour cream and a knife to shave the little girl's head bald.

Yeah, the case was getting to him. Beyond personal, beyond empathetic.

If the kidnappers had tricked Clara into going with them, then they wanted to play with her. If she'd been taken by force—brutally beaten into submission—she was dead. Discarded. No longer of use. But evidence showed they had taken her carefully.

Lt. Bit had called yesterday to say forensics had found traces of trichloromethane in powder form. Also known as chloroform, the powder was probably sprinkled on a wet cloth to activate. Taking her this way meant they wanted her alive, and unhurt. If it had been kidnapping with ransom in mind, the kidnappers would have still tried to get money, even if the girl had died.

That meant she was still alive. That meant Griffon was going to find her. That meant the idiot bastards who took her would suffer.

Griffon sent Bit an email about Teona and the possible connection. You couldn't build a case on a white van but it was always good to share information; clarify within your own head by laying the parts out. He'd call the man but it was his day off, and Bit got so few of those.

Griffon had just finished checking his messages, email and voicemail, when there was a knock at his door. He thought for a moment that it was from the adjoining door. With a second knock, he realized it was from the hall. Liesel may have locked herself out of her room.

Griffon peered out the peep hole, and smiled. His brother Frank and Frank's wife Tammy stood on the other side, murmuring to each other. Griffon slid the chain out then opened his door. "How in the hell did you know I was here?"

Frank laughed and gave him a shove out of the way. "I paid Max twenty bucks the last time we were in Boise. We've been in the restaurant waiting to pounce. The last time, you didn't even call us."

Griffon nodded at Tammy and gestured to his small sitting area then turned his scowl back on his brother. Tammy was a couple inches shorter than the two Griffon brothers, slender, blond and rather timid. Griffon made an extra effort to be gentle around her so as not to scare her.

"I'm here on a case. Just like last time. If it was a vacation, I'd stay at your house, eat your food and play with your girls." Now how to get them out so he could get over to the police station? "I'll be at Mom's for Christmas." Probably.

Frank had dropped onto one of the beds while Tammy stood beside him. "What you working on?"

"A couple of kids are missing."

Frank stared at Griffon for a moment and began to stroke his wife's hair, soothing himself. Griffon saw Frank's eyes cloud, and he felt his heart wrench in his chest. Frank was thinking about when Griffon had been missing. Griffon knew it like he knew his brother's shoe size; like he knew, though they loved each other, they wouldn't talk about it. Since Griffon's kidnapping, Frank didn't know how to interact with Griffon and he had gone to great lengths to protect his family.

"That's got to be tough. I can't imagine losing one of the girls." Frank stretched out on the bed with his hands behind his head and smirked when Griffon growled. "We're not leaving until you promise to come visit the girls."

At this point, his side of the adjoining door opened, and Liesel entered the room. Griffon noticed first that she had removed her jacket and unbuttoned the top three on her white blouse, a lovely bit of cleavage flashing as she moved. Second, her legs were bare. "Griffon, someone...." Her eyes were red and her skin had blotchy red marks.

She stopped and her eyebrows shot up. "Oh, hello." She blushed and shifted her weight, twisted her fingers together. It was so different from the measured confidence at the Johnsons that Griffon didn't know how to respond. She nodded to both of Griffon's visitors then turned back to him. "Have you seen," obviously trying to remember why she'd come, "my purse? I can't find it in my stuff."

Frank had raised himself to his elbows and was staring open mouthed at Liesel. Knowing the way of Frank's thoughts, Griffon crossed his arms over his chest and scowled. "I don't have it."

"Okay." She stood there another moment and looked back and forth between the room's occupants. Her face went through several emotions and when he didn't step forward to introduce them, she blushed even deeper. She lifted her eyebrows at Tammy as if to say

"Men." She turned back to her room shutting the door behind her.

"Business? Yeah, that's right. Business," Frank said.

His older brother was an odd mirror image of Griffon. The features were the same; dark hair prone to curl, strong brows and deep eyes, full bottom lip. They were hairier than what was strictly GQ, and their beards, when they let them grow in, were full and dark. But Frank was...approachable. Maybe that was the word for it. Frank had a thoughtful nature and a relaxed attitude that poured out of his physical characteristics. You couldn't always say what was different, whose nose was bigger or who was taller, but no one ever thought Frank was anyone but Frank and Griffon, well, people tended to be weary around Griffon.

"Frank!"

"What?"

"If your brother says he's working a case then he is," Tammy said.

"Thanks Tammy." Griffon smiled at her like he did her daughters, careful, reassuring. "I am working with her. Liesel knows both of the families and the kids that are missing."

"Okay, I guess that's believable but I could see where this case might be more fun than the rest." Frank smirked at his brother, until he saw his wife's frown.

"Meaning what?" Tammy asked. Tammy and Frank had met in college. Tammy, there on scholarship and Frank, the dark brain, there on financial aid had clicked instantly. Tammy was round of face and had beautiful laugh lines around her eyes. And they made beautiful children together.

"Hon, I love you. You're gorgeous. But my poor sap of a brother needs a gorgeous girl, too." He sat up and pulled his wife onto his lap, wrapping his arms around her. Frank nuzzled her neck a minute.

"Now you have to leave. No making out on my bed."

"Use the other one." Frank, his voice husky with lust, nodded to the other bed and Tammy elbowed him in the gut. He gave a little cough and let her up.

"We need to go anyway. We wanted to come by and make sure you come for dinner tomorrow. You will be here that long? Won't you?" Tammy asked.

"Well...." Griffon said.

"Come on Jimmy. You got to eat and you can bring the girl." Griffon saw a totally different plea in his eyes. Big brother needed reassurance that his little brother was really okay. Or at least getting better.

"Please, Jimmy. The girls will be so upset that they missed you. Bring," she seemed to be trying words in her head, "your business partner."

"I'll ask her and we'll call you guys tomorrow."

Tammy pulled on Frank's hand and headed for the door. Frank smacked Griffon's shoulder in farewell.

After getting his gear together, Griffon tapped on the adjoining door then opened it when he got no response. Liesel was gone. He set one of his wireless cameras on top of the T.V. and aimed it toward her hall door. He reminded himself to tell her it was there, so she wouldn't feel like her privacy was being invaded. He had one in his room as well and could see both shots on his special PDA device. It was habit and probably unnecessary, but they had come in handy on more than one occasion. He had access even here in California to the surveillance cameras at his home and office.

Liesel didn't strike him as being all that modest but women had weird ways.

Chapter 18

Detective Barnaby was treating the case as a runaway. Griffon didn't tell him about Clara Larkin. The guy was overworked and showed definite signs of major burn out. When you stopped caring about the people, it was time to get out. Griffon's problem had been caring too much.

It was almost seven o'clock but felt much later. Griffon checked the video feeds on both his and Liesel's rooms and the third camera he'd placed at the end of the hall. All three empty. He grabbed the large bag from the office supply store he'd stopped at and climbed out of the car. His cell phone rang and he pulled it out of his pants pocket with his free hand. "Hello."

"Hey." It was Max. "My guy got back to me about the agent assigned to the case. Did you know he's looking for a job? Retirement is slow I guess. You're looking to hire another aren't you? I told him you were."

Didn't take him long after all. However, anything longer than ten minutes was long for Max.

"Max, you know I have trouble getting enough work for me." Griffon picked up security work when things were slow. He had only been a private investigator for a year. He needed more time to establishing a name for himself. If it wasn't for the freelance work he did for the government, he'd be eating Ramen more often than not.

"What are you saying?"

Griffon shook his head. "Who's the agent?"

"Sting." Max ruffled through papers. "Assigned here in Boise. Doesn't have a task force or anything like that put together. But got thumbs up from my contact."

"Good. E-mail me his contact info and then go home. It's Sunday."

"So, did you hear about the break-in?" Max said, neither acknowledging the request or disconnecting the line.

"What?' Griffon bobbled his cell phone, switching hands to catch the large bag. He needed to buy one of those blue-tooth ear things.

Max told him the address of a robbery. It sounded familiar.

"Have you been listening to the police radio?" Griffon kept one in the office and could see Max, feet on the desk, drinking coffee and listening to dispatch.

"Little Bit called. I know better than to call him that to his face. Though his wife calls him big—"

"Max. Wait. That's Liesel's address," Griffon said.

"Bit said to let you know. Hooked to that JV record you had me pull."

Liesel's JV record. "Yeah. What happened?" Griffon had stopped just outside the hotel. He didn't want to take the chance of losing the signal.

"Middle of the day. Went through a window." Max said.

"Go to the station and get me a copy of the report. After they run the prints. Take a box of Krispy Kreme with you." Though police files were public record that was only after the investigating officers finished them. Before then it was like stealing eggs from vulture nests.

"Sir, yes sir." The rude one finger salute was clear.

"Please."

Griffon heard Max laugh as he disconnected the call.

As Griffon entered the hotel lobby, Liesel was talking to the front desk clerk. "Hey." He leaned a hip against the front desk and nodded briefly at the clerk. "Forget your key or something?" He stowed his cell in his pocket. Did Liesel know about the break-in yet?

"No. It seems I have a few messages." She held a stack of pink papers.

"Doesn't this place have voice mail?"

She didn't answer but thanked the clerk and walked away, stopping a good distance in the middle of the lobby. Griffon followed her. She looked through the papers then looked up at him, wild eyed. "Are you hungry? Let's go someplace, I'll treat."

"Okay. But first tell me what's wrong."

She shifted her weight on the balls of her feet, checking the lobby with her eyes and her body squared with his, almost hiding. "I'll explain, in detail, later. But for now...someone wants to talk to me and I don't want to run...into them."

"Will these details include another story?" Like why her house was broken into?

She laughed, her eyes crinkling and shining. Man she looked hot when she smiled. Sexy, and touchable. *Way to think with your dick. Remember who she is and what she can do.*

"There is a good possibility."

She means for another story. Down boy. Griffon placed his hand on her forearm and steered her toward the entrance. "What do you want to eat?"

"Want to eat? Nothing."

He let that hang for a moment and opened her side of the car. Then leaned into the open door after she climbed in. "What do you mean?"

She shrugged, looked embarrassed. "I just get tired of eating. I have to eat but I get bored."

"Sounds like you need something different. Any allergies?"

She shook her head. He liked standing there above her and felt weird about liking it. He closed the door, stowed his shopping bag in the trunk and went around to his side.

"Eat much seafood?" He pulled the seat belt across his lap and snapped it in place.

"Shrimp once in a while. Salmon of course. You have to eat Salmon in Idaho."

"Right. Like Potatoes." They smiled at each other and Griffon felt silly. He was quickly remembering all the reasons he wanted her body, enjoyed her company. He needed to get out of the car and keep his fucking distance. "Seafood it is then." What was he, twelve? That he was going to intentionally ignore the warning bells chiming in his head over a hot piece of ass. Guess so.

The place was cleaner and better lit than most dives. It didn't have valet parking or linen napkins. It was a perfect balance. They were seated in a corner booth and the waitress took their drink orders. One root beer, one water.

"Did you come here with your family growing up?"

"No, we didn't eat out much as kids. Hot dog stands and taco shacks once in a while. Me and Frank, the one on the bed this afternoon, sorry I didn't introduce you." He kept his eyes on his menu. It felt a little weird talking about himself. "It was just us and Mom. She had a lot of medical problems, arthritis, and couldn't always work. But we got by and she's doing great now. Finally qualified for disability." Crap, why did he tell her that?

"When my mom was diagnosed with breast cancer, she had to take a lot of time off work. Karma really stepped in and helped out. She already had a few kids by then, but we just lived together and made it work, like you said."

"What about your dad?"

"He died when I was little. Car accident." She twirled her straw in her ice water. "It was hard for Karma, she being older and all. But I also think it was hard on Harriett, my baby sister."

Liesel didn't ask about his dad. What the hell, he'd volunteer the information. It would keep them talking. "My dad was in the Air Force. Stationed at Travis Air Force Base here in San Fran. He died in a training crash."

"I'm so sorry."

Why hadn't he thought to say that about her dad? Griffon shrugged his shoulders.

"Is that why you joined the military?"

"No, Dad's best friend watched out for us. When he was on leave from the Navy. He was military police. I figured it was a good way to pay for college."

"And you were an M.P. too."

"Yeah, but I was in the Army. Fort Irwin."

The waiter came and took their orders. Liesel ordered one of the largest platters they had but only one, and Griffon ordered the chowder and a salad.

Once the waiter had left they continued talking. "You said you would eat less but you worried about your curves." Okay, Griffon, you idiot, he thought. Nice distance you're keeping by talking about her body.

"Did I say that? Well, it's true. I run and stay pretty active. If I didn't, I wouldn't need to eat as much as I do. Everyone is like that though. But with me, well, I start looking gaunt, drawn, if I don't eat enough. Unfortunately, the first place I lose weight is in the chest." She came to a stuttering halt and her cheeks reddened. "Sorry."

"Well, I for one am glad you're maintaining your weight." He teased, looking at her breasts. "Let me order you a second helping of dessert." He laughed as she blushed even deeper then took the playful pop in the arm. It didn't hurt, not even a sting. Just a good solid push. He sighed in relief. His body trusted, even if his mind didn't.

Freddy had gotten popped earlier. Did that mean she saw Griffon in a brotherly light? She didn't kiss like any sister he knew.

"So, tell me about this person we are avoiding."

Her cheeks were still red and she fiddled with her water some more before taking a long drink. "There are a few people in the area." She seemed to choose each word carefully, making her cadence slow. "People I've met through my website. They want to meet me and I'm not ready to meet them."

"Aha," he said in mock disappointment. "I was looking forward to a Liesel story."

"A story, huh?" Liesel waited until their waiter finished delivering the food, to continue. She pulled the pile of pink slips from her pocket. "The reasons these are on paper instead of voice mail, is because these actually came to the hotel. There are seven of them, though these two may be the same person." She waved two of the slips in the air with her left hand and then returned the paper to the table. All seven spread out in front of her.

"A mister Fioja, though I may be pronouncing that wrong, is married to an Amazon and wants my advice. He doesn't know what to get him for their anniversary. Like I know anything about anniversaries, let alone their relationship."

Griffon was sure his eyes where round with shock. She took a few bites of food.

"This is a lady from a national chain-gym or franchise or whatever they call them, who wants me to advertise for them. She is most definitely not an Amazon and doesn't think we have met because I was not what she expected. If that makes any sense. I'm doing my best to get her off the message boards, I've banned her twice but...." Liesel shrugged.

"This guy thinks I'm also—" She double checked the pink slip. "Amazingkisser78—that must be someone's online name—who isn't me but I'd have to check to see who it really is."

"What is your user name?" Since he'd gained access to the websites he'd scanned through her research but hadn't read any of the message boards. The latest translations were the most popular topic and she got a lot of heavy traffic each day.

"Oni. Spelled O N I."

"What does it mean?"

She smiled. "It means daemon or dragon in Japanese. It works well with the name of my business, Daemon Designs. I'm not sure about these other four." She waived the pink slips to indicate the ones left. "Just gives the person's name and that they want me to call. I feel like a Hollywood director or New York editor." She smiled at him. A dewy, secretive smile. She kept talking about different members, their triumphs and her excitement for them.

If it had been lust in her eyes, he would have known how to handle it. This made him agitated. She cared about these kids, about her family. She seemed to believe things need to be fair, equal. He wanted to test his new footing. See how far his body would let him go. But didn't want to get halfway to Orgasm-land and get derailed by a panic attack or performance anxiety. All systems were pleasantly go, his cock and balls tight and heavy in his pants, but could he keep it that way?

Griffon took her hand on top of the table and ran a thumb back and forth across her palm. There was no glimmer in her eyes to indicate she knew what it meant. He placed her hand back on the table, then trailed his fingertips over the back of her hand and down the length of her finger tips, then back up her hand. The touch was making his heart pound in an effort to rush all his blood to his crotch. He looked in her eyes and gave her his best smoldering look.

"You look tired. Sorry, I've been rambling, when I'm sure you want to talk about the case," Liesel said. Her eyes were dilated and glassy. She must feel something.

"Yes. What did the neighbors have to say about Teona?" Griffon kept his voice sultry, multi-tasking.

"Freddy worried about my reception. So, he came with me. I don't know if people were intimidated by him or not but they were very willing to give me information. I can pin the time between one and three-thirty. Herschel was home at lunch time. No van and Teona sulking in her room. Then Betty was home early that day, at 3:30. Neighbors say the van's license was smeared with dirt."

"You seem distracted," he said.

She smiled and blinked slowly once. "It's nothing. But I do need to make a phone call."

He'd meant distracted in a pleasantly aroused way. So much for seduction.

"Anna?" It was Liesel Grant on the phone and Anna Marie was relieved to hear her voice.

"Or Marie, or A. M., or Fort-Porter or Kompfee or Rogue. I'm not too particular." Just pissed off. And confused. The phone was tucked into her shoulder as she sat on the edge of her couch. It was her couch, her bed, her dining room chair and occasionally her hamper. It, and the coffee table in front of her, were her only pieces of furniture. But since she didn't spend much time in the apartment, it didn't matter.

In one hand she held a joint, rolled it back and forth between her fingers. Anna couldn't smoke it. She'd had it for over a day. She just didn't want it.

"I've been worried. Do you—"

Anna interrupted Liesel. "No, I don't want to talk about it. I'll figure it out."

"I know you will." Liesel was all calm assurance. She waited for Anna to talk. She didn't take offense to Anne's tone of voice, now or before when Anna shouted obscenities and stormed out of Liesel's house.

Maybe it wasn't that Liesel didn't care. That wasn't what stopped Anna from lighting up and getting high. Maybe it was that Liesel would care, about Anna, whether she smoked pot or not. Whether she fucked up her life or made something of herself. Liesel would care about her. Like her. Trust her. Anna wanted to be worthy of that.

"I'm...I'm...THERE IS NOTHING WRONG WITH ME."

"No, there isn't," Liesel said.

"Nothing wrong with you," Anna said, as if it was a point of argument. There was nothing wrong with Liesel, so it followed that there was also nothing wrong with Anna.

"I snore. Oh, and I've got this annoying habit." Liesel set up her sucker line.

Okay, Anna would walk into it, but it didn't count if your eyes were open. "What annoying habit?" Anna did use her insolent-pride-shit tone, though.

"I expect people to respond like me. I think it's funny, surely everyone else will too. If I know who Pele is, it must be common knowledge."

Pele, the Hawaiian goddess of fire. Said to protect the islands, and known to bring bad luck to those who displeased her. Anna put the joint on the coffee table. She'd sell it and put the twenty bucks back into her college fund. Pelé was the famous soccer player.

"And if being an Amazon is exciting and almost...'of course.'" Liesel said the last as if she had searched for the answer then had a great epiphany. "Then others will surely respond the same way. It's just that I feel so normal, so average." Liesel sighed. "I'm sorry. I didn't handle it well."

"It's okay," Anna said. The response was a knee jerk reaction to any apology, polite manners. But it wasn't okay. Not yet.

'I'm sorry I wasn't there for your birthday; Rome was just too good to pass up,' her mom had said. 'Too good to pass up' just meant nothing was better, including Anna. One year it was Rome on her birthday. Other years it was Tokyo at Christmas time. Even the Nile on her first day of school. Plenty of apologies and the required acceptance. The knee jerk, 'it's okay.'

"Penelope is missing. She hasn't returned the calls I've made to her home and her cell phone has been disconnected." Another sigh. "And the McKinnon leather was stolen."

Shit. Anna's hold on the phone slipped and she tightened her grip. "She took it."

"No, it was a break-in. I want to make sure she is okay. If I had gotten a hold of her, I would've sent her to check on you. "

Anna shook her head. Liesel may have been fooled but Anna knew something was up with Penelope.

"Can you tell if someone is lying? Like how you can tell if someone is an Amazon by touching them?" She'd seen that on the website.

"I don't need physical contact to know who is an Amazon. Unfortunately, lying and deception are still only visible through hindsight. I'm glad you've been to the site. My first few calls were to encourage you to take a look at it. There are lots of people going through the same things you are. Just figuring out that they are different. They're not sure how to handle that."

Neither spoke for a moment.

"I also thought you could use my library. It helped me to learn as much as I could."

Anna picked a quarter off the coffee table, fiddled with it in her hand then rolled it. She could feel the grooves across the edge of her finger. "And the last few calls?"

"I was wondering if you could go to Penelope's house to check. Just in case I'm wrong," Liesel said.

It was theirs, the leather pages. Their past, their heritage. A place finally, finally, where she belonged and there was no way in hell it would be taken from her. The quarter fell from her fist and landed on the coffee table. It was bent at a ninety degree angle.

"I'll go."

Chapter 19

"I've put almost all of my profit back into buying the latest in, well...computers, cameras, security. I have this portable security monitor." Griffon pulled out the portable monitor device that looked a lot like a PDA and was connected to the cameras in his and Liesel's room. It had a high resolution digital liquid LCD display. He clicked through the menu screen bringing up his hotel room. Then turned the device toward her. "I put security cameras in each of our rooms. They are like mini-web cams. They're wireless and have an amazing battery life."

The elevator settled and the doors slid open to their floor. "I put one at the end of our hallway." He shrugged.

"It's okay." They stepped off the elevator. She sounded distracted, her eyes unfocused, her body turned away. Which just added to his geeky-awkward feeling. He switched camera views to bring up her room. There was movement, a big bulky blur just off screen. Griffon grabbed her arm. "We have a visitor. Stay here."

"What?" She hadn't been listening.

"Stay here. There is someone in your room." He handed her the portable monitor and pulled his gun from the holster at his lower back. The weight and feel of the warm metal centered him. Her eyes got big and he just shook his head. "Stay. Here."

The elevator was at one end, their rooms at the other. Fourteen rooms, seven doors on either side of the hall. If the intruder escaped he'd have to run past Liesel to get to the stairs or elevator. Better make sure that didn't happen.

He'd given her the PDA device because he didn't want to rely on it. There was a three second or more delay. Front door or connecting door from his room? The connecting door would give him the surprise element, but would leave the front as a possible and easy escape.

He'd gotten her key as they came up, planning on escorting her to her door, gallant shit.

His gun was always the first thing he unpacked, and since he was licensed to carry concealed in the state of California, he usually didn't have problems traveling with it.

He inserted the key card, then re-griped the gun with both hands as the little light flipped to green and elbowed the handle down. He powered through the door.

Liesel yelled, "Gun!"

He dove for the floor and rolled into a crouch in the door frame of the hotel room's bathroom. No shot was fired. The intruder ran for the open door. Jim dove for his knees. Their bodies slammed against the wall in the tiny entrance way. The mirrored wall echoed the movement of their fight.

A black taser fell from the man's hands and tumbled into the hall.

Griffon tried to bring his gun up but the man's knee caught Griffon hard in the sternum. He gasped and hit the guy with his free fist in the jaw. At the same time he shoved the guy against the wall with his legs. He aimed his gun but the man lay slumped like a crumpled brick wall. Griffon pulled air into his lungs. No additional weapons, no broken bones, his or mine. He blew the breath out as Liesel stepped into the room.

"Oh, you've got him." She had volted the guy with his own taser and he now lay unconscious. Griffon kept the gun in his hand and bent to check the man's pulse.

This scenario was fucked up in more ways than ten. Why'd Liesel yell gun? It could have been the video delay and that she saw the taser, or was she trying to cover something up. Maybe her yell of 'gun' was to warn the man in her room. He wiped sweat from his brow and bounced once at the knees to stand in a fluid motion, holstered his gun and took the taser from her stiff fingers.

Now that she'd tasered him, Griffon would be unable to question the guy before security or the police came. She hadn't told him about the burglary though he knew she'd called that employee with the record, Anna Fort-Porter, during dinner. Max was checking her insurance. But he knew she wasn't in desperate need of funds.

Griffon would just have to keep the intruder for a while; ask him some questions, once he came around.

Liesel didn't protest as Griffon tied the man to one of her chairs. It felt creepy tying him down. Knowing where to tie. Surprisingly the confrontation hadn't brought any of the other hotel guests out of their rooms. Griffon used the telephone cord and a tassel from the drapes to bind the man to the chair. He kept the gut wrenching, sweat and flashbacks to a minimum.

The guy came around after a few minutes, flexing against his restraints but not really struggling. With sharp cheek bones, a lean physique and straight black hair, the man was probably Native American. Liesel sat on her bed, just out of the man's peripheral vision.

Griffon held up the man's wallet. "Mr. Dillon Gehr," he read off the California driver's license. He pulled out a business card. "Private Investigator. Even B and E in the line of duty is illegal." He raised his eyes to meet Dillon's. "No comment, Dillon?"

The man remained silent.

Griffon unhooked his own cell phone from his belt, flipped through his contacts list until he came to an entry titled Licensing. Phyllis worked records at the Bureau of Security and Investigative Services for the lovely state of California. P.I.'s weren't licensed in Idaho. California was a bit stricter. She picked up after the third ring.

"Hello, Griffon."

"Surely Phyllis, other people call you at work. Even this late at night on a Sunday." It seemed Phyllis was always working. He kept his eye on Dillon, watching for movement.

"Whatcha' need?" Phyllis said, all business.

He had never actually met Phyllis but pictured her looking like that sweet old lady that worked as a cashier at the grocery store in the mornings. Hair obviously dyed, hands twisting with arthritis, always flirtatious with the male customers. But she was probably early twenties with a two-pack-a-day smoking habit.

"I want to check a fellow P.I.'s status." He gave her the name and info off the card. She gave him all the technical data, length of licensing, physical description, etc. Then she offered up a few opinions.

"He works with his family. A brother and father, I believe. They are on the high-end fee wise. No complaints have been filed."

"Thanks Phyllis. Is there a contact number for the brother?" He wrote that number down on the back of the business card then thanked Phyllis again and disconnected the call.

"So Dillon," he said the name as if he believed it was a fake name, "who hired you to investigate Liesel Grant?"

He had strapped Dillon to a beast of a wing chair with heavy wheels hidden beneath a decorative skirt and fringe along the bottom. Griffon picked it over the lighter ladder back chair for its weight. It would be harder for his captive to run with it still attached.

"That is privileged information," Dillon said with a measured tone. His face clearly said where Griffon could take his questions.

"Oh, I shall feel most privileged knowing." Griffon was using his own colorful body language.

Dillon cocked his head to the side and narrowed his eyes. "I can't tell you who hired me."

"But it's me you're investigating?"

His head jerked around, finally realizing they were not alone in the room.

Dillon pushed his lips together.

"What did you steal when you searched Liesel's house?" As Griffon asked Dillon, he looked at Liesel to see her reaction. She eyes widened and she straightened her back, looking into Griffon's eyes.

"Whatever." Dillon sneered.

"Computer files, her underwear?"

"I was only hired yesterday." Dillon shook his head.

"Before we came? And someone was already working in Idaho?"

Dillon pushed his lips together again. Griffon walked around the chair, slowly. When he had circled and was behind him for the second time he said, "You usually do insurance fraud and divorce cases." Most P.I.'s paid the bills that way, but Phyllis had also mentioned the insurance fraud. He'd timed it just right so that he stood in front of Dillon as he finished talking and could see his reaction. "Who works at the hotel and gave you the all clear to search the place?" Again he was back around front to see Dillon's reaction. "Didn't bring anything with you but the taser. No camera to get evidence and no little slides to collect fingerprints." Another slow circle.

"You looking for a missing item?" He stopped and gripped Dillon's wrist feeling the pulse. Waited. "No missing or stolen items." Almost to himself. He started walking again, feeling the waves seep off Dillon. Waves of fear and tension. "So a pure dirt finding mission, but for who."

"Did you tie him up or tie him to the chair?" Liesel asked.

Engrossed in the power play, Griffon had almost forgotten Liesel was in the room. He stopped in front of Dillon again and crossed his arms over his chest. He thought Liesel's interruption was frustrating and odd. It threw off his momentum but he hid it behind a blank face.

All glaring scary eyes and Dillon was scared. Griffon could see it in Dillon's reaction, the way he shifted within his bonds.

"I tied him to the chair." He kept eye contact with Dillon as he spoke to Liesel.

"Good." She stood and walked toward Dillon and for a moment Griffon was sure she was going to hit him, Dillon seemed to think the same thing because he pulled back, raising his shoulders to protect his face as best he could. Liesel placed her hand beneath Dillon's chin, tilting it her way. His chin shook, obviously trying to resist. "I'm Liesel. I'd be willing to answer any questions you may have, if you contact me over the phone or email me. I'll even give you my business card." She held one up in her left hand so he could see it, then slipped it into his pant pocket. It bunched a bit. Then she slid her hand from his chin to his Adam's apple.

Dillon's eyes mocked her, and Griffon was embarrassed for her. If she wanted to threaten the guy it would be better to let him do it. No one would believe that a slightly soft, twenty something girl could hurt a man with her bare hands. Dillon's eye's got real big and the chair creaked as his weight was lifted off the wheels. "I don't care who is investigating me." She planted her feet in front of him and grabbed his shirt front with her left hand. Dillon croaked as his wind pipe closed, and his eye's started to roll back into his head. The wheels left the floor, just an inch but Liesel still managed to lift a two hundred pound man and the heavy chair. "Just make sure you tell them that I like my privacy."

She let go and the chair smacked the floor with an uneven clatter of wheels. Dillon's head jerked forward and he gasped and sputtered air back into his lungs. Liesel grabbed her bag from the bed and left the hotel room.

Griffon couldn't believe what he had just seen. Sure he could lift a man off his feet by his shirt front, but from a bent position? With the chair attached? Shit. Using the hotel phone, he dialed the number Phyllis had given him and waited for the brother to answer.

"Strong Investigations."

"You're brother, Dillon, is here." He made his voice jovial, slow. Leaving his precise location to Caller ID. "Drank too much in the hotel bar. He needs a ride and said to call you."

There was a deep sigh from the other end. "I'll be there in ten minutes."

As he put his cell phone back on his belt, an idea came to him. He dug out a transfer cable from his briefcase and patted Dillon down for a cell phone. Back left pocket, bingo. He attached his cell to Dillon's and within seconds had the incoming calls and outgoing calls downloaded to his cell.

"What the hell do you think you're doing? That's a violation of privacy. That's theft."

"You tell them about your B&E and I'll tell them how I was able to get your cell phone to download these phone numbers. Oh, and lookie, lookie. Some pictures of Liesel from this afternoon. Delete. 'Am I sure I want to delete?' Yes. Delete. Delete. Delete. Oh, lovely picture of you and...."

Dillon had a very fluent and vulgar mouth.

Griffon only deleted the pictures of Liesel. It was tempting to erase the whole cell's memory. Very tempting.

Griffon tucked the cell phone in Dillon's belt, put the taser on the floor in front of Dillon, then—making sure his captive saw—Griffon tucked the gun into the front waist band of his jeans. He grabbed Liesel's room key from the floor, then pushed the chair over the taser. It gave a rather pleasant crunch.

"Shit man that cost me—"

What it had cost Dillon, Griffon didn't hear. He stuck a wash cloth into Dillon's mouth. He rolled Dillon out of the hotel room and down to the elevators, nodding at a few curious guests as they passed.

"Bachelor party," Griffon said.

He pushed Dillon into the elevator, undid the knots holding the phone wire, pushed the button for the first floor and just before the elevator doors slid closed removed the cloth. It would take Dillon all five floors to get untangled. He waved the white washcloth in farewell.

He headed back to get his tracking device from his room. It was going to be a real treat seeing Liesel's reaction to his planting a bug in her purse, but this was the very example of how such a thing could be so useful. He didn't need to track her though. She was sitting on his bed staring at his PDA, she watched him walk up the hall from the camera he had placed there.

"There's a three second delay," she said in a quiet voice, body shaking.

Griffon knew women; what they wanted. Not too different than men. He knew what they were capable of. Multiple orgasms were pretty unfair, until he was the one giving them those orgasms. Mrs. Cockney had been especially energetic in thanking him for her third and fourth 'O.' When you were tall, handsome and innocent enough to be 'devilishly adorable,' the desperate housewives could eat you alive. Or better yet, let you eat them. He'd been thirteen the first time. Mrs. Rodriguez on Chatmore Street—not Mrs. Rodriguez on Fifth, that was when he'd been seventeen and knew what he was doing—but the first Rodriguez thought he was sixteen. Or so she said. Not that three years was a big difference when she was thirty-three.

It wasn't romance, not for either of them. It was curiosity.

Then with the others it was maintaining his rep. And all the perks. Sometimes it was the money. Though those were more gifts then payment. All the women thought letting Griffon come in something other than his hand, was payment enough.

He'd learned a lot. Boy howdy. But it made him jaded as a crack baby. The conservative city of Boise, Idaho had been a real eye-opener. Not that there wasn't crime, but there were also nice people. Sincerely nice. It was like walking through Mayberry. It was freaky. People looked you in the eye, said good morning as they passed you, and neighbors waved to each other.

Frank had never understood the appeal, nor the mental strain of being a sex toy. Of course Griffon didn't realize he'd been damaged until he was far enough away to see it.

He'd started dating in the Idaho Police Academy. Really dating, not just sleeping with women. He saw the difference, believed in women and their intrinsic goodness. For the first time he sought his mother out as a person, not just as his mom.

Then his police partner had been a corrupt cop with a capital 'F,' for sale to the highest bidder. But he still believed, hoped, that he would find a woman who was good. Then Ashley kidnapped him.

Ashley and her partner had used three of the five points of torture. They wore earplugs and played loud heavy rock. His left ear still couldn't hear certain higher pitches. The sadistic bitches broke beer bottles over his head—but only after he had wounds that would sting from the alcohol—then imbedded the glass into his skin.

They took a cricket bat, flat instead of round, to his arms and legs until they heard a bone break. Took a while since they were high and didn't swing very hard and couldn't hear over the music. When they passed out, he prayed they were dead. They had plenty of supplies and neither left the room, not even to pee. On Sunday he started crying and on Monday he would have begged. Thankfully, Monday didn't come.

The second girl liked to stick her fingers in his mouth. He bit her the first time and got cracked over the head with the flat bat. She'd run her finger around the inside of his cheek and pull. They could have removed body parts or blinded him but they didn't. Maybe eventually they would have.

After the police found him, it wasn't long before the nurses refused to work with a mean-as-hell patient. Then a female nurse, brand new, young and petite had brow beaten him into behaving, had even befriended him. Which is when he started worrying, because beautiful blondes usually did it for him, heavens it didn't take much to do it for him. Same with the female physical therapist. Nothing. So he started seeing Dr. Brown.

He was still working through all this shit. Yet, he was totally zinged as Liesel brushed against him at her office. A full military, Attention! and prepared to salute. Why her? Was it only her? But gee, she was convenient and she made him into such a prude, like it was new all over again, and Mrs. Rodriguez was asking for his help reaching the top shelf. Kissing her was newly awkward and easily the hottest kiss he had ever shared.

"Is he okay?" Liesel asked.

And maybe that's why his body was all prepared to worship at the holy gates of Liesel. She cared. Cared about the B&E idiot posing as a P.I.

"Yeah."

"Do you want to have sex?"

"Yeah." And wasn't that something to celebrate.

"With me?"

He opened his door and hung the do-not-disturb sign on the handle. He slid the chain in place as he closed the door. He needed time to think. Of course his body was done thinking and was to the chomping-at-the-bit phase. He locked the connecting door, the whole time feeling her eyes on him.

He turned and looked at her. "I want to have sex with you Liesel. Powerful. Body, mind and world numbing, sex."

She blushed and smiled but kept eye contact.

"Perhaps we should talk first." He sat next to her and slid his fingers across her clasped hands, curving them around her hand to add to the hand pile. "You think you know. About the court case."

About my torture.

He could see in her eyes that they were talking about the same thing.

"But you don't. No one does. Hell, I don't think even I know. I haven't," just say it, "slept with anyone since. I don't know how I'll react. So, be patient, okay?"

She nodded.

"And I want us to both understand. This," he pointed back and forth between them, "is just sex. Comfort sex." His first and best subject growing up.

"Not for me," Liesel said.

Crap. He didn't want this. He lifted his hand away.

"I have adrenaline I want to burn off. And I'm hoping it'll help me sleep."

He laughed, and she laughed and then they were kissing and it was good. Good and hot.

She felt the tips of his fingers slide back and forth over her mouth. She slid her tongue out to moisten her lips and taste him. Nipping the tip of one finger, watching his eyes darken and lids droop. It was so sexy, that drowsy look.

When they went to dinner he'd gone from furious to distant to outright conscientious and since fighting the intruder there was angry energy around him. She'd tried to tell him earlier about the break-in. It was a shock to walk in, red-eyed from crying her heart out to her baby sister, to see her longtime supporter, sitting next to a soft clone version of Griffon. She pieced together Tammy being Griffon's sister-in-law which meant Tammy hadn't told Griffon that she was an Amazon. Each time she played the situation out in her head, he asked why she hadn't told him sooner and she would lie about Tammy. Which wouldn't be good.

He stood and pulled his gun from the front waist band of his jeans, checked the safety and placed it on the night stand. He shrugged, one rolled shoulder at a time, out of his suit jacket. His movements steady, neither slow nor fast, content to let her watch him strip. He toed off his shoes and sat beside her again to yank at his socks.

"Do you have condoms?" Griffon said.

Condoms. As in Plural? "I was hoping you had some."

"I do." He pulled her close and kissed her, his hands, fingers spread wide, slid from her stomach to her back. He tasted like fresh fruit and the cleanest, coolest water. His mouth warm and firm, it guided her lips to open. To enjoy. He slid his tongue along hers, at the same time he pulled her tighter against himself and it was as if she'd been breached. All defenses lay defeated. Including her bra. How had he gotten it undone without the awkward fumbling? But then she didn't care how, only cared when. When would he touch her there? When would he grasp her breasts with his hands? With his mouth?

He changed his rhythm at her mouth from deep exploring strokes, to sips and nips. "I'll get them." He smiled at her obvious confusion "The condoms." He headed for the bathroom.

Her bra hung underneath her shirt still around her shoulders, uncomfortably brushing against her sensitive nipples. She stuck one of her hands up her opposite sleeve to pull the strap down her arm and realized Griffon had planned it that way. She'd be out here removing her bra, while he was getting condoms. But he wouldn't expect her to remove her shirt too. And that's why she did. Quickly tossing the blouse and bra in the direction of his jacket, she turned to see him, eyes wide and a breath taking smile on his face, walking back with a box. He put the box on the night stand and a single foiled package on the bed.

"Wow. You look amazing." He extended his hand. Slowly, slower. Liesel looked down wanting to see the first time he touched her breasts. Her nipples tightened and darkened and she leaned back to jut her chest forward. His hand touched her shoulder and slid over the top and down her back. Down her back, away from her breasts. Away from her breasts. She looked at him and he was grinning, almost laughing, knowing what she wanted.

Two could play this game. She placed her hands on his hips and pulled him closer. A quick jerk forward, she swiftly swooped toward his mouth. All her actions conveying her power and intent. Then she kissed him. The lightest, barely there connection of their lips and her pink tongue traced his, as if licking frosting off an Oreo cookie.

He laughed and she liked feeling it against her as well as hearing the sound.

He took control of the kiss then. Trying different things, learning what she responded to, showing her what he liked. But what she liked? All of it. The taste of his mouth. The smell of laundered clothes and man. The feel of his hands as they slid over her back dipping into her skirt band to kneed her waist and then finally, finally sliding around the front.

Chapter 20

She was so responsive. Little noises from her throat, little and big flexes of her muscles to press her body into his hands, into him. Her skin so smooth, a sexy contrast to his rough hands, scented from her adrenaline and the powder scent of her antiperspirant.

He brushed just the pads of his thumbs along the underside of her breasts, felt them firm and rise.

He pulled back so he could watch, so they could both look as the thumbs made a slow path back and forth, slowly upward to her nipples then he was touching her. Her whole breast in his hands, his thumbs stroking back and forth. Her head tilted back and she groaned. It was incredible and beautiful.

She was going to erupt and she still hadn't gotten her panties off. It was too much and she pushed his hands away and reached for his shirt and pulled. His arms went up and the shirt was off.

He didn't touch her then, except where they had their hips next to each other. Didn't look at her, just waited. The scars she'd seen a glimpse of before covered his torso and shoulders, ranging from one inch to one centimeter. Rather than raised and puckered like she had first thought, they were sunken, at least a hundred of them. They reminded her of Karma's stretch marks on her stomach. Liesel reached out her hands, fingers wide like he had, and smoothed over his skin. Her finger tips dipped into holes then she slid her hand around to his back and felt the ones there. He looked like he'd been riddled with bullets.

"Jim."

He looked up at her. His eyes flat, dark and intense, predatory eyes. His face quiet, menacing. Her hands stilled for a moment then she brought her hands back to his stomach, maintaining eye contact, making him look at her.

His stomach was flat and he flexed in response to her touch. She could feel the definition of his abs. His pecks were just tight enough to be defined, but in no way bulky. She slid her thumbs over his small nipples and then gasped as her right thumb dipped into the biggest scar yet. Right over his nipple. "Jim. Oh, my god Jim."

"It's James. Call me James. When we're like this." He tried to kiss her but she avoided his mouth and leaned forward to run her tongue along his scared nipple. It grew pebble hard and Griffon's breathing increased.

He couldn't keep his hands to himself any longer. He gripped her hip and felt around her skirt for a zipper.

"James." She said it as if trying it out. It wasn't his real name. He'd been born Jim Emanuel Griffon. His family called him Jimmy, everyone else called him Griffon. Everyone except Mrs. Rodriguez, both of them, and Mrs. Cockney. As if Jim made him older. Made what they did together okay.

"What happened? What are these from?"

He found the zipper, pulled it down over her hip. "Glass. Pieces of beer bottles." He slid a finger under the elastic of her panties. "You're wearing neon green panties."

"They were on sale. Besides, I like them."

He leaned her back on the bed and pulled the skirt off. She was wearing another pair of those sexy stockings that only reached mid-thigh. He stuck his thumb in the top of one, slid it back and forth over her thigh. "I like the view from here," he said.

Her whole body flushed. Oh, she was glorious, curvy and smooth. His hand slid up her thigh and he watched as her whole body responded to the touch. Her eyes closing, her breast heaving, her back arching, her thighs falling open, waiting. She was so wet.

He quickly shucked his jeans, his last piece of clothing and he slid up the bed. He wanted to be closer. To feel her reaction against him, to see it in her face. He was surprised to find Liesel tearing at the foil packet, unembarrassed and quick, her shaking hands were sliding it on and he was helping and she was straddling his hips. His disappointment that he didn't get to play lasted all of one second. Because she was up, then he was in her and she was coming, coming hard and loud with one stroke. "James." He loved being called James.

She lay spent on his chest, breathing hard and quivering. Loving the feeling of being pressed full length against him, of him still hard inside her. She lifted her head enough to look at him. He had such a look of concentration, holding desperately still to give her a chance to recover. His hands, she realized weren't holding her, but gripped the bed covers and the side of the mattress.

She moved, slid up him once. He bucked and she smiled, feeling powerful. Then all thought was gone as she moved again. She didn't count, couldn't, and he was coming, not saying a word but his movements fully sound-tracked by his groans and heavy breathing. And she was coming too, faster, longer than before.

"Ohm. Wow?"

She laughed and he felt it resonate against his chest.

"Bigger words...." big breath, "not happening." He knew he was prattling but didn't care. His hands were numb where they had gripped the bed so hard. He was blissfully drained and energized at the same time. He lifted her off him and pulled her to his side, conscious of the condom. He'd get up in a minute and remove it. Liesel cuddled up to his side, his arm between her breasts and her leg over his thigh.

"Thank you." She yawned and he felt her relax even deeper.

He pulled away, getting out of bed, and pulled a blanket up. He cleaned up in the bathroom, than came back in the room. She was asleep.

He looked at the door to her room, considered sleeping in there. Then moving his gun to the other side of the bed, he slid in behind Liesel. Pulled her naked body back into the curve of his own. Breathed in the musky scent of their bodies. Best experiment he'd ever conducted.

Of course, if it had been just an experiment, he supposed he would have slept in her room.

Chapter 21

Penelope lived in a nice complex of condos, the ones you could actually buy, in west Boise. They were geared to privacy, with more stairwells and entrances then Anna cared to count. The complex twisted, serpentine like. The planners probably thought it was charming, but it was just confusing.

Anna finally found the right building. She'd dressed to kick ass, in jeans, heavy boots and a t-shirt. Not all that different from what she wore normally, except the pants actually fit and she'd tucked in the t-shirt. Her hair was pulled back so she could see.

There were marks on Penelope's door. She probably owned a dozen cats. But it didn't smell like cats. She thumped the side of her fist on the door. No answer.

She gave the door knob a twist and it broke apart in her hand. In the movies, the metal doorknob came off or was crushed, which is ridiculous. The wood around the metal was weaker. With her twist, she pulled the knob through the wood enough so the bolt wouldn't hold in the frame. Holy crap, that was scary, being able to do that. A week ago she wouldn't have even tried. You couldn't do that. But now she knew she could, and she tried everything.

She pushed the door open, yelling. "Penelope Glass! Where the hell are you?" Then she saw where Penelope was. Anna ran back into the stairwell, retching. She scrubbed at her eyes to remove the image from her head.

Penelope was dead. The contents of her head splattered behind her, a hole in her forehead.

Once Anna was able to breathe again, she went back to the apartment and took out her cell phone. She dialed the police. Not 911. She knew the direct line to Lt. Bit. Better someone who could protect the crime scene than Joe Rookie, street cop, messing it up. Plus, Lt. Bit might believe her explanations about the door and her fingerprints on it.

He'd had the painful pleasure of making her acquaintance before.

The conversation was brief. Lt. Bit asked her to leave the apartment before she got off the phone. Looking for the manuscript would have to wait. Or so she told him. Only the phone and the doorknob had her fingerprints, she was careful enough to make sure.

She visually searched the kitchen and living room, using her box knife to lift things without touching them. She stepped down the short hall and turned into the bedroom. Steel bands clamped around her upper arms and neck, locking her into place against a cement beam. She realized the steel was arms, as a man lifted her off the ground. Her wind pipe closed. She swallowed, trying to pull in air, and her ears popped. She couldn't move her head a single inch. She kicked her legs.

Life slowed way, way, way down.

Her box knife was still open and she swung backward at the elbow but couldn't clear her own hips to make contact with her attacker. Her arms were pressed too tightly to her body. She knew she was several inches off the ground, her eyes were level with the top of the door jam.

She had the inane thought that someone had forgotten to paint the top of the trim.

She dropped the knife. It slipped from her numbing fingers and panic, slimy and sweet, slipped into her gut. She raised her hands and clawed her nails across the sleeved arm. She couldn't reach the one around her neck. She lifted her legs at the waist as if sitting flat-legged on the floor, her feet 'entered' the door in front of her, using all the muscles in her stomach. As black spots collected to form black lakes across her eyes, Anna swung her legs down with all her might.

She felt the briefest moment of free fall, heard sirens, then felt the wood floor smacking against her crumbling legs. Her head hit the bedroom door jam. As she blacked out, her mind filled with questions.

Why didn't he snap her neck? Why didn't he crush her windpipe? Why was she still alive?

Kick ass? What a complete fool.

-#-

"Are you hungry?"

"I'm hungry." Griffon mumbled into his pillow. "But I think it best if I just stay in bed."

Liesel laughed.

Griffon smiled. He liked hearing her voice in the darkness. "Just go back to sleep." He reached for her, tried to pull her close.

"Can't. I've been awake for a while. I can't seem to ignore my stomach." She sighed.

Griffon groaned and rolled to the side of the bed. He reached for the edge of the blanket, about to pull it back, when an image popped into his head. The image of Liesel, pregnant with child, sending him out to buy ice cream or pickles, or both. It freaked him out.

"Then do something about it." He rolled tighter into the covers.

Liesel shoved him in the shoulder. "Grouch." She climbed out of the bed and switched on a lamp to find her clothes. She pulled her shirt over her head, grabbed a pair of jeans from the pile. Griffon watched, curled on his side, peeking from beneath the covers. She stood to slip the jeans up her legs. Long, amazing legs. And that behind. Oh, man, she had a great butt. She started fastening the jeans, button fly, and the butt disappeared.

Wait a second. Liesel hadn't been wearing jeans. Those were his. He was about to protest but realized how it would sound. It would sound like a childish fit. He punched his pillow a few times and tucked deeper into the warmth of the sheets. She laughed.

When he woke later, it was to her slipping back into bed with him. This time it was her naked body pressed against his back. Her arms came around his torso and pulled him close. Her hips flexing as she curved to his sleeping form.

His breath caught in his chest, waiting for the panic. But it didn't come.

"Hold me."

"I am." Liesel's voice was already sleepy. She smelled of him. She smelled like them.

"Tighter."

She squeezed, a flex and release of her arms. Half-awake or half asleep already, she didn't understand what he was asking. But Griffon wasn't sure what he wanted her to do either.

"Liesel," His voice was urgent, louder.

She was awake now. "Yes?"

"Hold me tight. Really tight."

Her arms loosened and her body stiffened against his back. "What's wrong?"

"I'm not panicked."

She lay behind him, just breathing, and then adjusted her arms. One was beneath his neck and over his shoulder. The other circled around his waist, pulling him tight. She added a leg over his and her hold constricted even more. His breath shallower out of necessity, he pulled away. Or rather he tried to, but he was unable to move. He put all his strength into getting free. At first, he tried not to hurt her. Then the panic hit. His skin was clammy and his heart pounded. His struggle to get free became fierce, almost brutal.

He couldn't get free.

He couldn't get free.

It registered in his subconscious, the blankets twisted around them, that she was talking. "Please, Griffon. Please."

What is she saying?

"Ask me to let you go. Please."

Not how to ask, but a plea that he ask.

"Let me go." He was calm. His body totally limp. The closest he had ever been to submissive. It was scary as hell and he was horrified by what they—he—had just done. Everything in him yelled to retreat. To get the hell out of that bed and keep going until Liesel was a distant thought. His naked body flushed with ice.

Before he could get up, she reached across the bed and touched his shoulder, gently rolled him. He couldn't look at her. Her hand stroked his cheek, sliding along his bristled chin, then back to his hair. When she spoke, he heard her voice quiver.

"Just because I'm stronger than you, doesn't mean you don't have power over me." She was crying. He could hear it and when he looked up, into those wet, green, beautiful eyes, he could see it.

Though they were lying close, he could only describe what she did next as climbing into his arms. She pressed against him, shaking. Shaking like a leaf about to fall from the trees. His arms were limp. He couldn't touch her. But her sobs were painful and he couldn't stand it.

Griffon wrapped his arms around Liesel, much like she had him. But their fronts pressed together. For the first time since they found him in the deserted warehouse, he cried too.

Freddy Rayne sat at the Johnson's kitchen table, reading the new posts from France where they were just starting their day. His equipment spread out, his elbows propped on the table, his chin in his hands. He'd called his sisters and they were okay. Worried about him and teasing about the girl in his life, but fine. The three needed each other and were close. Nothing quite like violence to bring a family together. But they were so different. Abigail, tall, smart and redheaded like her mom, in college studying business. Bethany, short, giddy and brunette, a senior in high school. Beth would have to work two years before it would be her turn for college. Then Freddy would work another year after high school, before it would be his turn. If he went.

His hands were cold. He couldn't warm them. He clicked through a few pages on the website then he sat on his hands to keep them warm. He pulled his right hand out occasionally to scroll down the screen.

Same old discussions. Where do you buy clothes for your daughter who is six feet tall and only twelve years old? Clothes for six feet tall women were much too mature for young teenage girls, the message board said. Freddy thought the mature part meant they needed tits to fill them out.

He sent reminders to people who had violated the sites code of conduct. Cussing, reference to pornographic sites, and derogatory comments about another member, were not allowed. Two warnings in a year and you were kicked out. Everything else was allowed. Discussions of religion, or sex, or Sponge Bob Square Pants and his love of an Amazon squirrel. The racy loops had ratings. The younger groups had loop moderators almost twenty-four, seven.

So far, nothing about another missing Amazon. But Freddy read everything starting a month ago, checking for a casual reference to someone who hadn't been on in a while. A couple of these he'd called on the phone, using Liesel's access files, to check in with the person. Life was busy and they hadn't had the time. Everyone was accounted for.

The teen loop had rampant posts from students who would soon be back at school. He scanned the headlines of some of the threads, or discussion topics.

It was hard to go through by date. If a person hadn't been online for several weeks, they could read back through the discussions they had missed and post a response to them. The website would list it as a recent post, and update the 'last post' date. Anyone else who had missed it the first time, would see it listed as a new post, and read the thread. A thread, or discussion, could stay active for months.

Today there was a new post from K457. The heading read 'weird e-mail.' K457 was a girl from the Midwest. Freddy had read her posts before and she was very active on the site. He clicked on the hyperlink to bring up the new thread.

K457 had an animated avatar with a stick person making paper airplanes. The one inch square, or thumb print-sized box, showed the short cartoon on a continuous loop.

I just got this weirdaxx email from Jiffy's roommate. Take a look.

> *Hey,*
> *You're on Jordan's email list and I know he emails you a lot. Can you ask everyone else on that online fraternity if they've seen Jordan? He's probably sleeping it off at one of your guy's house. Let him know that Coach called him and he'd better show for practice today or he could be in hot water. K?*
> *Thanks, Ameri*

Weird huh?

Freddy had seen Jiffy post, but didn't remember much about the dude. There were already three responses to the post. One said, "I didn't think Jiffy was the drinking kind." The second agreed that the email was unusual and added, "I haven't seen him posting lately, but with the cross country track season starting, I figured he was busy training." The third response asked if Jiffy was named after the peanut butter.

Freddy hit alt-tab and brought up Liesel's access files. He typed in Jiffy and Jordan into the search options and hit enter. It would, he knew, take time. The database was large and he was accessing it from a distance.

Chapter 22

Griffon's eyes felt gritty. He rubbed them with the side of his fist and reached for his ringing cell phone.

"Griffon."

"Little Bit called me this morning," Max said.

Griffon formed a sarcastic remark about 'why would he give a flying fuck this early in the morning' but then saw the nightstand clock. It was almost eight am. Nine in Boise. They'd had sex again once their tears had dried up, quick and hard against the headboard.

"How is he?"

"He took Anna Fort-Porter to the hospital a few hours ago."

Shit. He looked over his shoulder but Liesel wasn't in bed next to him. The connecting doors were both open and he could hear the shower running from her hotel room.

"Car accident?"

"She was found roughed up at a murder scene."

Double shit. "Okay, Max. Stop piece mealing me. What happened?"

"Anna called Bit from the apartment of a...." his tone shifted, tightened, perhaps checking his notes, "Penelope Glass. She'd gone to check on her co-worker, or so she says. And found Glass dead, shot. When he arrived at the scene with CID, Anna was unconscious." CID, Criminal Investigations Department, was the CSI of the Boise Police.

"Is she okay?" Griffon tucked the phone into his shoulder so he could pull on his jeans. The image of Liesel in the same pants hours ago, combined with his lingering morning wood, sent a wave of desire rocking through him.

Looked like systems were functioning just fine today.

Max asked him a question and he missed it. "What did you say?" He left the jeans on the floor and headed for Liesel's shower instead.

"The murder is obviously connected to the robbery. But do you think this Anna girl is involved?"

Good question. Right up there with, was Liesel involved? She'd called both her secretary and Anna last night. "I'm going to ask Liesel some questions and I'll get back to you on this."

Griffon paused just outside the bathroom door. "Last night we came back to the Hotel to find a California P.I. searching Liesel's room. Name of Dillon Gehr. He wasn't forthcoming with the info. Let Bit know. He can call me if he has questions. Oh, and let Bit know I'm glad he kept us in the loop."

"More Krispy Kreme doughnuts and a copy of the report?" Max said.

"No, this time take Bit a milkshake from Half Moon Café. This is definitely milkshake worthy. We'll save the big guns for when forensics gets back, which won't be for at least a week, even if rushed."

Liesel gripped the Kleenex, twisted between her fingers and pulled until it shredded. "But Anna's going to be okay?" She sat on his bed. The one not in total disarray from them sleeping in it.

"You said she was an Amazon. Should be just fine."

She looked at his eyes a moment trying to read his thoughts. Emotionally, she was fudged up good and plenty. She'd slept well, when she'd slept, and her body had that rather delicious languid feel that came after good sex. Or so it would seem since they'd had good sex—great sex—and she felt amazing. But with the invasive search of her hotel room, Griffon's emotional demons, and Penelope's death she was seriously fried.

"The P.I. from last night—"

"Dillon Gehr."

"Do you think it's connected to the missing manuscript?"

He shrugged. "Lt. Bit knows about it. He's the best detective they have at the department. Probably in the state. If it's connected he'll figure out how."

He walked over to the mirror in the entry way and slid the glass to one side to pull out a new pair of slacks from the closet. As he dressed he spoke over his shoulder. "How did you hear about the robbery?"

The tone was too precise, too casual. He was in interrogation mode and Liesel went from fried to Cajun crispy. "I called my sister Harriett. My mom went for one of her three month cancer checks and...." She felt a tear slide down her cheek and tried to decide if it was for Penelope or herself. "Harriett reported the break-in. That's what I came to your room for, when Tam—when your brother was here."

She gathered the pieces of tissue back between her fingers and tore it further. "Griffon. I sent Anna to check on Penelope. The killer was still there and I'm...." She rolled her jaw and nose, trying to stave off the tears. Sending people into danger, getting them killed. Great job, Liesel.

She sighed. "I'm just glad she's okay."

"The sirens probably scared the guy off."

"With a gun you don't need extra time to kill."

"True." He was buttoning his shirt. He grabbed his shoes and sat on the bed next to her. "Max discovered that Penelope had received a large amount of cash and deposited it in her accounts." His assistant Max had called with that bit of news while they were in the shower together. "Bit doesn't know about it yet and since Max's method of discovery is a little illegal, let's keep that quiet for now but, well, if she'd been paid to steal the manuscript, why the broken glass at the house when she had a key?"

"To delay suspicion?" Liesel said.

"Sure. But she's worked for criminal lawyers for years; she's smarter than to deposit ten grand into her checking account. Could be she didn't have anything to do with it, or that she was in charge of it and got overthrown. Might not ever know."

"That would suck. To not know."

"Yeah it does."

He finished putting his shoes on and leaned back on his elbows. He turned slightly and placed a kiss on her bare shoulder, brushing her hair out of the way. "You'll get cold. Go get dressed."

Liesel curled her toes and pulled her towel around her chest. "I will." But she didn't move.

"What's the manuscript say?" Griffon asked.

"I don't know."

"Yes you do." He jerked to his feet and turned to look down at her.

"I'm working on translating it. I know what it contains but not all of what it says." This was exactly the way she wanted to spend the morning after having sex. Under suspicion by her lover. "And you can apologize. I'm not the bad guy here and I don't deserve the harassment." She crossed her arms. Rubbed a hand over her shoulder he'd kissed seconds ago.

Her lover, who had waited until after they took a shower together to tell her about Penelope, questioned her alibi. He waited until after pinning her back against the tiled wall and sliding into her wet heat and pounding to mutual completion.

"What does it say? It wasn't stolen for the money. It might be old but by all accounts it isn't a famous document."

"Yet." She threw the tissue away and stood. "I'm going to get dressed." She turned to walk into her room and spoke over her shoulder. "The translator, the original one, a young girl named Brigid, believed the story she was translating. It was part of her...." she couldn't quite put her finger on the word, "heritage? Anyway, the story goes that Zeus slept around and his illegitimate daughters were the founders of the Amazon society." She tossed the towel onto the bathroom floor and slipped on a pair of panties. "Because the Amazons enjoyed a certain amount of 'notoriety' the gods then created another race called the Mightys. Unlike the Amazons, their strength was only passed on through their sons. But like all historical tales, this was just a way for Brigid's people to explain what they were. What they could do." She finished getting dressed and sat to pull on her tennis shoes.

"To me, the story's significance explains that there was Amazons clear back in 500 BC and probably much further. It also speaks of genetic malfunctions; refers to them as cursed births. Punishments meted out because an Amazon and a Mighty joined in sin."

Before AIDS, before the Clap, the Greek gods created Blue Hairs.

"On the website I call them Double-Amazons but they've started calling themselves Blue Hairs. Before O'Grady sent me the McKinnon leathers, I'd never even heard of the term 'the Mightys.' Okay, not never, but I, as I am sure many historians have, felt the reference was an adjective rather than a noun."

"Anyway, when a Mighty and an Amazon have a son, if he gets both Amazon genes from his parents—though now we might have to call them Mighty genes—he is born with a genetic mutation. In the case of one of my friends, Dr. Sergei Sky, blue hair."

"If a male carrier and an Amazon have a daughter, she has twenty-five percent chance to be a Double-Amazon."

"Not a United States Postal carrier but little ay, capital Ax," Griffon said.

Liesel ignored his poor attempt at humor. "If she does she will also have a mutation. The super strength is still there, but something additional, an ability or physical trait, will also manifest. For Dianne Fender, another member, it is uncontrollable psychic abilities."

"So Mighty plus Amazon equals freak show. Gotcha." His tone dripped disbelief.

She tossed her pillow at him then dug into her bag and withdrew her red notebook. "This is some of what I've translated." She flipped to the end, skimmed down to the passage she was looking for. Her other notebook with the newer translations had been in the file cabinet; gone now except for a few pages of notes in the copier.

She held the notebook out to him. Griffon had taken up a position between the two hotel rooms, hands deep in his front pockets and his shoulder against the door jam. His face expressed neither interest nor doubt, but he didn't take the notebook. "It's all about rules put in place to keep them—worthy—of their strength.

"Athena told her sisters 'I set now upon you my laws. You must obey them above all.'" She scanned down the page. She felt the bed shift as he sat next to her.

"'First, no sister is to slay an unarmed opponent. For sisters, you are stronger, faster and'—more durable or tougher—'then they. Second, you must never abuse those who are weaker. It is your duty to protect the weak as they cannot protect themselves. Third, respect your enemies and underestimate them not. Should you kill them in battle, honor their bravery. Should you capture them, contain them, but treat them as you would your own sisters. Fourth, do not abide cowardice, thieving, lies or dishonor, for they are the traits of the weak and the wicked.'"

"It then talks about worshiping this god over that." She closed the notebook and slid her hand along the top. "I have all kinds of original manuscripts. It isn't about if the mythology is true or real. It's about understanding the why. Why create a history? Give them rules? Except to explain our abilities. Can we learn from history? From other's mistakes?"

"You posted your findings to your website. You're looking at a couple of thousand who know about it?" Griffon said.

She'd just read words written over two thousand years ago, words that had taken her hours to translate, and he was still focused on who could have broken into her house.

"It was just another research project. One I was being paid for. I always discuss my research onsite. I figure it's...." my duty. My calling, my mission. My responsibility. Hell, she was always so excited about the information she found that she wanted to share it with the world. She'd been right when she talked to Anna last night. She was naive.

"Griffon. I am not...." responsible for the kidnappings. Why couldn't she say what she meant today? Had sex hindered her communication skills?

But what if it was her fault? What if she'd somehow gotten Penelope killed? "I want to share this part of my life, this knowledge, with other people. To help them. I didn't kill Penelope or have her killed."

"I'm not asking you to prove-"

"Yes. You. ARE." She swallowed back her anger. It shook her nerves to realize just how angry she was. She'd stay in control. She wouldn't yell. "You want me to say I'm not guilty. I'm not guilty. I am not involved. And I don't know how to feel about you needing me to say it."

"It's my job. Habit."

She picked up her room key and her purse. "Is fucking me part of the job? The deluxe package?" She'd wanted to sound pissed, tough. But her voice cracked. She rolled her jaw and sniffed.

His hands touched her face and turned her to look at him. "I don't think you killed Penelope." There was something in his eyes, perhaps surprise or confusion. "I slept with you because I wanted to. Period." He brushed his thumb over her lip. "We need to get to work. We'll let Bit focus on the theft and Penelope. We're here to find the kids."

The hospital's sliding glass doors opened and Anna made good her escape. Since she was still a minor—for all of two weeks, three days until her eighteenth birthday—the state of Idaho would cover all her medical expenses. Good thing because the ambulance alone would have wiped out her college savings.

Rather than skipping out on the bill, she was escaping because a wheelchair escort to your ride home was still a hospital tradition. She didn't need a wheelchair and she didn't have a ride home. She pulled Lt. Bit's jacket around her shoulders. He'd left it in her room when he'd questioned her about her attack. He called it her attack; she called it her moment of idiocy.

As August was dwindling to an end it was giving off as much heat as possible but the jacket covered the bruises on her arms.

"Anna?"

Busted. Anna looked up, checking for the quickest way around the speaker, who surely was a hospital orderly, instead of looking at the obstacle itself.

"When Liesel said you were smart, I knew you'd pick this door to make your exit."

"Do I know you?" That was a politer version of who the fuck are you?

She was about the same height as Anna, she had her hair pulled back into a ponytail and her strong bone structure totally pulled it off. She wore jeans, t-shirt and work boots, not all that different from the clothes Anna wore but unlike Anna they looked comfortable, relaxed with several washings and the body and person underneath the clothes could handle any situation.

"I'm Liesel's sister Harriett. Harry." One-shoulder-shrug. She didn't offer her hand to shake. "She's worried about you."

"I'm okay."

"Sure you are." She pulled her hands out of her pockets and jangled a set of keys. "Can I give you a ride?"

Looked like she had a way home after all. But she didn't want to go back to her apartment. If she asked to go to Liesel's, would Harry trust Liesel's judgment or would she judge Anna based on her blue and purple coloring—purple hair, blue bruises around her neck.

"I need to go to the office. Check to see if anything else was taken."

"Okay." She turned without another word and headed for the parking lot. After a moment to recover from her shock, Anna jogged to catch up. When she was alongside, Harry said, "I could use your help actually. I've got the window replacement in the back of my truck. I need an extra pair of hands to get it in place."

"I'd be glad to help."

"Got your cell phone?"

"Yeah."

Harry unlocked Anna's side of the pickup truck but didn't open it. She stood close and made direct eye contact. "What. The Hell. Are you doing not calling her? She's worried about you. Having someone like Liesel worry about you.... Well, you'd better be grateful to have her in your life, and you'd better call her. Now."

Anna, feeling both pale and red, took out her phone, fumbled it a bit before she could swipe it open. Harry went around the truck and unlocked her own side. She wasn't done talking. "Since she isn't family, the hospital wouldn't even verify that you were here, let alone if you were okay."

"I'm sorry. You're right." The cell started to ring. Anna the Idiot was also the heartless, ungrateful bitch.

-#-

The doorbell rang and Freddy pushed back from the table to answer it. Herschel was at work. No matter life tragedies, you still had to work if you were going to eat. But the worried father had called home, both on his coffee break and at the beginning of his lunch hour. Betty met Freddy at the door. She was working on lesson plans in the living room, the phone inches from her elbow.

Betty opened the door and let Liesel and Griffon in. Betty's hands shook as she closed the door behind her. She'd been hoping it was Teona, too. Freddy rubbed at the back of his neck and sighed to the floor, wanting no one to hear. It was fucking stupid to hope she'd just walk in the door. This whole thing was bullshit.

Griffon had a large poster-board and a bulging folder in his hands. "I thought it would be a good idea to get your take on my theories." Griffon lifted the board. "Where can I put it up? Some place with good lighting."

"Let's put it in the living room," Betty said.

Griffon used silly putty to fix the board to the wall and stood back. It had columns with headings like Parents, Location, and Activities. Then four rows, the first two labeled Clara and Teona. Griffon pulled things from the folder and placed them on the board. He talked as he put pictures of each girl on the board. "Freddy did you get that list for me?"

"List of Teona's c-coaches? Yeah. Mrs. Johnson helped. The list of C-Clara's was harder. Her mother had a couple but the rest I had to be creative in finding." He handed the lists to Griffon.

"Great. Thanks." He was distracted, still adding things to the board. Then he turned to his audience. "There is no connection between the two except Liesel's site. The parents aren't related for at least five generations. They went to different colleges and as far as I can gather, have never met. Parents or children." He turned back to the board, perhaps checking it out for a clue. "They both play basketball but never in the same state." He scanned the lists that Freddy had handed to him.

"I checked. No names that are the same. Not even two S-Smiths," Freddy said.

"Maybe there isn't a connection. Maybe the white van is just a coincidence," Liesel said.

"Unfortunately, we won't know for sure unless others are taken." Betty pointed to the two empty rows on the board. "Maybe then we'll see a pattern."

"Actually, I think Freddy might have been the third." Griffon got tall and crossed his arms.

"Meaning?" Freddy said.

"The marks. Yesterday you had some bruises." Griffon pointed to his own temple, his lip. "How'd you get those?"

The ex-cop was being awfully careful, trying not to sound accusing. Like what, Freddy was a newb? "I was attacked at work. Some g-guys wanted to steal a network s-server. I turned them into the police." But not before he'd gotten the new watch and beaten the shit out of them.

"But they weren't there to kidnap you?" Liesel asked. She touched his chin, tilted his face side to side, to check for herself that he was okay. Griffon unfolded himself and turned to look at the board.

"Naw. They wanted the hardware. Besides, don't play sports and c-clear on the other side of the country. Not a girl. I don't fit."

"Except for Liesel's site," Griffon said.

"How could the connection be my site?"

Freddy watched Liesel toy with her purse strap. It sounded more like she was asking how it could be her fault.

"Online predators," Griffon said. "People pretending to befriend the girls to get information out of them. Where they live, how much money do their parents make, are they pretty?"

Freddy shook his head. "To join the site you have to ask for an invitation. That r-requires a full name, address and phone number. Then Liesel runs a background check on them before issuing the invite." It was getting easier to talk to these people. If he was worried about how they would respond to his stutter, it worsened. Once he relaxed, it was much easier. Then, as long as he was careful, he didn't stutter at all.

"It's not a full background check, unless they don't have an obvious connection through family and then Griffon puts together a report. At least for the American members. I've got a retired FBI agent in New York that does everything overseas for me. "

"Then she and the moderators keep a close eye on the message boards," Freddy defended Liesel. How dare Griffon make her feel bad? Sick, twisted bastards, populated the world. That's how it was. Liesel wasn't in that part of the world. "If someone was h-harassing kids—"

"We don't read every word," Liesel interjected again.

"But it could be something subtle," Griffon explained. "Gentle questions about the type of weather and then the kid answering with a full description about where they live."

"Teona isn't stupid. She wouldn't give out her info to just some j-Joe online," Freddy said.

"No, just a Freddy." Griffon crossed his arms over his chest again and Freddy felt the urge to thump him. Before he could tell Griffon to fuck off, Griffon added. "I'm not saying you weren't safe. I'm saying that given time, you can get people to trust you."

"She didn't tell me online. She called me on my cell phone. Which wasn't posted anywhere." Freddy smiled. In his wallet, the very thin, always empty wallet, was a picture of his beautiful Teona. She'd mailed it to him for Valentine's Day. "Teona still won't tell me how she did it."

It amazed him. This classy girl was into him, Freddy Rayne, the scrawny kid who sounded like a wacked out, homeless guy when he tried to talk. If she knew what he could be like when he got angry, she'd be marking his emails as junk and blocking his calls.

"Clara was never on the message boards. Her mom got on a few times to ask questions and check the threads, but not Clara," Liesel said.

"They're both girls, both basketball players." Griffon rubbed the back of his neck. "I'm checking out the sport camps. They both went in June. Different camps in different states but—"

"Why?" Freddy asked.

"Well, the police, on Clara's end, are doing checks on her teachers, neighbors, family. But not the people at the camp." Griffon sighed. "I may need to go to Teona's camp. They've been uncooperative. Probably, just covering their asses."

"You'll figure it out. I just know it." Betty grasped Liesel's arm and squeezed. Liesel smiled. It was the same type of smile doctors wear when they have bad news.

"Anything else on the site come up?" Griffon asked.

"Most things flushed out to be nothing, but I was working on s-something when you got here. A college kid. His roommate says he's just drunk somewhere but p-people on the board say he isn't a big drinker." Freddy turned to head into the kitchen. Betty stayed in the living room to continue working on her lesson plan.

Once in the kitchen, Liesel looked over his shoulder at the computer screen. "I have his information up and I'll give him a call. Jordan Mathews." Freddy read from the screen. Sounded familiar. "Hmm."

"What?" Griffon leaned against the kitchen counter, ankles crossed.

"Just saying the name sounds.... I know." Freddy knuckled dragged the memory to the top of his thoughts. "He's the athlete that refused to do a third drug test. He's been clean for the other two. It's been in the news."

"Yeah, runs cross country or marathons or something for University of Montana," Griffon said. "I heard about it on the radio. Thought Mathews was a girl."

Liesel shifted her weight next to him. The longer she stayed by Freddy's side, the more agitated the P.I. got. Wasn't that just cracking? But dude had to know he was here for Teona, not to score on some other man's skirt. Even if she did smell amazing. He gave Griffon a smile. I-know-your-annoyed-and-I'm-all-for-making-you-squirm, kind of smile.

Freddy dialed the phone number Liesel had in her database. It was listed as 'Dorm.' The second number was listed as 'Home.'

"Yo," said a male voice.

"Hey, is Jordan there?" Freddy said. He took it slow. When you didn't need to impress someone, the words came easy.

"Nope. Can I take a message?" If Freddy had to guess, he'd say the roommate was white, middle class and from some tiny no-where-ville place in Montana.

"This is Freddy," he said it like he knew the roommate would recognize the name. "I saw online where you hadn't seen him. How long's it been?"

"Jerk's been gone since Wednesday's practice. No problem until Thursday's practice and he didn't show. Coach 'bout shit a brick."

"Yeah, I hear he's a real d-drill sergeant. Listen, anyone ask about him before he left. You know, someone looking around for him?" People always said Freddy sounded older on the phone, he hoped it was true.

The roommate's tone changed. "I don't think so. Something going on?"

"Just surprised is all. I mean Jordan loves running, right? Why would he miss?"

"Yeah, maybe. We weren't roomies last year, so I wouldn't know. I'm a freshman." Freddy hoped that the freshman would think of something new. "You know there was a guy watching Tuesday's practice. Thought maybe he was one of those US Olympic scouts, you know?"

"Yeah." He knew exactly what the freshman meant, or his voice said he did. The thing with people was, if you let them talk, wait them out, they usually told you everything.

"But he didn't talk to any of the runners or the coach. Just watched. Then took off in his van."

Freddy straightened in his chair and looked at Liesel. Loud enough for the others in the room to hear him, Freddy asked, "What c-color was the van?"

"White. California plates."

"You sure?" Be sure. Be sure.

"When you run long distance along the road, you play car games with the team. I got all fifty plates one summer."

"I got to head but hey, take my number and have Jordan call me. Ready?" When the roommate said he was ready, Freddy gave him his cell phone number. "Thanks dude." He disconnected the call.

"White van?" Griffon asked.

Freddy nodded. "California Plates."

Liesel sat down in one of the kitchen chairs. She looked like she was going to cry. Freddy heard Griffon growl behind him. What was that about? Dude had issues.

Liesel laughed, then sobered. "I'll call his parents."

Chapter 23

"The parents didn't know about my site." Her body shook with the effort to not cry.

"So we gathered from your conversation," Griffon said.

She jerked her head up to look at him. It was weird having conversations with him. Yesterday, before they'd slept together, every look, word, gesture, was interpreted differently.

"Jiffy hasn't been registered all that long. He was referred by one of my moderators so I didn't have a background check done on him. He was old enough, he didn't need parental permission. I only have basic information. Nothing on his family."

"What did the parents say?" Freddy asked.

"They were getting worried themselves. His coach called this morning to see if he'd gone home without telling anyone."

"Three missed practices and he finally calls?"

With Clara the abduction was so obvious and with these older teens it was easier to believe they'd taken off to a friends or runaway. Easier to be angry at their possible actions then afraid. Afraid they were dead or hurt.

"I guess there was some controversy about the drug testing. The mom was very vague. I guess the coach thought he was hiding, because he knew he would fail or something." Liesel's head pounded. She placed her fingers on her forehead then separated thumb and forefinger, pressing firmly around her eyes, sliding them across her face, the fingers coming back together at her nose. Then she used the heel of her hand to scrub her forehead.

She had put all thoughts of Clara, of Teona, of even the wretched nomination, out of her mind when she'd slept with Griffon. Now the thoughts were sharper for their absence.

Added that to the self-recrimination for thinking it was more than just sex. Hell, he'd told her it was just sex, she said it was just sex, and now it felt all weird. It wasn't like he was acting any different. It was all in her head. She'd thought that their mutual vulnerability had changed it to more, deeper. A few shared tears and she started spinning imagery, *we* scenarios. What was wrong with her? What about her did he not want? Why did a possible relationship even matter when a week ago it wasn't even a consideration? Shut up. No more internal whining. Jordan, Teona, and Clara needed her, needed their help.

"The sports camp theory is out. College kids don't attend sport camps. Plus, different sport. Basketball and Cross Country," Griffon said.

"I'll Google him, read everything that has been in the news," Freddy offered.

"Good." Griffon placed a hand on Freddy's shoulder and Liesel watched as Freddy stiffened. Griffon ignored or didn't notice the movement. "Let's do a search for any other children, zero to twenty-one, that has gone missing in the last two months. See if the van is anywhere else."

Freddy, still stiff, said. "I can c-check the 1-800-THE-LOST website but it m-may f-flag me. D-draw notice."

He nodded. "With three kids that we know about missing the same way, I think it's time to bring in the FBI." Griffon stood straight and crossed his arms over his chest.

"Liesel, what do you think?" Betty had come into the kitchen at some point and gazed with worried eyes at Liesel. The three of them turned, surprised by Betty's presence. Liesel drew herself up to look more poised.

"Griffon knows what he's doing. If he can bring in someone he trusts then I say we trust Griffon." Betty nodded at Liesel's words. She glanced distracted around the kitchen. "Betty...." *What? It will be alright?* Hooray for the great asinine clichés. Liesel didn't believe her own words but knew it was what the woman wanted to hear. "I'm going to make sure everything is okay. We will find them."

Griffon had pulled out his cell phone and was talking to someone. "Hey it's me. Listen. We've found a possible third victim." He tucked the small cell phone in his shoulder. "Maybe more and I want to bring in the FBI. Send me a text with his contact info. Who am I supposed to say referred me?" He shook his head. "Thanks Max."

"Who's Max?" Freddy asked.

"My secretary. I swear that's what he calls himself. He's a retired L.A. sheriff. He has connections." He said the last bit with disbelief.

"We don't need to go to Montana, do we?" Freddy asked. Now that Griffon wasn't touching him, Liesel noticed his speech evened back out.

"Probably not. We'll let the police gather anything they can up there. I'll track down the officer assigned to the case and ask him to call me with information like I have with the other two." He looked around the room for a moment. "Betty, do you mind if I make this call in the other room?"

Betty nodded, her eyes still cloudy with her thoughts. She'd started unloading the dishwasher. Her actions mechanical, she stood staring at the empty bowl in her hands. Clean or dirty? Forgotten in the second it took her to stand.

"They're done," Freddy said. She nodded and placed the bowl into a cupboard. "What have you decided about the n-nomination?"

She had specifically avoided thoughts of it. It was always there, like an achy tooth, but if she didn't push on it then she could pretend it wasn't there. All the little things that had made her think of it she curbed.

"I don't know if I would call it that," she said.

"I think you should be our leader. You already are." Betty sat down at the table but didn't look at anyone, she'd left the dishwasher open. Just gaping and full of dishes still needing to be put away. "You've done so much for us already." Betty's voice was tiny and Liesel wanted to take the weight off her heart. They had to find Teona. Alive. The constant-panicky-unknown that Betty and Herschel must feel couldn't be easy.

"I built a website. That's it." Didn't they realize how inadequate she was for this? Yeah, she'd pretty much decided that she would represent and fight however they needed her to but that didn't mean all misgivings had vanished.

"You've done all that research," Freddy said.

"Yes, but—"

"You have good rapport with the group starting in Europe," Betty added.

"Still—"

"She helped start the group in Brazil," Freddy told Betty. They turned toward each other, smirking and enjoying Liesel's blush and obvious discomfort.

"No. I just suggested—" Liesel protested.

"She's working with that genetics doctor," Betty said. "That's how we know about the Amazon gene."

"And all those articles she's written," Freddy said.

They didn't understand. They couldn't possibly understand. "Those things—"

"Oh, and what about—"

This time Liesel interrupted Freddy. She smacked the kitchen table with the palm of her hand. The table wobbled. She tried to smile. "How can I run an organization of over two thousand when I can't even finish a sentence with two people present? One thing we'd advocate for is to make sure underage Amazons," she raised her eyebrows to let him know just who she was talking about, "aren't being used in slave labor or laboratory testing."

Freddy just smiled right back at her. "It's three t-thousand two hundred fifty-three. I checked this morning. You have fifty r-request for invites."

She groaned, punched his arm in slow motion. He quirked an eyebrow and grinned.

"He gets a kick out of teasing you. Are you like that with your sisters?" Betty asked Freddy.

"I'm glad you guys are getting along." Liesel said. "Teona will be pleased." It was a dumb way of changing the subject but she put as much energy into the words as she could.

"My daughter has always chosen her friends well. I expect you guys to be careful though until you're older." For Betty there was no other outcome. They would find her daughter and bring her home. So she would continue to talk as if Teona were still here.

"Easy thing to do, when we haven't even met each other," Freddy said. "She doesn't care that I'm different, you know? And it's more than the Amazon thing."

"Yes. She understands being different."

-#-

"Hold it while I check the level," Harry told Anna.

The window holding position gave Anna the delightful view of her own image. The young girl's eyes were still red, her neck looked like someone had tried to separate her head from her shoulders using barb wire, and she held the one hundred pound glass window like it was made of paper. Was she that girl?

The level was good. Harry hammered the frame in place. "Sorry I was hard on you earlier."

"Yeah," Anna said.

"Liesel defended you. When the burglary report came in. Your name came up as a suspect and she said 'no way,'" Harry said. She used a caulking gun to seal the window.

Looked like she was that girl. Confused and scared, she swallowed back tears. "Are you an Amazon?" Anna asked Harry.

The ride in the truck had been a silent one. Neither woman was comfortable with the other.

Harry tossed her hammer into the truck bed. The clanking noise of metal and wood bouncing among her other tools echoed off the trees around them. "Nope."

"How does that work?" Anna said.

Harry stood and stared at her for a moment. She rubbed a hand across the back of her neck. "Have you been on the website?"

"Only a little."

"Well from the way I understand it, it's a gene that's passed on from the parent. If your father's mother was an Amazon you could be an Amazon or if your mother was you'd have fifty percent chance to be one."

"So a dominate gene?"

"Yep. The windows done. You can let go now." She pulled a rag out of her pocket and used it and some window cleaner to clear the finger smudges off the glass. "Thank you for your help."

"I'll go look around inside."

Harry just nodded. The large tree branches overhead shaded

Liesel's yard and held back the heat but Anna felt sticky and she finally took off Bit's jacket, cinched it around her waist.

"They didn't find the manuscript. The McKinnon Leathers." Anna told Harry. Okay, so maybe she was talking to a brick wall but what better thing to bounce ideas off of. "Lt. Bit said there was maybe a P.I. in California who was involved."

Then the wall talked and she was just as amazed as if the wall really had been made of bricks rather than flesh. "Dillon Gehr. He was hired to look for missing research material. Sent a retainer and nothing has come of tracking it backwards. Casey is researching Gehr's past clients a bit further. If for nothing else, to make his life difficult."

Casey? Then clear in the back archive of Anna's brain she remembered who that was. Bit's first name was Casey. "How do you know the lieutenant?"

"We went to high school together. Boise, for all intents and purposes isn't all that big." Harry—done cleaning the window—gathered up the rest of her tools and jumped into the back of the truck. One graceful leap. "Penelope was dead or unconscious when she was shot. The bullet lodged behind her head in the floor." Looked like Harry was a fount of knowledge too.

"Sting." The voice sounded irritated.

"My name is Jim Griffon. Pluto said I could call you." And if Max had set him up for a prank he'd confiscate the police radio for a month. "He said you were working the Larkin case."

Pluto was Sting's ex-partner down in L.A, or so Max had said. Sting got moved to Boise for health reasons and Pluto thought Sting's new partner was driving him a bit bat-shit with his overeager attitude.

"Yeah, the little Larkin girl." Griffon could hear him shift through the files on his desk. "How is Pluto?"

"We haven't met. I work with his friend Max Wallace." Looked like Max got to keep his radio. He scanned the kitchen, glad to see Freddy was less twitchy and that Liesel was back to her stoic, school teacher persona.

"So, what do you got on the Larkins?"

"I'm a private investigator and I came across two other kidnappings with similar M.O.'s."

"Grand, just grand. We were working with the idea that an estranged aunt had taken the girl to piss off her brother. This'll be a whole lot more complicated. Go ahead."

"A Ms. Teona Johnson of San Francisco, missing two weeks, African-American female, age sixteen. Parents have reported to local police but a Detective Barnaby thinks it's a runaway. White van and Caucasian males were seen around house on the last seen date. Mr. Jordan," Griffon paused to check his own notes. "Mathews. Age nineteen. Student at the University of Montana but originally from Iowa. Last seen Monday, white van, California plates. A Caucasian male was seen at track field where Mathews was running." It sounded like not nearly enough information to do a damn bit of good. "What else do you need?"

"How these are connected would help." Sting sighed. "White vans are seen near almost every crime ever committed. They often turn out to be work vehicles for utility companies. That is if we find them."

"All three know each other." He couldn't keep the hesitancy out of his voice. Yeah, he thought they were connected somehow he just hadn't unearthed that portion of the puzzle yet.

"A seven year old girl, and two teenagers? From where?" Silence from the phone. "This is when the paranoid conspiracy buffs hang up or gave their very longwinded and convoluted explanations."

Tell me how you really feel, Sting. "The internet."

"I'll tell you what. Since Pluto is going to vouch for you, I'll roll with this. I'll see if there are any other cases in the last couple of months with this M.O. But I need more details."

Now Griffon would see if he could convince someone to believe in something he still couldn't fully wrap his brain around. "All three are registered through the same online site. A combination chat room/message board. If you have a list of any others, I could run them through the site's database and see if they come up," Griffon said.

"I'll need the site's name."

"Triple W dot H dot O dot A dot X dot com."

A name like HOAX was sure to encourage confidence. He could hear Sting typing on his computer. "What's the site's password?"

"He won't be able to," Liesel motioned at him across the room.

Griffon covered the mouthpiece. "How did you manage that?"

"Mr. Griffon?" Sting tried to gain his attention.

"Sorry. Um, the site designer and owner is here. She says that your firewalls and security won't allow you access to the site."

"Can I talk to her?"

Sounds like the perfect time to hand the reins over to the Amazon expert.

"Mr. Sting, this is Liesel Grant. The site is designed to read the accessing computer's memory and obtain a password stored in a cookie." The cell phone was still warm from Griffon's grip and smelled like his aftershave.

"Ah, now the convoluted part. A cookie? Snicker doodle, half a dozen."

Liesel ignored the sarcasm. "A cookie is a hidden file that your computer stores so that you don't have to re-type information. You go to check your Hotmail or Yahoo account and it already lists your email address because that information is stored in a cookie. If you pay your bills online and check the little box for them to remember your banking information, then you've created a cookie to store the bank information." She did her best to sound confident. Betty had finally put away the dishes and was making noises about cooking dinner. Griffon was offering to order them all pizza.

"The site doesn't use a password just searches your files for a cookie containing the original invite information. If it finds one, you gain access."

"Fine." Sting wasn't impressed. "Can you get me access a different way?"

"I'm not home to make those kinds of changes. And my own

security prevents me from doing it here in San Francisco," she said.

"Where are you normally based?"

"Boise." She continued, "The site is for kids and adults that feel... different."

"Some religious, god made you special thing?"

"No." This time Sting waited her out. "It's a site for Amazons."

"Right, Amazons." Dead pan, not too quick. But there was something there in his tone.

"It doesn't matter what the site is for." Her voice was all business now. She'd wasted her time and was now getting off the phone. Have a nice day. "But I do feel there is a connection between the missing kids and if you come across any others, I would like to check my site and—"

He interrupted. "I have four."

"Four?" Liesel gasped, her eyes felt the need to climb out of her head.

Griffon took back the phone and put it on speakerphone. "What part of the country?"

"Two from Chicago, one from L.A. and one from Seattle. Nothing on the east coast. Last Seen Dates are too close to have one van drive through all five states. Give me your email address and I'll send the names." Griffon rattled off his email address. "Contact me if any of them turn up on your database."

As the call disconnected, Freddy startled and started typing furiously. "Oh swipe. We're being gangked." Liesel ran to read over his shoulder. "No. NO." He groaned and lay his head down.

"What happened?" Betty asked.

"They crashed my server." Liesel pulled the keyboard out from under Freddy's bowed head and tried to get the system to reboot remotely.

"But first they were copying to whole fu—" he cut himself off. "You're being photocopied. Total back up in progress. Who'd have access like that?"

Liesel looked at Griffon's cell phone. The FBI? But that didn't make since. She wasn't hiding from the government, hell she'd given access to the cyber division of Homeland and regularly published on her own website updates on her research and the type of sites she was building.

The Senator led the way into his study. He missed his D.C. office but family would always come first. The Amazon threat would need to wait until they'd recovered Jordan and destroyed those who would dare touch what was his.

"The book you requested."

Commanded you get and protect. "Excellent and our contact in Liesel Grant's office?" the Senator asked.

"Dead."

"And you are following tradition?" He watched the young killer for signs of remorse. And gladly saw none.

"Gunshot to the forehead. Yes."

"Well done. Well done indeed. Let me see the book."

The new Mighty passed him the large pages, his movements reverent and careful. Perhaps he too felt the damaging power such a document could have on the thousands of years their ancestors had ruled in secrecy.

"What language is this?" The hieroglyphs, like tight little chicken footprints, moved across the page.

"My skills lie outside of books." The young fool smiled at him.

"Get me a translator." The Senator sat behind his desk and smoothed the pages across its marble top. The savages had probably made the leather from human flesh. The idea gave him a bit of a thrill.

"Don't know any. Plus, it's too hot of an item to just say, 'hey, can you read this?'

"Watch your tongue," the Senator said. When the Mighty didn't apologize he felt a begrudging admiration. Mightys did not apologize.

"I did get some files. Probably Liesel Grant's initial translations." He pulled a manila folder out of his shoulder bag.

The senator held his hand out expectantly. Her writing was tight and precise. The legal pad pages rustled as he paged through to read them.

And so it came to pass the kingdom of the Amazons started its reign. Our sisters followed the decrees of Athena and focused on family and prospered. For (translates to 20 years) they lived unharmed, growing wiser and stronger. Building cities and a culture but keeping to themselves. For they knew the minds of men and knew they would be feared by those who knew not of the gods' ways and they desired only peace. Sadly, their tranquility did not last.

For five and twenty years did our sisters build in peace. Then in that year the kingdoms of men surrounding them began to raid the lands of the kingdom. A council of elders was called and Athena's wisdom was sought. After much prayer and thought, our sisters knew they must conquer (or had to conquer) those who would conquer them. Thus began the war of conquests against the surrounding lands. It would last for many decades. For with each push against our sisters they—

A half a page was blank.

—and thus the Mightys were created. Men, children of Zeus, children of Apollo. Among them Hercules and Azure, called so for his skin. We lived for a time, separate. Mightys and Amazons. Men and Women.

"She's gotten further than we thought. Do you wish her eliminated?"

"No. Something more important needs to be dealt with first." The Senator closed the file then rubbed the bridge of his nose. "My nephew, Jordan. Your cousin, and one day our Patriarch. He's been kidnapped."

The man looked him right into the eyes, good sign of bravery and intelligence. The Senator had chosen well. "My Harvest Team is still in transit from their last deployment. I need boots on the ground. I want him back and the idiots killed that took him."

"They will be eliminated."

-#-

No matter how good the digital pictures were of the dead boy, Griffon wished he could have been there. Which just showed how twisted things got when you were a detective.

Ming Poulsen. Chris Ward. Jesus Corby. Three of the four names were in Liesel's access files. Liesel had called the three sets of parents and they all knew who she was, but she didn't recognize their child's name, let alone who they were; a handful of people among a list of thousands. All white vans, all athletes. But the girl from Seattle was a golfer, the boy from Chicago played hockey and the boy in L.A. played baseball. None had met any of the others that the parents knew of.

Griffon got the detectives in both Seattle and Chicago to fax over files, pictures and stats for the board. Liesel and Freddy drove to L. A. to get information on the baseball player.

Griffon checked on a sports camp in Chicago. It was different than Teona's and Clara's—some hockey camp—but was owned by the same corporate conglomerate. It seemed pointless but Griffon felt the need to fill in his chart.

He had just finished putting all the new pieces on the board when Sting called with bad news. They'd found a dead body.

He flipped the digital photo page, then turned his head this way and that to look closely at the body and crime scene. Shea Strausser, the kid not on Liesel's database, had been found in a dumpster in Searchlight, Nevada. The body, decaying in the heat, had been put in the dumpster after the teen had been dead for a day.

Griffon didn't know how they'd figured that part out, but Sting would know if Griffon was inclined to ask.

You couldn't quite get the feel of a crime scene by just looking at the photos. But one positive, his nose didn't have to suffer. The smell always made your gut clench and your throat desperately swallow, even before you identify the scent as death. Small, shallow, quick breaths.

Did this eliminate the kid from the case or did it foretell the fate of the others? Was this now a separate crime? Or still part of the puzzle?

Griffon skipped forward several thumbnails, twenty shots taken from a traffic camera. They were vehicles that the local cops would run, the list would be added to the report.

Freddy was looking over his shoulder. Too young to see this and far too fucking young to look without being sick. Griffon realized Freddy wasn't reacting physically to the images. Liesel was crying silent tears as she stared out the window, her body stiff and silent. Griffon looked at the man standing next to him and shook his head at his own sentimentality. Yeah, he'd been that battle worn at the same age, maybe for different reasons, but still sure nothing more in life could shock him.

"Feds say he was dead several days before they found the body. Caucasian, male, age fifteen. Tied at the wrists. Probably nylon climbing rope." Griffon whispered the words with a jagged voice.

"Parents...." With a deep shoulder rising sigh, Liesel continued, "Have the parents been—"

"Yeah," Griffon said. Identifying the body of your child; listed under the category of 'things parents have blood curdling nightmares about.'

"I think we should tell the Feds to come to California," Griffon said.

"Not Nevada?" Freddy asked.

Shaking his head, Griffon pointed to the side of the dumpster. SWM, then spelled out underneath, Searchlight Waste Management. "The town. It's like ten miles from the border." Griffon shrugged, considering the time in his head. "Maybe four hours from L. A."

"But Las Vegas is even closer," Liesel pointed out.

"You dump a body in Nevada, you bury it in the sand. So, no one finds it. Why the trash? Unless you wanted people looking in Nevada." Griffon clicked the thumbnail of the first picture to take him back to the beginning.

"Makes sense." Freddy reached around to close the pictures. Guess they were starting to get to him too.

"Chris Ward and Shea Strausser. They actually knew each other and were taken on the same day," Liesel rubbed at her forehead. "So is Chris in a different dumpster?"

-#-

I did this. Liesel wanted to be out running. She was so close to the ocean that the air was thick with salt. She'd just go out the front door and run until she got to the beach. Then she'd strip her shoes off and run in the sand. Her lungs would ache and her muscles would tighten. Sea spray smacking her eyes. Then the adrenaline would kick in and she'd vibrate from its intoxicating power.

"Liesel?" Griffon said.

"Yeah?" She opened her eyes and talked to Betty's table. She had her head down on her crossed arms and could only see the wood grain.

"My brother and sister-in-law invited us to dinner. I already put them off once."

"Yeah?" She asked the table again.

"It would do you some good to get out of here for a while. You need to eat and Betty can't keep feeding two Amazons." He'd said Amazon without derision or doubt for the first time. Wow.

Liesel lifted her head as if she had a hangover and squinted one-eyed at Griffon across the table. She was glad to see that Betty was still gone. She would hate for her act of frustration and dismay, getting back to the site. Betty had been at her school all day setting up her classroom. Desperate, she said, to stay busy.

"You sh-should go." Freddy peered at her over his monitor. "I'm going to send out that n-notice you wrote up and get some s-sleep. Was up all night, getting the server back on line."

"Thank you for your help."

"Have to do something." He shrugged. Betty wasn't the only one needing to stay busy.

Dinner with Tammy's family? She could do that.

Chapter 24

Griffon said he was taking Liesel to see his nieces. He was right, she needed to feel human again; to remember goodness and feel hope. He said he needed the reconnection of family, something to blot out the crime scene pictures.

Frank and Tammy Griffon lived in a nice suburban area. It was built far enough out of the city center that the road was level but the homes were still three and four stories high, tall and narrow. Griffon parked the car in the small driveway and came around to get Liesel out. He'd opened doors, held her chair and such, when they'd gone to dinner. This time it was to make sure she got out of the car.

Frank stepped out the front door as they approached, a wide smile on his face. "I'm glad you guys came. Maybe you can save me from the chaos inside." He nodded over his shoulder than hugged his brother. One of those stiff, brief hugs that suggested they could love each other and still be men. It made Liesel smile, watching them together. See, plan was working just fine.

"Leslie, right?" Frank offered his hand.

"Liesel. Actually. Like Diesel with an L."

"Liesel, nice to meet you. I'm Frank." The door behind him swung open and Tammy came out carrying a little gamine girl, her short black hair tucking perfectly behind her ears. "This is my wife Tammy and our daughter, Riley."

Liesel's smile turned natural as she looked at the mother and daughter. "I'm so glad to meet you." Then to the little girl. "Hello, Riley."

"Hi," she said shyly then glancing at her mom she added to Liesel, "Mom wants you to be mother." Tammy was HeartsOnFire, who had recommended Griffon, and one of her most active members. Liesel hadn't realized the family connection until she'd walked into Griffon's hotel and seen Tammy sitting on the bed with her husband back at the hotel. What she hadn't done, was figure out why Tammy was keeping the truth from her family.

"Riley," her father cautioned. Tammy tried to laugh off the words.

Liesel's heart pounded. Not only was this an Amazon—someone she needed to impress—but Griffon didn't know that his favorite nieces were descended from an ancient race of warrior women.

"I think it would be wonderful to have kids one day." Liesel turned to Griffon and laughed at his startled expression.

"No. She wants—" Riley tried to clarify, determined to make everyone know that Liesel should be the mother or leader of the Amazons.

"Riley would you like to show me your house?" Liesel interrupted. "Is that okay?" She asked Tammy.

"You're always welcome in my home." All formal. Sure hope that was her normal greeting.

"Thank you." As the three girls walked into the house Liesel could hear Frank and Griffon behind her.

"Is she that determined to marry me off?" Griffon asked his brother. Nope, not Tammy's typical greeting after all.

"Weird. She's usually much more protective of the girls," Frank said with a shrug.

"Frank's been seeing a therapist." Tammy kept her gaze on the salad she was tossing as she spoke.

Griffon stared at the crown of her honey-colored head. Lovely and good, she was perfect for Frank. Riley was introducing the furniture to Liesel and Frank was making sure Amy, their oldest, had clean hands before dinner.

When Tammy spoke, the muscles in his shoulders and chest had tightened. He felt them pull as he leaned against the kitchen wall. Making sure they were alone, he watched her for a second then said, "Is he?"

"It would probably embarrass him but I thought you should know." She stopped and looked at him.

He nodded his head as if considering this information for the first time. "What do you think about him going?"

She gave a little shrug and looked back at the salad.

"Why is he going?" he added.

She quickly looked up again. She lost all color to her face. Her eyes widened. They were dark brown, her eyes, and an odd contrast to the naturally blonde hair. "Because...when they couldn't find you...and then when they did, he did...." She couldn't finish her sentences.

"He told me he feels guilty about not knowing I was missing at first. Said he has nightmares." Griffon watched to see if she was annoyed at his deception, pretending he didn't know his brother had gotten help. "Frank even feels guilty for going to a specialist when I was the one tortured."

She flinched and placed a hand on his forearm. It felt good there. Comforting. Sisterly.

"I've been seeing someone too," Griffon said. "A psychologist, which means he's got me on an antidepressant." Did he just tell someone that? "I'm counting down the days, forty-six, until I can wean off them. They make it hard to sleep. Most I get is six hours." Well, look who's got verbal diarrhea. But it was somehow easier to tell her than Frank and Griffon knew she'd tell her husband everything he couldn't. "Still, better than not sleeping at all. I'm glad you're here for Frank." He un-tucked his hands and placed one hand over hers on his arm. "Don't hesitate with him." His grin was self-mocking. "He loves you."

"I know." She managed. Her eyes bright. "He likes seeing you with a girl. I think he was worried you would swear them off."

"I worried my body had. Turns out my mind and body are definitely welcoming of the women."

She blushed, picked up the salad and headed to the table. Laughing, he followed her.

Dinner went well; if *well* meant worse than a dental visit but better than a blind-date from hell. Frank asked polite, get-to-know you questions. Griffon smiled. Liesel relaxed. She was cutting up Riley's food as she spoke.

"I never played sports though. I'm such a klutz." She passed Riley's plate back and caught Griffon looking at her. "What?"

He nodded to Riley's plate. "Do that often?"

"I'm sorry." Embarrassed, she turned to Tammy. "Habit."

"No. It's okay. You did it just right. Riley can you thank Liesel?"

"Than ou," Riley said.

"Don't talk with your mouth full," Amy, Frank and Tammy's oldest, admonished her sister. Amy had her mother's blonde coloring and at nine, felt more than able to keep her much younger five-year-old sister, inline.

Liesel nodded at Riley. "I have four nieces and two nephews. I've been an aunt longer than I've been an adult." She reached to her other side and scooted Amy's glass back from the table's edge.

"How many are—" Griffon said.

"Different? None of them are at all alike." Liesel's cheeks were hot. If he started talking about Amazons it might shine a flash light on his own family. "So, Frank. What do you do?" She couldn't believe that she had asked that question. One she hated when asked her. But it worked as a distraction. Liesel nodded along as Frank explained the type of work he did for banks.

Tammy Griffon was one of her strongest followers in California. Liesel didn't have a lot of say in the matter of followers. If she closed the site someone else would set up and run a different site. The new site would still need a leader. She was realizing that avoiding the issue didn't make it go away.

Some of what Frank was saying filtered through her thoughts. "So you do anti-counterfeiting security for banks?"

"Precisely. Though I can never sum it up like that. I develop everything from watermarks to voice activated safety deposit boxes," Frank said.

"That's amazing. I'm coordinating a conference in Las Vegas in a few months. We're trying to figure out security measures to control access to certain places. Would you be interested in offering advice? As a consultant? Our budget might prohibit it—" Actually, she was hoping Sergei was wrong about the number of people coming but finding out this type of information might be helpful.

"I might need to work onsite." Frank seemed to like this idea. Griffon was frowning and looking back and forth between Tammy and Liesel. "Tammy wants to visit her sister in Las Vegas with the girls. I wasn't planning on going—her sister drives me nuts—but this would be perfect." He looked at his wife and Liesel turned her head to look as well. "You already know she drives me nuts." He told her. Her face was pale and creased with worry.

"Which week?" Frank asked Liesel.

"Last week of October." Liesel watched Griffon—his thoughts processing on his face.

"It's even the same week you were thinking of going." Frank, still getting the uneasy look from his wife, quickly backpedaled to reestablish safe footing. "Check out my website and let me know what you would need. We'll have to see."

That is when it clicked for Griffon. Liesel could see the shock of realization. His eyes narrowed as he considered each of his nieces and studied Tammy carefully. He shifted in his chair and glared at Liesel. She looked down at her plate and ate a few bites before looking back up. Griffon was still glaring. "Liesel, could I talk to you for a minute." Not asking. He slid back from the table.

Frank looked bewildered. Tammy's fork clanged against her crystal glass. "Sure." Liesel slid back as well. "Excuse us, please."

He grasped her elbow tightly, giving it a little jerk and steered her into the kitchen.

He talked quietly. His jaw clenched, the words hissed out between his teeth. "Is my sister-in-law an Amazon? Or is Frank one of those male carriers?"

Postal jokes were probably inappropriate at this point. "I think it's Tammy's business what she is and what she does about it." She kept her voice down as well, but her blood was pounding in her ears.

"Don't give me that shit." No longer speaking softly. Eyes going all scary. They darkened, his eyebrows pulled forward, and at the same time, his eyes got bigger. She smiled. Not nearly as scary, when you look at it that way.

He didn't appreciate her smile.

"Look, I didn't know this would be an issue. She recommended you but didn't say how she knew you. She was one of the first ten people on the site. I only knew her as HeartsOnFire before the other day." She shut her mouth and looked around the kitchen.

"What?" He was back to the hissing whisper.

"I recognized her in your hotel room." They both kept their voices down, very aware of the tight silence from the dining room. He stepped close to talk in Liesel's ear.

"I can't believe this. They've been married over ten years. And she hasn't told him."

He would never hurt these people but she battled a brief instinctual urge to protect them. Lover or not, Griffon was scary. And lover or not, Liesel was an Amazon and would protect the innocent at any cost.

Liesel's ire rose at his words. "She hasn't magically changed, just because now you know she's an Amazon."

"So, she is an Amazon." He placed his hands on Liesel's hips, flexed them, almost painfully. Wanting her close or making sure she stayed?

She growled. Surprised at her own actions, her next words were softer. "I don't know why she hasn't told Frank. It's not my business, nor is it yours." She wanted to kiss him. More. Take him to oblivion and back. That brief flare of protect had lit the kindling that she'd been stacking up since Clare's disappearance. Still no way to immediately act on the need to save, to defend and she felt that desire twist inside her. Glow amber hot.

"They are my nieces and his daughters."

"And?"

"We should know."

"Why?

"I just. Told. You." He was having a hard time keeping his voice quiet.

"Why don't you know?" She shook her head then stepped back enough to look him in the eyes.

"What?" Taken aback, his voice rose again. She placed her finger on his lip to shush him. Left it there. His mouth was formidable.

"Have you not seen them? I hear Amy plays baseball and already hits home runs. A nine year old little girl. Riley climbs up the poles on the swing set using just her arm muscles. Why don't you know?" Liesel pulled her hand away. Loving the play of emotions on his face, in his eyes.

"They're just little girls. I figured they were gifted, naturals."

"Exactly. They are." Liesel gave him an equal glare.

He grabbed her hand and pulled her to his side. Her waist bumped against his hip and he kissed her. Lips sliding. He slid his hand up her arm, around her neck, squeezed. His other arm stayed at his side. She smiled. She couldn't help it. When they were like this, touching, it seemed okay. All okay. Their tongues stroked and it was sweet.

And then it was very, very hot. He pushed her back into the counter and she slid her leg up his thigh to pull him in even closer. His hands kneaded at her lower back and his tongue tangled and stroked her mouth. Wet heat pulsed between her legs and she considered pushing him to the floor, unsnapping his jeans and palming his dick while he tongue fucked her mouth.

She stepped back and caressed his face. She gave them both a moment to regain their breath. She headed back into the dining room, a bright smile on her face.

"Is everything okay?" Tammy said. She held her husband's hand across the corner of the table. Her thumb jerking back and forth nervously over his knuckles.

"Yes." Liesel sat back at the table and lifted her fork. "This lasagna tastes great Tammy. Thank you both for having us to dinner." She tried giving a little mysterious smile, hoping to indicate they'd been making out rather than arguing.

Frank's eyes and lips had a knowing smirk, so the mysterious smile must look somewhat decent. It probably helped that her hair was tousled and her cheeks were flushed.

Conversation returned to normal and soon Griffon rejoined them. As they were finishing, the doorbell rang. Tammy looked to the door then back to Liesel. "I invited Jessica over. Just to meet you."

"Who?" Frank asked.

"Just my friend." She assured him and scurried into the entrance hall. They could all hear the quick whispers between the two ladies. Liesel felt the burn again to her face, knowing she blushed. She quickly stood and began carrying dishes into the kitchen and helping little Riley from her booster seat.

"No, I'll get those. You're our guest." Tammy spoke from the doorway into the dining room.

"Don't be silly," Liesel said to Tammy. Not daring to look back at anyone. She wasn't ready, wasn't prepared to meet anyone. She headed for the kitchen. One chant of her mantra first. Funny, she couldn't remember it. "I'm just as capable of helping." She called over her shoulder. She set the dishes in the sink and felt Griffon come up behind her with another stack of dishes. He placed them on the counter and stood right behind her. Not touching her with anything but his heat.

"Hiding?" His voice was playful. Liesel sucked in a breath. The wall she had been building to protect herself from this new person, crumbled. His hot and cold mood swings were driving her nuts. Where did she stand with this man? Besides in the Kitchen. Real helpful there Liesel.

If it was just sex, why couldn't she ignore his temper? Why was she afraid? Her knees shook and her eyes watered. He leaned in and kissed her cheek, leaving his lips close to her ear. "You'll be fine."

I'll be fine. She breathed in. Then out. Then turned to walk back into the dining room.

When Frank followed his brother out of the kitchen, the three women were whispering together at the table. Frank found it odd, Liesel calling Jimmy 'Griffon.' It was part of the older brother credo to use nicknames, but calling Jimmy 'Griffon', his own last name, didn't fit.

Jimmy had talked Frank into loading the dishwasher. "To give the girls a chance to talk," Jimmy told Frank. Frank was hoping it helped because his wife was acting weird. She'd talked about going to Vegas for weeks. Yet tonight, she acted as if that would be the worst thing in the world. Unless, it was just him going with her. He didn't like that thought so ignored it.

Jessica wore jeans and a sloppy t-shirt. Her one good feature, glossy red hair, rippled down her back. It made her look almost pretty. Her eyes were blotchy. Frank knew the moment his brother realized the girl was crying. He came to a sudden stop, a foot in front of Frank and Frank had to do a quick sidestep around him. The mouse. Afraid of crying women.

"Frank, let's go get everyone ice cream," Jimmy said.

"We've got some in the freezer."

"What kind?" Smart brother. Don't say what kind you want, until you know what kind they already have.

"Vanilla and Rocky Road." *He'll want Blue Bunny. I could really make him work for this.*

"I feel like peanut butter cup. Blue Bunny."

Pegged it in one.

Liesel beamed at Jimmy, and wanting the same look from his wife, Frank agreed.

As they stepped into the entrance hall, Liesel hugged Jessica. "He is such a jerk," Liesel said as Jessica blew her nose into a Kleenex.

"Do you think they mean one of us?" He asked his brother.

Jimmy shook his head. "You have some pretty amazing daughters Frank."

"I sure do. They're both taking piano lessons this year." He pulled his keys out of his pocket and double-checked that his wallet had cash. Tammy had the habit of using it without telling him.

They were quiet until they reached Frank's SUV. "Aren't you proud of their sport abilities?" Jimmy asked. His voice was weird and Frank darted his eyes to look at him.

"Of course. Amy is already pitching for her little league team. Throws an eighty mile an hour fast ball. It's amazing."

"Do you think it's too amazing?"

He clicked the doors open and Jimmy opened the passenger door.

"What do you mean?" He was thinking about ice cream and whether they sold Blue Bunny at the corner grocery, or if they'd need to go farther to the big chain store.

"Other kids can't do those things." It was Jimmy's tone, almost accusing, that made him stop.

"There is nothing wrong with my girls." Frank paused halfway into the driver side. What was Jimmy saying? Frank curled his fists. It had been a long time since they had fought physically. But Frank had every confidence that he'd bloody Jimmy's nose before Jimmy got a shot at him. He had no illusions. His brother was trained to defend himself. But Frank was quick.

"I love those girls." Jimmy said, his voice fierce. "You know I will, and have done everything I can, to protect them. I was talking weird shit. I meant like prodigies." Frank knew that Jimmy lied, there was something going on. But decided to let it go.

The therapist would caution him. But he only wanted to flatten Jimmy's nose. Either way, Frank was getting better. It was a whole ten seconds, before the image of Jimmy's bloodied body, came to mind.

Fuck it. "Let's get that ice cream."

Chapter 25

Lab Rat 8.20-18

Liesel stood at the kitchen sink, her hands wrist deep in soapy water, as she washed the lasagna pan and a few dishes that the guys had missed. The two girls sat behind her at the kitchen counter coloring.

Tammy had decided to drive Jessica to the transit. Poor girl, Liesel thought. Jessica had met a guy through the website. When they had finally met in real life he had broken things off. He'd envisioned her a bit more like Wonder Woman. The jerk.

"Hey, give that back."

"Make sure that you share the crayons," Liesel said, not turning to verify the offender. She waited a moment then added. "No kicking." The soft thumps stopped and Liesel smiled.

The pans were draining on the counter next to the sink and the dishwasher hummed. She dried her hands on the bottom of her apron then untied it.

She lifted her head and glanced out the window again. A man stepped into her line of sight. A neighbor? "Amy, who's this guy?" But as she asked she realized he was carrying a bat. Liesel's blood froze and the hair on the back of her neck rose. There were two more men behind him.

They're coming for me. They got my name from the website and one of Tammy's well-meaning posts on the board told them I was here.

The idea that they were here for the girls flashed through her mind. But she discounted it. Tammy was so protective of her daughters that she had only mentioned them on the site's forum once over six months ago. Having never met Tammy, Liesel had pulled a list of all her posts before she took Tammy's referral of Griffon. And the girls themselves were too young to participate in the message boards.

Liesel turned from the window and hurried to the girls. Trying not to frighten them, she said, "I need you guys to come with me. It is really important." She grasped each girls hand and marched them down the closest hall. She could hear someone at the back patio door. An odd shaped shadow passed behind the blinds. She led the girls into the bathroom and crouched before them.

"There are angry, mean men here. I'm going to lock you into this room and I'm going to go call the police. Stay quiet and don't let anyone in. Okay?" She directed her question to Amy. The girl nodded and clasped her little sister's hand; their eyes huge.

Liesel pushed the button on the door knob to lock it and pulled the door shut behind her. She didn't know the house's layout. The kitchen and front door were to her right, the backyard to her left and a small hallway behind her. She hadn't seen a phone in the kitchen, and though she couldn't hear anything but the dishwasher's hum, she knew she wasn't alone. She walked down the hallway, keeping her steps quiet. Maybe there was an office with a phone this way. It would be beyond stupid, to go upstairs and get trapped. Why had she left her cellphone at Betty and Herschel's?

The first room was a play room, the floor covered with toys. The second had bookcases and a desk. On the desk was a phone. In relief she hurried into the room, noticing too late that French doors stood open onto the backyard. She grabbed the phone anyway and dialed 9 1 before the phone was yanked from her hand.

She stomped backwards, hard on the man's foot then swung around with her elbow raised. His nose folded like foam then spurted blood as he fell backward onto the floor. He didn't move. Please, don't let him be dead. Liesel moaned, fear pumping through her body. How much more damage would she have to do to protect herself? Why hadn't she learned to fight, learned to pull her punch, to restrain her strength.

There were two men at the door into the hall and three stood at the French doors. "I don't want to hurt anyone else," Liesel said. "Just leave." They hadn't hung up the phone. If she could only hit another '1.'

"Doesn't want to hurt anyone." The shortest of the five stepped forward, his accent guttural London, toeing the body on the floor with his boot. "Always was an easy faint."

The men wore different things but all were tattered and unshaven. Two, the ones by the door, had dark skin and the bulky look of ex-weight lifters, their muscles still strong.

The short man circled her.

"Let's take her," one of the guys by the outside doors said. Robin Williams looked waxed bare compared to how hairy this guy was. Was this Tara's hairy man? Maybe these men would take her to the others; maybe they weren't just killing them. But she couldn't just let them take her, when she didn't know the outcome.

Hairy's companion stepped forward. He carried the baseball bat. Looking at it made Liesel's knees quake, not wanting to think of what that bat might have done. The images flooded her mind anyway, of Shea's battered body in that dumpster. Why the hell had she looked when Griffon told her not to? Her stomach heaved and rolled; she tasted bile in her mouth and nose.

When he was close enough, she grabbed the bat. His eyes showed his surprise. She didn't know what her face showed. But she was angry. She yanked the bat, bringing the man a step closer, than pushed it toward his face. This time it was the man's chin that cracked. He let go and Liesel swung the bat into his ribs, remembering to pull back, just before it hit. He still crumpled to the floor. She thought she might cry. She was so stupid.

The short man, closest to her, crouched slightly waiting to spring. But no one moved toward her. She blinked to clear her eyes. "Give me a reason."

"I'd rather you not hit me with that. How about I give you a reason not to hit me." He'd smirked with the last and Liesel realized he meant to charm her. He grabbed his crotch, clarifying what was up for the offer.

"No, I mean give me a reason to go with you." Liesel thought only to stop herself. Hoped they'd take her with them.

"If you don't, we'll beat the bloody hell out of your hide."

She channeled aggression, giving her best shot at looking tough. "Not before I take more of you out."

There was a clank and one of the girls screamed.

She had her reason. "No! Leave them alone. I'll go with you. Just leave them alone."

At the hallway door the two black men parted and a new thug came in carrying a kicking Amy. She thrashed another moment then was still. Her mouth was covered with his hand, a white cloth jutting between his fingers. Chloroform, they're taking them alive.

She turned the bat down, barely holding the bottom with the tips of her fingers. "Please, I'll come. Let her go." She cracked the bat in half and threw it away. A simple snap between her hands.

"It's not you, we're after. But hell since you're so willing...." the short man said. It was totally stupid to come at her with the pieces of the bat between them on the floor. But thugs weren't known for their brains.

She had turned her back to the French doors when Amy had screamed. Hairy man grabbed Liesel from behind; the air whooshed out of her. His arms banded around her arms, above the elbows. The newcomer handed Amy to one of the black men and stepped toward Liesel, pulling a bottle from his pocket. She kicked and struggled. The hairy man staggered forward, almost losing his grip. Save, protect. Move, move, move.

"'urry the 'ell up." He had the most arrogant French accent she'd ever heard. She relaxed as the sweet sent filled her nose. She would go with them. Perhaps her only chance to find her missing kids. And once found, she would save them. She felt the prick of a hypodermic as the chloroform made her limbs flop to her side like useless tentacles.

"Stop. Stop the car." Griffon jerked the car door open and ran flat out across the front lawn. Leaping the low hedge, not feeling the pull on his thigh muscles, the adrenaline already running high.

The front door stood open, the frame splintered.

He quieted and moved into stealth. Shutting down every urge to run through the house yelling, he looked for his girls. All four of them. If there was an intruder....

He felt rather than saw Frank come in behind him and he put up a hand to hold Frank still. Searching, he moved through the house. He heard a whimper and Frank was shoving him in the shoulder.

"Riley!" He dropped to his knees at the bathroom door, pale but cooing to his daughter. "Daddy's here Riley. What happened? Where's...?"

Griffon left them and headed farther down the hall. Two feet stuck out the office door. Heavy, thick soled black dock boots, twisted and in sharp contrast to the light tan Berber carpet. He checked his perimeters. Registered the familiar smell of gun smoke and blood; felt a breeze from the office. The feet connected to a body—always nice when they were still attached—he crouched and felt for a pulse. Kept his eyes on the room. His hand came back wet and sticky but he ignored it. Another man laid feet away, face down in his own blood. No need to check that pulse. With a broken wood bat sticking out of his chest, the other half of the bat feet away on the floor, there was no chance he was still alive.

Tammy called from the front door, unaware of what happened. "Frank?"

Everything that was still a cop inside Griffon said 'Crime Scene. Protect the Crime Scene.' He swiped his cell phone awake and dialed the Police. He looked at Tammy, asking with his eyes if Liesel or Amy was with her. She shook her head no. He barked orders for Frank and Tammy to take Riley while he searched the rest of the house.

His mind narrowed and he focused on two levels. Former police detective, relaying information to dispatch, and frightened uncle and lover, rolling between hope to see Amy and Liesel hiding upstairs, relief that their bodies didn't lie on the floor twisted and bloody, and apprehension that he would never find them. But he knew one thing to his very core. Liesel would protect Riley and Amy at the cost of her very life.

He'd read the report on the canal rescue. He had seen her family, strategically maneuvering to protect their own, stand against the world.

Where Amy was, so was Liesel. This was his worse fucking

nightmare come back to haunt him with a special directors cut of hell. But Liesel would do everything in her considerable power to keep Amy safe. He hoped it was enough. That she would know to hold out for the cavalry. He was coming for them.

"What is she doing here?" Murket didn't ask who the new lab rat was. Maybe the muscle head already knew. Dr. Savon couldn't read his face, but some of the anger still pulsed around them.

The labs with their cool cement and muted colors felt like the old basement locker rooms from football stadiums. A familiar smell of sweat, sport ointment, and the waxy scent of medical tape, clung to the walls. Murket looked in his element here. His home team locker room. As the coach, he needed to remain calm and pass on only encouragement to his players. Dr. Savon tried to contain his derision. He had little trouble twisting the man around to whatever path he needed him to take.

"Your thugs brought her in with the soft ball pitcher," Dr. Savon told Murket with disdain. He spoke with a specific tone so Murket would know that Dr. Savon viewed him as something filthy the good doctor couldn't get out of his lab coat. "I think they wanted a diversion."

"You let them rape her!" His head snapped around and he put all of his rage in his eyes. The doctor shook, stamped viciously down on his smile. Oh, how lovely those eyes looked all heated with anger and a touch of fear as his plans started to unravel. Like cell samples under his microscope, branching, morphing, and drawing him in.

"No. Besides, I don't let them do anything. They are...hesitant to go in there." He indicated the cell where Liesel was lying unconscious. "I guess she beat up Lawrence and Rae."

Murket turned back to the control booth's television monitors, watched the new unconscious lab rat. Missing children were common enough to allow them to stay hidden. But her disappearance would bring hell down on their heads. How would Murket see it? Time to forfeit the game?

Chapter 26

Liesel lay on the floor. It was hard and cold, which probably meant cement. But she didn't know because she kept her eyes closed. Her right arm throbbed at the inner elbow, her stomach clenched and her head pounded. The last two were probably side effects from being drugged. The only noises were a hum, like an air filter or air conditioner, and her heart.

Amy. Where is Amy? Save Amy.

Liesel tried to open her eyes, thinking to keep them mostly closed and survey the area beneath her eyelashes. The left one wouldn't open and she could only see blurry images from her right. She raised her hand to feel her left eye. Pain shot through her head at the barest touch of her fingertips. She gritted her teeth and felt along her eye lashes. They were crusty and puffy. Maybe they'd decided to beat her anyway but other than her arm and head, she didn't hurt anywhere else.

She ran her fingers down her arm to the ache in her elbow. There was medical tape and a cotton ball. Someone had taken her blood. If it had been an injection, they wouldn't need the cotton ball to absorb the run off.

She opened her right eye, blinked several times and the images finally cleared. It was dark but a lighted area wasn't too far away. It made her feel like she stood on an empty sidewalk, too far away from a street light, to be in its circle of light. She sat up and looked behind her. It got darker. She wiggled her toes and felt her knees, then stood up. Her head didn't encounter anything and she raised her hand up slowly, than stretched. Nothing.

She turned toward the lighted area then took a step. Legs held just fine. Slight throb to her head. Still good. She took another step, looking at the ground ahead of her. There was something a few more feet ahead of her. It moved. Liesel turned her head to the left so her right eye could get a more direct look. It was a person. Sitting on the floor.

"Hello?" She heard herself speak but there was no echo to her words. "I'm Liesel. Where are we?" The person didn't say anything else but waved again. Liesel took another step forward. The person nodded and waved. But this time Liesel realized it wasn't a wave but more of a roll in the wrist, beckoning her to come closer. Two more steps and she could see that the person was oddly shaped as if pressed up against a wall. Then the image shifted and Liesel realized it was a wall, a clear wall between her and the person, preventing sound. Cautious, she put out a hand and stepped slowly the rest of the way, like swimming to the edge of a pool.

It was a young man, slender and long. It was hard to distinguish his features but she could tell his hair was long on top and wavy. She thought he spoke but couldn't hear him. He shook his head and motioned again for her to come closer. She sat next to him on her side of the floor. A murmur of sound turned to words as she leaned closer. "—against the wall or we can't hear each other." Rapid words than sounding relieved; "Can you hear me now?"

"Yes."

"Are you okay?"

"I think so. Someone's taken my blood." She rubbed her forearm.

"Hopefully, that's all they took. I saw them bring you in about an hour ago. Not sure though on the time, they took my watch the first day."

"You saw them bring me in?" She had to repeat herself for him to hear her.

"Yeah."

"I was with a little girl, where did they put her?" Thinking of Amy, heart pounding again. She was relieved that he was apparently unharmed. A good sign that Amy would be too.

"A few more cubes down." He nodded behind her. "Cells, I guess." He corrected himself, brushed his hair back and studied her. She wanted to ask him if he was okay but couldn't. It sounded like a stupid question. Of course he wasn't. Neither was she. Okay was scraping your knee. Being locked in a cell was bad.

"Do you know how many people there are?"

He shook his head. "I think you and the little girl make twelve, but I'm not sure. And I don't know what happened to the one already in your cube. They took her out sometime yesterday. I haven't seen her since." He shook her head. "I wish you weren't here, but I'm glad to see another adult." He was quiet a moment.

Liesel wished she could see more of his face. She saw more the outline of where things were, eyes, ears, nose but not the features themselves.

"I'm Liesel Grant. What's your name?"

"Shit." He spit the word out with a jerk of his head as he pulled back from the wall. She couldn't hear him for a while. But she could see more of his features. He was beautiful. She tapped on the wall and he leaned back against it. "I'm Jordan Mathews, Jiffy on your site. So it *is* because we're Amazons?"

"I don't know. They came for the girl and she hasn't been on the boards. They said they weren't there for me."

They sat without talking for a while. Her head hurt and she wanted to climb into a warm safe bed. Even better if it was Griffon's bed. Still warm from his sleepy body; feel his naked flesh pressed into the curve of hers.

Twelve counting her and Amy? That meant there was at least ten others and she and Griffon had only had a list of five from the site.

"Does anyone even know I'm gone?" She almost didn't hear him, his voice was so quiet. She could tell, even from just his voice that he was losing hope, that being here for so long was taking its toll.

"Yes. The first night they didn't know. Your roommate thought you were out partying. When you missed practice the third time your Coach called your parents to see if you had gone home."

"Four days? Before anyone said anything?"

What could she say to that? "You're at college. You probably only call home once a week and the roommate is new. They're looking for you. Be glad it wasn't later." She gingerly rotated her damaged eye, slowly testing the healing. "It's not like you missed classes. They don't start for another week." Classes, brilliant Liesel.

"What else?" Jordan said.

"We don't know what the connection is. A girl named Clara

Larkin was taken and her parents contacted me." How long ago? It seemed like so long ago. "When we realized there was more from the website who were missing, we contacted the FBI."

"She's in the cube on my other side. Clara." He nodded toward the other side of the light. "Blonde, grey eyes?"

"Is she okay?" Alive, Liesel thought, alive and here. Thank god.

"Yes. Scared. We're the ones that figured out the sound thing." He indicated them sitting so close. "We've passed the knowledge to everyone."

"Teona Johnson?"

"You're in her cube."

A cube he'd said was empty for quite some time. Liesel pressed her forehead to the wall, closed her eyes. Allowed a moment for the tears of relief, of frustration, to gather before blinking them away.

"We have to get out." She tapped the wall between them with a knuckle.

"I've tried." He sounded young and desperate before he firmed his voice. "I can't break the walls. And the door slides from the ceiling."

"What about when they take you?"

"They tranq your food. We figured that out the last time they took Clara. But when I didn't eat, they used a tranq gun instead. You've got a bucket for a toilet and we get some kind of über oatmeal once a day. It's got protein, calcium, vitamins. The full spectrum. I can tell. It's like eating one of my nutrition bars." He smiled. It was a tastes-like-shit smile.

Two more street lights, both farther down the street behind her, flipped on. It was enough. She stood and turned trying to see as much as she could, walking away from the wall. Other children stood. Ten or more feet separated each. Their silhouettes varied in size.

Hairy and Short Man entered the ring of light that had already been on. Skirting the perimeter, they disappeared into the darkness just before they reached Jordan's cell. They pushed a wheelchair, a black girl hunched forward in its seat. She still wore the clothes she'd disappeared in and Liesel knew it was Teona without seeing her face.

In her peripheral vision, Liesel saw Jordan throw back his head, fists clenched at his side and yell. She didn't hear it, even though his whole body shook with the effort.

The light above Liesel flipped on and she squinted in the harshness to see where they took Teona. The short man carried a black and wood pistol in a thigh holster. But he carried a shotgun in his hands. They stopped at what she realized was her cell's door. It opened and the short man came in first pointing the gun at her.

She stood, her hands down at her sides. Hairy tilted the wheelchair. Teona slid to the hard cold cement. She regained consciousness enough to brace her fall with her arms. She rolled to her back and lay looking up at the harsh lights. Still. Straight. They backed out, keeping the shot gun on Liesel.

As soon as both men had left, Liesel hurried to Teona. She leaned over her. Blocking the light.

Teona blinked several times. "You're Liesel Grant. I voted for you."

What was she? The President?

"What happened to your eye?" Teona breathed heavy, mouth wide and gasping.

"Hi Teona. Are you okay?" Liesel looked down at Teona's body. She had marks across her wrists as if she'd been bound. Her shoes were gone.

"I don't want to talk about it." She turned her head away. Tears seeped from her eyes, streaming into her hairline and pooling at her nose.

"Fair enough, since I'm not answering about my eye." Liesel could barely get the words out. Her whole body shook with anger. Her imagination giving her plenty of images. She went from shake to full vibrate.

Teona shook her head but didn't meet Liesel's eyes. She took the girls hand, pleased when her hand was gripped firmly. "I've seen your parents. They're worried of course. Freddy is staying with them. Trying to help us look."

"Freddy? Really?" There was hope in her eyes. Her voice jagged from tears. Her breath leveled out.

"Yeah." She rubbed her thumb over Teona's hand. "We've got local police and even the FBI looking. They'll find us soon." And Griffon. Griffon will find us.

"Maybe." She'd stopped crying but still wouldn't look at Liesel.

"I'm going to talk to the other walls, before they turn the lights off. I'll be back."

Teona closed her eyes and nodded. Liesel walked to the far wall and motioned to the boy to come to her. She thought it might be the hockey player from Chicago. He had on a Chicago cubs t-shirt and was built like a mini linebacker. He leaned against the glass, looking absolutely petrified. His blue eyes huge. "Is Teona okay?"

"I think she will be."

"What happened—?"

"I'm Liesel. What's your name?" She interrupted him, not wanting to speculate on Teona's trauma.

"I'm Chris."

Chris Ward. Her stomach dropped like the down slope from a rollercoaster. He had dark, prominent eyebrows and blonde hair, bleached from the summer sun. His nose was slightly tweaked at the bridge, perhaps from a wild hockey puck.

"I want you to pass the word. The FBI are looking for us. We'll be out of here soon."

His eyes glassed and watered at her words.

"Can you do that? Can you tell the next person over?"

He nodded.

"Thank you."

He drew himself together, so much older than his thirteen years.

"I came in with a girl named Amy. Tell her I'm okay."

He nodded again. But kept by the wall, shoulders squaring. Liesel realized that she often did the same thing. Drawing herself up. Squaring off and heading into battle.

"Go." She watched him turn and walk into the darkness of his cell, barely able to see the figure pressed against his far wall, unable to see who it was.

She checked on Teona again then walked toward Jordan's wall.

He was waiting for her.

"Is she okay?" He asked before she was close enough, so it sounded like she turned up the volume with each word.

"I don't know what they did. She won't talk about it. But I think she'll be okay."

"I think they...." He turned his head to look away from her then just his eyes darted a quick look back. "I think they...took some of my sperm."

She could see him swallow. She placed her hand against the wall and he placed his over it. In this together but separate.

"Bastards."

"We'll find it. We'll stop them." For a moment, he blurred in her good eye then, blinking, the tears dripped down her cheeks and she could see him again.

She said, "Go tell Clara about the FBI coming and that—"

"I did. While you talked to Chicago. She'll pass it on. I told her to tell them that you're here, too. That'll give them hope."

Ah, great. Yet, she couldn't help but be glad because he was right. She'd move hell to get them to safety.

Liesel sucked in her breadth. "I'm just.... I'm going to sit with Teona."

Jordan nodded then walked to the opposite wall.

Teona stared wide eyed at the lights above her, not caring at how harsh the lights must be. Her eyes surely ached at the brightness and little dots must fill her vision but she didn't look away. Liesel leaned over her, casting the intended shadow. "You have the messiest room I have ever seen." Liesel had only been in her room once and only briefly. It had been a typical teenage room.

"What?" Startled, Teona gaped at Liesel.

"I mean all those posters of boy bands." There hadn't been a single one. "And those pizza boxes everywhere. Oh, and the argyle socks." Her eyebrows raised as if to ask 'what's up with that?' She shook her head, dismayed.

"You are so weird." Teona sounded awed.

"Thank you."

Teona gave a little laugh and smiled. No grimace of pain with either.

"My sister works for social services, and volunteers at a women's shelter." She was trying to approach the subject carefully. At the same time off balancing her with the quick change of subject, knowing that it would help to talk.

Teona shook her head and gave a little grin that only affected her mouth. "It wasn't like that. They strapped me to a treadmill. Made me run. I must have been on that thing for hours. My legs feel like wet noodles. I'm afraid they won't ever hold me up again."

"What else?"

Teona looked around the cube. It was several minutes before she answered. "They'd take my blood pressure and took blood while I was running. They talked but I couldn't hear much over the pounding of my heart and feet. Something about adrenaline affecting the samples." She shook her head and finally looked at Liesel. "They did a pelvic exam. Clamps and scrape. But it scared the shit out of me at first because I didn't know what they were doing." Annuals, necessary evils, could be very painful when forced.

"Did you see the doctor's face?"

"Yeah. We've all agreed to memorize their faces. If we escape, we want to make sure they pay."

"They will." She caught movement out of the corner of her eye. Jordan was waving to her. "I'll be back."

Jordan waited until she was pressed against the glass. "How is she?" His eyebrows pulled forward.

"They made her run strapped to a treadmill. They do anything like that to you?"

"Had me lift weights. To see how much I could handle. I stopped counting after two hundred. They ran out of weights to add but I don't know how much that is."

She wasn't surprised by the weight, just his hesitance to know how much he could lift.

He shrugged. "My shoulders still quiver like I've let them sit too long." He rubbed a shoulder then said, "I want to try something."

She raised her eyebrows as an indication to continue.

"I've tried breaking the walls and doors. I don't know what this stuff is, maybe some weird kind of Plexiglas. But maybe if we try together." He explained his plan and they decided to wait for the lights to go back off.

It was almost half an hour before darkness descended. They had both stayed against the wall. Though only a few inches apart, they could no longer see each other.

"Are you ready?" He asked.

"Yes." Liesel placed her left hand on the wall, planted her feet slightly apart and clenched her right hand into a fist.

"Count to three. One...."

Chapter 27

She couldn't hear the other numbers as he stepped back from the wall but counted on her own. Two. She dropped her left hand and pulled back with her right. Three. She hit the wall as hard as she could. The noise was deafening like the inside of a giant church bell. The heart beat after her fist connected so did Jordan's. Her hand vibrated with his hit. She leaned against the glass. Her heart thumping against her ribs. "I think our rhythm is off."

"Okay. Count with me. One, two, three. One, two, three."

"One, two, three," they said in unison.

"Let's try again." They were trying to hit right next to each other, without over lapping, to cause as much stress to the wall as possible. Liesel's hand only stung slightly. She may have shitty aim and not know how to control her strength, but her knuckles could take the damage. "One." She got ready again, counting with him. "Two." She waited until they started to say three to pull back her arm so its backward motion would add momentum to her forward punch. "Three." The clang of the bell again but then the crunching sound and slight high pitched whine of folding steel. Liesel didn't lean forward to start the counting again. She hit the wall twice more, feeling Jordan doing the same thing. If they could get Jordan onto her side of the cube they could then try the same thing on one of the outer hallway walls. Though neither of them thought it would work.

"Move to your right," Jordan shouted. Though the wall was definitely cracking, it did not shower the floor with glass. Like glass in automobiles, it seemed designed to fold instead of shatter. Liesel didn't know why he told her to move but took a step to the right and hit the wall for the fourth time. The lights came on and a siren sounded. She blinked then saw Jordan. He was clawing at the wall, his fingertips bloody but a hole was emerging and bits of the wall lay at his feet.

Whew-o, Whew-o. The siren kept going.

Liesel reached for the hole and pulled at the edges on her side. Large bits crashed to the ground and she went back for more. Then she saw Hairy and Shorty and the two black guys running toward them.

Whew-o, Whew-o.

She dug, frantic, at the hole, now big enough to fit her hand in. Her door slid open and Teona, crouched and ready, ran at them. A gun went off and echoed through the hole on Jordan's side.

Whew-o.

"No!" Liesel shouted. She took a running step toward Teona and faltered as the pistol swung toward her, another report and her arm jerked back without her command. She could feel the dart's drug seep into her body pushing through and twirling serpentine with her relief. Teona was fine.

Whew-o.

A second dart slid by her arm, as the black man grabbed Hairy's arm. "Give it a chance to take effect. You don't want to kill her."

"Who says," Hairy said. Liesel realized she was on the floor but didn't remember falling. She looked back at the hole and saw Jordan lying down as well. Bloody chunks of glass surrounded him. Shorty and his black companion hovered over him. Teona's shot hadn't echoed, Jordan had been tranquilized as well. The lights started turning off, the furthest ones on either side first, then ones closer. Until finally she lay in blackness.

"When this is over, how about you explain why Amy has a tracking device embedded in her tooth," Agent Sting said to Griffon. They stood together waiting for instructions. The L.A. Feds were in charge of this. Griffon gave them the frequency for the tracker. If they thought he would sit idly by and allow them to go in without him, they were idiots.

"Chalk it up to being paranoid and liking gizmos," Griffon told Sting. Sting and his partner Marks had already been on their way to L.A. when Griffon called them. Like the twenty odd men around them, they were dressed in full S.W.A.T. gear. Kevlar vest, helmets, guns and all of it black. A few of the leaders had infrared goggles.

This side of Barstow, a couple hours north of Los Angeles, was full of manufacturing plants. The totally non-descript building matched the surrounding blocks. No residential areas for at least a mile and at this time of night there was no activity.

The plan was to shut off power to part of the building, enter, detain the bad guys and rescue the kids. It was more intricate than that but Griffon wasn't thinking about the plan. He looked again at the men standing around him.

Griffon had asked to come on the mission. He had been told no. Not a 'laugh-in-your-face no' but still, it should have deterred further requests. Instead of bargaining, he just made a phone call. "This is Jim Griffon. I need you to vouch for me." No one need know that he'd worked this out with Max's brother the General beforehand. Then Griffon had handed the cell phone to the L.A. Director and waited. Feet shoulder-length apart, arms folded across his chest, that steely look in his eyes, his I'm-about-to-start-a-bar-fight look.

Even before 'the call' the other agents gave Griffon his space. The call cinched it. He looked and felt like a street thug. A real bruiser. He projected menace with each movement, every look.

The Director had identified himself then listened for several seconds. Scanning Griffon up and down. He had flipped the phone closed then handed it back to Griffon. "So you're Jim Griffon?" As if they hadn't been introduced by Sting a few moments before. The Agent in Charge didn't say another word and leaned back over the compounds blue prints.

"The government evacuated this building just over two years ago. Budget cuts." Not another 'no' but not a go-the-hell-away either. "It was sold to a private buyer eight months ago." He pointed to several areas on the blueprint. "As you can see it was a detaining facility and has cells in these sections. Amy Griffon's signal is here. We will be entering here as I've said. Sting, you and Mr. Griffon will be in charge of moving the children through this set of corridors." His finger tip flat to the paper moved snake-like to the back of the building. "There will be a medical team and transport waiting for you." Griffon dropped his arms and stepped forward. No bar fights tonight.

-#-

Jordan lay on his side looking across to Liesel and Teona. He was glad they hadn't tranqed her a second time. He had been shot in the t-shirt, twisting the last possible second so it didn't puncture his skin. He dropped to his side like expected and waited. Muscles bunched. Heart racing. If they tried to drag him out, he'd fake unconsciousness then fight like hell to get the other doors opened.

Whew-o. Whew-o.

The taller of the two men stepped toward Jordan and nudged him with his boot. He relaxed and let his body shift to the pressure. But they didn't take him. The siren shut off and his door closed and the last light turned off.

His hands itched and ached. He had once helped his grandfather re-insulate the attic. They'd used the pink style of rollout fiberglass insulation. He'd worn gloves except during clean up and the micro fibers of glass covered and cut his skin. Afterward, he'd washed several times but could still feel glass slivers in his hands for days. His hands felt that way now.

He laid still. Waiting. Aware that they were watching. Then he pulled the dart out of his shirt and clutched it in his hand. He'd have a weapon when they came back. He thought about working on the whole some more, but without Teona's or Liesel's help, he wouldn't be able to break the other wall.

His mind raced with thoughts of the steroid tests and the irritation he had felt over it and—now he could admit—the fear he had felt.

Last year, as a freshman, he had set a new record for his school and placed tenth in Nationals. Both times they'd wanted to test him. One had been a urine sample while a judge watched. He'd done both tests knowing it wasn't random. Knowing they only tested one of the other top ten runners.

He didn't have an unfair advantage by being a Mighty, or as Liesel called them, an Amazon. His muscles were more thickly woven then a non-Amazon. Yes, it gave him strength but it also made him much heavier than the average six-foot-one, nineteen year old boy. It required more strength to move his body. How was that an advantage?

Plus, if a kid was a math genius, raised by famous mathematicians, would they disqualify him from competing in a competition? Would he be turned down from college or for research grants because he had a natural ability to add and subtract?

Jordan worked hard. Just like everyone else on that team.

Then two months ago in June he'd ran a marathon for charity. He came in 27th. 27th and they wanted to test him again.

He thought of his fiancé. Simoné in her tight blue t-shirt. The one that proclaimed "Feminism: The belief that women are people too." It was his favorite. He hoped she wasn't worried and hoped that she was. He would miss their weekend if he wasn't out soon.

He closed his eyes, thinking of the hole, proud of finally breaking the wall. Thinking of running, of his coach. He'd been awake, tense for so long. He was just drifting to sleep when he heard his door open.

They'd get out. All of them.

Chapter 28

Griffon had run mock prison raids of the Federal Correctional Institution in Herlong, California just outside of the Sierra Army Depot. Ah, those had been the days.

His official OS, occupation specialty, was MP, military police, and he had been stationed at Fort Irwin. But he was a spec ops favorite Grey Ghost, Red Fox, or guerrilla agent. They'd pull him and a few others off duty and give them the new job of creating chaos in the Nevada desert or hiding in the Sierra Mountains. So clearing this building was doable but better yet, when they finally got there, it registered why the blue prints had felt so familiar. They were just lines on a page but the single story building plus basement he viewed through his night goggles was familiar. He knew this place. Not that he'd been to this specific building before but the government had the habit of reusing house plans.

The OC, officer in charge, was the L.A. FBI Director and though his team was a mix of Rangers from Fort Irwin and HRT's, the Federal Bureau of Investigation's Hostage Rescue Team, the Director had everyone's complete attention and respect. Ah the spirit of cooperation.

One of the Agents was a woman. Griffon noted it and also noted that she did not stand out. She was an agent and was treated like one of them. No deferring to female sensibilities, no guarding her. No aggressive desire that she be anywhere else. Griffon realized he was just fine with her too. He could tell, just from his brief look, that this was a knowledgeable operator.

They were outside of Barstow, a few miles from a USMC strategic planning base, South of Fort Irwin and even the famous route 66 passed through town. Not only was the building close to several major airports but there were plenty decommissioned air bases in the area as well. And Sting said, most important of all, it was a few hours drive from Searchlight, Nevada. A small town with the huge drama of a missing Chicago teen discovered in their trash.

So they'd found the place, in no small part to the homing device implanted in Amy, and they had the blue prints, but Griffon didn't see this as an easy in and out.

He'd played Red Fox and Grey Ghost because, though he was well-trained and a great MP, he was not special ops. He didn't think like them and he didn't have their training. You want a Ranger or SEAL to defeat a target. Call it done. But throw a wrench in the gears and things got interesting and the teams came out better for the wrench. Training against other Special Operation Forces, you started to predict how they would handle situations, because it was how you'd handle it.

"This building here." Griffon tapped the paper spread out in front of the director. As the only nonmilitary, non-government guy it felt good not using protocol.

The director cleared his throat and one of the Rangers, easy to spot despite his total lack of identifying marks, crossed his arms, spread his feet shoulder-length apart and leaned toward Griffon. Nonverbal for watch-it, you-fuck-up. Heard loud and clear and clearly ignored.

"Maintenance building? For this little of a compound? It's too big. They could be using it for something else," Griffon said.

"We aren't ruling that out. But yes, that is what the building was used for." He was about to continue when Griffon interrupted him again.

"All kinds of interesting tools and things that go boom in maintenance sheds."

The Ranger gave a single nod and melted backwards.

"Lieutenant, we'll have you come in via that side. Check the building and radio-in a report before we execute into the main building."

"Yes, sir," said the aforementioned Ranger.

"Anything else to add Mr. Griffon?"

"You've got civilians, medical teams, standing by at the extraction point. The area is going to be pitch black with the power out." He moved his thumb across the point he was talking about. "We don't want them exposed to danger, and we want to be able to see each other. What kind of lighting can we guarantee back there?"

They finished the initial briefing and then went over it a second time. Key things to know: the labs were in the basement; the old cafeteria was probably being used for barracks for the 'hostiles', a very technical term meaning the bad guys; security points included a rear guard tower, a security guard station in the lobby—probably unmanned—and a security room with all the cool gadgets. And the cool gadgets were the reason they were shutting off the power. Just as soon as the report on the shed came in and they were in place.

A grove of trees, which was a mix of evergreens and palm trees and a dash of California desert, was on the south side of the building. The location of his 'position.' And here Griffon was in position. Check.

Now the wait. Maroon 5's Harder to Breathe was playing via iGriffon. The heavy thumps of the initial measures mixed with the beat of his heart. Amy was okay, had to be. And so was Liesel. They'd be in one of the basement labs or they'd be in the containment cells. Griffon would find them. They would find them and then they'd get them to safety. But in his head—separate from his calm, tactically ready exterior—he was struggling to keep the emotions out of it. Keeping the memories of his own rescue separate from the mission.

"Flower shop has been trashed, but clear of shop keepers. Evidence of missing chemicals," the communication man of the ranger team said. They all heard it via their earpieces. "Backup generator in here. Will pull the plug on mark."

No need to tell the guys that those chemicals could explode. But Griffon doubted any of the others knew what it felt like having a weed killer sprayed on your cuts. If they were using poisons to torture these kids, they'd need more body bags. Not a single shop keeper would come out of this alive.

"Time to mow the lawn." That was the signal. The power went out.

-#-

Little boys playing seek and destroy know how to shimmy along a wall, dart a glance around a corner. Soldiers didn't need to glance, they watched the shadows, they listened for movement, they felt the target.

Griffon thanked the fourteen Holy Helpers including Saint Christopher that he was going in with professionals. But following the fucked up luck that was his life, the hostiles were trained professionals too. They had a guard at the front entrance that was so well hid—he was behind a heating duct and bushes that both covered his image as well as his thermal heat indicator, and radio silent—that they didn't know he was there until he opened fire. The FBI were faster and with two silent pops, he fell to the ground. Surprise over. One advantage lost.

The first few booby traps were found and disarmed by the Rangers going in from the rear. The hostiles set the others off themselves; originally configured to surround, trap and eliminate intruders while they escaped. Sounded like the Rangers had thwarted that plan.

Griffon could smell the acrid smoke as he followed Sting through hallways to the basement stairs. A smell of a chemical burn, it stung the eyes like no wood smoke could. The frontal team—Griffon, Sting and the local FBI—worked silently, signaling with their hands. Griffon stood watching their backs as the others descended the narrow and steep stairs to the basement labs.

It felt good kitted up in tactical gear again. Not safe, never that. But powerful and freeing. The short sub-machine gun, MP5, fit into his shoulder perfectly. He had a 9mm at his hip and his own Berretta at the base of his spine. They had stacked at the front door, the bullet sponge in front carrying a half shield—just in case that guard post was manned—Sting in back, playing leap frog. The first person taking up position, covering the team as they took the next position. Griffon was front man at the stairs and felt the attack coming.

A short robust bruiser tried to catch him by surprise and knock him over the metal railing. Instead Griffon thrust the MP5 into the man's jaw and rode him down the stairs. His elbow and knee banged the steps and railing but he felt nothing yet.

The thug, still intent on his attack, obviously hadn't felt the corrugated metal steps grind down his spine. Shorty pulled a K-Bar knife and swiped at Griffon's throat. It tore Griffon's skin like an orange peeler, pulling up the first few layers.

Sting stepped forward and twisted the KaBar out of Shorty's hands. The capable female agent had super glued Griffon's cut before he could blink. Shorty's gun had flung loose during the descent and the female agent checked the rounds then tucked it in her front waistband. The other's still silent, still controlled, covered the stairs and the two hallways that fed into their spot. The female agent used a plastic restraint on the now unconscious man, and patted Shorty down for a radio.

Griffon took the KaBar and sheath and followed his team to the next position.

The basement's noise containment rivaled any sound studio. "They constructed an escape panel in the floor of the cafeteria," radioed the Rangers. The warning came just as the front team entered Lab One. Once inside the lab Griffon could hear the fire from the second floor

The lab was the size of a basketball court and had several work stations, tables and equipment covered in plastic and dust, they reflected the emergency lights from the hall and the flames from the fire. The stations were L-shaped islands, great for taking cover.

Squirming from the ceiling the thugs dropped to the ground. It was evident that more had come through here. The lab doors across the room still swinging on their hinges. The agents yelled "Freeze." The Rangers descended among billowing smoke and flames. The hired thugs knew the land better and were ready for them. The Rangers took two out with headshots. Body armor or not, a sharp shooter can take you down.

As they took cover, both sides, the FBI told them to surrender.

Griffon saw a man crouch low and head toward the exit. The rat was focused and he thwarted each attempt to stop him without turning and being on the defense—like a quarterback heading for the goal post. And no one was in front of him. It was different from running away. There was no fear or screaming, no cussing. And he was headed toward the containment cells. Major wrench in progress.

The remaining thugs opened fire and Griffon's team returned the shots. Griffon was careful, watching placement of the Rangers to prevent cross fire. If he missed he didn't want to hit a friendly target.

A single shot to the forehead took out his current opponent. The lead Ranger stepped to Griffon's flank, running in tandem with him and taking out road blocks like ducks in a shooting gallery. Seeming to bend bullets around Griffon. Relying on his cover Griffon focused on the rat. They dropped into the sub-basement, guns ready and facing opposite ways, Sting dropping down between them.

Griffon signaled the way. Normally they'd switch back to stealth, not knowing what was up ahead. But Griffon went first and prayed for the best. Rat man had wrenched a security door open and whipped inside as Griffon rounded the corner. He tried to pull the door closed, activating the security lock, Griffon stuck his fingers in the way and braced his foot against the frame. The runt had the hydraulic hinge on his side and Sting wrenched his fingers free just in time.

They stepped back and the Ranger shot the lock once and twisted the hot metal handle to open the door. Again Griffon went first. This was his rat chase he didn't want the other's hurt because his gut said this guy was trouble.

"You're too late," the Rat said. He reached for a red switch large enough to be visible from across the room. Fuck, whatever that switch did was very bad.

The Ranger, back to bending bullets, dropped the guy. He came into the room checking via radio with his team. They were making systematic searches of each nook and cranny for any hiding men.

It looked like the room was a security hub. It had to have a separate generator because the equipment was still on. The monitors was divided into sections showing each dark cell.

The power came back up with a whoosh of sound. Time to head down to the cells.

-#-

The body on the cement floor turned and jumped at him. Griffon had no time to react, not even seeing the dart until it was stuck in his Kevlar vest. He fell backward with the weight and force of the attack but rolled, using the body's weight to flip his attacker. The body shifted and Griffon realized it was a young man lying next to him. "Shit," the body said, looking at the dart. They both scrambled to their feet.

"It didn't get my skin," Griffon said.

The body reached over and yanked out the dart throwing it to the ground.

"Thanks." It seemed the appropriate thing to say. "We're getting you guys out."

Sting was up in the control booth opening doors and keeping an eye on the building for additional men. Three more agents were gathering children from the first few cubes.

Griffon hurried to the next cube and spotted two bodies. The whole area only lit by emergency red lights.

The young man pushed past him into the room. "See if you can lift Teona." He pointed to the one closest to the door. "I'll get Liesel." Griffon was going to argue—surely he could lift more than this slender guy—but Liesel's name made him hesitate long enough that the guy had her picked up before he could protest. He bent and checked Teona's pulse.

"I'm Jordan." Jordan's voice wasn't at all strained. He had simply dropped to one knee, grasped one of Liesel's hands, and pulled her over his shoulders, his other arm held her behind the knees. Then stood up.

"Griffon." Griffon staggered a bit as he lifted Teona. Taken off guard by how heavy she was—she looked petite compared to Liesel's length and curves. "What happened to them?" The power came back on, a signal that the basement and cafeteria was clear, but only every other cell or so. They were in a dark cell.

"We were trying to escape." Jordan nodded to a section of wall between their cells. The wall was webbed with cracks and had a hole as if a demolition crane had smashed into it. "They've just been tranqed."

They headed through the door and followed the children and agents already gathering at the end of the corridor. No weeping children to hush. No one, but the two unconscious women, were being carried. The rest of the doors were opened and the children came out cautiously. All the little eyes looked at Liesel in concern then Jordan for guidance.

"These guys are going to help us. Keep together. Be as quiet as possible," Jordan said. Several little heads nodded. This was going surprisingly well. The itch in the back of his eyes, waiting for that second boot to drop, kept him looking for that looming threat.

"What happened to Liesel?" Jordan's newly designated shadow was a boy about thirteen years old. He wore a Cubs shirt that was smeared in more than just blood. His eyes were flat, his tone empty. God, what these kids must have gone through.

"I've got her," Jordan told the boy instead of answering him.

Griffon saw Amy then, pressed against the walls, her eyes large and puffy from crying. "Amy." Griffon whispered her name. She was safe and she could cry as long and as hard as she wanted. He might never leave her presence again. His heart unclenched for the first time in hours. He swore it had stopped beating altogether when they'd found Riley. Amy looked up at her name and smiled. When she was close enough to reach, she grasped his leg tight. He gently slid his hand into her hair and let the heat of her radiate into his cool skin, ground him. He blinked once to clear his eyes.

Agent Sting joined the group, gave the all clear, and led them out into the twisting corridors. An agent, gun drawn, brought up the rear. Liesel's arms hung straight like a stored puppet over Jordan's shoulder, swaying with each step forward. Amy kept a tight grasp to Griffon's pant leg, which kept his gun hand free.

The walls were bare of everything but paint; the floors, cement. In the dark, tomb-like-air, all noises were in sharp resolution, a megaphone. Each whisper or rustle of cloth against cloth as bodies moved, was magnified. Crisp.

The dark, utilitarian look to the place, the echo of sound off the cement, it was like being in that basement again. Cold. Smothering.

His need for air, for freedom became a sharp, compulsive force. Griffon bit back the urge to scratch at his throat, or push at his wind pipe. He needed to keep it together for a bit longer. Just because the clear signal had come through did not mean there wasn't still a threat.

The escapees reached a hall junction.

Sting signaled them against the inner wall and checked the next hallway. Gunfire pelted the outer wall across from them. The corner's edge where Sting ducked back to safety, blew out puffs of white dust. The children screamed and clutched each other. Griffon leaned down and pressed Teona's back into the wall before carefully letting go. She slumped there still under the drug's effects. Sting, at the head of the group, returned fire.

Almost there. They'd made it to Sunday.

Griffon had his rifle swung down from his shoulder before he finished standing. He dove and rolled, firing the gun at his two targets. A bullet thumped into the cement above his shoulder. It was the only round fired before the gunmen dropped to the ground. Looked like he could still bend his own bullets.

"Hold your position," Sting yelled. Sounded like he might have pissed off the FBI agent but that clutch and swallow to his throat was going to escalate if he didn't get his girls out. Now.

Griffon checked the hall again from his new perspective. A hand gesture to Sting for cover and Griffon checked the back way.

It was a large parking lot. Two armored SWAT vehicles parked sixty feet back. Yellow, dull emergency lights hung from the building's roof. Griffon could hear the click of guns being cocked. He pulled a flare from his belt, flipped the top off to activate it and tossed it to his left out the door and along the building.

The flare was another signal. Griffon walked out, holding the door open, scanning the perimeter. He signaled to Sting, who proceeded the kids out and EMT's poured around the SWAT vehicles to help the kids to ambulances parked behind the trucks. The last out were two agents, one carrying Teona and one, gun at the ready, covering the rear.

Griffon counted heads, splitting his focus between Amy, wrapped in an army blanket, and Liesel, still over Jordan's shoulder. A couple of the EMT's tried to get Jordan to put Liesel down or transfer her to their arms. He shook his head. "She's heavy. Just show me were to put her. On a stretcher or something."

Pop, Pop. Gunfire.

The last agent fired his rifle then fell backward, a splash of red from his shoulder hit the ground. The children screamed.

The hairiest man Griffon had ever seen, stumbled out the door, assault rifle at the ready. Griffon's weren't the only bullets that hit the man and with more than a double-tap to the head, he dropped to the ground dead.

Chapter 29

Agents and office personnel were putting in overtime to get the kids settled into the Federal building in L.A. The security was, of course, high and any safe house they had ready wouldn't hold all of them. Questions needed answers. Including her own.

"Griffon. Please, I need to talk to you."

His classic, normal, everyday eyebrow lift. But it looked so wonderful, seeing it again when Liesel thought she wouldn't. With gentle hands, he guided her to a quiet corner.

"The men. At your brother's house." Please understand. She couldn't form anymore words. She'd seen them last, crumpled on the floor, as the chloroform cloth was placed over her mouth and she decided to let them take her.

"Dead."

She dropped, suddenly. Her muscles lost all strength. He grabbed her elbows and shouted for a chair and Jordan and Chris were there, guiding her down. Griffon dropped to his knees at her feet and the kids swarmed her, a literal wave across the room, leaving the adults standing like dock pillars. They'd been out of that building, out of their cells, for over two hours. Yet, it seemed like seconds, like inches away. It was so close to their skin; their minds.

"Did the paramedics check her out?" Chris asked.

"Yes," Jordan said.

"But maybe they should've—" Teona said.

Clara, the youngest, started keening and the sound pulled Liesel out of her half faint.

"No, I'm okay." Liesel reached down and pulled Clara onto her lap, stroking the girl's hair. Her eyes focused and she straightened her shoulders; remembered Chris doing the same hours before.

A cold shiver ran over her skin. "I'm so proud. Of each of you. Look what you accomplished, figuring out the glass so you could talk. Being there for each other, so no one was alone. You are no longer teens from separate parts of the country, but survivors. Conquerors."

"You know, no matter what you face, that we...." she indicated them in the room, "will be with you." Two girls held hands and smiled at each other, and even the youngest boy stood taller, prouder. "I'm so proud. Now. Go eat."

They scattered, happy. Still, she didn't get up.

"Chris?" Griffon said. Chris had stayed at Liesel's side as the others went to load paper plates with food. "Would you get something for Liesel to eat?"

Jordan took Clara into his arms and carried her. "I'm hungry." He growled like a bear and pretended to eat her shoulder. Clara giggled.

"What is it?" Griffon whispered once they were alone.

She stroked his head, feeling his hair slide between her fingers. "Dead?" Be brave, Liesel. You can take the truth.

"Yeah, I came in, maybe fifteen minutes after they...." He couldn't say the words. A haunting pain in his sharp eyes. "Did they hurt you? Shit. I'm such an idiot. I can see...." His thumb gently stroked beneath her bruised eye; the horrors of his own abduction, plain on his face.

"Dead?" Just tell me. Just say it. I killed. She could feel the vibration of her shivers intensify.

"Yeah...." but then he realized that it was destroying her. "No. Liesel." His hands slid to her chin. "It wasn't like that. They were shot."

He took her face in his hands, brought her close, so that all they could see was each other's eyes. "They were both shot in the head. Probably, while they were unconscious. Both bullets were lodged in the floor. You didn't kill them. The others didn't want to hassle hauling them when they had...No, not like that." He growled.

Her face felt wet. Was she crying? Was she awake? Or was this part of the hideous nightmare that began on a cold cement floor. All the worse for the hope escaping had given them.

"They didn't want them slowing them down. Damn it, stop that. You did it right, Liesel. You did it right." Perhaps not knowing what else to do, and desperately wanting to do it anyway, he kissed her. There were giggles and whistles and tiny hands clapping around the room.

Tears slid down her face anyway. It's okay, now. It's okay. And when she put her brave face back on, it was sincere. That's how his touch always made her feel, like they were, life was, everything was, okay. She'd do it right from this moment forward. She'd learn the proper way to kick ass. She wouldn't fight it like an addiction. It was part of her and she'd embrace it.

Later, Liesel sat in a wing chair, Clara, asleep, curled in her lap. The Amazons had taken over a lounge in the Federal building. The FBI had offered rooms to sleep in, but no one wanted to be alone. Instead, they pulled the back cushions off the couches to make more 'beds' and a few of the agents had dragged cots into the room. Varying bodies were spread across the room, all breathing peacefully. Finally, even Teona had fallen asleep. Liesel and Jordan were the only ones awake.

He sat in the matching chair. They were sentinels, guarding the door. A table against the opposite wall held what remained of the food. A half of a peanut butter sandwich, an apple, several empty water pitchers and crumbs. The trash can next to the table was full of potato chip bags, paper plates and cups.

Jordan stood and walked across the room for the sandwich. Once back at his seat, he chuckled quietly. "Do you think they'll feed us again? Or just take us to some all-you-can-eat restaurant?"

Liesel smiled at him. The food had probably been meant for the Agents, too, but the kids had plowed through the food like locusts. Slightly alarmed, the Agents had let them.

She remembered Griffon's reaction. "Won't they get sick eating so quickly? If they've been starved, their bodies need time to adjust."

"They fed us," Jordan had explained, eating his first of three apples. "But we're like Saiyan. We use up all our energy, or if we are denied food, then we have to reload. "

"Goku and Vegeta? Dragon ball Z," Griffon said.

Jordan nodded.

"Holy cow. How can anyone afford to feed more than one?" He

shook his head as even Amy started her second sandwich.

Liesel's real surprise was Jordan's natural ease with Griffon. No intimidation or posturing. Confident without needing to add macho airs. Most people, even the federal agents, tensed in Griffon's presence. They assumed that he had an extra three feet of personal space and went out of their way to stay out of that space. But not Jordan.

Jordan spoke, bringing her out of her musings. "I wonder if they've figured out the why yet." It was a question they'd asked each other before—Jordan, Teona, and Liesel.

"I sure hope they have an answer before the parents get here. It's not going to be a smooth event anyway. But if we don't even know why you guys were taken...." She shook her head.

Griffon was somewhere down the hall, answering questions and helping to contact the parents. What would he tell them? Five of the kids had never heard of her or the idea of Amazons. She had touched each child. Reassuring, getting contact information and looking for an answer. If Griffon said they were Amazons, what would the FBI do? She had told Sting but it didn't mean they understood or that he'd believed her.

"I talked to my parents. I think they'll bring the whole family to come and get me." Jordan shook his head. Liesel turned to look at him. He sounded distressed at the very idea and a bit bewildered.

"It's our nature to be protective." Amazons were primal in guarding their young.

"Perhaps," Jordan said. "But six angry M...Amazons aren't going to help this situation." He licked a smudge off his thumb and stared at the apple across the room. "If that was a green apple, I'd be all over it."

Liesel laughed but hushed quickly as Clara stirred. "I thought Teona would insist on going with each child as they were questioned." Even in sleep Teona was trying to protect them. She lay in front of the cots and couch, where the youngest ones slept; a guard between them and the rest of the room.

"Probably would have, but they questioned them all at the same time."

"It was a good idea you had. To have each child responsible for a different composite sketch." She stroked Clara's head, breathing the air, feeling safe. No harm would come to these kids and she would help them heal.

Jordan didn't respond in any way to her compliment. "Too bad they'll need to use them." The doctor and a man the children referred to as 'pierced and scary', had both gotten away. Everyone else was accounted for.

"It was good for these kids. It helps them feel like they can make a difference. Be helpful. They can start getting rid of the victim mentality."

They were silent for a while.

"Have you decided about the nomination?"

Pulled from her thoughts, her response was a knee jerk reaction. "An organization, or body of government, has to exist to nominate a leader." She'd used the line before, a hundred times in her head, so it came out easily. She was trying to distract him but it wasn't going to work.

"Have you decided to establish said organization and accept the role of leader?"

"What's your major? Poly-Sci?" Without waiting for his response, she said, "Yes." She tried to make it sound firm, self-assured. It didn't. "Maybe. I've always believed the purpose of clubs, groups, whatever, was to exclude people. To make people feel superior. I don't want that to happen and I don't know if I can prevent it." It seemed so odd to struggle with what exactly the problem was and have it finally fall into words. It had been rattling around in her head but not until she had voiced it, did she realize what it was.

"What do you mean feel superior? Aren't we, in some ways, better?" Jordan said with a neutral voice.

"I know you don't believe that."

"No. I don't." He sighed and rubbed the long sleeve of his shirt at the wrist on his forehead. "I believe people are put in power to prevent evil, to serve. But why don't you? Tell me a story."

You are very charming and sneaky, Mr. Mathews. "A man becomes a lawyer. He spends eight years in both college and law school, which cost him hundreds of thousands of dollars." Her voice was lyrical and Jordan's eyes glassed over as he opened his mind. "He studies and passes the bar exam. A set of rules that dictate his qualifications. Then, to establish a name for himself, to pay back all that money, he must work endless hours, charge a high rate. After all of that, he has to be proud. Look what he accomplished. Not everyone has the drive or the focus to do those things." She played with Clara's hair, twining it around her fingers.

"He is a lawyer. But he could be any number of things. A senator. A famous basketball player. A heart surgeon. It's not the profession in particular, I like lawyers just fine," she said.

"Is he better than his mother? A mother without a college degree?" Her own eyes saw everything but nothing of the room in front of her. "A mother who still works at the age of sixty because she doesn't have a retirement fund. Smarter? Yes, he is probably smarter. But is he better? He most likely thinks so." She gently tugged her finger free of Clara's hair.

"So power corrupts," Jordan said. He had a smirk on his face which made Liesel remember his youth. This may have been his first big trial in life. She didn't know if she was relieved to see his attitude untarnished or worried.

"Yes," Liesel said.

"Yet, your desire to not be corrupted is a good sign."

"Perhaps."

"I know what you should do."

She turned and looked at him, their eyes focusing. The way he tilted his head and looked at her, waiting for her response, was a heavy shade of confident. Jordan continued, "Don't give yourself, or the ones that follow, power. Give the organization power."

"How?"

"A constitution. Senators have more say then you or me, but it's us that put them in power." He snorted in derision. "I should know. My uncle is a senator and my grandfather served in Regan's cabinet."

"You're pretty smart." Liesel's mind filled with possibilities. The McKinnon leather tried to establish rules, so her ancestors would have some guidance on what the hell they should do. Could she do that? Could they? Build in protection for their kids? Give them a path forward?

"For a kid you mean."

She jerked her head back to look at him, taking a second to transition her thoughts. "I'm not even ten years older than you. I've got a sister I'm thinking about introducing you to. You're not a kid."

He smiled. "I'm spoken for."

What do you say to that? After another companionable silence, she asked, "Want to tell me about the Mightys?"

"Can't, can I? Not yet, anyway."

She was content with that. For now. But any doubt on who he was, was gone. The Mightys still existed and she was probably sitting next to one of their future leaders. Rulers without kingdoms.

A few agents came into the room with Griffon. "Jordan Mathews? I'm Agent Sting. This is my partner Agent Marks. We'd like to ask you some questions now."

"I'm surprised you waited so long." Jordan stood and stretched.

"Wait. I think you should hear this too." Griffon put a hand up to the three men and looked at Liesel. "They know why. The men we captured said the doctor was trying to develop a natural steroid. One that would pass drug testing. He was analyzing your DNA and the adrenaline you produce."

Jordan had sat back down. His eyes scanned the kids that slept around them. "He was keeping us alive for what? So he could keep harvesting our blood?" Jordan said. "We're not sure," Marks said. "The doctor kept records but it will take a while to go through it all. It's not likely they would have held you forever."

"I think the Doctor may have...." Liesel thought he was about to tell the agents about his possible coerced sperm donation. She shook her head and nodded to Chris who was awake and listening. His t-shirt had been swapped for a black FBI one. His square frame was buried in black cotton and he actually looked his age.

Jordan stood again. "I'll tell you when you question me. I'll be back. Don't leave without me." He smiled and Liesel saw again the breathtaking beauty she'd glimpsed in the cube. Yet, it felt like museum art, look but don't touch. Griffon's handsome face, though often stern and dark, always pulled her in closer, asked her to feel, connect. Jordan led the two agents out, confidently taking point, knowing they'd follow without further direction.

Chapter 30

Liesel waited for the door to close, then stood and placed Clara on her seat. The little girl curled into a ball and continued sleeping. "Chris? I'm going to walk down the hall and use the bathroom. You're in charge."

He nodded and sat up, crossing his legs, scanned the room.

Once they had left the room as well, Griffon said, "What is Jordan going to tell them?"

"He thinks they used electric shock to get him to ejaculate when he was drugged."

"Shit." Griffon stood a moment in place, pressing his knees together and shaking his head.

She'd pulled him to the hall to tell him this. This and more. She needed to touch him. Could almost smell the pain rolling off him. "I think he is worried they put it in Teona." Liesel whispered. Whispering is such a powerful tool, soothing and private.

"They examined her. They examined everyone but you and Jordan. Everyone's fine."

Jordan hadn't let them, saying he'd been poked and prodded enough for this week, only letting them bandage his hands. As an adult he had the right to refuse medical treatment.

They started walking, slowly, so they wouldn't get too far from the room. "How is your eye?" His firm hands reached up to gently touch the bruise.

She knew from looking in a bathroom mirror that it looked almost normal again. She was relieved Griffon hadn't seen it when she couldn't open her eye. Less than a day later, it was a little tender, slightly puffy on top, and already yellow, as the bruise faded. After washing her hands, she could hardly tell she'd been cut by the wall. A few angry red lines were all that was left.

She shrugged in response to his question. "Any word on the doctor?"

"They found him. Dead. Pierced and Scary, too."

"Where?"

"The men we have in custody, they told us about a hotel. They'd all been hired and contacted from there. These guys were just guns for hire, out of work, criminal records. Just random really. Anyway, they sent a team over to check the place. They found both men."

"Did they kill each other?" She asked on a yawn and stretched, her shoulders popping. She'd been tranquilized for a few hours but it hadn't been restful sleep.

"They don't think so. It looks like a third, unknown party." His voice was distracted, husky.

She stopped and turned toward him. He looked so inviting. He still wore the black cargo pants and boots but had removed his vest and guns. The black T-shirt stretched across his shoulders and pecs. She placed a hand on his chest, feeling his warmth, his heartbeat. "What did you tell them about Amazons?" She asked to have something to say. She was way more interested in the dips and curves of his defined abs.

"I didn't. They avoided it like the plague. It was pretty odd. I figured they knew but didn't think I knew, so were trying to keep it a secret or something. Every time I'd try to reason on why these kids, they'd steer the question in a different direction." He looked down at her hand as it stroked him.

"Could it have been an internal leak? I mean do you think they have a file on all of us and one of theirs got the information?"

He shook his head. "I don't think so. I mean, why use children? From what I've been told—which I don't think is even half the story—and what I've seen, you guys get stronger as you get older." He picked her hand off of his chest, looking at it. He slid his finger along her knuckles. "You heal quicker, too." They'd had to still clean and bandage Jordan's cuts.

It felt good, him holding her hand. She stepped a little closer to his warmth. He looked into her eyes and his pupils dilated, darkened. "Your eyes aren't really scary. Not really."

She kissed him or he kissed her. It didn't matter, the result was the same. They were kissing and all the pent up emotions, good and bad, the things they'd felt in bed but hadn't expressed, the feeling caused by her abduction, by his, all of it and more, much, much, more, was in that kiss. There was no way to express all that in a single kiss. No way to release all that with their clothes on. Hands slid into hair and they pulled each other closer, tighter.

There was a cough behind them and her body jerked at the noise but he didn't let her go. He gave her a chaste kiss to seal her mouth then leaned back, far enough to look at their audience but close enough to keep her within his arms. His strong arms. The place, she realized, she wanted to be.

"The parents are arriving. I'd appreciate your help, Ms. Grant," the Director said.

"Of course." She tried again to step back from Griffon but he wouldn't let go. He wanted her close, wanted to be touching her. She looked questioningly at him. He took her hand and turned back to the lounge and the elevators.

They followed the Director back to the elevators. The Director pushed the down button just as the elevator doors slid open. Five men, all six and a half feet tall, broad shouldered and menacing, filled the elevator. It was like looking at the starting lineup for the Utah Jazz.

"Senator Mathews." The Director extended his hand to one of the men.

The Senator ignored the Director and fixed his eyes on Liesel. Her skin crawled, like it was covered in little bugs. She wasn't frightened of this man and he wasn't looking at her in a creepy lustful way, more of an I-know-all-your-secrets, smug, superior way. "Ms. Grant, queen of the Amazons, or so I am told," he said. Secret number one.

She nodded at the men, deciding to ignore their rude behavior. "You all must be Jordan's family." They looked like a family. Something in their eyes and, oddly, in their necks made them all look alike. A man on the far side, slightly pudgy and with graying hair, kept his hand on the elevator door to prevent it closing. "If you—"

"You will address him as Senator Mathews," said the twin on the left. Of the five there was the grandfather, the senator, a set of twin uncles and one she thought might be Jordan's father. The father's face was pale, eyes shot red from lack of sleep and tears. It was his expression, his love that gave her patience. He alone looked around the hall hoping to see for himself that Jordan was okay.

Okay, so they were rude. Arrogant men, especially wealthy males, often used abruptness to gain control of a situation or perhaps.... It was no use, her temper wasn't buying it. These were Mightys and though she didn't understand what that fully meant, she wouldn't allow them to treat her like that. "Then you may address me as ma'am or your highness." She said it to point out how inappropriate their behavior was. She said it because it was ridiculous, thus perfect for the situation.

"We do not and will never recognize your false authority," the other twin said.

"I don't know what the problem is. I haven't asked anyone to pledge fealty to me. Be rude, arrogant, assholes for all I care." She kept her tone below sarcastic and shrill. Just barely. She pushed her hair away from her face. "Now, if you would like to know about Jordan, like if he is okay? Try your best to behave and the Director and I will answer your questions." She turned her back on them, head high.

"Director, can we use the conference room down the hall?" She knew the angry stares they must have, her back burned with it.

"Gentleman," the Director said. The word conveyed a stern reprimand. Usually, only librarians perfected such a talent. Liesel couldn't help but be impressed, something to aspire to. He nodded and indicated that they should follow him.

Liesel stood next to Griffon for a moment, wishing he would take her hand, so she could feel his reassuring warmth. An unpleasant prickle along the back of her neck had her gut clenching. The Mathews men couldn't make her feel that way. Only the ones that mattered had ever been able to hurt her. She looked at Griffon.

He was angry and he wasn't trying to hide it behind his stony, unreadable expression. The scary eyes were working overtime, plus holiday pay. Was his anger in support? To show her he disliked the Mathews? He maintained constant control, each action had a purpose. Anger, she'd already figured out, he hid with silence and detachment. There was something very loud about this glare.

"Are you angry with me?" She kept her voice low.

"Queen?" The leash was finally put back on the scary eyes, his face going blank.

The last Mathew had entered the conference room. "People want...I've...Yes, though I'm working out a different title. The group needs a leader. Someone who can give them structure, a code of conduct. Speak for them."

"Like laws." Big time closed and angry body language.

What the hell had she done now? She pinched her eyes closed. "Something is obviously wrong, but we'll have to deal with it later. Check on the kids." The conference room didn't need any more male hostility.

She was a good person. It pissed her off that her feelings were hurt. Couldn't he trust her? But she knew he saw her as a woman of power. As an Amazon. The word took on the meaning freak for the first time in her head.

They wanted her to be their leader, to set up rules and govern them accordingly. Just like a judge. She'd sit up there on her throne of superiority, feeling she had to have complete control and say over their lives. Otherwise they might question her power, her authority.

Griffon shook his head and started walking, away from the lounge, the elevators. Away from her.

But this is Liesel. Not your partner. Not the neighborhood whores.

But a voice taunted him. Look at the way she used her body. Turned him on with the way she dressed, the things she said. Then acting so innocent.

His thoughts scared him and that took the edge off his anger. The images in his mind were over lapping. He couldn't separate them;

lay them flat in his mind so he could truly see them. Liesel was innocent and she was unaware of the effect she had on him, on people. She didn't see herself as an attractive woman. She didn't see why Griffon would want her. Why people would follow her.

The other images weren't even her. Those images were barriers built from lies.

Liesel was none of those images. She made his skin vibrate and his blood rush. She was kind and patient with others.

Griffon wandered back to the lounge. Chris was sitting on the arm of Clara's chair. Scanning the children. Alert. Amy slept peacefully on one of the couches. Griffon leaned against the open door and scanned the room with his arms crossed. Liesel had helped save these kids. She'd never believed anything but this eventuality. Something inside of him seemed to open, suck in this new truth. He hoped. And it was all because of her. She'd make a good queen. She would.

The elevator door opened down the hall. The Johnsons hurried out, frantically looking left and right.

"She's in here," Griffon called.

They were running and calling for Teona. Griffon stepped into the lounge before them and had time only to place his hand on Chris's shoulder before they burst into the room. Chris was up and in defense mode. Snap, just that quick.

"It's okay," Griffon said.

But Chris just stood there, watching.

Teona was up and quick as sound into her parents arms. They talked at the same time and cried together. Griffon decided they had enough of an audience and stepped back into the hall.

Freddy leaned against the wall just outside of the lounge. He turned his head away, wiped at his face, as Griffon came out. "Is s-she okay?"

"Yeah. Tired but not hurt."

Freddy nodded. He had one leg bent, sole of his shoe pressed against the wall. He crossed and uncrossed his arms. His brain not processing a single thing.

They stood in silence. Freddy gave a little twitch and stuck his hands deep into both pockets when his cell phone vibrated. The digital display was for a 503 number. "Yeah?"

"Hey, this is Johnny Ameri."

Who the hell was Johnny Ameri? The voice sounded familiar but Freddy's memory wasn't clicking. Hell, nothing was clicking. His brain had been bricked.

"You guys find my roomie yet?"

Freddy mouthed 'Jordan's roommate' to Griffon. "Yes, Johnny, we found Jordan," he said just to make sure Griffon understood. Freddy lifted his eyebrow, asking Griffon about Jordan.

"In questioning," Griffon said.

"He's being questioned right now...."

"Friggin A. That's great. I've been feeling pretty shitty about the whole thing. Should have said something sooner, you know?"

"It happens," Freddy said.

"Yeah." There was a noise, Freddy figured was probably a snort. "Man, the reason I called was because I remembered why I thought that guy was a recruiter. Woke me the fuck up."

Teona was okay. Not dead. Not even hurt. He hadn't realized, not allowing himself to, how much he was totally, fucking, fire-brand scared. His body started to shake.

"You know, the one with the van, checking Jordan out."

"The recruiter, right." He was so, so tired. He slid to the floor, trying to keep the phone in his hand. He registered on some level that Griffon stepped toward him "What?"

"Jordan said he was a recruiter," Johnny repeated.

Freddy handed the phone to Griffon.

"This is Griffon. What did you say?" If the roommate was concerned about the switch in phone companion, he didn't say anything.

"That's how I knew he was a recruiter. Because Jordan said. Said he'd met the dude in Washington D.C. at one of them president fitness things." As Johnny continued, Griffon was already hurdling down the hall looking for Jordan. Freddy was up and following on his heels.

"Old guy. Lots of grey hair."

None of the captured men had grey hair. Not even the doctor. Hadn't he seen a picture of lots of grey hair? "Johnny, can you hold on a sec." He'd found the room and wrenched it open.

"Sure man. I'll hold."

Jordan, Sting and Marks looked at him, startled by his abrupt entry. "Jordan, the day you were taken, your roommate said you recognized a sports headhunter. He was there watching you train."

"Yeah. Murket. Sam Murket. I met him last year at the President's National Fitness Day in D.C. He wants to be my agent, get me sponsors to run the pro-circuit."

The name stirred around his memory bank. "Your roommate says he saw the guy driving a white van with California plates."

"Everyone else was taken by a group of men," Marks said catching on, flipping through his notes as if he needed to double check.

"Maybe he did this one solo. Draw less attention," Griffon said. He still held the phone, the other hand gripping the door.

"Maybe I was a last minute addition," Jordan said. He sat across from the two Agents at a small table, his eyes heavy with fatigue and his hair tousled. His hands tugged on the bandages they'd wrapped his hands in, agitated. "He'd asked, again, and I told him I wanted to finish college."

"Let's go ask the others. See if any of them know this guy." Griffon put Freddy's cell phone back to his ear. "Johnny?

"Yeah?"

"Can you give a statement of what you saw?"

"Yeah."

Griffon thrust the phone to Marks then pivoted out of the room, hurrying back to the lounge. Sting, Jordan and Freddy were right behind him, their long strides close to a jog.

As they drew closer, he heard Jordan moan behind him. "You could have told me my family was here."

"Sorry."

Jordan stopped just outside the doors and braced himself as his father and uncles converged from the conference room.

The Johnsons sat with Teona and two other children sat with their newly arrived parents. Tears streamed down many of their faces. Freddy stayed by the door. Griffon cleared his throat to get everyone's attention. "Did anyone else attend the Presidential Fitness Celebration last year in D. C.?" Half the hands went up. All of the younger ones. Only Teona, Chris, Ming Poulsen—the golfer from Seattle—and Amy were left. "Has anyone been contacted by a recruiter named Sam Murket?"

"I have," Chris said. Seattle girl raised her hand and gave a little nod.

"He wanted to know who my supplier was," Teona curled her lip in disgust. "He figured I'd have to be on something to be so good."

Only Amy was left. She'd sat up on her knees and was leaning over the side of a couch. Griffon sat next to her. "What about you Amy?"

Amy shrugged, watched his face.

"Little League Hall of Fame," Ming Poulsen said. "You are Amy Griffon aren't you? Broke the Jr. Fast Ball record at age nine. Eighty-seven miles per hour."

Amy shrugged again. "I like batting better."

"Did you do any interviews for sports magazines?" Sting asked.

"Sports Illustrated for Kids but it wasn't a very good photo."

Griffon laughed and kissed Amy's forehead.

"There's more," Freddy said from the door. Teona gasped, perhaps seeing him for the first time, and walked over to him as he spoke. Her legs unsteady from random muscle spasms. "I've been working on.... Well, you're Ming Poulsen. Chris Ward. Jesus Corby." He pointed in turn to each of the three missing kids from Liesel's database, his voice questioning.

They nodded.

"You all f-five, with Clara and Teona, went to sport camps in June. You all gave b-blood as part of a physical. Who else?" He slipped his hand in Teona's, keeping his eyes on the room. But

Griffon saw him shake as he took his girlfriend's hand for the first time, a full head to toe shiver.

"I was invited to that camp. On scholarship," Jesus Corby said.

Mr. Corby said, "No such thing as a free lunch."

The room was in shock as they processed that and Griffon realized where he had heard the name before. In Coeur d'Alene, at the basketball camp, the manager had said the old man in all the photos had been Murket.

Sting was pulling out his cell phone and Agents were scrambling for their offices and phones. "I'll see what we can find out about this Murket guy." Sting left and Griffon realized that Liesel wasn't there. She needed to hear this. It would ease her mind to know it wasn't her website that had exposed these kids.

I'll let Jordan tell her, he thought, or Freddy. Not yet trusting himself to fuck it up with his short temper. But Jordan was still surrounded by his family. From where Griffon sat he could only see the broad backs of the uncles. Freddy was answering questions from the newly arrived Marks.

Griffon looked at Herschel and waited until they made eye contact. "Where is Liesel?"

"She's gone down to security to greet the parents as they come in," Herschel said.

Griffon gave Amy a reassuring hug and told her he would be back. Chris, still taking his job seriously, sat next to Amy and nodded his head in a very mature 'I've got her' sort of way. It was unnerving because Griffon didn't doubt the boy for a second.

Griffon took the elevator down to the first floor. He was still angry at her, wasn't he? His blood still pumped with anger. Hot and slightly sour. But he needed to see her. Wanted her to explain in a way that made it okay. She just needed to say that she hadn't told him because...because, hell, she was just trying to figure out how to trust him. Like he'd been trying to figure out with her.

The elevator opened into the lobby. In front of him was the security checkpoint. They had better equipment then L.A.X. Metal detector, thumb print scan, camera hooked to an image database, even a bomb dog. Though it was very early in the morning, two of the three stations were busy scanning people in and out.

He didn't see Liesel anywhere. He asked the security supervisor, a man behind bullet proof glass monitoring computers, if he'd seen her. The man nodded. "Was greeting parents like some kind of foreign diplomat."

"Yeah, that was her." Not really a question but answered anyway.

"One of the fathers had left his I.D. in his rental car. She offered to walk him out." The man checked his watch. "About ten minutes ago."

"Thanks." He went through security, making a show of emptying his pockets, car keys, hotel key card, and wallet. Making sure he left only with what he came in with. He'd been required to relinquish his gun, not being federally approved to carry on site. The exit guard waved him through and he gathered his stuff back up. The main parking lot was to the left side of the building. As soon as the automatic doors swished open he felt a chill clutch his gut. Something was wrong. He had learned to listen to his gut over the years but unfortunately it still spoke 'Internal Organ' and he only knew "I'm hungry" and "I'm sick" in that language.

Was it something upstairs? No. It was Liesel. It was the fact that a rental car made no sense. Who else could have made it to L.A. this quickly? Why would they take the time to rent a car? Who had only a father that would come? He didn't know the answer to the last one, but it just didn't fit.

Instead of heading into the well-lit parking lot, he walked to his right, toward Veteran Avenue. It was a towing zone, nothing allowed there for more than a few minutes. With the Oklahoma City Bombing and 9/11, parked cars and federal buildings didn't mix. A block in the other direction was the long, endless lines of white gravestones at the veteran cemetery.

He could see a couple of people a block and a half away standing next to a car. It was too far to see who the people were. He took off at a jog to get a closer look.

It was two teenagers delivering morning newspapers, the sun still struggling to rise. "Have you guys seen a lady about my height and a guy? They came out of the Federal building ten minutes ago." They were probably headed back into the building, while he stood out here looking like an idiot.

"I told you something weird was going on," one of the boys said to his friend.

The second one shook his head and shrugged.

"Yeah, we saw them. They stood talking for a few minutes then headed that way," the first boy said. He pointed behind Griffon to Wellworth Avenue, a perpendicular street blanketed in apartment buildings and alley like yards stuffed with trees.

"Why did you think it was weird?" He looked back from where they pointed.

"They shook hands," the first boy said.

"Everybody shakes hands, idiot," his friend said, his voice much deeper than the other teen.

"Yeah, but she got this weird look on her face." He spoke to his friend but Griffon didn't have any problems hearing them.

"We weren't close enough to see her face."

"We were still down there right across the street from the entrance. You might not have seen—"

"What'd the guy look like?" Griffon tried to interrupt.

"I'm not going to let you drive anymore. If you can't see that far. All I need is to get grounded because you crash the car." He mumbled more then opened a newspaper dispenser, filling it and taking the change.

The second teenager, ignoring his friend, said, "Lots of grey hair."

Chapter 31

Griffon turned and sprinted down the side street, looking between cars and into shadowed doorways. He could still hear the teenagers as they started shouting at each other.

Then he saw Liesel. She stood between two parked cars, facing the mouth of a small delivery driveway. The buildings on either side, cast the drive into darkness. But he knew the bad guy was in there. Liesel had her hands up.

He tucked in, running faster, weaving in and out of parked cars. He slowed his movements and quieted his steps as he got closer. Liesel didn't turn her head but he knew she saw him.

She raised her voice. "I don't know who you are. I don't care. Take this chance to just get out of here." How long had she been standing there? She couldn't dodge to her right or left, the parked cars were in her way and if she turned to run out into the street, the assailant would still be able to shoot her before she could get to cover.

He heard a gun fire and his body lurched, his heart convulsing in his chest. Eyes wide he watched as she shook. But the bullet had hit the car next to her. Within seconds, he could smell the gas. A few more feet and he would be at the driveway and could reach Murket.

He felt his body. It was ready. He sniffed the air, sensing more than just the gasoline.

"Why are you afraid of the bullet? Aren't you bullet proof?"

From the sound, Griffon judged him to be only a few feet into the alleyway.

Her tone was scathing. "I'm strong, not invincible. I'm human, not an alien with antennas on my chest. I get sick and I can die just like everyone else." Eerily, the image of his former partner being shot, juxtaposed his vision. If only he'd shot her. He'd said it before. Wished it. Then he'd be the one in control, rather than the victim.

"Oh, but you're not like everyone else," Murket was yelling.

"I am," Liesel whispered.

"Nope. You're like those kids. Better. Perfect." Murket's voice was now sweet, charming.

"I've got two left feet. Absolutely no hand eye coordination." She was desperate to convince Murket and maybe Griffon too.

"No, I know. I know. You're like those kids." The smell of gas was getting stronger. Griffon needed this to end before the man fired another round and ignited the gas tank. It wouldn't explode but the fire could flash and consume Liesel

"And I knew the minute we touched that you weren't. You said you were Chris's father but you're not his biological father, and you couldn't have made it from Chicago this quickly."

"I had to find out how much you knew," Murket said.

"Knew what? Who you are? Well, I think that you're the one who found these kids. But no one knows. They all think, somehow, it was the doctor." Liesel still hadn't looked at Griffon but seemed to have the same plan. Keep him talking.

"Yeah, I'm the one. I can say it. What fame!" Murket's voice was self-mocking. "The only person who could tell the world, has to die." He must have raised his gun to fire again. Liesel did the smartest thing in the world. She looked at the opposite side of the drive as if she saw someone there, eyes wide in shock.

Just as a bullet zipped across the opposite corner, Griffon rushed into the darkened path and tackled the gunman. Their bodies hit the cement, folding up, jarring. Griffon stayed on top of the older man, so Murket would absorb the shock of impact. The gun skittered further into the shadows. Griffon planted a facer as hard as he could and the man didn't move. Liesel had run in after him and picked up the gun. She didn't aim it at Murket, just turned it handle side out to Griffon. He took it, checked the bullets and aimed it at the prone figure on the ground.

Griffon had gotten an elbow or knee to the stomach. He rubbed absently at the ache, wiped sweat from his brow. The punch of adrenaline still thumped through his body, despite the brief fight. The transition always made him queasy.

He could hear sirens in the distance. The teenagers must have called the police at the first gun shot.

Neither of them talked for a moment, breathing hard. Griffon pulled out his wallet, letting it flip open to reveal his PI license. "So they won't shoot us."

"Thank you," she said.

He nodded.

"Thank you for saving me. Again."

He nodded.

The moment was too sharp, his emotions too high. This wasn't the place or time for their confrontation. He shifted his weight, leaning on different legs, kept his eyes on the unconscious body. But he couldn't wait.

"Queen? When were you going to get around to telling me about that? Why do I always get information from you," he was yelling now, "in bits and pieces?"

"So you didn't know I've been asked to be queen. So what? It's not like we're even dating. We've known each other for like, what, a few months? And you have to know everything about me?" She yelled right back.

Her chest heaved and her eyes flashed. "I don't know how to dance but I can swim a full mile non-stop. I don't like peas. I own four pairs of shoes but forty pairs of earrings. So what? How much do you have to know for us to be okay?"

"I'm not talking likes and dislikes. This is big." He looked at her and his chest tightened to see her. Eyes passionate, still filthy from her ordeal and mussed. But inexplicably beautiful. She looked good, heated with temper.

"No. Shit. But who says you have the right to know about it? Where is it written in the friendship handbook, that I must divulge all details of my life by day three?" She drew a deep breath, lowered her voice. "I don't know your mom. I don't know why you chose to be a private investigator. Or how long you've had a problem with authority figures. Does that mean I can have a hissy fit?"

"I am not having a hissy fit. And I don't fuck my friends." The man at his feet stirred. Griffon kicked him once to make him lie still. The sirens had reached the end of the drive. The car's lights filled the path, bouncing off the walls, distorting his vision. Liesel held up her hands, badge facing the police officers as they poured from their cars. Griffon lowered the gun and stepped back from the body.

"I'm not really a redhead," she yelled over her shoulder. "Are you going to pout about that, too?" He flicked his eyes in her direction and scowled. He liked her red hair.

Then Griffon smirked. He already had concrete proof what her real hair color was.

The cafeteria at the Federal building had worked overtime to provide enough scrambled eggs and toast to feed everyone. More of the parents had arrived and Liesel answered questions and made sure everyone had something to eat. They were making sure the parents had information for counseling options in their own areas, establishing points of contact if questions came up later on either side.

The Director asked for a moment of her time and they rode the elevator up. A lady in a blue power suit and short hair stood at an office door. If those weren't clue enough that she was about to speak to someone with a hell of a lot of clout, the Director cinched it by treating her with stiff formality.

She was the type of woman Liesel always assumed was southern. Not from an accent, she hadn't spoken, but because everything she did said 'I am grace and manners personified.' A true lady in the classic definition.

"Ms. Liesel Grant, this is Special Agent Valdez." After introducing them the Director left.

The lady smiled, though stiffly, and ushered her into the office. Professional. Not friendly. "Please sit Miss Grant." She indicated one of the leather wing back chairs in front of a large desk which Valdez sat behind.

"Let's simplify things. We of course know of your internet site and the group of people that frequent it. You sent us the link and web map when you first started," Agent Valdez said sitting very straight.

"I figured it would save time later, if the U.S. government didn't freak out that I had pretty high security on such a site. I've never wanted to work in secrecy. My members often feel differently," Liesel said.

"We would like to establish, among other things, a line of communication. The government does not want to have any misconceptions about the handling of Amazons. We don't want it ever said that such people were persecuted or taken advantage of. We have enough image issues." Was this really happening? Simple as that, lets introduce you to the public liaison. Felt like it was more than just a CYA, cover your ass, move.

"I'm a patriot, Ms. Valdez. I think this country is great. The people that live here aren't always as wonderful." Liesel's eyes were heavy and her clothes smelled like gasoline. Or maybe it was her eyes that smelled and her clothes that were heavy.

"We are working to make sure those people don't ruin it for the rest of us. Case in point." She flipped one of the files across her desk to Liesel.

Case in point? Only lawyers say case in point. Now is not the time to pick up Harry's habit of giggling when tired.

The file was folded open and the papers attached to a top bracket. The Doctor's character sketch lay on top. Chris had done an excellent job drawing him. "The FBI has tracked down phone records verifying that Murket and the doctor have been in contact for over a year. The doctor, John Savon, had lost his medical license and tenure at a University. He'd been developing steroids for asthma patients. But he used the college's football team for guinea pigs."

She pulled another folder out. Thumbed the pages. "Sam Murket is a sports agent and has in the past represented some of the biggest names in basketball and football. The last four years his client base has diminished because of allegations of embezzlement and drug use. That's all we have on him so far. But give us another hour." She re-clasped her hands and after waiting, perhaps to see if Liesel had a question, continued her explanations.

Sam Murket wanted a drug that would be undetected by the sport authorities, Valdez explained. Dr. Savon believed this was possible using natural adrenaline. They had come up with the idea to study and harvest adrenaline from superior athletes. The body, however, can only handle its own adrenaline. Excess could easily lead to death.

The next file she left closed. "Shea Strausser."

"Sting gave us that name. He wasn't on my site." But the images would always haunt her.

"Yes," she said, agreeing, confirming. "He went into anaphylactic shock. It is a severe hypersensitivity reaction; in this case to a horse sedative. Someone administered epinephrine intramuscularly...." She stopped, seeing Liesel's face. "When that failed, Murket took Mr. Jordan Mathews. Perhaps as a replacement. They flew from Montana to L.A. The FAA is checking the smaller airfields for more information. We want to know how, exactly, he was able to transport an unconscious boy and possibly a depressurized corpse."

No sperm was found in the lab. Murket swore the doctor would never use electric shock to extract sperm from a body. Which didn't rule out the possibility. It was decided that Jordan had been tasered by one of the guards. Pierced and Scary had three tasers in his possession when they found his body. Nothing could be discovered to why Teona was examined. "Probably was a sick bastard and got his jollies scaring people." It was Valdez's most human sentence and thus unnerving. They had also rigged the controls to lock down the lab and it would have taken a vault cracker a week and divine intervention to breach the tomb-like bunker.

"We of course will know more as the profiles are finished. All the lab's computers are being analyzed. I'll be available for questions. This is my number and e-mail address." She slid her card across the table; there was no name on it.

Liesel took the card and held it in her hands, rotating it and flipping it over between her fingers. Surely there was more. Sting could have told her all of this.

"Ms. Grant, are you familiar with the term μπορεί?" The Greek word for Mighty was said perfectly.

Liesel decided, that if she was going to be interrogated, the least they could do was put her in a room that let her know that was their purpose. This room made you relax. It was not personalized in anyway, not even a photo on the desk but it was plush. Leather wing chairs, paintings of historical buildings of importance like the Pentagon and Jefferson Memorial. There was a large window that probably looked out over the parking lot but the drapes were closed.

"It means the Mighty. I've come across it in my research of old documents."

"We are concerned with...." Agent Valdez lifted her head and looked Liesel in the eye, "your safety. We are more than willing to let sleeping dogs lie. But it has been brought to our attention that you have...awoken a few dogs."

"That was amazingly precise and helpful."

"You're right." Agent Valdez smiled in response to Liesel's sarcasm. "I agree. And, I wish I could say more." Valdez kept her face neutral but Liesel could see that she was weighing her options. "Your secretary Penelope Glass was killed with a single shot to the forehead. The two bodies found in Frank Griffon's home were killed the same way. As was the Doctor and Pierced and Scary. Check your sources for the traditions of the Harvest Teams."

Harvest Teams? Liesel had no idea what to say. Were their groups of Mightys seeking vigilant justice? And had she just mouth offed to their starting line up? Oh, shit.

"For now our concern is the children." Valdez waited to see if Liesel would say anything. Valdez had done that a lot. Perhaps trying to be polite but it just made Liesel feel like an idiot. Valdez continued, "Please, feel free to contact me." She stood and Liesel knew she had been dismissed. Liesel reached forward and shook the agent's hand. Holy crap. The Amazon Agent's hand. Griffon was right. She did have a secret connection to the FBI.

Chapter 32

It was hours later before Liesel and Griffon returned to their hotel rooms. It felt like days. Clara, the child that had started their hunt, was the last to be reunited. The Larkins had trouble flying out of Boise. They brought Tara with them and it was wonderful to see the two sisters together.

It reminded Liesel of her own sisters, who were angry that she hadn't called them sooner. They were posed to pounce and mother the hell out of her as soon as she got back so could she hurry the hell up and get back to Boise.

Once they reached the hotel, neither spoke. They both automatically went into his hotel room. Griffon started unloading his gear. He placed his gun on the night stand. His movements just as tired as hers.

She started pacing. As if they hadn't stopped hours ago, she picked up their fight, mid rant. "I'm a girl. Just like all the rest." She laughed. "Of course, you know that first hand."

"You're a girl but not just a girl." He kept fiddling with his briefcase, his voice neutral.

"What?" She spun to look at him. She was so tired and sore, she was going to take off her shoes. Only her shoes. And fall into bed and not move until the smell of herself bothered the neighbors. Then she would sleep in the shower for a while.

Griffon grabbed her and wrestled her to the bed, wrapping his legs around hers. Their hard bodies bounced against each other for a moment as they settled into the consenting contours of the mattress. They lay on their sides, their breaths coming quick and jagged.

He thought it would be harder to pin her, but she went willingly, and it made him feel like a manhandling jerk.

"What do you want me to prove? I can get loose." She glared at him.

"Shut up a minute. I wanted to touch you. And I was tired of you pacing."

Her body flexed and pressed into him. He groaned and she stopped; confusion on her face. "Did I hurt you? I know you're sore. Or is it—"

"My turn to tell a story." He interrupted her, pressing a kiss to her slightly parted lips. He brushed the hair from her face, distracted. "Is it as dark as your thatch?"

He'd seen her roots, having traveled past her belly button but lots of women had lighter hair on their heads, exposed to the sun.

"The story," she reminded him.

"When I first was hired at the police department in Boise, I did a year in a squad car. I worked nights and so had a partner. The day shifts you can ride solo. My partners name was Ashley Morgan." He waited to see if she would recognize the name. She knew this but he needed to say the words. "She was taking bribes. Money from business owners to plant false evidence or to stay clear of certain areas. She would also sleep with suspects and let them off the hook from speeding tickets or whatever. I figured it out pretty early. She was so arrogant about it; wasn't very careful. When I turned her in, she tried to implicate me as well, but I'd documented everything."

"That must have been really tough." Her voice was husky and his body began to respond. He shifted their positions so his arousal wasn't pressing between her legs.

"It just made me so angry. She'd sworn to protect and to serve but she was taking advantage of these people."

"It sounds more like they were taking advantage of her greed, her desire for power," Liesel said. "Oh, I'm not saying she was a victim. But the ones they hurt—the bystanders—those people deserved better. They should have been safe. You should have been safe."

"After she was sentenced, they were transporting her to the prison in Pocatello." He had made detective by the time the long trial went to sentencing. "One of the transport guards was an old accomplice of hers. Ashley had managed to keep the girl's record clean, so when she applied as a guard, they hired her. They killed the other guards. Escaped. Then came after me." They'd used the same restraints, Ashley's chains, to capture and hold him.

"Frank felt a lot of guilt. That we hadn't stayed closer. That he didn't know right away I was gone. He was there when they found me. Not a pretty sight."

"The stuff of nightmares."

"Yes, it is," Griffon said. He stroked her hair. Noticed, for the first time, a star shaped freckle on her cheek. He almost remarked on it.

Instead he continued with his story. "He had homing devices implanted in his girls. Tammy too. Took a small second mortgage out on the house to pay for it." Their bodies had relaxed against each other as they talked. Companionably comfortable verging on raging horniness.

"My whole point in telling you all of this, besides to explain a few things...Well, I realized you're not like them." He kissed her, took a moment to just enjoy the feel of her beneath his hands.

"So, where does that leave us?" She asked.

"I want to know you well enough to answer that question."

She smiled at him. "So, we could, like date?"

"Yeah."

"Dating with perks?"

"Oh, I definitely see sex in our relationship. Often and soon."

"Oh, the sex is nice. Incredibly. Amazing. But I was thinking about the jeans. Specifically, me wearing your jeans."

He laughed and stroked the bare skin he had uncovered at her waist. His hands heated her skin. He had found Liesel Grant, a powerful woman, who he could trust and maybe love. And wasn't that the miracle of the year.

"I decided to let myself fall for you."

She blinked at him and paled.

"I know. Scary shit."

"I was so caught up in everything else that I didn't...."

"Guard against it? Yeah. Well, much too late to fight it off now."

She laughed. "I can live with that."

The End

About the Author

Amberly lives in the Northwest with her husband, two children, and their cats, Cat and KitTon. Their home has become a PC graveyard where games and gadgets are discarded for the latest shiny. She likes to read in bed, write in coffee shops, knit, and cuddle while watching Netflix or Hulu. Amberly acknowledges that she has issues with being too succinct. Feel free to ask her questions about herself. She's not shy. Follow her strange life on her website at www.amberlysmith.com or look for her on facebook.

Thank you for reading Bravery Not Included. I hope you enjoyed it. If you did, please consider putting a review on Amazon. It's easy and reviews are what writers live and die by.

Some Assembly Required
Rise of the Amazons: Book Two

Amazons are real and taking over Las Vegas.

Renowned photographer Dianne Fender was too late to save her Grandma Maggie. Now, no matter what she has to do or suffer, she is determined to control her psychic abilities so she can protect Liesel Grant, the new Amazon Matriarch. The odds are against her since Liesel has been shot at, kidnapped, robbed, and pissed off by the Mightys—a secret race of superhuman men.

Doctor Sergei Sky must find a cure for the harsh Amazon gene mutations to help his family and others. Dianne, a double Amazon, is his best bet to test his early research. Plus, once he teaches her how to use her powers, she can find Liesel's stolen codex—an ancient record of the Amazons.

Together they travel to Las Vegas for the first International Amazon conference. Assassination attempts, all you can eat buffets, a Harvest Team out to slaughter those who would expose the Mightys, and a Vegas wedding— Amazon style. Yep, things are totally going as planned.

Excerpt:

Chapter 1

Dianne Fender knew, even before she left the hospital, that her Grandma Maggie was dead. Liesel Grant was alive, for now, and the plan was to keep her that way. Dianne's thoughts, and those of the hundreds of people in the church, flipped through her mind like a carousel set on extra fast.

Grandma Maggie should have been buried in an Indian ceremony not this grand scale chapel and graveside service. Dianne was pretty sure that thought was hers. With little effort she could take a mental survey on A) how many people felt the 'service was lovely' or B) those who wished there'd been candles instead of the brightly lit overhead electric chandlers. Option C) that Maggie had never died in the first place. Dianne choose that one.

At least the pallbearers would be Amazons.

The solid wood pews were worn. The funeral flowers were buried three arrangements deep, ten across and had no scent. Dianne adjusted the long sleeves of her dress, pulling with a nervous twitch to cover her burns. Part of her mind knew the burns were no longer there but she tugged at her sleeves anyway.

A young girl sang the words to Britney Spear's Toxic. *Damn it.* How dare they allow such a song to be part of this sacred ceremony? But Britney was in somebody's head. Or rather, some young girl had the song stuck in her head. When Dianne laughed the thoughts flooding her mind switched to thoughts of Dianne. Which was freaky-ass creepy. The drugs must be wearing off.

Escaping now would be good. At least to the rafters, her camera in her hands. The rafters weren't anywhere near far enough to avoid the torrent of thoughts nor would the camera shield her. But to have her equipment, to be dangling from a high dangerous point, that was familiar. Hell, necessary.

The only reason she'd ventured forth was Maggie.

Grandma Maggie had taken her to her first pow-wows. Before her abilities kicked in. Rich memories of colors, the sharp swish of shiny beads and the chanting rhythm. Her first photos had been of dancers, bonfires, her white grandmother, and the tribe that had adopted her a hundred years before. Pictures of people. Before being that close caused pain; before she became a hermit.

Liesel, the young Amazon leader, gave the eulogy. Tears streaked Liesel's face as her kind voice eloquently paid tribute to a lost friend, a mentor. Liesel had worked tirelessly to connect all Amazons and Mightys—women and men of extraordinary strength. She had guided them to the answers they so desperately wanted. Dianne and Grandma Maggie included. Dianne owed Liesel more than just her devotion and respect.

Liesel had explained why she was different and not alone. Her Amazon mother and her father, the stiff empty man sitting next to her, the son of Maggie Mountain Fender, both carried the Amazon gene. Two Amazon genes were unmixy. Made a Blue Hair. In Dianne's case a FOBAR human. And the drugs that helped block all the thoughts, that made the pain tolerable, breathable, were fading.

Dianne fumbled in her purse for a glass vial. Barney, her agent, had taken her to Wise Woman Daisy, a Navajo Indian who sold herbal medicines. She'd needed something for the pain and none of the drugs at the hospital had worked to block out the mental noise of those around her. The doctors had thought her quick recovery from the fire was a blessing from God for her great self-sacrifice. *Please. As if.* There was nothing shiny enough in her karma bank to pay for something like that.

"Maggie lived a life to be proud of. She died peacefully in her sleep and now is with her soul-mate. In her own words—" Liesel said. What Grandma had said Dianne didn't hear.

The carousel in her head paused a short second longer on a man. The man knew that Maggie had been killed. Just like Dianne knew that Maggie's death wasn't a quiet passing in the peace of sleep. The slide was gone, and with the cold vial clasped in her hand, seconds away from peace, she closed her eyes to focus. All the thoughts, not just the mourners, but the thousands of people in a three mile radius, flooded her. Hot painful air caught in her throat. Her mind staggered under the weight. His oily presence was torn out of her grasp. She could no longer find him in the sea of noise. She couldn't do it, not even for Maggie.

She tipped the vial into her mouth, painting her tongue with the tart fluid and felt her father place his arms around her. His grief and fear of loneliness made her black out for a second but then she felt him. Not his mind or his thoughts or anyone's thoughts, him. Just the physical feel of her father. Solid, warm.

It was the first time that she had physical contact with another person in…a very long time. Unless you counted the painful touch of each doctor or nurse; of Barney, helping her walk out of the hospital.

"Liesel is stalling," her father whispered. "You've been out for almost ten minutes. Are you okay?"

She straightened and nodded at Liesel. Sending a mental thank you. Probably a bit loudly, if Liesel's jerk and then smile was any indication.

Dianne yanked at her sleeves again as she stood with the congregation. Her whole body shook as if she had Parkinson's and her mind could only focus on the immediate.

Stand. Wait. Watch. Watch as six women, dressed in long black dresses, spread around the coffin. Who was in that coffin? Oh, Grandma Maggie. Right.

And the women weren't wearing black, she just couldn't take the time or effort to figure it out. She was watching.

The ladies lifted the solid mahogany casket easily—Amazons, her mind explained—and walked out of the church, carrying it on their shoulders to the waiting hearse.

Was it too bloody much to ask that her powers make sense? That they be useful? For almost fifteen years Dianne had lived on her own, traveled, photographed and finally, *finally* found peace. Found acceptance. Then she has a vision. What the fuck? If she was meant to make a difference, to help, was it too much to ask for a guide? Her very own Doyle or Gandolf? Instead a vague sense of doom and she was sleeping on a couch in a city. Bringing her mental baggage to Liesel who deserved her own peace.

Yet she was the only one that believed Maggie was killed. So, until she knew what happened to Maggie, she would stay close to

Liesel. She'd have another chance to make this right. She just needed to suppress her powers enough to cope.

Having psychic abilities was like reading a novel with all points of view present. Today, because of some street-acquired Mary Jane, Dianne only heard the points of view of the five women present.

"I don't need a point guard," Liesel said and thought, *My life is so screwed up.*

They might not believe Dianne's vision had predicted Maggie's death but they were determined to protect Liesel. She'd already been kidnapped, shot at, her home broken into. Plus, there was a very powerful family of Mightys that had done their best to show their displeasure of HOAX, the rising Amazon community. All of which didn't include inside factors.

"All queens have, at the very least, a set of body guards," Tammy Griffon said. Tammy personified the suburban housewife, conservative dress and manners in neutral colors.

"I am not the Queen." Liesel buzzed around the room, sorting through mail, wiping off the kitchen counter. She was doing her best to be polite to these women but was growing weary of their bossy insistence. She even smiled, thinking how ironic it was to be designated queen. She didn't have enough influence to get them to stop pestering her about a guard detail. Again.

All four women were shorter than Dianne's obnoxious 6'1" height and worse Dianne was suffering major hair envy for Liesel's red curls. A thousand black exclamation marks covered Dianne's head. She placed her hand over her recently bald scalp, as if that would hide her short hair..

Liesel tried again. "I can't be called Queen, that's just ridiculous. This isn't a country. I'm a political figurehead for an organization. A web-based organization."

Dianne's drug oblivion from the funeral had lasted the night and she awoke on Liesel's couch ashamed of her retreat. That man in the congregation had known something about Maggie and she couldn't suck it up long enough to learn his secrets. Whether or not he was the killer. If Maggie had been killed at all. Like a selfish child she'd hidden behind the drug, used it instead of fighting.

Dianne stayed on the couch as Liesel's baby sister Harriett started loading the dishes. It would be nice to stay busy by helping but she couldn't risk being that close to everyone.

"So Madame President, you still need to consider—" Harry, the only non-Amazon in the room, didn't broadcast her thoughts like the others. If Dianne concentrated on the blonde she could read emotion and surface thoughts. But the whole point of the marijuana was to not think. Harry blocked her mental scan. How? Dianne was busy not thinking about it and envying the long, straight blond hair.

Liesel interrupted her younger sister, "I don't like President." She was putting leftovers from a late breakfast into the fridge and looking out into the backyard where Tammy's girls chased each other.

"What about Monarch?" Tammy said.

"The butterfly?" Liesel asked. She rolled her eyes and pictured herself lying in a huge bed, thick blankets and a warm male body surrounding her. Jim Griffon, the boyfriend and Tammy's brother-in-law. Dianne felt a deep ache of desire in Liesel's stomach that made her own skin flush with heat.

Dianne shook her head to get out of Liesel's thoughts. Out of Liesel's and into Anna's, Liesel's assistant. Anna Marie Fort-Porter's brain was like a super computer. Dianne wasn't sure what a super computer was but had learned not to ask Anna questions. Dianne would get encyclopedia level details.

Monarchs, Danaus Plexippus, Greek for 'sleepy transformation'. Related to the Greek myth, the daughters of King Danaus of Libya. The information rolled through Anna's mind, who ignored it.

Each adult butterfly lives four to five weeks. In autumn a special generation are born that survive seven or eight months. In human terms 525 years old.

"Then isn't that fitting? Since we live a long time. Or can," Dianne said to Anna. Unlike Anna's thoughts, Dianne spoke out loud.

The two sisters and Tammy looked at Dianne. Anna groaned and slumped further down in her chair in the corner. Liesel thought, *I don't know how to help her. I need to get a hold of Sergei. Maybe he can help.* At the same time Dianne heard Tammy's *Freak.* Dianne brushed their thoughts away. Whatever. Nothing new there.

"Who's Sergei?" Dianne asked.

"Even though you can read people's minds," Anna said, "doesn't mean you should say what they say in their heads. It's in there for a reason." *We're all hiding something.* Dianne knew Anna's cynicism, unlike other eighteen year olds, stemmed from battle weary experience.

"Let's get something clear." Liesel smiled. "Tammy, you live in San Francisco with Frank and the girls. You can't be my bodyguard. Harry, you're my sisters and I love you but you need to work and can't be here twenty-four seven. Anna is in her first year of college. Nuff said."

They were due in Las Vegas for the first national convention of HOAX, Home Of the Amazon eXchange, their community on the web. There Liesel would be voted in as leader—title to be determined—and a board of directors appointed. Surviving in Vegas would make Dianne's visit to Boise look like a fun field trip to a sunny park.

And me? Dianne asked Liesel.

Liesel smiled at her. "We need to figure out a way you can survive in a city." She rubbed her fingertips against her temple.

Preferably without weed, Anna thought.

"I heard that." Dianne glared at Anna.

Anna just smiled and said in her head, *Welcome to my mind, Jean Grey.*

"Who?"

Anna laughed again and got up to get a glass a water from the fridge. Her mind filled with old comic book pictures of a redheaded superhero who could move things with her mind.

"I'm not telekinetic," Dianne clarified.

"What?" Tammy asked, irritated.

"She can't move things with her mind," Harry explained.

Stop. Stop. Liesel pushed at her temple, feeling pain throb there.

Dianne didn't think about it, she just scooped Liesel up like a young child and carried Liesel to her bedroom. The weight of her queen in her arms, the scope of light bleeding into shadows, were still muted by the drugs she had taken during the service and the marijuana. So it felt like carrying a pillow in a dim room.

"What the hell are you doing?" Harry demanded.

"She's in pain." Careful not to touch Liesel skin to skin, Dianne angled sideways to avoid bumping the narrow hallway walls. The house was both home and office to Liesel's web design company and headquarters for HOAX. What if the threat wasn't a potential killer but an illness? Breast cancer ran in the Grant family. Dianne checked Liesel's mind for her last physical.

"I've just got a headache. Dianne, put me down," Liesel said. She wasn't frightened of Dianne, but still she was fully capable of walking to her room on her own.

"No," Dianne said. Liesel had a full exam and blood work done after she was kidnapped. Everything looked fine.

"D, you need to chill," Anna said.

Tammy, angry, had her dander up and Dianne sent a mental command to stay the hell back, do not touch. Sometimes they listened.

The women followed them down the hall into Liesel's room. It was messy, and Liesel cringed in embarrassment.

Then as she realized Dianne was carrying her she jerked still in her arms. *Dianne!*

Understanding her friend's concern, Dianne said, "I'm being careful not to touch skin." She stumbled at the bedroom's threshold as it switched from hardwood to carpet. Startled, Liesel grabbed Dianne's neck.

In that brief instant of touch, nightmarish images took over. Dianne stood in a glass cube where Griffon bled from deep gouges. Her sister Harry sobbed and a small child, muscular like a circus carnies' sideshow, cowered in the darkness.

Someone tortured Griffon. Sliced deep. Blood pumped in rhythmic streams down his body. Harry, the gray of decay, dripped pungent water and didn't breathe. Dianne tried to offer Harry comfort, save Griffon and lead the child into the light. Her muscles tore away from her bones, pulled in three different directions.

Dianne dropped Liesel onto the bed. She experienced a brief

moment of black sharpness before all the other thoughts flooded back in. And not just the house. Dianne swayed on her feet and fell like a cut tree. Liesel made it out of the way just in time. She lay stomach down, face turned to the side on Liesel's bed.

Before Dianne succumbed to unconsciousness, she saw Liesel reach out to brush the hair out of Dianne's face. Oh god she wanted that, a motherly touch, soothing, strong. Liesel stopped, remembered not to touch.

I'm so sorry.

It happens.

How was she supposed to help protect and support Liesel if she couldn't be within miles of a city without her life being totally fucked up?

Doctor Sergei Sky ran his hand over the top of his head, feeling the short blue bristle of his hair. He was wet. Runny wet. If you stand in the shower or in the rain then you are dripping wet but water from inside—sweat—runs off skin. Runs at different speeds in rivulets; runny wet. He grabbed a grungy towel he kept for the purpose and wiped down his muscular arms and scrubbed his head. His t-shirt and the towel were tossed in the hamper and he took the single step required to go from home gym to office.

Enjoying a rush of endorphins and adrenaline, unwinding a bit before his vacation revved him up. He flipped a page in his battered notebook and read page three for the eight hundredth time.

"Nice abs," crackled across the walkie-talkie.

Sergei started and laughed looking outside to the apartment building across the way. He placed a finger in the notebook to keep his place. Yeah, as if he would forget what it said. Somehow the answer would present itself. It had to.

He picked up his walkie-talkie and pressed the send button. "Well, Veranda, that's why I leave the drapes open. To enhance the view." He made his voice slick and flirtatious. He turned his body toward the window and undulated his hips once to really show off the goods. He laughed at how ridiculous he probably looked.

"If you got a gym membership you'd have a reason to get out of the building. Maybe meet someone."

"Veranda! Are you breaking up with me?"

His neighbor had a motherly tone to go with her sassy, wise-woman persona. "Darlin' I'm too much woman for you."

Sergei laughed and tossed the notebook into his carry-on. Every word Liesel Grant had translated from ancient texts, the gene research, even the sporadic bits of the Amazon codex before it was stolen, was in that notebook. Everything he'd ever found on Blue Hairs.

"I'm going to miss you next week," Veranda said. He pulled his water bottle out of the fridge and chugged it while she spoke.

"You could come to Las Vegas with me." He wiped his mouth. "We'll take in the Blue Man Group and get married in one of the cheesy chapels." Sergei walked to the window and waved to Veranda.

The seventy year old woman was wearing her favorite bubble gum pink sweater. It engulfed her frail body and made Sergei think of those coconut stacked sweets—pink, brown and white.

"Can't afford it." It was a difficult subject, money. Veranda lived on bread bought at wholesale and the 'discounted groceries' Sergei took in twice a week. Shortly after moving in, Sergei saw the old woman, who he smiled at in passing, fall on a loose rug. It was late and hard for him to see but Sergei knew she didn't get back up.

He alerted the police. She'd broken her hip. The walkie-talkies were his idea. Him eating his only non-microwaved meals at her apartment was Veranda's idea. She was a nice enough lady that he occasionally felt bad for taking advantage of her generous nature. The groceries were an attempt to make up for his general lack of a heart. Okay, as a doctor he knew he had a heart but not much of a soul. Those great tasting meals and the home-like-feel of their visits was worth the price of compliments and the time Sergei spent.

"You'll bring back pictures?" Veranda said.

"And shot glasses and pink M&M's from M&M world." He could see her laugh even from this distance because her whole body shook. "Your nephew Tony's coming on Monday and his wife Sarah on

Wednesday—" The walkie-talkie squawked and stuttered as she interrupted. Her version of sticking her fingers in her ears and going 'La-la-la.'

He released his button.

"Get cleaned up and come over. I'm making spaghetti."

He rearranged his mental schedule and kept his sigh to himself. She'd be alone until Monday and it wasn't like he had anything to cook here. His chest twinged with guilt over his reluctance. She was a good person. She deserved a faithful and grateful friend. Instead Sergei dragged his feet.

"I need to check my email. Half hour?" Sergei said.

"Ten four, Blue Hair."

Sergei set his walkie-talkie down on the small coffee table that also doubled as a kitchen table. The place was small but just a block from the D.C. hospital where he had done his residency. If he had had student loans to pay back like most new doctors, there was no way he could afford it.

The flat consisted of three rooms: bath, bed and catch all. The minuscule bathroom had needed a shower head extension, which he installed the first day. The old one didn't reach above his shoulder. At least on the top floor the ceilings were all high. Just as long as he remembered to duck in the doorways.

He turned on his radio and set the volume to the piece of tape marked 'approval line.' Above the tape and the neighbors started pounding to turn it down. He nodded his head a couple times and gave a snap to The Ramones' Blitzkrieg Bop. Above the radio hung a framed photograph of a Life Flight medical helicopter landing at sunset. A blanket, his only successful sewing project from Home Economics class, lay on his bed. Every remaining shelf, surface, and floor space held his medical books.

He left the radio on as he checked his email. Credit card offer. Couldn't they just stick to snail mail? Monthly subscription to an online doctor's magazine. He'd read that on the plane. Save on your car insurance. What? No, penile implants? The last was an email from Liesel Grant with the subject line 'I need your help.' His body tensed, the press of his heartbeat against his chest so much stronger than when he'd been exercising.

Serg,

Maggie's granddaughter Dianne is a Blue Hair with extreme psychic abilities. She's suffering in Boise but refuses to leave. I know you don't start your new job until after Vegas but could you recommend something?

Liesel

Crap. He knew exactly what was wrong and didn't need the hassle. He had finished his residence. Three years of being the bottom of the totem pole. Little sleep, almost no social life and every spare moment filling his notebook. Not only was this his first adult vacation but he hadn't had more than two days off in nearly four years.

He would start his new job for NEWCo Labs in a couple of weeks. The company had helped him obtain his research grant to study the effects of different medications on Schizophrenic patients. A disease the world believed his father suffered from. He wanted to help Blue Hairs before it was too late. Help those who suffered like his brother had, like his father did. Like Dianne was suffering.